The Dead of Oban

By

Allan Martin

TP

ThunderPoint Publishing Ltd.

First Published in Great Britain in 2024 by
ThunderPoint Publishing Limited
Summit House
4-5 Mitchell Street
Edinburgh
Scotland EH6 7BD

Cover Image: Photo 176737575 | Oban © Eddie Cloud | Dreamstime.com
Cover Design © Huw Francis
Map: © PredragLasica / Shutterstock.com

ISBN: 978-1-910946-91-6 (Paperback)
ISBN: 978-1-910946-92-3 (eBook)
Printed and bound in Great Britain by Clays Ltd, Elcograf S.p.A

www.thunderpoint.scot

Dedication

As Always, to Vivien

Scotland
Inner Hebrides
Oban
Dundee
56°
Glasgow
Edinburgh

Prologue

Kaali meteorite crater, island of Saaremaa, Estonia

Franzisca Schmettlinger arrived at the lip of the crater at seven o'clock that morning. Her objective was to photograph the circular depression, less than a hundred metres wide, and the small lake at the bottom, twenty-five metres below, as the winter sun rose. She hoped it would shine down through the trees to speckle the surface of the water, before any tourists arrived.

From the rim of the crater, it was difficult to get a good shot. The birch trees clinging to the steep sides obscured her view, so she made her way down the steep staircase to the viewing point fifteen metres below. This was a lot better; an uninterrupted view of the lake – or was it more of a pond? – the muddy shore, and the side of the crater rising around it. She set up the tripod and fixed the camera – a Canon EOS R5, a costly but necessary investment – in place. It was still too dim to see much in the pre-dawn gloom. The pond and its surroundings were sketched in shades of faded blue. A couple of shots sufficed to capture that. Then she waited.

Her mind drifted back to the previous evening, and the Swedish couple – both women – she'd met at the hotel bar. The place was small and homely, a comfortable old villa looking across a lake at the heavy walls of the Bishop's Castle in Kuressaare, the island's capital. The Swedes were planning a documentary about the island's history – they were going to call it 'Saaremaa, Hidden Jewel of the Baltic' – so they had plenty to talk about, including the meteorite crater. She'd stayed up later than planned, and those two glasses of wine hadn't helped. She began to doze.

She came to with a jump as she caught sight of the first rays of the sun slanting over the edge of the crater, colouring the water a lurid and sickly shade of green. Must be algae on the surface of the stagnant water. She put her eye to the viewfinder and then saw, breaking the livid green of the surface, an aureole of pale orangey red. She zoomed in. And gasped.

The orange patch on the water was the floating hair of a woman – no man could have hair like that. Looking closer, the outline of the body beneath the water could be discerned. It wasn't moving, and the head was floating face-down beneath the greasy surface of the pond.

She clambered down, clinging to the birch trunks, and took a closer look. There was no sign of any movement. The woman was undoubtedly dead.

She pulled her phone out, to call the emergency services. Then hesitated. She'd miss a fantastic photographic opportunity. And if the woman was dead, she wouldn't mind waiting a little longer to be fished out of the water. She took several pictures over the next twenty minutes. Finally she moved gingerly forward to look closer. But she hadn't realised the mud was so soft and keeled over onto one knee. Extracting herself rapidly, she packed away her equipment, climbed back out of the crater, and walked over to the nearby Visitor Centre to report what she'd seen.

In thirty minutes a police car and an ambulance arrived. Franzisca showed them the body. She was asked by the police if she'd taken any photos. She told them she'd been going to, but as soon as she saw there was someone there, she'd given up the idea, and gone down to help the woman. She said she'd slipped in the mud trying to get close to her, but had realised then that she was dead.

After talking to the police, she was asked to move back behind a police tape which kept her well away from the action. She went back to her hire car and left. However, she resolved that the pictures she'd taken would not be wasted. One of them would later win second prize at the annual competition of the Photographic Society of Linz.

1

Oban Police HQ, Friday 25 November

At ten o'clock sharp Detective Inspector Angus Blue tapped on the door of the Super's office.

"Come in. Ah, Angus! There you are. Coffee? I needn't ask."

"Thank you, sir." Blue sat down facing the expanse of polished wood that was Superintendent Campbell's desk. He wondered if, were he to lean forward over it, he would see his reflection.

When the gleaming Italian coffee shrine had delivered its two tiny cups, the Super could get down to business. "Estonia, Angus! Ever been there?"

"No, chief, sorry. I'd like to get there sometime. The old town of Tallinn is well worth a visit. Since regaining their independence they've … Ah, but you wouldn't ask without a reason."

"Of course not. You see right through me, Angus. No. I'm not asking you to actually go there. But at least you've heard of the place, which is more than I can say for most of the folk in this building. So perhaps you can help with a matter that's just come up. A man has phoned in to report his wife missing. In Estonia. He's coming in to see Sergeant Morgan at eleven. But she feels we need someone with some international experience in there too. Given the circumstances. Perhaps you could have a chat with her, and then go along and see what the fellow has to say."

"No problem, chief. Were they on holiday there? In Estonia, I mean. Or on a cruise?"

"No, no. She was on her own. She's Estonian, you see. Anyway, Sergeant Morgan has the details. Oh, one other thing. I know you've been a bit short since DC Craig got onto the graduate scheme. However, I've some good news. We have a new officer just completed her CID training. I think you know her – DC Vunsells."

"Lena. That's excellent news, chief. She'll make a good detective."

"I hope so. You did recommend her, after all."

He found Sergeant Morgan in a cramped office halfway along a corridor on the second floor. At the back of the building. On the door a paper sign blue-tacked on the door said, 'Missing Persons.

Lost and Found.' Sergeant Morgan dealt with all things lost and found, be it people, dogs, cats, or umbrellas. No, not umbrellas; there are limits. A grandfather clock stood in the corner of the room, ticking loudly; it had been left by persons unknown on the ferry from Islay. Sergeant Aelwyn Morgan sat behind a small and ancient desk, found in an abandoned van, filling in a form. Her dark hair showing signs of grey at the roots, she always reminded Blue of one of his French teachers in school, a superb organiser with a deceptively homely aura.

"Hi, Aelwyn."

"*Bore da*, Angus, how are you?"

"Fine, thanks. But I'm afraid I don't know much about Estonia."

"There you have it, Angus. 'I don't know *much*.' All the rest of us would simply say, 'We know bugger all about Estonia.' Besides, everybody knows you know all about geography and history; you're our resident intellectual, after all. Plus, I suspect a detective would be useful here – I'm sure there's more to this than meets the eye. Just a feeling, you understand, but I'm sure his wife's not just run off with a gigolo she met in a nightclub in, um..."

"Tallinn?"

"Exactly. Point made."

"I guess. So what do we know so far?"

"The guy phoned reception at 9.30 this morning. They passed him on to me." She glanced at a pad on her desk. "Paul Carselaw. Lives over at Ganavan, in one of those new flats."

"The ones right on the shore?" Blue remembered the fuss there'd been a few years before when the developers had announced plans for the apartment blocks at Ganavan, just a couple of miles round the coast from Oban. They were up-market and very modern. But, being so close to the shore, they also changed the aspect of Ganavan Sands, a popular spot for Oban residents.

"That's the place. His wife's name is Aino. Pronounced 'ah-ee-no'. He took great pains to coach me on that when he phoned. But she's been in the UK since 1989."

"Not long before Estonia got back its independence. That was 1991."

"So they're not flighty young things. Anyway, three weeks ago she went over to Estonia, to visit family and friends. And didn't come back. So she's missing, but in Estonia, not here. Mr Carselaw is naturally worried, and wants to go out there to look for her. But, very wisely, thought he should have a chat with us before he went. He'll be here at eleven. I said I'd bring along our international specialist officer …"

"Specialist officer?"

"That always makes people feel more reassured. Knowing that we have specialists for every eventuality."

The meeting was organised for the so-called End Room. This was a bright and airy room, situated at the end of the first floor corridor, at the corner of the building, with windows at the front, overlooking the bay, and at the side, looking towards the Corran Halls. When a Chief Inspector in Traffic Division, whose office it had been, retired, Superintendent Campbell had commandeered the room before any of the other senior officers who'd cast greedy eyes on it could get there. He had then turned it into a space where interviews could take place with non-suspected persons. He felt that the interview rooms for suspected persons did not convey the right atmosphere in which victims of crime or witnesses could be interviewed. His colleagues had to admit that his decision had been correct. The cameras were unnoticeable unless you knew what to look for.

There was a table with four chairs round it in the middle of the room, and a coffee table with two comfy chairs by the front-facing window. A box of tissues sat on the coffee table. There was even a small kitchen off the room. The walls were painted a tasteful but subdued magnolia with a hint of rose. Superintendent Campbell had taken a lot of time to choose exactly the right colour.

Morgan and Blue were there by ten to eleven. Blue made it clear he was happy to let Morgan lead the questioning. She was, after all, the Missing Persons Officer. He would only intervene if there was a point he wanted to probe. They made themselves coffee and waited.

Paul Carselaw was shown in at 11.02. He was of medium height and, thought Blue, had once been slim, but was now beginning to put on a little weight. His neatly trimmed hair was dark, with hints of grey, and thinning on top. He wore glasses with black rims, and what might be a permanent frown. Perhaps he was simply short-sighted. Or was it a sign of concern over his missing wife? He wore a blue corduroy jacket over a light blue shirt, black trousers and black leather shoes.

They both rose from the table. Sergeant Morgan smiled at Carselaw, held out a hand to shake. "Mr Carselaw?"

"Doctor Carselaw, if you don't mind." He paused, looking down on her, as if asserting his superiority.

"I do apologise. I'm Sergeant Morgan, our Missing Persons Officer. And this is Detective Inspector Blue. He's our international specialist."

Dr Carselaw looked at Blue, as if curious about the nature of some new specimen, and gave a hint of a nod. Blue held out a hand and Carselaw shook it reluctantly. His hand was cold and limp.

"Do have a seat," continued Sergeant Morgan. "How about some tea or coffee?"

Dr Carselaw sat down opposite the sergeant at one of the longer sides of the table. "Yes, tea would be fine. Earl Grey if you have it." His expression suggested that he already knew they didn't. "Otherwise whatever you've got. No milk or sugar."

Blue went to the kitchen and made the tea, using the anonymous tea bags in the plastic cylinder marked 'TEA.' He brought in the mug of tea, put a place-mat celebrating Oban Whisky on the table and the mug on it, then sat himself at the table end, as instructed by the sergeant – "Two people facing him would seem like an interrogation."

Sergeant Morgan opened the conversation. "Thanks for coming in to see us, Dr. Carselaw. And for calling us this morning. It was absolutely the right thing to do. And I'm sure we can help you. So, I hope you don't mind talking through what's happened with us."

"Yes, of course. Where would you like me to start?"

"Let me just have some basic details about yourself first. To make sure we've got them right. Oh, just a moment." She took out an iPhone, tapped it a couple of times, laid it carefully on the table. "I'd like to record our conversation, so that we don't miss anything. But I need your permission for that. If you'd rather I didn't, my colleague will take notes."

"I'd prefer if you didn't. I'm sure your colleague is perfectly capable of writing."

"I can assure you that I am, sir," smiled Blue. He took one of the lined pads from the centre of the table, and laid his black gel pen on it.

"Better than the average, then. Most policemen I've encountered seemed barely literate."

For a moment the atmosphere chilled.

"I'm sorry," said Dr Carselaw, "I didn't mean that remark to apply to you two. I shouldn't have said it. Put it down to anxiety over my wife's disappearance."

Sergeant Morgan nodded. "We need to begin now, sir, by just confirming some basic details. Your name is Paul Carselaw?"

"Yes. That's correct."

"Do you mind telling us when and where were you born?"

"Why do you need to know that? It's my wife that's missing, not me."

"I'm sorry, but it's important that we establish your identity, as well as your wife's. We'll come to her in a minute. But unfortunately we do encounter people here who are not who they say they are, and are looking for someone for reasons that are not in that person's best interests."

"Yes, all right, I was born in Stratford-on-Avon in 1962. That's in Warwickshire, in case you don't know. In England."

"A very pleasant little town," put in Blue.

"I wouldn't call it 'little,'" retorted Carselaw irritably. "The population is over thirty thousand."

"I'm sure you're right, sir," said Blue, nodding. "It's been a while since I was there. A school trip to see some Shakespeare. *The Tempest*, I seem to remember."

Sergeant Morgan cleared her throat. "Thank you, Dr Carselaw. Let's move on to your wife now. Perhaps you could tell us how you met." Blue appreciated that his colleague was trying to create a good atmosphere by beginning with what he assumed would be positive memories.

"That was a long time ago. My wife is missing now. What's all that got to do with it?"

"I know it may be tedious, but we need enough background to be able to focus our enquiries. It will be worth it in the end."

"I certainly hope so," said Carselaw. "Well, it's not a secret, after all. We met in Cornwall. A place called Mount Edgcumbe."

"Perhaps you could tell us the story."

Carselaw sighed, as if he was dealing with a pair of simpletons.

"Oh all right. From the beginning then. I got my BSc – first-class, by the way – and MSc at Warwick University, then went on to Exeter to do my PhD. Electronic systems. Then I was recruited by a company called X-Syst-X, based in Plymouth."

"What was your job?"

"Digital systems architecture."

"Is that, like, computer programming?"

"No, not at all. We had other people to do that, mostly in India. Our own people in Plymouth then put the modules together. You see, building a system is really about working out what the client actually wants, then designing a structure that gives them that."

Blue noticed the man's voice had changed, he seemed more alive. At last he'd reached a topic he liked to talk about.

"We have to do a lot of talking with the client," Carselaw went on, warming to his theme. "You see, many clients haven't thought through exactly what they want the system to do. Occasionally it's straightforward – they have a piece of machinery that can perform only a very limited range of operations. Let's say it's a washing machine. So they want to be able to select the operation, add some parameters – sequence and number of cycles, temperature, addition of softener, spin speed and duration, and so on. That's a simple example; most systems are a great deal more complicated. Sometimes the client doesn't even know what their machine is capable of. So we have to read the technical handbook, and ask them exactly what they want the machine to do."

"It sounds really interesting work," commented Sergeant Morgan.

"Believe me, it is. Big systems can take months or even years to design and construct. And after they've been built they need to be tested – that's whether they work – and evaluated – that's the extent to which they do what the client wanted. Here's an example. This company had developed an intelligent lawn-mowing machine, and ..."

"It's okay, sir, we've got the picture. What sort of things were you working on in Plymouth?"

Carselaw's face seemed to close up again, and he paused as if to compose his response. "Sorry, I can't tell you that. There could be legal complications if I say anything."

"That's fine, I was only curious. Anyway, you were telling me how you met your wife."

"Do you know Plymouth at all?" Both Morgan and Blue shook their heads. "I thought not. Well, there's a little ferry that goes from Plymouth across the mouth of the river Tamar to Cremyll, that's on the Cornish side. It only takes ten minutes or so. Not far from the ferry landing there's an estate, Mount Edgcumbe, it's called. It's open to the public for free and lots of people go there from Plymouth for the day, especially at weekends. Well, I and two of my colleagues went across one Sunday morning, it was in June of 1989. We were going to walk to Picklecombe Fort. It was built in the nineteenth century, to defend the entrance to the Tamar from the French, but was converted into flats in the seventies. Nevertheless, you can still see a lot of the original features. Anyway, Jeremy's the history buff, he was keen to show us round.

"On the boat was this girl. I only noticed her because of her hair, long and gingery red, not dyed, the real thing. She must have spotted me looking at her because the next thing was she came over. She said she'd only been in the UK for a few weeks, and was starting to explore the area; and she wanted to know what there was in Mount Edgcumbe. 'Was there a mountain?' she even asked. You see, in Estonia they don't have any mountains. The highest point in the country is called Suur Munamägi –that means 'big egg hill' – and it's only 1,043 feet high, that would be, er, 318 metres. It's down in the south-east corner, near …"

"Then what happened?" interrupted Morgan, smiling.

"Hm. Well, the upshot was that I offered to walk round the estate with her, and Jeremy and Dean went over to Picklecombe." He permitted himself a hint of a smile at the memory, and sipped his tea, then grimaced. Clearly not Earl Grey, not even Assam.

"And that was it?" asked Sergeant Morgan.

"Yes, as you put it, that was it. And we were married a year later. September 23rd, 1990."

"Can I ask what Aino was doing when you met?"

"As I said, she was on the boat…"

"I'm sorry, I meant what sort of job did she have? Why was she in Plymouth?"

"Oh. She was doing a course at the polytechnic. She'd learned English in Estonia, and it was an advanced course in English for non-native-speakers. It's now a university."

"Do you know what Aino's maiden name was?"

"Of course I do."

"Perhaps you could tell us it."

"Aino Kuusk." He said it again slowly: "A-ee-no-Koosk," then spelt it for Blue to write down. "Kuusk means 'spruce' in Estonian. The tree, that is. A lot of Estonian names come from trees. Not off the trees, literally." A short, nervous laugh. "I mean, named for them. You see…"

"And can I assume she wasn't married at this point?"

"Of course not." He hesitated. "Er, but she had been married before."

"Tell me about that."

"Is it necessary?"

"We really need as much background as we can get. The more we have, the more chance we'll have of finding her."

"I suppose so. She'd got married while she was still at university, Tartu University, that is. That's the main university in Estonia. Founded by Gustavus Adolphus of Sweden in sixteen, ah..." He paused and frowned. "Hm. Sixteen-something, I can't remember the exact date."

"She was quite young, then?"

"Yes. But they encouraged that during the communist period, they wanted to keep the population up. And being married was a help in getting accommodation, which was always in short supply."

"What was she studying?"

"English and Literature. Her husband was another student, a bit older than she was. His name was Lind, Kalev Lind. Kalev's one of the heroes of Estonian mythology, you know. He …"

"Sorry, sir," interrupted Blue, "how do you spell that?"

Carselaw sighed. "K – A – L – E – V. Just like it sounds."

"So," put in the sergeant before Carselaw could get back to his exposition of Estonian mythology, "Aino Kuusk married this Kalev Lind, do you know when, I mean, what year?"

"It must have been about, um, 1986, I think."

"And what did she do then? Did she finish university?"

"If Aino starts something, she always finishes it."

"And did she get a job?"

"Oh yes. They had to. She was in a government office, translating documents that they needed from English. This was in Tallinn, that's the capital. It means 'Danish town.' That's because it was founded by the Danes in ..."

"Did they have any children?" interrupted the sergeant quietly.

"Oh, yes. Yes, they had one girl, Tiina. She was born in 1987. But things didn't work out between Aino and Lind. She thought they were married too young. They got divorced in 1988. She stayed there, in Tallinn I mean, for a while, but eventually felt she had to get away. Her husband had custody of the child, you see."

"That's unusual. Do you know why that was?"

"He had influence with the judges, she said. She could only see Tiina once a month, and couldn't keep her overnight. She hated that. So she came over here, I mean, to Plymouth."

"She intended to stay here?"

"She says she might have gone on to the US. But she met me."

"And that was it. Okay, do you know Aino's date and place of birth?"

"She was born in 1965. Kuressaare." He spelt it. "On the island of Saaremaa." He spelt that too. Blue nodded his thanks. "It's in the Baltic." Blue knew how to spell that.

"So she's now fifty-seven?"

"Yes. Her birthday is the fourteenth of September."

"Thanks. So once Aino had finished her course in Plymouth, did she get a job there?"

"Yes. Through a contact from her course. In a bookshop in Plymouth. An independent one. They were quite flexible in terms of holidays, which allowed her to get back to Estonia, to visit her family. And she was also able to meet with Tiina now and then. The father didn't seem to object to that, now the girl was a bit older, and Aino was living over here."

"How often did Aino go to Estonia?"

"Usually four times a year. For a week at a time. Occasionally a fortnight."

"Did you go with her?"

"Not usually. I couldn't take holidays whenever I felt like it. I tried to get out with her at least once a year, but even that wasn't always possible."

"We'll come back to that in a minute. Can I ask if you have any children?"

"No. We don't." Said with some firmness, thought Blue, or through gritted teeth. Was that an issue between them?

"And when did you move up to Scotland?"

"2004. The company got a big contract in Scotland, and needed permanent staff there. So we moved to Helensburgh. That's on the river Clyde."

"Yes, I think we know it," said Sergeant Morgan. "Did Aino get a job there too?"

"No. But she worked three days a week, as a volunteer, with a charity. I don't remember which one. Some condition I've never heard of. They had a shop: clothes, furniture, books, all sorts of used stuff. After a couple of years she set up a bookshop herself."

"New books?"

"No. Second-hand, collectible and antiquarian."

"Is there much business in that?"

"It made a modest amount."

"Okay. And when did you move up to Oban?"

"That was in 2013. Aino suggested we move here. We'd been a few times for short breaks – there's plenty of good walking round here – and she took a fancy to the place."

"How did that fit in with your work?"

"I can do a lot of the design stuff and the admin at home. I go down to Helensburgh for three days every second week. That was this week, by the way."

"What about Aino's shop?"

"She closed the Helensburgh place, of course. However, she knew someone who was looking to open up a bookshop here, so she went into partnership with him."

"Where is it?"

"Stairfoot Lane. Near the distillery. There is actually an old stone staircase at the end, that leads up to Ardconnel Terrace."

"Is the business doing well?"

"As far as I know. It's quite specialist. Academic stuff and rare books, mostly about northern and eastern Europe. Out of print or hard to get hold of, but still in demand, by academics or collectors."

"Is there much demand for that in Oban?"

"Most of the business is online, but occasionally people do come in."

"Are you involved in it too?"

"No. I don't know anything about books."

"What's Aino's partner's name?"

"Ishmael Balfour." He looked at Blue. "Shall I spell that?"

"I think I can manage, thank you."

"Is he local?" asked Sergeant Morgan.

"No, I don't know where he's from. He owns several bookshops, in different parts of Europe."

"So he's not directly involved in running the shop?"

"Obviously not."

"Does anyone else work there? Apart from Aino."

"There's a young woman. Anna something. A Ukrainian refugee."

"Does Aino have to do any travelling connected with the business?" asked Blue.

"She goes to book fairs, and to look at collections that are being sold off. In the UK or sometimes abroad."

"That's good," said Sergeant Morgan. "Now let's focus on Aino's visits to Estonia. Did Covid affect her travelling, by the way?"

"It did get troublesome. The regulations for travel between here and Estonia kept changing, sometimes at their end, sometimes here. A couple of trips had to be cancelled."

"When you went with her, where did you stay?"

"Oh, hold on a minute," interrupted Blue. He pushed forward an A4 sheet. "This is a map of Estonia I printed off the internet. So we can see where the places are. Do carry on, Dr Carselaw."

"Hm. To start with we usually stayed with Aino's parents in Tartu." He pointed to a spot on the map. "There it is. However, Aino's sister Maarja and her husband live in Nõmme, that's near Tallinn, so we'd stay there too. That was when Aino would meet up with Tiina. She usually met her in a café in a shopping centre in Tallinn."

"Did you accompany her to these meetings?" asked Sergeant Morgan.

"No. Aino felt it would be better if I wasn't there. She said Tiina was loyal to her father, and might be quite hostile to me. I didn't mind too much. They'd just be talking in Estonian anyway."

"You don't speak it?"

"I did try. But it's a difficult language to learn. The grammar is fascinating, from an academic point of view, very different from English. But speaking's a different matter. Most Estonians tend to speak far too fast for me. And once they realise I don't understand, they just switch to English."

"Where did Aino go when you didn't accompany her?" asked Blue.

Carselaw studied the map. "She's also got cousins in Viljandi – that's in the south – and Pärnu – it's here on the west coast, at the top end of the Gulf of Riga." He pointed out the places on the map. "But she has old school friends all over the place."

"Have you met any of the cousins or friends?"

"No. Aino sees them when she's there without me. When I'm there we stick to Tallinn or Tartu, with occasional trips out to see places. Like some of the old castles built by the Teutonic Knights. Or Suur Munamägi. As I said, it's not very high, but you can see a lot of the country from the tower they've built at the top. Most of Estonia is very flat."

Sergeant Morgan studied the map as if taking it all in. "Well now, let's come to her latest trip. I take it you weren't on this one."

"That's right. We hadn't been for a while, due to Covid in fact, and she was really wanting to see lots of people. She suggested going on her own. I didn't mind. I had plenty to do here. Lots of work, as usual. And there's also my model railway."

"You have a model railway?"

"Didn't I just say that? I've built a base for it in the garage. I try to add a couple of new features each year. A branch line or a station or tunnel. So I didn't object too much. Two weeks on my own would be a great opportunity to get some upgrading done."

"Now we need the details of Aino's proposed visit. She sounds well-organised."

"Yes. She always made the arrangements, even when I was going too. So there would be a plan of where we would be right through the trip."

"Do you have the plan for the present trip?"

Carselaw frowned. "No. Some of the details were only confirmed quite late, and she said she'd give me it on the morning of her departure. But we had to rush to be at the airport in good time."

"Sorry to interrupt," said Blue. "Which airport would that be?"

"Glasgow. We had to set off in the middle of the night. I remembered about the plan after she'd gone. When she phoned that evening, I asked about it. She said she'd email it, but it never came."

"OK," said Sergeant Morgan. "When was it she set off?"

"The eighth of this month. A Tuesday. 6.05 am to Amsterdam, and from there to Tallinn. With KLM. She would have got there about two o'clock. She was staying that night with her sister, so Maarja would have collected her from the airport in Tallinn. She phoned that evening. Everything was fine. She said she'd phone again in a couple of days."

"Did she always phone you?"

"Yes, usually. Of course, she liked me to phone, but she said it helped her relax if I didn't. Said she'd get uptight waiting for me to call. You see, if I said I'd phone at the same time each night, well, something can come up, like, with the railway or work, and then I don't call till later. She really doesn't like that."

"When did she phone next?"

"Two nights later. The tenth. Thursday. She was still at Maarja's. She was going to Tartu the next morning, the Friday."

"And did she?"

"Yes, she texted me from the train, and phoned from there in the evening."

"Okay. So on the fourth day she's in Tartu. Staying where?"

"With her parents. Then I heard nothing until the Sunday."

"That would be the thirteenth."

"Yes. She phoned me about ten in the morning. Said she was going to visit an old friend who lives in Valga – that's on the border with Latvia. She could get the train directly from Tartu."

"What was the friend's name?"

"I can't remember. I'm sure she mentioned the name, but it wasn't one I recognised. You see, a lot of Estonian names are quite unlike ours. For instance, ..."

"Let's keep focused, shall we? When was the next contact?"

"I got a text on the Tuesday evening, that would be the fifteenth, saying she was still in Valga. Then there was another on Thursday morning."

"The seventeenth?"

"Yes, it would be. Said she was now back at her sister's. I texted her later the same day, maybe about four in the afternoon. The following evening – Friday – I got another text, saying she was going to her parents' place on the following day. Since she hadn't phoned for a few days, I tried to call her, but it seemed her phone was off. I texted her, but got no response. Same again on the

Saturday and the Monday."

"Did you try phoning her parents or sister?"

"No. I'd done that once on a previous trip, but Aino got very angry. Insisted that if I had to phone, I should only call her own mobile. I tried on the Tuesday morning, when she was due to be back, that would be the twenty-second, but again, nothing. I thought she might be on her way to the airport or something. The plane was due in at Glasgow Airport at 10 pm – the last one in from Amsterdam – so I drove down there to meet her. But she wasn't on it. The KLM desk at the airport said she'd not checked in for the flight, maybe she'd decided to wait until the next morning. I stayed overnight in a hotel near the airport, tried phoning with no response. I was there for the first flight the next morning, the Wednesday, that is, but still she wasn't on it."

"You're doing fine," said the sergeant. "What did you do next?"

"I decided to risk phoning her sister, but no-one answered. So I tried the parents. They'd expected her to stay the night before she returned here, but she'd phoned them to say she'd go directly to the airport. And she hadn't been in touch since. At least I think that's what happened. Her father is somewhat deaf, and her mother hardly speaks any English."

"Did you think of coming to us at that point?"

"No. She could easily just turn up and ask why I was making such a fuss."

"So she's done that before? Returned late?"

"Yes, a couple of times, last time was back in January. She'd not shown up at the airport, and I was getting worried, when she phoned up, told me she'd decided to stay on a couple more days, and had changed her flight. She wondered why I was getting so uptight."

"Let's come back to the present. So what did you do next?"

"I went back home. I thought she'd let me know when she was coming back. But I heard nothing then or the next day, the Thursday. That evening I decided to contact you."

"What made you do that?"

"Well, isn't it obvious? I was worried about her. She's never been this late coming back."

Morgan nodded thoughtfully. "Dr Carselaw, can you think of any reason why your wife might not wish to come back?"

"What do you mean by that?"

"I mean that in cases like this, the most likely reason for a partner not returning is a domestic issue. A falling out. Or occasionally something more substantial."

"Are you suggesting my wife has left me?"

"I'm not suggesting anything, Dr Carselaw. I'm just asking you whether some relationship issue could account for your wife's delay in returning."

"Are you saying it's my fault? This is ridiculous. I come here to ask for help and you start blaming me for it. You know nothing about our relationship."

"That's exactly why I'm asking. Please calm down. I'm simply suggesting that you consider whether your relations with your wife could have triggered her delay in returning. We are trying to establish whether there is a possibility that her delay could be voluntary."

Blue cleared his throat politely. "Dr Carselaw. If we don't ask these questions, the Estonian police certainly will. Even if you answer us, they will ask them again, simply because, as Sergeant Morgan has explained, a common cause of such events is a marital difficulty. We do need to know whether this is a possibility."

"All right, all right." Carselaw took a swig of his tea, which must be cold by now. "Obviously, like any couple, we have disagreements from time to time, but these are always resolved. Amicably. There is no big issue between us at the moment. Aino isn't like that, anyway. If there's a problem, she will say so, and we have it out. She doesn't go off in a huff. I understand the point of your question now, which I don't think you made very clearly. But I can't see anything at home that would have caused her not to come back. And I'm worried about her. That's why I'm here."

"Thank you, Dr Carselaw," said Sergeant Morgan quietly. "I know some of this has been difficult, but the more we know the better."

"That's all very well, but is there anything you can do about it? Otherwise I'm going to have to go to Estonia and see if I can find her."

The sergeant turned to Blue. "Inspector Blue, what could you suggest?"

"Well, we can certainly take steps from this end that would be difficult for you as a private citizen. We can contact the Estonian police and make some basic enquiries. For instance, it's possible she may have had an accident and ended up in hospital without her phone. Or has been mugged or got lost or something like that. If that draws a blank we can ask our Estonian colleagues to contact relatives and friends there. I'll get this moving right away, so I'd suggest you wait at home till I or Sergeant Morgan get back to you, before you decide on your next move. It'll only be a day or two. But it could well clear things up, and help you to decide what to do."

"I would agree with Inspector Blue," added Sergeant Morgan. "If you do feel you want to go to Estonia immediately and see family members there, we certainly won't stop you. But waiting a couple of days could make things clearer."

"Yes, thank you. I'll have to think about it."

"There are just a couple of things we'll need, Dr Carselaw. Do you happen to have a recent photograph of your wife? Remember I asked you to bring one when we spoke earlier."

"I have one here." He took his wallet from the inside pocket of his jacket, extracted a folded paper, and opened it on the table. A colour printout from an inkjet printer. Aino was immediately recognisable by her long red hair. Not out of a bottle, but, as Carselaw had said, the real thing. She was slim, of average height, standing with her husband and an elderly couple – Blue guessed they were her parents – by a low wall, beyond which was the muddy water of a river, and on the far bank a park with people walking about or sitting on benches by the riverside. She was smiling, but there was a seriousness in the eyes, as if smiling was not her default expression.

"Can we keep this?" asked Sergeant Morgan.

"Yes, of course. That's why I've brought it."

"It would be even better if you could email us a copy of the original file. That way we can get it quickly to the Estonian police. Can you do that as soon as you get home?"

"It's on my phone here, so I could send it now."

"That's great. Here's my card. Just send it to the email address there."

She waited until he'd done that, checked her iPhone to make sure the image had arrived, then nodded. "That's great, Dr Carselaw. Now, when you get home, see if you can get the names and contact details of her parents and sister. And any other relatives or friends of hers over in Estonia. Even just names if that's all you've got. Then email them to me. Oh, and if you do hear from her, or she turns up, ring me right away. Remember, we'll be back in touch in a day or two, as soon as we've heard something from Estonia. Then you'll be in a better position to decide what to do next."

2

While Sergeant Morgan took Carselaw back down to the entrance, Blue made coffee for both of them. In five minutes she was back. After a thoughtful sip, she asked him what he thought.

"I guess the first question is whether we can trust Dr Carselaw's account. It's always possible he's done away with her and is making it all up. She could be buried in the back garden. Then it would make a lot of sense to report her disappearance before people start asking questions. But the Estonia story would be asking for trouble. It's too exotic not to attract attention. And we can check her flights and so on. Much easier to say they had a falling out and she's gone off to stay with a friend, but he doesn't know who or where. Or that she said she was going to Glasgow to do some shopping and never came back. But that's just my suspicious mind. I'm thinking he's on the level. More or less. I just wonder if he's telling us everything."

"That was my feeling about him too. He did seem worried about her. Though I'm really just a sentimental softie."

"I don't believe that for a moment," said Blue, with a smile.

"But I think he's a bit frightened of her too," Morgan continued. "Her objections to him phoning and reluctance to call him very often worries me."

Blue picked the photo up and peered at it. "Do you think she was happy?"

"We can't tell, Angus. Not till we know a lot more. Right now we just don't know how serious it is. It's possible Aino is on a flight home at this moment, or just picking up her mobile to tell her husband why she'd been delayed. But it's equally possible she's lying in a coma in hospital after being hit by a car on some dark rural road, or been assaulted by a mugger in an alley in darkest Tallinn. So whatever we think, we've got to take it seriously."

"There's another possibility too," said Blue. "Mrs Carselaw isn't in any danger, but doesn't want her husband to know where she is. She could even be leading a double life, spending weeks every year with some other man, in a cottage in the countryside or a city hotel. Or just being on her own for some reason. Who knows, maybe she's writing a novel."

"We really need the details of her friends and family."

"Let me make some initial enquiries with the police in Estonia.

I'll probably have to go through some red tape to make that happen. Why don't you come along to my office on Monday at nine; the rest of my team will be there and we can decide how to take it further. Hopefully by then we'll have an initial response from Tallinn to help us too, and we can get back to Dr Carselaw."

"Sounds good to me. We can still hope Aino will turn up at home tomorrow or Sunday."

No sooner had Blue sat down at his desk than there was a knock at the door. A youngish woman, not tall, not particularly pretty – prettiness isn't a help in the police force – but with an air of stolidity and intelligence. At least that's what it seemed to him.

"Lena! Good to see you. Come on in." Lena Vunsells, who'd been a uniformed officer in Oban, had helped him with a murder case there during the COVID-19 lockdown in 2020, and again the previous year in Appin. He'd recommended her to move to CID. And here she was, a welcome addition to his team.

"How was the training?"

"Very interesting, sir. I learned a lot." Blue nodded. He knew that she'd have made the most of it, taken every opportunity to learn. And also to question. To know the reason why, and to consider the alternatives.

"What made you decide to come back here? You could have headed for the big city."

"I liked working here before. And I think I'll get a more varied experience here, as well as a much better environment. I can't think why I'd want to go to Paisley or Aberdeen, when I can enjoy what's on the doorstep. Besides, I haven't done all the Munros around here yet."

"Good. Well, I'm pleased you've come back. Since Deirdra left for the Uni we've been a bit short-handed in CID. Luckily there have been no big cases. But enough to keep us occupied. For instance, the llama-rustling."

"Llamas?"

"A wildlife place opened up last autumn near Dalmally. Goats, exotic sheep, Shetland ponies, birds, snakes, lots of things for children to look at. Big play park. And a very nice café But somebody targeted the animals. That's the trouble with anything out of the ordinary; it has a price. They took all four of their llamas one night."

"Did you get them?"

"It took a while, but yes, we tracked them down. After a month they tried to sell them to another wildlife place, near Ipswich. We'd already circulated all the wildlife parks with their description."

"The rustlers?"

"No, the llamas. They were very distinctive, apparently. And we got DNA ID too. The place in Ipswich tipped us off, and we got the gang when they arrived to deliver the animals. That's the thing about llamas, they're hard to disguise. Anyway, I've a feeling our next case has just started. We'll have a team meeting at one, Meeting Room 3, same as we used for that case last year. You'll need to sort out a locker and so on. See if you can find Arvind and Enver and say hello to them too. Anything you need from me at this point?"

"No, chief. It's not as if I'm new to the place, or the team."

"See you at one then. And Lena."

"Yes, sir?"

"I'm glad to see you back. You'll be a real asset to us."

"I hope so, sir."

Blue emailed the other members of his team, Sergeant Enver McCader and DC Arvind Bhardwaj, asking them to meet him in Meeting Room 3 at one. Then he headed for the little café by the ferry terminal, buying a goat's cheese and rocket roll and a cup of Fair Trade coffee to take out. In ten minutes he was sitting on the bench at the top of Pulpit Hill, eating his lunch with the harbour and the bay below him, the island of Kerrera behind it and to his left, and the town laid out below and to his right. And beyond the bay the bulky mountains of Mull rose in misty outline. This was a place he could think things through.

Although so far there wasn't a lot to think through. Some feeling in his gut told him that the disappearance of Aino Carselaw, if that's what it was, wasn't going to be as simple as it might be. That could only have been a subconscious reaction to what Paul Carselaw had told them, and the way in which he had told it. They needed to get to work on the case that afternoon.

Blue arrived at Meeting Room 3 just after one, to find McCader, Bhardwaj and Vunsells waiting. The atmosphere was relaxed.

Four cups of coffee sat on the table. There was no need to introduce Vunsells, or to explain why she was there. They could get straight down to business.

"Afternoon, everyone," he began. "First of all, you've noticed Lena's back, and that's good. We don't need to waste time with introductions, and so on. Thanks for the coffee. The next round's mine. Now, to work. We've been given something that might turn out to be quite interesting."

"More interesting than llama-rustling?" said Bhardwaj.

"Indeed, Arvind, possibly so. Let me explain. I've been asked to assist with a missing persons case involving the wife of a man named Paul Carselaw. His wife's name is Aino. A, I, N, O, that is. She's from Estonia, and over there's where she seems to have disappeared. Sergeant Morgan and I spoke to Dr Carselaw this morning, so I can give you an outline of what we know so far. Here's a printout of a timeline to get us started."

The timeline he'd compiled was based on what they'd gleaned from Dr Carselaw.

1962	Paul Carselaw born in Stratford on Avon
1965	14 Sept. Aino Kuusk born, Kuressaare, Estonia
1986	Aino Kuusk marries Kalev Lind
1986	Paul Carselaw gets PhD, moves to Plymouth
1987	Aino and Kalev Lind's daughter Tiina born
1988	Aino and Kalev divorced
1989	Aino Kuusk comes to Plymouth, in June meets Paul
1990	Aino and Paul married, Sept 23rd
1991	Estonia becomes independent
2004	They move to Helensburgh
2013	They move to Oban

2022

Tues, 8 November:

morning, Carselaws drive to Glasgow Airport
6.05, Aino flies to Tallinn, stays with her sister
evening, Aino phones Paul

Thurs, 10 November:

evening, Aino phones Paul

Fri, 11 November

morning, Aino texts Paul from train to Tartu

Evening, Aino phones Paul from Tartu
Sun, 13 November
10 am, Aino phones Paul, says she's going to Valga
Tues, 15 November
evening, Aino texts Paul that she's still in Valga
Thurs, 17 November
morning, Aino texts Paul that she's at her sister's
Fri, 18 November
evening, Aino texts she's going to her parents on Saturday
Paul phones and texts back but no response
Sat, 19 November
Paul texts; no answer
Mon, 21 November
Paul texts; no answer
Tues, 22 November
Paul phones; no answer
10 pm, Aino doesn't show up at the airport
Wed, 23 November
No Aino. Paul phones parents. Goes back to Oban
Fri, 25 November
morning, Paul phones police

He talked them through the timeline, giving them plenty of time to digest the information.

"Okay," he concluded, "There are several possibilities. The simplest is that his wife decided to stay on a bit longer and neglected to tell him. If that's the case, she'll get in touch with him in the next few days, and that'll hopefully be that. The next is that she's had some sort of illness or accident, or got involved in something else that is delaying her return, and her family don't know about it. Maybe she had a car accident and ended up in hospital. Or got involved in something illegal and is sitting in jail. Well, if that's the case, an enquiry to the Estonian police will give us the facts.

"Those are the most likely scenarios. There are, however, three more possibilities. One is that his wife has left him and isn't planning on coming back. If that's the case, she'll most likely get in touch with him, to tell him that, because the last thing she'll want is him roaming round Estonia chasing after her. The final two possibilities are darker. One, she's been abducted or even murdered in Estonia. And two, Dr Carselaw murdered her himself before she left for Estonia, and is trying to cover it up. The good news is that these last two are very unlikely, and we don't need to consider them at this point."

"Unless we discover something that points us in those directions," added McCader.

"Quite. Lena, what do you suggest we do now?"

Vunsells paused, thinking about the question. She never gave answers without thinking. "Contact the Estonian police."

"Exactly," said Blue. "I'll do that this afternoon. I'll also check with the airlines whether Aino Carselaw actually flew out to Estonia, and if she flew back. Or, indeed, whether she flew somewhere else altogether. Anything else we might be doing, Arvind?"

"Er, find out more about the missing woman?"

"Good answer. The more we know about her, the closer we get to why she's not come back. That's something I'd like you and Lena to follow up. Have a chat with Sergeant Morgan first, and take on board what she knows. Then see what else you can find out about Aino Carselaw. Start with the basic facts that'll be on paper. I'm guessing she now has UK citizenship, so there will be records about that. And she married here, so there's more paperwork. Then there's the shop she worked at. And anything else. Facebook might be worth looking at. But don't phone up anyone who might know her, we'll get to that later. We're just looking for basic facts at this stage."

"Not much different from what we used to do in uniform," said Bhardwaj.

"Plenty of CID work isn't that different. You've always got to start with the facts. And there's always plenty of legwork too. Enver, can I ask you to dig up whatever you can about Dr Carselaw. He may or may not be trustworthy, and we can't rely on his say-so for the facts of the case. Okay, we'll meet up here again at, let's see, four thirty, and see what we've got."

Blue's first call was to Superintendent Campbell. He reported on his meeting with Carselaw, and what his team were doing.

"Good, good. Now, you'll be wanting to talk with somebody over in Estonia, of course."

"Yes, chief, soon as I can. We need to get things moving, just in case..."

"Yes, of course. I've got the OK for us to work with the police there. I've emailed you the contact details for their liaison officers. Let me know how you get on."

He checked the time zone for Estonia and found they were two hours ahead of Scotland. So it would be nearly four there now. He'd need to get on to it right away.

His call was answered by a female voice in perfect English. "Police Department of Estonia, International Liaison Office. How may I help you?"

Blue gave his own details and the case reference number. The woman asked him to outline the facts of the case briefly, so that she could categorise his enquiry.

"Thank you, Inspector," she concluded. "This is categorised for the present as a missing persons enquiry. Please send an email to the address I will give you, describing the exact nature of your enquiry and providing whatever information you have at this moment, including a photograph of the missing person. We will then direct your query to the appropriate agency and location. They will make inquiries and report their findings back to you. This will happen, if possible, tomorrow or the following day. Do you understand?"

Blue said he did, and that was that. Before settling down to compile the email, he phoned Glasgow Airport and was put through to the KLM office there. He spoke to a woman who introduced herself as Diane. It did not take long for her to confirm that Aino Carselaw had indeed left Glasgow on the 6.05 am flight from Glasgow to Amsterdam on Tuesday 8th November. She had then boarded the 10.30 flight to Tallinn.

"I suppose she'd have spent most of her time in Amsterdam in the queue for non-EU citizens," he commented.

"That all depends. Can I ask if the lady is of non-UK origin?"

"Yes, she's Estonian by birth."

"Does she have an Estonian passport?"

"Good question. I'm afraid I don't know."

"If she does retain dual nationality, she could present her Estonian passport at the security gate in Schiphol. As an EU citizen, that would have got her through the checks quite quickly. Our records here show that she presented a UK passport at the security gate in Glasgow, but I'd have to contact Schiphol to see what she presented there."

Of course, thought Blue, he should have realised she'd retain her Estonian citizenship. It would make all those trips back to her homeland so much easier. He asked Diane whether Aino had returned from Estonia, either on the day she was supposed to, or some other time. Diane confirmed that she was booked on return flights on Tuesday 22nd November, but had not travelled on those flights. She would need more time to check whether she had come back using any other flight, and promised to phone back as soon as she had the information.

This at least confirmed that she'd gone to Estonia and not come back on the planned flights. Now he could get on with the email to the Estonian police. The timeline was a very useful prompt, and an hour and a quarter later he sent the email off.

After that he began his report. Writing up reports was the most tedious aspect of police work, and Blue liked it no more than any other officer. But he realised it had to be done. Rather than waiting till the end of a case, he preferred to begin the report at the beginning of the investigation, updating as he went along. This could be time-consuming, but gave him the opportunity to think through the updates and additions, and get a sense of the daily changes in the picture they formed. As the chief investigating officer, it was his job to keep that picture in front of him.

He was about to head for the canteen when his phone rang. Diane from KLM. "Hi Inspector. I've done some checking. We've no record of an Aino Carselaw on any KLM flight on the twenty-second, or on the twenty-third or twenty-fourth. Or even this morning. I could ask my colleagues at Schiphol to see whether she has passed through there on those days, using a different airline, if that will help. By the way, at Schiphol security, she presented her Estonian passport."

Blue considered this. "Thanks, Diane. I may get back to you on that later, but what you've given me will be very useful for the moment. Many thanks again for your help." Aino Carselaw had not returned as planned, that was clear. If she wasn't still in Estonia, she could now be anywhere else in the world. He would have to see what the Estonians would come up with.

They assembled again at half past four. Blue began by reporting on his contacts with the Estonian police and KLM. Then he asked Bhardwaj and Vunsells what they'd found out about Aino Carselaw.

Bhardwaj began. "Well, boss, we had a good chat with Sergeant Morgan, and she gave us some useful pointers. The first thing we tracked down was the Carselaws' wedding. 23rd September 1990 at the registry office in Plymouth. Her name was given as Aino Kuusk, his as Paul Marcus Carselaw. They had separate addresses. The registry office told me she would have had to show proof of her divorce before the marriage went ahead; just saying it had happened wouldn't be enough."

"Unless she didn't mention her first marriage at all," added Vunsells.

"That would be bigamy!" gasped Bhardwaj.

"That's a good point," commented Blue. "If there was no mention of her divorce, or of her first marriage, in the form submitted to the registrar, it tells us something about Mrs Carselaw. I think you need to get back to the Registrar's Office and find out what was submitted by Aino in terms of her first marriage. What else have you got?"

Vunsells looked around the group to get their attention. "I looked for Aino Carselaw, or Aino Kuusk, on social media. Not a sausage! Searches across the internet got no responses relating to her. Aino Kuusk is not an uncommon name in Estonia, and there were several. I checked each one out and none of them are her."

"OK. We'll have to talk again with Dr Carselaw, and ask him what sort of activities his wife was involved in. We're not getting a very clear picture of her yet. Enver, what about Dr Carselaw?"

McCader glanced at a pad on the table in front of him before speaking. "Birth details as he said. Went to primary and then grammar school in Stratford, then Warwick University in 1980. BSc in electronic engineering, 1983 and MSc in systems analysis, 1984. This is where it gets more interesting. He enrolled for a PhD in electronic systems analysis in 1984. But it seems that after two years full-time, he then switched to part-time. I'm guessing that's when he got the job with X-Syst-X. But there's no record of him submitting his thesis or getting the degree."

"Then he's not actually Doctor Carselaw?" said Vunsells.

"That's right. Though he clearly likes the title. I'm guessing no-one questions it. After all, to do that you'd have to do what I did, and sweet-talk the university records office."

"Surely X-Syst-X would have asked for proof?" asked Bhardwaj.

"Not necessarily," put in Blue. "I presume he got the job on the basis of his first two degrees, and good reports from his PhD supervisor. Then all he had to do was tell the company he was going part-time. Two or three years later he'd simply tell them he'd got the doctorate. They'd congratulate him, and change their records accordingly. Why should anyone question it? But it does tell us that Mr Carselaw can be dishonest when it suits him. OK, anything else?"

"I checked out X-Syst-X," said McCader, "but they don't make it easy. Their website tells us little more than that they exist. There's no means of contacting them given. Their head office is in Anguilla, that's a tiny British-owned island in the Caribbean. That doesn't mean they're doing anything illegal, by the way, just means they're avoiding paying tax. The Chairman and CEO is one Anthony Farnley-Montserrat; he has a nice house in Sussex and a villa in the South of France. Not doing badly, I think. As to what they do, it's systems analysis and design. I haven't found who their clients are yet, but if both they and Mr Carselaw won't say, it's probably government-related. And Plymouth suggests to me the naval dockyard at Devonport. I'd guess Carselaw was working on warship systems of some sort. Then they move to Helensburgh. Where's that near?"

"Faslane!" said Bhardwaj. "Nuclear subs. Maybe he was working on intelligent torpedoes. Or nuclear missiles."

"As with X-Syst-X," continued McCader, "it doesn't mean that he's up to no good. But it does explain why he's cagey about it. If he is doing something like that, he'll have signed the Official Secrets Act, so he daren't say anything."

"All right," concluded Blue, "that's filled in some of the background. But we need to find out more about Aino, so that'll be something for Monday. I'm hoping the Estonian police will get back to me before then. Let's leave it there for today. We'll meet here on Monday at nine. Have a good weekend."

3

Saturday 26 November

Angus Blue sat at the old kitchen table, of much-scarred and much-scrubbed oak, at breakfast. A mug of Assam tea (milk, no sugar) and a plate of toast and marmalade lay before him. The toast from his home-made bread (although he did use a machine), and the marmalade of his own manufacture. Opposite him Alison Hendrickx preferred coffee (real, black, no sugar) with her toast. Their dog, Corrie, a black-and-white border collie, sat in her bed in the corner of the room. She'd already had her morning walk, and looked forward to being fed once the leaders of the pack had eaten. Nevertheless she kept a close watch on the eaters, just in case something should fall from the table.

Blue had recounted the main points in the case of Aino Carselaw to Alison the previous evening, over a meal of baked salmon in oatmeal, roast potatoes and parsnips sautéd in butter, with a delicate Hollandaise sauce. He did not keep anything from Alison. He knew policemen who'd tried to keep their work rigidly separate, and therefore secret, from their loved ones, and knew that it didn't work. He also knew he could trust Alison to give nothing away to anyone else. And being involved in police work herself, as a forensic archaeologist, she knew how to be discreet.

But that didn't stop her having an opinion. "I'd say there's a fair chance that she's had enough of him and has decided now's the time to clear off. The husband sounds more interested in his train set than in his wife. Some men never grow up. Or is it a need to control something? Inanimate objects that are easier to deal with than people?"

"You don't think she'll come back?"

"I'm only guessing, Angus. But her hardly contacting him, saying she doesn't like him calling, not letting him know her plans, it all looks to me like she's keeping him at a distance."

"You think there might be another man? Or woman?"

"I'm not so sure about that. It's a kind of male conceit, isn't it, to think that if a woman leaves her partner, there must be another man. Maybe she just wants to be her own boss for a bit. Perhaps that's what all the visits to Estonia are really about. Not so much visiting friends and family as just being able to do exactly what you want for a while. Go where you want, eat what you want. Even to speak to others using your own mother tongue. Him not learning Estonian speaks volumes to me. It doesn't matter how hard it is, he should have been trying."

"Well, we'll see if she returns over the weekend."

"I wonder if he's more annoyed than worried about her. Resentful that she does her own thing. Not behaving as a woman should."

"Needs to be taught a lesson?"

"That's not what I was going to say. But you can't tell at this stage what he'll do. You need to find out more about him as well as her."

"What if he does go over to try and find her?"

"That could make matters worse. She could have briefed family and friends to keep him in the dark. Then he'll get frustrated and who knows what could happen. You could even have a murder on your hands."

"Thankfully it would be the Estonian police, rather than me. Anyway, there's only one jar of marmalade left in the cupboard. I'll have to make another batch soon. That could mean going to the supermarket sometime this weekend."

"You know how to give a girl a good time, Angus. Better start making a list."

They were back from the supermarket by eleven, and thinking about what to do with the rest of the day, when Blue's phone rang. It was Katie from the reception desk at the police station. "A call from Estonia, sir. Is it convenient to take it now? I can switch it through to your phone."

"Please do. Thanks, Katie."

He switched on the speaker on the phone. "Inspector Blue here."

"Good morning, Inspector," came a woman's voice. "Please wait a moment." He listened to an accordion playing a lively waltz, he supposed an Estonian folk tune, until the line picked up again.

"Inspector Blue?" An older woman, he guessed, than the first voice. "I'm Sergeant Riita Haavik, Missing Persons Officer, Tallinn Police Headquarters. Thank you for your email, it's very helpful when things are explained in writing. We have already contacted the hospitals, and there's no record of their having treated anyone with the name Carselaw. Similarly we have no reports of any incident involving her. I've emailed the image you sent us to the police network, and if that produces any response I'll get back to you. If you have details of her relatives here, we can contact them."

"She may be using her maiden name, Kuusk, or even her previous married name, Lind."

"We can check for them. Kuusk is a common name in Estonia. It will take longer to check."

"Thank you. I'll get back to you as soon as I have more information."

"Thank you, inspector. Please do. Then we can do more for you. Goodbye."

He was impressed that Sergeant Haavik had got off the mark very rapidly. It would have been straightforward if they'd found Aino Carselaw unconscious in a hospital, or even drunk in a police cell. Case solved. But it wasn't usually as simple as that. They needed more information on Mrs Carselaw. Then Sergeant Haavik might come back with something positive, or even suggest ways in which they could widen the search. She knew the country and its people; he didn't.

"What are you thinking, Angus?"

"It's just got a bit more complicated. But not necessarily worrying. Not yet, anyway. Let's see where we are on Monday. So, what about today? Where shall we go? The weather's not looking so good, but at least it's not raining. And Corrie could do with a good run about."

4

Monday 28 November

Blue was in his office at eight. He and Alison had spent the previous evening looking up all they could find about Estonia on the internet. He now had a rough outline of its history and geography, and had seen some impressive images of the Old Town of Tallinn, a frequent stopping point for Baltic Cruise ships. It looked like a place worth visiting. Neither he nor Alison were into lounging on a beach when there were historical sites or interesting walks available. Alison had headed off at half past seven, taking Corrie with her, to get to the Police College at Tulliallan on time for a planning meeting. He'd received no further messages about Aino Carselaw since Saturday morning, and there were no emails about her waiting for him.

He met Sergeant Morgan on the way up to the meeting room. Bhardwaj, Vunsells and McCader were already there. Blue began with his phone call from Tallinn, then asked if anyone had anything to add.

Vunsells raised her hand. "I managed to speak to someone at Plymouth University after the meeting on Friday. In the registry. They fished out Aino's file. Wouldn't tell me her marks, that's confidential, but did say she passed with a very good grade. The address on her application form was care of her parents in Herne Street in Tartu. Her address whilst at the uni was a bedsit in Plymstock, that's on the eastern edge of Plymouth. She attended the graduation in June 1989 and collected her certificate. They keep a note of the first jobs their students get, but she didn't return the form, so they assumed she'd gone back to Estonia."

"That's useful, thanks Lena. Anything else?"

"Well, yes," said Vunsells, "I've got a bit more. I found the website for her bookshop, Eastwards Books. It didn't give the name of the owner, but described itself as 'an independent antiquarian bookseller, specialising in books of European origin.' The address is there, but there's also a contact form, so that enquiries can be made from anywhere in the world."

"Was there a catalogue or list of the books they had for sale?" asked Blue.

"No. But it did say that requests for specific information could be made using the contact form."

"OK, thanks Lena. Aelwyn, I suggest we take a look at the bookshop today. By the way, everyone, this is a missing persons' case, and we must make no assumption that a crime has been committed. Sergeant Morgan is therefore in charge of the inquiry. Aelwyn, you know where we are now. What would you suggest we do next?"

"Thanks, Angus. We need to talk to Mr Carselaw again, so I think a surprise visit to their flat might be a good idea. That would give us the chance to get a feel of their home, as well as get more information from him. We need to find a bit more about his wife, and see any documentation he has on her: birth certificate, marriage and driving licence, club memberships, official letters, and so on. An example of her handwriting, in case there's a note somewhere. And more pictures."

"Mr Carselaw should be able to give us the mobile number she's using over there," said Bhardwaj. "That could be useful in locating her."

"That would be very useful," agreed Sergeant Morgan.

"What about pictures of her in Estonia?" suggested Vunsells. "Especially ones that he didn't take himself. The backgrounds may tell the Estonian police where they are."

"That's a useful idea too."

"Example of her DNA?" put in Bhardwaj. "In case the worst comes to the worst. Better to have it now than come to him and say we found a corpse and can we have her hairbrush. We could say it's purely for identification purposes. In case she's lost her memory, or something like that."

"I don't usually go down that line so soon," said Sergeant Morgan. "What do you think, Angus?"

"I'd say the more we can give the Estonian police the better. We know she did go there, and that she didn't return. That means she's probably still in Estonia. If not, she could be anywhere else in the world by now."

"Or at the bottom of the Baltic," added McCader.

"What about finance?" asked Vunsells. "What did she do for money out there? She may have had a separate bank account in Estonia."

"That's another good point," said Blue. "We'll ask her husband about that."

"He may not be aware of it," said Vunsells. "What if she wanted to leave her husband? Setting up separate financial resources could be part of the plan."

"It's certainly a possibility. Aelwyn, can I suggest the team continue to investigate the Carselaws, while we visit the flat and then the bookshop."

"That's a reasonable suggestion, Angus. Thanks for your help. It would certainly have taken me a while to get to where we are now on my own."

Blue and Morgan took a pool car. Turning left by the Corran Halls, they passed grand Victorian or Edwardian houses and hotels, then left the town to follow the road hugging the coast. They passed the ruins of Dunollie Castle on their right, and in five minutes arrived at Ganavan, and parked in the car park facing the bay. In front of them lay the beach, deserted on a cold and blustery morning, and to their right the path up the hill favoured by dog-walkers. To their left the modern apartment blocks reached onto the shore, almost cutting off part of the bay. Only a narrow path remained to give access to the war memorial on the grassy point overlooking the water.

At the entrance to the first block, Blue noticed that above the panel of doorbells was a camera. The sergeant rang the bell, and they waited. After a minute they heard Carselaw's voice from the speaker. "Yes, who is it? Move in front of the camera please."

"This is Sergeant Morgan and Detective Inspector Blue," said the sergeant. "We'd like to have a word. We have some news regarding your wife."

"All right, just wait there. I'm in the garage. I'll be round in a moment."

Working on his train set, thought Blue. Taking his mind off his wife's disappearance? Or relieved that she was no longer around, and he could get with the things he really liked?

A few minutes later, Paul Carselaw appeared around the corner of the building and came towards them, frowning. He nodded briefly to Blue, ignoring Sergeant Morgan. "What is it, then?" he asked. "I'm right in the middle of something. You could have phoned me, rather than coming here."

"We're sorry to disturb you, sir," said Sergeant Morgan, "but we have some news, and we need to talk with you about it.

Preferably in private." She said nothing more, and moved aside to allow Carselaw to reach the door.

"All right, if you must," sighed Carselaw. He punched a code into the numeric panel, and the door clicked open. They followed him up the stairs to the second floor, and the door of Flat 2.2. Blue noticed there was no name plate on the door. Carselaw unlocked the door and went in, beckoning the two police officers to enter.

He pointed them through the entrance hall to a bright and spacious lounge with French windows opening onto a wide balcony overlooking the bay. The room was sparsely furnished with a sofa and matching armchair, and an anonymous coffee table. A large TV screen was fixed on the wall opposite the sofa. A couple of prints in frames hung on the magnolia walls, bland scenes of beaches and palm trees. There were no family photos; perhaps they were in another room.

Carselaw waved them to the sofa and sat himself in the armchair. No offer of tea or coffee, noted Blue. "Have you located her, then?" he asked, directing his gaze at Blue, and glancing at his watch as if to suggest that the answer should be delivered as concisely as possible.

Blue looked at Morgan, who replied. "No, sir, not yet. However, the Estonian police have informed us that she is not in a hospital, or other public institution, and that they have no record of any incident in which she has been involved, at least under the name of Aino Carselaw."

Silence ensued as Carselaw processed this information. "So where does that leave us?"

"It means she has not had an accident, or come to the attention of the police in any other way. We have asked them to carry out the same check using her maiden name of Aino Kuusk, or her previous married name of Aino Lind."

"You could have phoned just to tell me that."

"I'm afraid not, Mr Carselaw..."

"*Doctor* Carselaw," he snapped, "If you please."

"Which university awarded you this doctorate, Mr Carselaw?" asked Blue quietly.

"What do you mean? Why are you asking me this. Didn't I tell you yesterday? It was Exeter."

"I'm sorry, sir, but Exeter University have no record of

awarding you a PhD. According to their records you went part-time after two years, but did not subsequently submit a thesis. Perhaps it was some other university? We can easily check."

Carselaw paused, staring at the floor as if seeking inspiration from the bland grey carpet. Receiving no response, he looked up at them again. "All right. You win. I don't actually have a PhD. But the title gives our customers confidence that I'm the right person to deal with them. And the only reason I didn't complete it is that I was head-hunted by X-Syst-X. And why the hell are you poking your noses into my background? It's my wife you're supposed to be finding!"

"It's not a question of winning," said Blue, "simply of having accurate information. If we are to do our best to find your wife, we need to be sure the information you give us is reliable. That's why it worries us that what you told us about yourself is not accurate."

"You're blowing this up out of all proportion. After all, people can call themselves anything they want these days. There's no law saying I can't call myself Dr Carselaw. Anyway, what is it you want now?"

"Any further contact from your wife since Friday?" asked Sergeant Morgan.

"No."

"It is possible she may be using her maiden name, Aino Kuusk. But this is apparently a common name in Estonia, and it will help the Estonian police if they get more information about her before they can make further enquiries. Any information, especially of an official nature, would be helpful. For instance, does your wife have an Estonian passport?"

"Yes, she does." Carselaw was more subdued now.

"In what name?"

"I don't understand. Aino Carselaw of course."

"Are you sure of that, sir?"

"Of course. Well, I haven't looked inside, but what else would she put in it? That's her name."

"It could also be in the name of Aino Kuusk."

"She's no longer Aino Kuusk."

"In some countries women retain their maiden names for various purposes. Even here it's not uncommon for a woman to continue to use her maiden name at work, even after being married. Do you by any chance have a record of the number of your wife's Estonian passport?"

"I don't. But there's a file with official details of Aino. It'll be in the filing cabinet in the study."

"Perhaps we could have a look at that file, sir."

"Yes, yes, I'll go and get it now. Wait here." Carselaw was evidently not keen for them to follow him through into the study.

He was back five minutes later with a slim brown cardboard folder. He put it on the coffee table and opened it up. Inside were a number of clear plastic folders. Carselaw quickly opened each one and looked swiftly at the contents, frowning as he did so.

"This is where all her personal data is kept. You know, NHS, HMRC, old P60s from work, that sort of thing. The NHS stuff is there, and the tax letters, and one or two other things, but that's it. Nothing else. I know her birth certificate was there. And there was a pile of stuff in Estonian: divorce papers and passport forms, and so on. But all the Estonian stuff's gone. She must have moved it to another file."

"When did you last look at this file, sir?" asked Morgan.

"Ages ago. I mean, why should I be looking at Aino's stuff? She's very sensitive about it."

"OK, sir, let's see what else there is. Does she have her own bank account?"

"Yes. She needs that for managing the shop accounts. I've no idea how much is in it."

"Do you know which bank it's with?"

"No. We keep our own finances separate."

"Does she have an account with an Estonian bank? For use when she's over there?"

"Yes. She gets cash with it. But I don't know which bank it's with."

"What about Aino's relatives and friends in Estonia? Do you have any details there?"

"Well, I've got the address of her parents and sister, they're in my address book. She has her own address book, but she'll have taken that with her, it was always in her handbag."

"Hmm. Can I ask if Aino has a laptop, or if she used a shared PC here?"

"She has her own laptop. She always uses that. I don't even have the password for it. And she takes it with her whenever she goes to Estonia. So it's not here either."

"What about her business records?" asked Blue.

"She has a spreadsheet on her laptop."

"Paper records? Printouts?"

"Any paperwork will be in her office at the bookshop."

"Can you give me the details for Aino's parents and sister now?" asked the sergeant. "Oh, and the mobile number Aino is using in Estonia."

Carselaw went back to the study and returned with a small black notebook. He carefully tore out a page at the back, then copied out the information they'd requested. He handed the sheet to Blue. "The mobile is an Estonian number, by the way. She always uses that when she's over there."

"Thank you, Mr Carselaw," said Morgan. "There is one further thing. We'd like samples of your wife's fingerprints, and some items from which DNA can be analysed."

"What do you need them for?"

"Circumstances can arise in which people who've disappeared are found, but have lost all means of definite identification. For instance, what if your wife has had an accident, without any documents on her, and is suffering from amnesia or concussion? Fingerprints and DNA would enable a secure identification. We're not saying this has happened, but if the Estonian police have her fingerprints and DNA profile, it could enable something like that to be dealt with rapidly. It's a simple matter for us to take these. All we need for the prints is some item touched by Aino before she left. For instance, if she put away some dishes, there may be clear prints there. For DNA, the best thing is a few hairs, so if there's a hairbrush of hers in the bathroom, we would just take a few."

"Yes. I suppose so." Carselaw didn't seem too enthusiastic.

Blue was meanwhile pulling on a set of blue nitrile gloves, and took from his rucksack a print-collecting kit. He followed Carselaw to the kitchen, and soon captured a good set from a large wine glass, and another set from a plate, which Carselaw said she had put away after washing them. Then they went to the bathroom where, using tweezers, he extracted several long ginger hairs from a brush, put them in an evidence bag and sealed it. As they returned to the living-room, Blue paused. "Just one more thing, sir. We'll need a set of your prints too."

"What! That's ridiculous. I'm not missing. What's going on?"

"Nothing's going on, sir. But we need to be sure the ones I've just collected are not yours."

"Didn't I just tell you they were Aino's?"

"Yes, you did, but we must be clear that there's no error. You are the only other permanent resident of this flat, so it's important that we can show that these prints are not yours. You can be sure that once Aino has been found, your prints will be destroyed."

"I don't believe that for a moment. But I don't suppose I have any option, have I?"

"Of course you can refuse, Mr Carselaw. But there is no point in us sending a set of prints to Estonia if we're not completely clear that they're your wife's and not yours."

Carselaw sighed and held out his hands. "All right, get on with it."

Blue took another kit from his rucksack and collected Carselaw's prints. Once he had washed his hands and returned to the living-room, Sergeant Morgan asked if he had any questions.

"Not that I can think of. I suppose you know what you're doing. But I think I might have to go there myself and see if I can track her down. I've got a meeting of the West Coast Model Railway Society on Wednesday, so it'll have to be after that. Maybe Thursday or Friday."

"That's entirely your decision, sir," said Morgan. "Tell you what. We'll give you a ring if anything turns up before Wednesday morning, and if you give us your mobile number we can keep in touch with you over there. We'll keep looking for her at this end, in case she suddenly comes back, and will be sure to let you know. Do let us know which flights you'll be on."

5

They returned the car to the police station, and set off on foot for the bookshop. Dark clouds hung over the town. Stairfoot Lane was a narrow alley, leading off the main road, with tenement buildings three storeys high on the left, and a ten-foot stone wall on the right, probably separating the lane from the distillery grounds. There was a café advertising its organic and vegan credentials on the corner, then beyond it a shop selling bracelets, necklaces, earrings and other small objects made of weathered glass recovered from the sea. The next small shop was unoccupied, the window roughly whitewashed on the inside, some time ago, it seemed, from the pile of junk mail on the floor that they could see through the glass panel in the door. Then came the entrance to a close, giving access to the flats above, and then the bookshop. Beyond it, the tenement continued to the end of the lane, with one further set of flats. At the very end a weathered stone staircase climbed a steep bank and out of sight.

The frontage of the bookshop had not been changed since its previous owner, or maybe the one before that, for on the board above the window was announced 'Baird's Bakery'. The shop window was dirty and peering through, Blue could only see a sign propped at the rear of the narrow display space reading 'Antiquarian Bookseller.' Aino clearly saw no need to attract local customers. If business was mainly done online, maybe the intention was even to dissuade casual passers-by. He glanced up at the flats above; but there were no lights in any of them, despite the gloom.

A bell tinkled as they entered. The interior was as dim as the alley outside, and Blue wondered if the shop was closed. Then they heard a door open in the darkness at the rear and a low wattage light bulb came on. In the light a female figure became visible. For a moment Blue imagined it was Aino, manning the shop whilst her husband believed she was at the other end of Europe. But no, this woman, although about the same height and build as Aino, did not otherwise resemble the image they had of her. She was younger – perhaps in her twenties – and her face more open in its expression that Aino's. And her hair was blonde. She stood behind a counter. Glancing round the shop, in the meagre light cast by the single bulb, Blue could see book-lined shelves on every side. Not the colourful spines of volume paperbacks, but the bland, monochrome spines of hardbacks without even the colourful flicker of a dust jacket. Breathing in, he could smell decayed paper and the dust of ages.

The woman smiled. "How may I help you?" she said nervously, in an accent from somewhere in Eastern Europe. Then the smile disappeared, and she put her hand to her mouth, and stared beyond him. Fear was written on her face.

Blue realised she was staring at Sergeant Morgan, a police officer in uniform.

"Good afternoon," he said, as pleasantly as he could. "This is Eastwards Books?"

"Yes, sir." Her voice had shrunk to a whisper.

They showed their warrant cards. "I am Detective Inspector Blue, and this is Sergeant Morgan. I wonder if we could ask you a few questions?"

"Yes."

"Can you tell us who you are, please?"

"My name is Anna. Anna Zeresova. What is it about, please?

"Do you work here, Ms Zeresova?"

"Yes, sir. My papers are in order, I swear it!"

"Please, Miss Zeresova," said Blue, "relax. We're not here about you, and we don't want to see your papers. It's Mrs Carselaw we're looking for."

The woman relaxed somewhat, and cleared her throat. "Mrs Carselaw is not here."

"Mrs Carselaw is the owner of the shop, is that correct?"

"Yes. And also Mr Balfour. But he is not here either."

"Have you worked here long?" asked Sergeant Morgan, smiling.

"Six months. I am a refugee, you understand. From Ukraine. We lived on the edge of Luhansk province. When Putin's creatures seized the district, we fled. We stayed with relatives in Kyiv. But my father was afraid it would get worse, and sent me here to be safe."

"Is your family okay?"

"Yes, thank you. So far they are safe. But who knows what will come?"

"It must be very difficult. As Inspector Blue said, we're trying to find Mrs Carselaw. We think she may be in Estonia. Is that right?"

"Yes, yes." Anna nodded vigorously. "That is where she is.

Where her family live."

"Can you tell us when she was last here, in the shop?"

"Let me check my diary." Anna took out her phone, tapped it a few times. "It was Monday the seventh of November. She was going to Estonia the next day. She came in, in the morning only, to make sure I had the things I needed to look after the shop."

"Did she say how long she would be away?"

"She said about two weeks." She looked at the phone again. "She was due back in the shop on the twenty-third. That was last Wednesday."

"Have you had any message from her, perhaps explaining her delay in returning?"

"No, not one."

"Is the shop open every day?" asked Blue.

"Monday to Friday, yes. We are not open on Saturday and Sunday."

"Wouldn't you get a lot of customers then?"

"Mrs Carselaw says on weekends the wrong sort of customers will come. Tourists looking for guidebooks or paperback novels. We do not sell these things."

"Ah. What kind of books do you sell?"

"Old books. Not popular books. Academic books. Also rare books and first editions. We specialise in books about Eastern and Northern Europe."

"May we look around?"

"Yes, sir, of course." She flicked a switch and the level of lighting rose significantly. Now Blue could even see the titles. "We have low lighting," Anna explained, "to preserve the books better. The light is turned brighter if there is a customer in the shop, or we must locate a particular book."

Blue walked around the nearest shelves. According to the handwritten labels stuck to the shelves, the books seemed to be organised by country, then by subject. Countries included Norway, Sweden, Denmark, Finland, Estonia, Latvia, Lithuania and Poland. Topics included history, geography, language, culture, and politics. Many of the books were in the language of the country concerned, although he noted that there were also books in English, German, French and Russian, as well as languages he didn't recognise.

To the right of the counter was a glass-fronted cupboard, with more books inside.

"Do you keep particular books in here?" he asked.

"These are old or rare volumes. Please look. The doors are not locked while I am in the shop."

"Thank you." Blue opened the left hand door and took a book at random, handling it very carefully. He looked at the title page. Virgil's *Aeneid*, published in Warsaw in 1767. The text was in Latin on the right-hand pages, with text in what looked like Polish on the left. A translation, he guessed, as it also seemed to be in verse.

"Fascinating!" he said. "How much would you sell this one for? I don't see a price marked on it. But I guess you don't want to mark such old books."

"That's right, sir. We have a catalogue, and the prices are there. I can look it up for you."

"Yes. Thank you. I don't want to buy it. I just want an idea of what it would sell for."

"The price in the catalogue is not always the price for which the book sells. Sometimes the customer will offer a bargain."

"Haggle?"

"Yes, that is the word. Forgive me, my English is not perfect. Please, give me the book and I will consult the catalogue." Blue handed her the book. She opened a laptop on the counter and typed a few words in, then stared at the screen. She looked up again. "Mrs Carselaw would ask for this book four hundred euros. It is not particularly rare, I think, but not easy to come by. And if Mrs Carselaw thinks you will pay more, she may start with a higher price. Maybe six hundred euros."

"Thank you. Are these the most valuable books you have here?"

"There are sometimes more valuable books. They would be kept in the safe in the office. I do not deal with such books. Only Mrs Carselaw and Mr Balfour."

Blue nodded. "Okay. Thank you. Tell me, when she's here in Oban, how often does Mrs Carselaw come into the shop?"

"Most days she is here, but not always for the whole day. Sometimes only for the morning or the afternoon, or even just an hour or two."

"Otherwise you are in charge of the shop?"

"Yes, sir."

"And what about Mr Balfour? Does he come in regularly?"

"No. Not at all. Sometimes there are three or four weeks when he is not here."

"So it's Mrs Carselaw who runs the shop, I mean organises the stock and so on?"

"Yes, that is correct. She catalogues the books, and sets the prices."

"So what does Mr Balfour do?"

"Sometimes he brings more books for the shop, or removes some. He has interests in other shops too. Much of the time he spends in the office talking with Mrs Carselaw."

"Are they close friends?"

Anna smiled. "No. I think their relationship is about business only."

"Thank you, Anna," said Sergeant Morgan. "Can we see Mrs Carselaw's office now? She has been reported missing and we'd like to see if she has any addresses of contacts in Estonia."

Anna led them past the counter, through the door into a dim corridor. At the end Blue could see a small frosted pane in a door, presumably leading to the back green. There were two closed doors on either side of the corridor, one immediately on his left, another about halfway down on his left, opposite a door on the right, and finally a door on the right almost at the rear entrance.

Anna opened the door halfway down on the right and switched the light on. "This is the office," she said. A much-begrimed window high up in the wall offered the only natural light available. The room looked as if it had not been refurbished for decades. Old grey wallpaper peeled at the edges of the strips, and a worn dark red rug lay on the fawn lino which covered the floor. An old wooden desk lurked under the window, a wooden upright chair in one corner, and a large iron safe in the other corner. The only item which looked as if it belonged to the twenty-first century was the top-of-the-range desk chair parked by the desk. As to the desk itself, the surface was completely clear. To the right of the space for the chair were three drawers.

"Anna," said Morgan, "we'd like you to look in the drawers for us. Just in case there's anything helpful in there. We're looking for an address book, or something like that."

"Yes, I understand." Anna opened the top drawer. All they could see was a jumble of clips of various types and sizes, pens, rubber bands, rulers, and so on. But no documents. In the second were padded envelopes and rolls of sticky tape. She took a key ring from the pocket of her jeans and used a small key to open the third and final drawer. In it were two thick ring binders stuffed with paper.

"What's in these?" asked Blue.

"These are the records of purchases and sales," said Anna. "In the purchase file is a page for each book, including details of the book itself, where, when and from whom it was purchased, and the price paid. In the sales file each sheet has the details of one sale. The date, title of the book, name and address of the purchaser, their email address, the price agreed, and the date and ID of the bank transfer, or cheque. Cash purchases are noted as such."

"We need to look through these, to see if there are any contacts in Estonia," said Blue.

Anna put the files on the desk and opened them up to let them flick through. Blue took the purchases, Morgan the sales. It took half an hour to look through them. Since the sales were recorded separately from the purchases it wasn't easy to see how much profit Aino was making on each book. But a few checks between the files showed that the markup was generous. One book, bought for £2.50, had sold for £64.00. Not a bad deal. However, the volume of sales was not high, averaging between twenty and thirty per week. And he guessed that even for sales at that level it was necessary to maintain a large stock, waiting for perhaps years until the customer who really wanted that particular book made contact.

By the end of their search they had discovered nothing that would assist them in locating Aino Carselaw. Many of the names and addresses of purchasers were missing. Anna explained that these were regular customers who were indicated only by an ID containing a letter followed by three numbers. Anna had no idea what these represented; Mrs Carselaw kept the list of IDs in a little book in her handbag. It was never left in the shop.

"Do you have the combination for the safe?" asked Blue.

"No. Only Mrs Carselaw and Mr Balfour have that."

Back in the shop, Blue asked Anna what was on the laptop on the counter.

"Only the catalogue."

"What about emails?"

"Emails from customers to the shop email address are forwarded automatically to Mrs Carselaw. She handles them on her own laptop. If she is not here, she phones or emails me with instructions."

"What if a customer comes into the shop?"

"That is not often. If the customer accepts the catalogue price, I complete the deal. If not, I phone Mrs Carselaw, and she speaks to the customer. If she is not available I contact Mr Balfour."

"Have you tried to contact Mrs Carselaw recently?"

"No. She told me, when she is in Estonia she is not available. If there is a problem, I must email Mr Balfour."

"Can you give me Mrs Carselaw's and Mr Balfour's email address, and your own, please?" asked Sergeant Morgan, taking a notebook from her pocket.

"Of course." Anna dictated the addresses.

"Do you have Mr Balfour's home address?" asked Blue.

"No, I do not know where he lives. When he is here he is always in a hotel."

"Sorry. Something I should have asked earlier. Are you the only person employed here?"

"I think so. The shop is closed at weekends, but Mrs Carselaw is sometimes here."

"One last question, Anna," said Sergeant Morgan. "How does Mrs Carselaw treat you?"

Anna paused for thought. "She took me on as soon as I arrived here, without questions. The pay is good. She treats me very fairly. If there's something I need to know, she explains it very clearly. She is not, how would you say, warm. She does not smile, and has no sense of humour. But I think maybe that is how Estonians are. We Ukrainians are very different. We are normally happy. But not so much now, with the invasion. The Russians will never be satisfied I think. They must recreate the empire of the Soviets, and the Tsars before them."

"Thank you, Anna," concluded the sergeant. "If Mrs Carselaw does return in the next few days, can you ask her to give us a ring and let us know? And if something odd, or something that worries you happens, give me a call. Here's my card."

Back at the police station, they went to the canteen for lunch.

"Where do you think we are now, Angus?" asked Morgan.

"Well, Aelwyn, it's looking increasingly like Aino Carselaw wanted to be completely out of touch for the two weeks in Estonia. The fact she's taken the Estonian stuff from the flat might mean she's not coming back. On the other hand, she's left a lot of stock in that shop, and given the impression that she is coming back."

"Could something illegal be going on at the bookshop?"

"It's possible. Anna looked pretty honest to me, but we don't know what pressure she might be under. On the other hand, they could be selling drugs there on Saturdays and Sundays! If Aino doesn't reappear soon, we may want to search the place."

Back in his office, Blue emailed Ishmael Balfour, asking if he could meet him, explaining that he was trying to locate Aino Carselaw. Then he took the fingerprints and the hairs to the forensics department. He would soon receive scanned images of the prints; the hairs would be sent to the police laboratory at Gartcosh for analysis. Then he needed to work on his report.

Aelwyn Morgan joined Blue for the team meeting at four thirty. The feeling was downbeat. The visits to Paul Carselaw and the bookshop seemed to suggest that Aino Carselaw's visits to Estonia might be more than get-togethers with family and friends. Bhardwaj and Vunsells had little to report. They'd persuaded the Plymouth registry office to email scanned copies of the documents Aino Kuusk had submitted in preparation for her marriage to Paul Carselaw. They confirmed her date of birth as 14 September 1965, that her name was Aino Kuusk, and that she was divorced. The divorce certificate was in Estonian, but there was an English translation with it stamped and signed by a lawyer in Tallinn. It confirmed that her divorce from Kalev Lind had been finalised on 18 November 1988 by the Tallinn District Court.

McCader had been looking into Paul Carselaw. He'd talked to a contact in the Ministry of Defence, who'd confirmed, off the record, that X-Syst-X did have contracts with the ministry relating to work at the Faslane naval base, and that they might relate to weapons systems. He'd also tracked down a front office in Anguilla, and threatened to close them down unless they supplied him with contact details for the company's actual head office. It turned out to be located in a former naval barracks on the Plymouth waterfront. He'd tried to phone, without success; the line was dead.

Blue asked them to reconvene at nine the following morning. He went home to Connel in a disgruntled mood. He phoned Alison at her flat in Clackmannan, not far from the Police College, and that lifted his mood a little. He took a home-made burger from the fridge and fried it with shallots and mushrooms, then added a slice of cheese, and put it in a roll, then ate it with a glass of stout. He tried to focus on learning more about Estonia. The concentration that involved helped put the questions about Aino Carselaw to the back of his mind, and he managed to get to sleep that night.

6

Tuesday 29 November

Blue was up at seven, and made his breakfast. It was raining steadily outside, and the cloud was so low that the upper parts of the Connel Bridge were lost in the mist. The swirling waters of the Falls of Lora, the rapids directly beneath the bridge, thrashed onto the rocks so close to the surface that their black humps gleamed intermittently in the thin light of early morning. He thought of dark memories, and forced them aside.

He was in his office by eight. The call came at quarter past. Blue picked up the phone.

"Ah, inspector, thank goodness you're in. It's Katie here. There's a call from Estonia for you."

"Put it through, please."

After a pause, a man's voice. "Inspector Blue?"

"Yes, that's me."

"I am *Komissar* Kõnekas. Similar to your rank of inspector. I am in the *Kriminalpolitsei*, the criminal police, in Tallinn. You inquired about a woman named Aino Carselaw."

"Yes, that's correct."

"Your email says her name may also be Aino Kuusk?"

"That was her surname before she was married."

"And you also say she may also use the name Aino Lind?"

"Yes. She was once married to a Mr Lind."

"Kalev Lind?"

"Yes, that's him. He was her first husband, according to the information we have."

"Where does your information come from?"

"From her present husband, Paul Carselaw. He reported her disappearance. He thought his wife had been married to Mr Lind from 1986 until 1988 when they divorced."

"I have some information for you, inspector. The body of a woman has been discovered."

Blue's heart sank. This wasn't the outcome he'd hoped for.

"Please go on."

"She was found five days ago, on Thursday the 24th November, at a location on the island of Saaremaa. The dead woman has since been identified as Mrs Aino Lind."

"It was a possibility that she would call herself Aino Lind."

"The dead woman carried identity documents in that name. They are genuine. The body has also been identified by her husband, Kalev Lind, as that of his wife. But she resembles the photo you sent of Aino Carselaw, and the information you included in your email also fits Aino Lind. The only difference appears to be that she was still married to *Härra* Lind."

"*Härra* Lind?"

"Excuse me, please. That is Mr Lind. *Härra* is the Estonian for Mister."

"Ah. Thank you. Are you saying Aino Lind was not divorced from Mr Lind in 1988?"

"There is no record of any divorce. *Härra* Lind has been her husband since 1986. Your email, which was forwarded to me only yesterday, has made the case more complex."

"In what way?"

"*Proua* Lind – that is Mrs Lind – was found in a crater lake in a place called Kaali, on the island of Saaremaa, in the Baltic. It is the westernmost part of Estonia. We do not know how she got there, or her activities in the two weeks before her death. Her husband says he expected to meet her but she did not come. He did not know that she planned to go to Saaremaa, although it is where she grew up. But if Aino Lind is the same person as Aino Carselaw, the puzzle becomes greater, does it not?"

"Indeed it does. But she did have papers confirming her divorce, an original in Estonian and a translation, attested by a lawyer. We have scanned copies."

"That is, strange. Please, send them to me. We will check them over here."

"How did she die? Was she drowned?"

"No, she was strangled. It was not an accident. Excuse me, inspector, I will get back to you when we have examined the divorce papers. Then we can take it from there."

"Sounds good. I'll get the scans to you right away."

"Thank you, inspector. I'll talk with you again later today."

"Goodbye, *Komissar* Kõnekas."

Blue put the phone down and thought. The news from *Komissar* Kõnekas offered two options. First, that the dead woman was Aino Lind, in which case it looked like her marriage to Paul

Carselaw had been set up by her as a falsehood; yet they'd been together over thirty years – that just didn't make sense. Second, that the dead woman was Aino Carselaw, in which case why should Kalev Lind claim she was still his wife?

He put aside his thoughts, and emailed the images of the divorce papers to *Komissar* Kõnekas. The fingerprint images had not yet come to him from forensics. Then he went up to Sergeant Morgan's office and told her about the phone call.

"This doesn't look good, Angus. It does seem like Mr Carselaw's wife is dead. And also that she wasn't even his wife. If that's true, then the divorce papers she gave him must be fake."

"They looked convincing, so I doubt the registrar would check with Tallinn."

"But what was the point of it all? Why pretend to be married to the man and stay with him for thirty years? I just don't understand it, Angus."

"It's a puzzle, right enough. Well, let's hope *Komissar* Kõnekas gets back to us. Then we'll be slightly clearer about it. By the way, you're welcome to come to the team meeting at nine."

"Sorry, Angus, I'm tied up this morning. I have to sort out a dog that was found on the ferry from Mull. I need to be at the terminal now. But do keep me informed. And involved, if that's possible. Though now it looks like a murder case, rather than a missing person, so I'll pass it on to you."

He went up to the meeting room, and went through what had just happened. It was met with a feeling of dismay all round. They'd all hoped Aino Carselaw would be found alive and well. Her marital status was a secondary consideration to the fact of her death.

"Does that mean Carselaw is a bigamist?" asked Bhardwaj.

"No," Vunsells answered him, "Aino was the bigamist. He was just an unwitting accessory."

"Let's focus on what's important here," put in Blue. "Aino's body has been found, and identified. This is a murder case, but the lead investigator is clearly *Komissar* Kõnekas. She was found on his turf. Our job must be to address any questions which his investigation raises over here. Meanwhile, anything we can find out about the Carselaws could be useful."

"What about Ishmael Balfour?" asked Vunsells.

"He's certainly worth looking into. We don't know anything about him at the moment."

"When do we pass the bad news on to Mr Carselaw?" asked McCader.

"Not till we've heard back from Estonia about the divorce, and have a definite identification. That could happen later today, so I'm thinking I'll be visiting Mr Carselaw this afternoon. Lena, would you like to come along? It's always best at these things to have a woman present. I'll inform Family Liaison, and they may send somebody too. It's the worst part of the job, I know. But somebody has to do it, and sooner or later it'll be you. So best to start now."

"No problem, chief," she replied.

Blue asked McCader to follow up with Ishmael Balfour, and Bhardwaj and Vunsells to continue digging up whatever they could on the Carselaws. He would come up to the workroom as soon as he heard from Estonia.

7

The call came at 10.45.

"Tere, komissar!" said Kõnekas.

"I'm sorry?"

"Some Estonian for you, inspector. 'Tere!' means 'Hi!' What friends and acquaintances say when they greet each other. But you have to say it right. Say 'ten' then take off the 'n'; then say 'red' and take off the 'd'; put what is left together, and you get 'te-re.' Say it quickly and there you are: *Tere!*"

"Ah. Thank you. *Tere, Komissar* Kõnekas! What have you got for me?"

"I sent the scans to our forgery unit. They say these are definitely forgeries. Good ones – they look realistic, and use all the right legal terms – but fake nevertheless. And they don't match any papers in the court records."

"Wouldn't false legal papers be difficult to obtain?"

"Back then, in the aftermath of the collapse of the Soviet Union, everything was possible. People in the newly-freed countries did not know how to practise western-style democracy. Or capitalism. No-one knew where exactly were the boundaries between what was acceptable and what was not. So many things happened. Some people made much money. The Russian oligarchs bought up state enterprises for tiny sums. Others were cheated of all their savings, like the victims of the pyramid schemes in Albania. The Baltic republics were not so extreme. Nevertheless, some of the politicians who had helped Estonia recover its independence got caught up in corrupt activities, simply through naiveté and ignorance. I suspect there was good business for forgers, as well as swindlers. Many people who were close to the communist regime would wish to adjust their identities, to distance themselves from their past. To obtain false papers, of any sort, in the first years of independence, would not have been difficult. And, as with everything else, there were many opportunists from the west who went over to make money."

"The question in this case, though, is why? Why go to the UK and pretend to be divorced? Then get married and spend over thirty years with another husband?"

"I agree, that is a puzzle. It would be easier to get a divorce than to find a forger and pay him a lot of money to produce good quality false divorce papers."

"That suggests she had a good reason for doing what she did. Perhaps she feared the husband would cause trouble for her if she filed for divorce."

"Yet *Härra* Lind says that he knows nothing of her life with Carselaw. He claims his wife worked abroad to earn money."

"Do you believe him?"

"I do not think it is plausible. I will need your help on this case, inspector."

"I think that will be fine. I'll have to clear the co-operation higher up here."

"It is approved by my senior officer. Perhaps we can talk on Zoom or Skype when it is time?"

"Sounds good. Now I'll have to see Mr Carselaw, and give him the bad news. Tell me, how did Mr, sorry, *Härra*, Lind react to the news of his wife's death?"

"With great calm. But then, he had only seen her for short periods each year for the previous three decades."

Blue went to the workroom to brief the team on his conversation with *Komissar* Kõnekas. Then he went up to the Super's office, and explained the situation.

"That's a bad one," commented the Super. "His wife is dead, but she wasn't even his wife."

"I'm going to have to tell him today, chief."

"Won't be easy, I'm sure. Anyway, about the co-operation. I'm fully behind you on that. I'll get on to the ACC right away. As long as it's not going to cost money, it should be OK."

Blue phoned the Family Liaison Office, and they suggested he wait until after lunch before going to see Mr Carselaw. That would give them time to send someone over while he was still there.

Just before twelve he received an email from forensics with images of the Carselaws' fingerprints, and the receipt from the lab for the hairs; the analysis would be completed as quickly as possible. He sent the image of Aino Carselaw's fingerprints to *Komissar* Kõnekas.

He and Vunsells set off at half past one, driving through heavy rain, and in fifteen minutes were at Carselaw's door. This time there was no answer to the bell. "We'll try the garage," decided Blue.

The garages were numbered to match the flats, so the right one was soon found. Blue rapped loudly with his knuckles on the metal swing-over door, until he heard a voice from inside shouting, "All right, all right, what the bloody hell do you want? I'm opening the door."

As the door swung up it revealed a large table filling most of the space, on which was laid out a complex array of railway tracks, the rails perhaps an inch apart, along with stations, buildings of all sorts, bridges, and even trees. And lots of little plastic figures of people. And right at the back, holding a mobile phone, stood Paul Carselaw.

"Oh, it's you again. Why didn't you phone? Can't you see I'm busy? I'm testing a new circuit. It's an impressive setup, isn't it?" Blue noted that his anger at their arrival had been dissipated by his wish to demonstrate his favourite toy.

"It is indeed. But I'm sorry, Mr Carselaw, we don't have time to take a good look. There's been an important development in the search for your wife and we need to talk with you right away."

"Fire away," said Carselaw, adjusting the position of a little steam locomotive, sitting on a siding near a station.

"It's imperative that we talk in your apartment, Mr Carselaw. We have some news from Estonia which we need to share with you. In private."

Carselaw looked up. He had caught the tone of Blue's voice. His face paled. "What's happened to Aino? You need to tell me."

"And I will. In your apartment," repeated Blue. "Let's go, shall we?"

Five minutes later they were in Carselaw's lounge. It was so gloomy outside, as the rain continued, that Carselaw switched the lights on. He motioned Blue and Vunsells towards the sofa.

"I think you should sit down too, Mr Carselaw."

Carselaw sat down. "The news is bad, isn't it? Is she…?"

"There isn't an easy way to say this, Mr Carselaw. The Estonian police called me this morning. They have identified a person whom they believe is your wife."

"I don't understand," cut in Carselaw. "Is she in hospital? Is she unconscious?" Then a penny seemed to drop. He spoke quietly now. "She's dead, isn't she? Please, tell me what's happened."

"Try to stay calm, Mr Carselaw. I know it's not easy. I'll be perfectly straight with you. A body has been found. It looks like the image we sent of your wife. It carried valid ID identifying the holder as Aino Lind. And the body has been identified by Kalev Lind as his wife. There doesn't seem to be any doubt. I'm very sorry."

"Can I get myself a drink?" asked Carselaw.

"Yes, of course."

Carselaw disappeared and returned a few minutes later with a glass of what looked like neat whisky. Blue restrained himself from suggesting a splash of water. The taste wasn't the important thing at this point. Carselaw took a good slug and grimaced. He sat down on the armchair. "Aino is dead. I want to be clear that that's what you said. It's so easy to get things wrong."

"Of course. Yes, I'm sorry to have to confirm that it appears your wife is dead."

"'Appears?' Are you absolutely sure?"

"It's what the Estonian police have told us. They're sure that the person they found is your wife."

"What do you mean: 'found'?"

"She was discovered in a crater lake, on the island of Saaremaa."

"Found in a lake. Drowned?"

"I can't tell you any more at the moment."

"How do they know it's her?"

"As I said, she looked like your wife, had ID identifying her as Aino Lind, and her husband Kalev Lind identified her."

"That's not right. I'm her husband. She's Aino Carselaw. What's he got to do with it?"

"It appears they were still married."

"But she was divorced."

"It seems the divorce papers were forged."

Carselaw took another swig of whisky. "What? What are you saying? That she wasn't even my wife? Not for thirty-two years? What the fuck is going on?" He drained the glass. He stared into the empty glass and shook his head slowly. "Not even married." He got up and walked into the kitchen, coming back almost immediately with another glass of whisky.

At this point the doorbell rang. Vunsells sprang to her feet and went into the hallway. Blue heard the door opening and subdued voices. Vunsells returned, leading a middle-aged officer, who introduced herself as PC Agnes Hare, from the Family Liaison Office, and offered to make everyone a cup of tea. Blue noted that she glanced with disapproval at the glass of whisky in Carselaw's hand. PC Hare disappeared into the kitchen.

"Saaremaa," muttered Carselaw. "That's where she grew up, you know. Where did you say she was found?"

"A place called Kaali, they said."

"Kaali. Yes, the crater lake. You mentioned that. I think we saw it. We only went to the island once, just for a couple of days. We got there on the ferry, then drove around for a day, and stayed overnight at a hotel in Kuressaare – that's the island capital. Next day we drove around again and got the ferry back that evening. A whistle-stop tour. I think she only went there because I wanted to see where she'd grown up. So why was she there? What was she doing?"

"They don't know yet," said Blue. "Tell me, did Aino still have relatives on Saaremaa?"

"There are cousins, I think. But we didn't visit anyone."

At this point PC Hare returned with mugs of tea on a tray. Everybody got milk and one sugar. PC Hare made for Carselaw's glass of whisky, but he poured it into his tea, and handed her the empty glass. "Thank you," he said to her. "My wife is dead, you know. And they say she wasn't even my wife. Can you beat that, eh?" He fell back in his chair, staring at the wall. Blue could not imagine what was going through his mind at this moment.

There was no point in staying. Blue stood up and apologised once more for the news he'd had to bring. "Constable Vunsells and I have to go now, but we'll come back in a day or two, and then I should be able to tell you more about what's happened. In the meantime, Constable Hare will see that you've got everything you need." He nodded to Carselaw and then Hare, before heading for the door. As he opened it, he heard Hare asking Carselaw, "Now, who do you know around here?"

The atmosphere in the workroom was subdued, as Blue reported on the visit to Paul Carselaw. Whatever they did now, they couldn't bring back Aino Carselaw.

"The body was discovered in Estonia," said Blue, "but I'm sure there's a link to here. We need to look closer into the bookshop, in case something was going on there. And here's a question: why would Aino pretend to be divorced, and even go to the trouble of getting fake divorce papers?"

"What if the husband wouldn't give her a divorce?" offered Vunsells. "And she felt she had to get away. Maybe she got the fake papers just in case she needed them. Not anticipating she'd meet someone so soon."

"I don't go with that," said Bhardwaj. "I think she came over here to find a husband. Someone in the west who would look after her financially."

"That's an interesting point," added McCader. "A lot of women from the former Soviet Union came to the west looking for husbands, after its collapse. A friend of my father's in Dundee married one. He was a fireman, saw her on a dating website, and three months later they were wed. And have been perfectly happy ever since. We mustn't assume all these women were gold-diggers. Many of them were just looking for security. A good man who'd look after them."

"That's interesting," said Blue. "Got anything else?"

"I had a word with someone at X-Syst-X. He gave me a phone number for Mr Farnley-Montserrat's PA. She was caught on the hop and passed me to personnel. They told me that Paul Carselaw left the company's employ in 2013. That's not what he told you."

"So what does he do three days a fortnight?" asked Vunsells.

"Well may you ask, Lena," said McCader. "In fact, there's more to it. He was asked to leave."

"Sacked?" said Bhardwaj.

"You could put it that way. It appears Mr Carselaw had been taking work files home with him, which was strictly forbidden, due to the sensitive nature of the projects they were working on."

"He was spying?" gasped Bhardwaj.

"Not necessarily. The person I spoke to thought he was simply a pathetic geek without a life. He was questioned by the firm's 'security consultants,' and admitted to taking work home, saying that he wanted to spend more time on the design, to get it just right. They had a look at his finances, but found nothing irregular. Nevertheless, they decided to terminate his employment as a precaution."

"And that's when the family left Helensburgh and moved to Oban," said Vunsells. "So how's he been occupying himself since then? Apart from with his train set."

"Probably with his boat," said McCader.

There was a pause while they took that in.

"I'm guessing we're not talking about a model of HMS Victory?" said Blue.

"Quite right, chief. I wondered about these three-day trips, and just on the off chance checked on the boats registered at all the marinas within twenty miles of here. It wasn't too long before I found him, or rather, his boat. A cabin cruiser called the *Jolly Mermaid*."

"Where is it kept?" asked Blue.

"Just down the coast. The marina at Gallanach Bay. Perhaps I should take a look at it?"

"Good idea, Enver. See if they have a record of its comings and goings. It would be useful to know what he does with it. It may be perfectly harmless, of course. Fishing. Seal-watching."

"Drug-dealing?" suggested Bhardwaj.

"Let's see what Enver finds out. Arvind, what have you come up with?"

"I checked out Eastwards Books on eBay. I thought, given the lack of information on their website, they might not be there. But they are. The kind of books they're selling matches what you told us about the shop, but it looks like they don't put the expensive ones on eBay. They looked mostly like academic books withdrawn or discarded from college or university libraries, on offer for anything up to a hundred pounds. And all in English. I looked for other sites where they could market the books in other languages. There are versions of eBay in other countries too, such as ebay.de and ebay.pl. In Poland Allegro is the biggest equivalent of eBay, and I found some of their books there. But again, nothing over a hundred and twenty euros or the equivalent in Polish *złoty*. It all looks above board, as far as I can tell."

"OK," concluded Blue, "if Enver can follow up the boat angle, we can perhaps see what Carselaw's up to those three days a fortnight. We could of course just go and ask him, but it's better to arm ourselves with some information before we do that. And right now, we can't be too hard on him. We've just told him his wife is dead."

"Should we keep an eye on his movements?" asked Vunsells.

"Let's revisit that one when we hear what Enver's got tomorrow.

We don't want to panic him. I think we also need to look at Mrs Carselaw's finances. I'll talk to the fiscal and see what can be done. Trouble is, I doubt we'll get any further till we can prove there's a crime here."

"Surely the discovery of the body in Estonia should be enough," said Bhardwaj.

"That doesn't indicate there might be a crime over here. In fact, we don't know yet if there is any angle to Aino Carselaw's disappearance in this country. It might be none of our business at all. Right, let's meet tomorrow for a quick chat at nine, and take it from there."

8

Wednesday 30 November

Blue met the team along with Aelwyn Morgan at nine. He'd no sooner greeted everyone than Sergeant Morgan's phone rang. She moved to the corner of the room and listened for a few moments, then said a few words and hung up.

"Sorry to interrupt," she said.

"That's OK, we hadn't started. I thought you wouldn't be long."

"That was Anna Zeresova. From the bookshop. She's just arrived at the shop. There's been a break-in. I said we'd be there in a few minutes."

"Good call," said Blue. "Can you send a uniformed officer to secure the premises and hold the fort till we get there? I'll meet you downstairs in five minutes."

Sergeant Morgan left to alert the duty sergeant.

Blue continued, "Enver, can you take Arvind with you to Gallanach Bay? Lena, you come with me and Aelwyn. We'll meet at half four if we don't see each other before that."

Blue, Morgan and Vunsells walked round to the bookshop. Turning into the lane, the first thing they saw was a police car almost wedged into it, stopped outside the bookshop. As they squeezed past the car to the shop doorway, Blue peered in through the open passenger window to see the plump and rumpled figure of PC Ron Beattie in the driving seat.

"What are doing?" asked Blue.

"Er, securing the premises, sir."

"Is there an entrance at the rear?"

"I don't know, sir."

"Why didn't you ask Ms Zeresova?"

"Well, actually, I can't get out of the car. I can't get the door open wide enough to get out. I'm kind of stuck here."

"Why did you bring the car? You could have walked here in five minutes."

"I didn't know where it was."

"So how did you get here?"

"The SatNav. It sent me along here."

"Didn't you look when you saw the corner?"

"But the SatNav said to go this way."

"Here's something to think about, Beattie. The SatNav is a computer program. It's not a real person. Now, get the car out of here. Reverse back down the lane, and make sure you don't kill anyone on your way out onto the street. Take it back to the station. Then come back here. On foot. I know that involves walking. But that's something police officers have to do sometimes. I want to see you back here in ten minutes. Do you understand?"

"Yes, sir. Right away, sir."

"I'd better give him a hand," Morgan whispered to Blue, as Beattie turned the engine on. "I've got the uniform, so I can hold up the traffic to let him out. And shout if he's going to hit anything."

She turned to the open window of the car, and began to talk to Beattie.

Meanwhile Blue opened the shop door and entered, Vunsells behind him. The first thing he noticed was the chaos of books, scattered on the floor and heaped in untidy piles, everywhere but on the shelves. And behind the counter, weeping quietly, stood Anna Zeresova. She wiped her face with a handkerchief as she recognised Blue, and attempted a smile. "Inspector, thank you so much for coming. This is so bad, so bad. Mrs Carselaw will never forgive me."

"Anna, this is hardly your fault, is it?" said Blue. "Did you lock up yesterday when you left?"

"Yes, yes. I am very careful always to do that."

"Well then, you're not responsible for what's happened. The only person responsible is the person who did it. By the way, this is Detective Constable Vunsells. Sergeant Morgan will be along in a few minutes. Now, can you first tell me what time you locked up yesterday afternoon?"

"It was five minutes after six o'clock. The shop closed at five, but I had to do some tidying and dusting of the shelves. Even if no-one comes in, the shelves become untidy."

"And you locked up behind you?"

"Yes. The front door. The door at the back, it leads to the drying area, the back green they call it here. It is locked unless I have need to open it. But I checked it before I left. Mrs Carselaw was very insistent that both doors are checked before I leave, even if I know the back one is already locked."

"And you didn't return here until when?"

"Nine o'clock this morning. The shop doesn't open till ten, but I must be here at nine in case there are emails or calls on the telephone."

"So just before nine you walked up the lane to the shop?"

"Yes."

"And unlocked the front door?"

"Yes. I keep a key to the front door only."

"And the door was locked when you got here?"

"Yes. That's right. I unlocked the door and went in."

"Did you notice anything odd about the door? Did it feel looser than usual, or in any way different?"

"No, I don't think so."

"Okay. What did you do when you got in?"

"I saw all this, this…"

"Have you tried to tidy anything?"

"No. It is clear to me that thieves or bandits have been here, so I immediately phone Sergeant Morgan. I have her card."

"What did you do then?"

"I wait. After a few minutes the police car comes. I go out, but the policeman says he will wait in the car. Until reinforcements arrive, he says. And now you are here."

By this time Sergeant Morgan had returned, and she greeted Anna. "I'll call forensics," she said to Blue, taking her phone out, and turning towards the doorway.

"Right, Anna," Blue continued, "don't touch anything. At some point we'll ask you to go through all this and work out exactly what's been taken. But first, just look around. Is there anything that's obviously missing?"

Anna did as she was asked, looking carefully around at the empty shelves and then the books littered on the floor. Then she pointed to the glass-fronted shelves by the counter. "The books from this cabinet, they are all gone, I think. I see none on the floor. The most valuable ones."

"That suggests that our thief knew what he was looking for, doesn't it? Now, while we're in the shop here, can you tell me how many people have been so far this week? Apart from Sergeant Morgan and myself. I'm guessing you don't get many customers, is that right?"

"Yes. Most of our business is by phone or email. Let me think. On Monday there was in the morning a couple from England, I think. They complained to me of the weather. The woman asked if I had any detective stories. I explained that we did not keep this type of book. Paperback novels of recent origin."

"You stock older paperbacks?"

"Only books with paper covers, from the 1920s and 1930s. For instance, we have a copy of *Must Ingel* by Aleksander Sipelgas, published in Tallinn in 1927. It's a crime story. In English it means 'black angel.' It has paper covers, but is now very rare. Ours is even an uncut copy."

"What do mean by that?" asked Vunsells.

"When the book is printed, there are several pages on a sheet. Then the sheet is folded so that the pages appear in the correct order. Then it is bound. The result is that there are folds at top edge of the book. Today when the books are bound, the top folds and any uneven edges at the side and bottom are removed by a cutting machine."

"Like a guillotine," added Blue.

"Yes, that is it. Then there is a smooth edge all round the book. But in the early days of books with paper covers, often the pages were uncut. The purchaser would then cut the folds with a paper knife in order to turn the pages and read the book."

"So the fact this book is uncut means it hasn't been read?" asked Vunsells.

"Yes. Of course, a book is not always in good condition even if it is uncut. The paper is cheap and deteriorates, the cover is faded or chafed. Maybe someone has spilt coffee on it. But, in general, an uncut paper-bound book is in better condition and will bring a higher price."

"You've learned a lot since you've been working here?" asked Blue.

"Oh yes. Mrs Carselaw is good teacher. Very firm. And I learn much. When I am back in Ukraine I will hope to open a bookshop."

"All right, Anna. Back to the customers. What about yesterday?"

"There was only one person, a woman, in the afternoon. Maybe about two o'clock. She looked at the books for a while. Then she took one out and asked how much it was. I said I'd have to phone the owner, but it might be five or six hundred euros. She said that was too much for her. Then she gave the book back and left the shop. She was very polite. Also, the way she held the book, she was very careful. I think she is familiar with old books."

"She didn't give a name?"

"No."

"What did she look like?"

"Slim. Taller than me. Older too. Blonde hair, tightly tied at the back of the head."

"A chignon?" suggested Vunsells.

"Yes, I think that's it. And sure of herself. Confident. She had a nice smile."

"What was she wearing?"

Anna paused to think. "She was very chic. A grey suit and a dark blue coat. A green, white and purple scarf. Black shoes with high heels. Black gloves. And an umbrella. She was very careful with the umbrella, folded it closed when she came in and propped it in the corner."

"That's helpful," said Blue. "We'll need to look out for her."

"You think she is the thief?"

"Not necessarily. But she may know something that will help us. OK, Anna. Now let's go behind the counter, and tell me if there's anything missing there."

Trying to avoid the books tossed on the floor, Anna stepped gingerly past the end of the counter, and looked around again.

"May I open this?" she asked, pointing to a single drawer of a dark wood beneath the counter.

"Let me do it," said Blue, taking a Swiss Army knife from his jacket pocket, and opening out a metal prong about six centimetres long. With this he grasped the handle of the drawer and pulled it open. A black laptop folded shut, a mouse and mouse-mat, and a cable were the only occupants.

"This is the laptop with the catalogue on it."

"Anything missing from this drawer?"

"No." She looked down into the space below the drawer. "The printer is still here too."

"Good," said Blue. "That suggests the books were the target. We'll go through to the back next. I'm going to put on some gloves. Try not to touch anything."

He put on a pair of blue nitrile gloves. Then he pointed to the door at the back of the counter area. "Is this door normally locked?"

"No," answered Anna.

Blue opened the door and led Anna into the corridor. Vunsells followed. Morgan remained by the shop door, awaiting the return of PC Beattie and the arrival of the Scene of Crime officers.

The corridor appeared empty. Blue saw again the rear door at the end of the corridor, with its small frosted-glass window, and the two doors on each side.

He began with the first door on the left. "Where does this door lead?"

"I don't know," said Anna. "It is always locked when I am here. I asked once Mrs Carselaw, and she told me it was none of my business. Maybe it is a store for more books, but I do not know."

Blue tried the door. It was locked. "OK. What about the one beyond?"

"That leads to the kitchen. In there I make coffee."

"Let's go in."

The kitchen had a window facing the rear of the building, through which long grass could be seen. There was a stainless steel sink with draining board, an electric kettle, and some cupboards beneath it. Blue opened them one at a time so that Anna could look in. There were a few mugs and plates, and cleaning materials. A drawer contained a scattering of unmatched knives, forks and spoons. Anna concluded nothing was gone.

Returning to the corridor, he tried the rear door. It was locked. The door at the end on the right was, Anna told them, a toilet. Again, she could not see anything amiss.

Finally the only door which remained untried was that to the office.

"Is the office door normally locked?" asked Blue.

"No," said Anna.

Blue opened the door and they went in. Nothing appeared out of place. Anna checked the three drawers in the cabinet below the desk. Again, nothing had been taken. The files containing the sales and purchase records were still there.

They returned to the shop. Sergeant Morgan was talking to a man clutching a top-of-the-range camera, and a slim woman with hair of a very light blue colour in a Cleopatra cut. Morgan introduced them to Anna as Andrew McGuire and Jill Henderson, members of the SOC team.

"I hope you haven't been poking around too much in there,"

said Jill sharply.

"Don't you worry, Jill," said Blue, "we've been very careful." He held up his gloved hands.

"We'll need her prints," said Jill, glancing at Anna.

"Anna," said Sergeant Morgan, "you'll have to come back with us to the police station so we can take your fingerprints. This will enable us to find the prints which are out of place."

Anna looked dubious. "Don't worry," said Vunsells, "they already have mine and the inspector's and the sergeant's, for the same reason."

"May I not stay here?" asked Anna.

"I'm afraid not," said Morgan. "The shop will be well looked after. PC Beattie is outside the main door to guard the shop. And Andrew and Jill are here too. We will also have to ask you to give us a statement. Then, once Andrew and Jill have finished, we'd like you to come back and try to identify what has been stolen."

Blue held back as the others left. "Jill," he said quietly, "can you have a look at the first door on the left in the corridor? It's locked, but we'd like to know what's behind it."

"Right you are," said Jill. "We'll probably have to get Dennis in. He'll get it open, no problem."

9

Back at the station, Blue asked Vunsells to take Anna to have her fingerprints recorded, then to go with her to the canteen and get her some coffee.

No sooner had he returned to his office than the phone rang. Katie from reception.

"Inspector, there's a Mr Balfour come to see you. He says you emailed him."

"OK. I'll come down in a minute and collect him. Is the End Room free?"

Receiving an affirmative, Blue phoned the meeting room, but no-one answered. McCader and Bhardwaj would be at the marina, and Vunsells was with Anna. He phoned Aelwyn Morgan, but no answer there either. He'd have to do the interview on his own.

When he reached reception, Katie pointed out a man sitting on one of the plastic chairs in the foyer, looking out of the window at the dark water of the bay. As Blue approached him, Ishmael Balfour rose to meet him. He was of average height, perhaps five foot nine, but well filled out, not obese, but well-rounded, with two or even three chins. He was clean-shaven, with little hair on his head, and a hint of wispy brown around his temples, though his eyebrows were thicker and darker, and his eyes a disturbingly bright blue. His age was perhaps around sixty. He wore a suit of a lightish brown colour, and a folded umbrella lay against the seat beyond him. He held out his hand, the fingers short and pudgy, to shake Blue's hand. Along with it came a waft of some scent; a hint of sage with an overlay of pineapple. His hand felt slightly spongy in Blue's, and was unusually hot.

"Detective Inspector Blue, I presume," he smiled. His voice had a rather artificial and old-fashioned air to it, as if learned from an ageing voice coach, or from copying the tone and diction of some film star of the 1930s. "I am so very pleased to meet you. Naturally, when I received your email, I took steps to respond as soon as I was able."

"Thank you for coming in so promptly," replied Blue. "If we go upstairs we can talk more privately."

"I'm perfectly happy to talk with you just where we are, inspector. As you see, there's no-one else around us, and I'm sure we shan't be disturbed." With that, Mr Balfour sat down again.

Blue had no wish at this stage to alienate the man, by forcing him to come to the interview room, so he sat down himself, not the chair next to Balfour, for the other man's excess bulk oozed onto the edge of it, but the next one along.

"A tea or coffee, Mr Balfour?" He knew Katie would fetch something if he asked nicely.

"Your offer is most generous, sir, most generous. But I fear whatever potation is offered would fall below the standards I'm accustomed to. I don't say this in any way to disparage the beverages available within this building, only to say that they would not fall within the parameters of my own tastes. For instance, I prefer my tea to be only the finest Darjeeling, with a combination of spices of my own devising added thereto. And as to coffee, you may imagine that I am equally discriminating. However, I am quite happy to do without for the moment."

"Of course. I'd like to talk to you about Eastwards Books."

"I'm sure the first thing you're going to do is to inform me of the break-in at the shop. There is no need, sir. I heard of it this morning from a reliable source, who observed a policeman there and asked him what had happened. The officer was more than willing to oblige."

Blue made himself a mental note to raise this with PC Beattie.

"I wonder if I might ask you for a few basic details. For our records. Your name is, I think, Ishmael Balfour. Is that correct?"

"Yes, indeed, sir, that is my name. And a most well-chosen one, don't you think?"

"Is it not your real name?"

"Ah, my friend, what is real, as Pontius Pilate might have said. Indeed, it is the name on my passport, though I will confess it was not the name I was given upon my arrival into this world. But times do change, as they say, and sometimes names must follow."

Blue merely raised an eyebrow.

"Ah. I see your curiosity is piqued. Or perhaps you worry that my passport is forged. May I offer it for your inspection." He took from the inside pocket of his jacket an EU passport and handed it to Blue, who opened it and looked inside.

"I see you are a citizen of Slovakia."

"Yes, indeed. Not the country of my birth, but a most welcoming location. For a very modest investment, they were happy to welcome me into their ranks, and greet me as a brother. Tell me, have you been to Bratislava, inspector?"

Blue shook his head. "It's not a place I've visited yet."

"A pity. You should go there. I think you would find it most interesting, for I can see that you are a man who has a genuine interest in the many and varying places around our tiny planet. Yes, it's a fine city. It lacks the pretensions of Prague or Budapest, but retains the good taste of its Hapsburg mentors. There is none of the crudity of Sofia or Bucharest, or the latent hostility of Belgrade."

"Yet you haven't taken a Slovakian name?"

Balfour laughed, a deep throaty laugh. "My passport may be of Slovakia, but I remain a citizen of the world. And I am a great admirer of small states. They are always in danger of annihilation, of being gobbled up by greedy and jealous neighbours, but in them there is so much more life than in the empires of the so-called great powers. And of all small nations, it is the Scots whom I admire the most. Your culture is ancient, yet vibrant, and your identity stands forth clearly from the mass of lesser nations."

"Hence your choice of name?"

Balfour leaned forward, almost conspiratorially, and leaned his hand on Blue's arm. "I must tell you this, inspector. There is no book which I have read in my entire life which has made such an impression upon me as that made by Stevenson's epic tale, *Kidnapped.* That is the source for my choice of surname. Many think it only an adventure story for children. But read it yourself, sir – I'm sorry, I'm sure that you have read it – and so I say, read it once more, and you shall see that it is the tale of a man who seeks his own identity in an alien landscape, as the Germans say, a *Bildungsroman*, a novel of growing up and self-discovery. Think of the interaction between David Balfour and Allan Breck Stewart. This is not simply an unlikely friendship with a possible murderer, for Allan Breck is David's *alter ego*, the part of himself which he must accept or deny, the risk-taker, the one who leads rather than follows. Well, I'm sure you can work out the rest. In the end David chooses to exclude some of those aspects of his psyche which Allan embodies. He opts for safety and probity. Not quite my choice, inspector, but I lean towards his essential sensibility, and therefore choose Balfour over Stewart." He smiled with pleasure at his exposition, and nodded his head. "And as for my first name ..."

It was Blue's turn to smile. "Call me Ishmael?"

"By Gad, sir, you're right! You are indeed a man of discriminating literary taste. Melville's masterpiece is another perfect work. But tell me this, inspector, why would I choose Ishmael, rather than, say, Ahab, or even Queequeg?"

"He survives?"

"The perfect answer! Yes, Ishmael is, like myself, a survivor. Also, something of a loner."

"And someone who may have adopted a new name. The opening sentence suggests Ishmael may not be his real name."

"My word, sir, you are, if I may say so, on fire! The criminal who crosses your path does not escape, I think. But I fear, in this little corner of Paradise, that you may not be offered the cases which will challenge your considerable intellect."

"Thank you for your kind words, Mr Balfour. Perhaps can you tell me your current address?"

"Ah, inspector, I tell you this, I am a person of no fixed abode. No, do not panic, you require an address and I give you one. It is the Queen Adelaide Hotel here in Oban. Not one of the most prestigious of establishments, but it supplies my modest requirements. I do not have a permanent domicile. Yes, there is a flat in a most tasteful apartment building in Bratislava, dating from the early twentieth century. And a modest farmhouse in the Dordogne, to which I will resort for May and June, and perhaps October. And a yacht, the purpose of which is only to get me from A to B in peace and quiet. But none of these is a home in the sense which you no doubt mean, only stopping places where now and then I lay my head."

This is going to take a long time, thought Blue. "Are bookshops your main business interest?"

"Books are my main interest in life, inspector. I have of course other interests, but, yes, I would say that the buying and selling of books is my central business endeavour."

"You have a number of book businesses?"

"A small number only. Having too many businesses smacks of the tax-dodger or money-launderer, does it not? Believe me, inspector, I pay all my taxes. And all my businesses are based in Europe. Not in the Caribbean, or even your own Channel Islands or Isle of Man."

"And you are co-owner of Eastwards Books?"

"Quite so. I and Mrs Carselaw are partners in the enterprise. I can add, for your further information, that Eastwards Books is the only business in which I have any interests in the UK."

"Can I ask what your role in Eastwards Books is?"

"You may indeed, sir. As you are no doubt aware, the day-to-day running of the shop is overseen by Mrs Carselaw, and our employee, Miss Zeresova, attends to the shop on a daily basis. My own role is more wide-ranging. I source many of the books on sale here, and am constantly on the lookout for new stock. This of course requires a great deal of travel, but, as I've said, to be a traveller is my nature, perhaps even my calling."

"When was the last time you were in the shop?"

"A good question, inspector, very pertinent, if I may say so. I consulted my diary in anticipation of such a query, and can say with some confidence that it was on Saturday the 5th of November. Your day of bonfires and fireworks. In the morning. I talked with Mrs Carselaw, to ensure that the period of her absence in Estonia was adequately covered. I offered naturally to be available for consultation by Miss Zeresova during that period. I might add, though you've not asked me yet, that I know nothing of Mrs Carselaw's movements in Estonia. I believe the visit was a private one. She expressed a desire to visit family members, and to renew some old acquaintanceships."

"Did she mention any names?"

"Alas, none at all. And it is not my nature to press for such things."

"How did you know Mrs Carselaw had not returned?"

"It was reported to me on the twenty-third by Miss Zeresova. I asked her to hold the fort – she is, I believe, a most competent operative – pending Mrs Carselaw's return. I was on the point of visiting the shop myself to assess the situation, when I heard of last night's occurrence. A dreadful thing, an abhorrence to a lover of books, that these unique records of our culture and learning should be cast about like so many…" He evidently could not think of a worthy comparison and shrugged, shaking his head in disbelief.

"Can you think of anyone who might want to do this?"

Balfour paused, as if thinking. "Alas, I cannot. There are of course rivals in the bookselling business, as in any other enterprise, but to do this, no, it is below any respectable dealer in books. But I am not in a position to comment further, as I don't know what has been taken. I wonder when it will be possible for me to examine the premises, and to assess the losses?"

"At the moment our Scene of Crime officers are examining the premises. Once they have finished, I would be grateful if you and Ms Zeresova could tell us what is missing."

"Would that be sometime today?"

"No, but I think tomorrow may be possible. Do you have a phone number, and we'll let you know as soon as it's convenient?"

"I'm afraid I don't carry a mobile telephone. They seem to make other people think that you are at their disposal, to be summoned instantly from whatever you are doing simply to talk to them. However you can reach me at the Queen Adelaide Hotel. I shall be happy to come over to the shop whenever I'm informed that it's clear to do so."

With some effort he heaved himself to his feet, and offered his hand once more. "It's been a huge pleasure to talk with you, inspector. I look forward to our further meetings."

"One further question, Mr Balfour," said Blue, standing up also. "I have to ask you where you were last night. It's a routine question, but we'll be asking everyone connected with the shop."

"Of course, inspector, there is no need to apologise for doing your duty. I was at the hotel last night. The staff will have seen me take my evening meal – the food there is remarkably good, by the way, you should try it inspector – and I went to my room at about nine pm, to do some reading before going to bed. I took breakfast at 8.30 this morning. But I think you will already have concluded that I am not a man who breaks into bookshops and throws the contents around."

Blue shook hands and thanked him for coming in.

He needed a coffee, and headed for the canteen. There he noticed Vunsells and Anna Zeresova at a table by a window, deep in conversation. He got himself a mocha, and joined them.

"Anna's been telling me about Ukraine," said Vunsells. "It's appalling what the Russians are doing there. We should be doing something to stop them."

"Putin tries to rebuild the empire of the Tsars," said Anna. "Our forces will give all they have, but they will need support from the West to maintain the struggle. Putin will not give up. If he does not win, the war could last for years, until all of our country is ruined."

"You're right, Anna," said Blue. "It's like Hitler in the 1930s. The longer Putin is left to do as he wishes, the worse he will get. Now, I'm sorry to change the subject, but I want to ask you a few things. I've just been talking with Mr Balfour."

"He is here?" said Anna. "In Oban?"

"Tell me, when did you last see him?"

"Perhaps four or five weeks ago, near the beginning of October. But Mrs Carselaw told me on the last day she was in, that he'd been in the shop the previous Saturday. If there were problems I was to contact him by email. When Mrs Carselaw did not return, I emailed him – on the Wednesday – and he replied quickly, telling me to carry on as before, and he would come in sometime this week if she was not yet back."

"Have you met him?"

"Yes. Only a few times, and even then only for short periods, when he brought new stock or came to see Mrs Carselaw."

"What's your impression of him?"

"I do not know what he is really like. It is as if he plays a part all the time, always very jolly, that is I think the right word. But what goes on in here" – she tapped her right temple – "I do not know."

"As a matter of course, I need to ask you what you were doing last night. You understand we must ask everyone involved in the shop this question."

"Yes, I understand. I was in my flat. It's near the harbour, and I share with two other girls. At 7.30 I had a meeting on Zoom with my mother and father and brother in Ukraine. That finished a few minutes after 8 o'clock. After that I was very sad about what is happening. The others suggested going out, but I was too sad for that. We played a few games of Scrabble instead, and then watched something on the television. I couldn't tell you what it was, I wasn't concentrating. There were people cooking, as if there were no problems in the world. I went to bed about 10 o'clock. I got up at seven as usual, and went to the shop just before nine."

"Thank you. I'll ask Lena here to take that down as a statement, and once you've signed it, you can go home."

"When will I be able to go back to the shop?"

"I think it will be sometime tomorrow. I'll ask Lena to text you as soon as it's possible. We'd like you to go through the books that are there and tell us what you think is missing."

Vunsells conducted Anna to the meeting room to take her statement, and Blue returned to his office, picking up a tuna mayo sandwich and a cup of coffee for his lunch.

He felt sure that there was only one case here; the trashing of the bookshop managed by a woman who had recently disappeared was too much of a coincidence. He knew that bookshops were seldom a target for burglars, and when they were, the main objective was to get any cash in the till, or carry off any piece of equipment that might have a resale value, such as a laptop. It was of course still possible that this was a carefully targeted robbery by a specialised book thief, who knew exactly what was worth stealing, and simply threw the other books around to give the impression of a cruder operative. And that Aino Carselaw's disappearance was completely coincidental. But Angus Blue wasn't a great believer in coincidences.

It was not long after two when he went up to the meeting room. Anna had gone home and McCader and Bhardwaj had returned from the marina. He decided to have the meeting right away, and began by briefing them on the attack on the bookshop, reporting that he had subsequently spoken to Ishmael Balfour. He then asked for comments.

"You're right," opined McCader, "it can't be a coincidence. But what would be the point?"

"There's another 'coincidence' too," put in Bhardwaj. "It happens just when Ishmael Balfour hits town. Could he have orchestrated it, to take advantage of Aino's absence and remove some of the most valuable books, which he would then shift to one of his other book businesses to sell?"

"There's another possibility," said Vunsells. "What if Aino Carselaw set up the robbery, meaning to sell the books elsewhere to fund whatever she planned to do in Estonia. Then she was murdered, but the plan went ahead as the guy she'd hired to do the job didn't know she was dead."

"What if Paul Carselaw was behind it?" said McCader. "He pretends to be ignorant of the book business but knows a lot more than he tells us. Yesterday he learns his wife is dead. So he decides to get something out of the business while he can, by taking the best books."

"There are other, perhaps remoter, possibilities," put in Blue. "For instance, Anna, having found out how much the books are worth, got some Ukrainian pals to undertake the robbery, or even did it herself. She could easily have slipped out during the night to do the job."

"I can't believe that," urged Vunsells. "She's genuinely upset about it. I think she's on the level."

"I wouldn't disagree with you," replied Blue, "but we have to bear in mind that it's a possibility. As is also the possibility that it was a robbery commissioned by a rival dealer, or even an opportunistic job by a local burglar."

"What about the customers who came into the shop earlier in the week?" asked Vunsells. "Especially the woman who seemed to know about books. Maybe she was casing the joint."

"We'll need to follow that up," commented Blue. "But Enver, I'm intrigued that you've suggested Paul Carselaw as a suspect. I'm guessing you found something on his boat that may have supported your conjecture. Time for your report, I think."

"You know me well, chief," smiled McCader. "OK. We went over to the marina, and had a chat with the manager, Emma McIntyre. She told us Paul Carselaw bought the boat in 2014, not long after he and Aino had moved up here. It's a small diesel-powered cabin cruiser. They don't keep a detailed record of the movements of all the boats, but they do have a general notion of what their owners do with them. According to her, he would turn up every second week and take the boat out for three days, out on day 1, back on day 3. But she'd no idea where he went or what he did."

"Did he have the boat taken out of the water each winter?" asked Bhardwaj. "My Dad has a pal with a boat at the marina at Inverkip, but he gets it taken out of the water at the beginning of November and doesn't put it back until the beginning of April."

"No, he used it all year round, irrespective of the weather. So, after we talked to her I thought we'd have a little look at it. Arvind kindly kept a lookout whilst I nipped inside."

"We didn't hear any of this," said Blue. "Remember that any evidence obtained by such means would not be admissible in court, and anyone who used such means to obtain evidence without the appropriate search warrant might be severely reprimanded. So, what did you find?"

"Not a lot, to be honest. Tins of beans and steak, instant mash, bottle of whisky, cans of lager. Spare clothes. No trace of drugs. But a cupboardful of porn mags, well-used by the look of them. And underneath them, this." He took out his phone, switched it on and soon held it out so they could see the image. A leather-bound book, the leather yellowish and worn. It certainly looked old.

"There's no title," said Bhardwaj.

"The title page is inside," said McCader, flicking the image sideways to show the next one. "*The Scottish Chiefs*, by Jane Porter. It gives the date as 1819."

"Possibly the world's first historical novel," said Blue. "I got a copy for my twelfth birthday. A present from my great-aunt on Jura. It's about William Wallace, and his sidekick Andrew Moray. It was a popular book and I think frequently reprinted. My version was printed around 1910 with splendid illustrations; it really turned me on to history. If this were a first edition, I suspect it would be worth quite a bit. I assume you put it back where you found it."

"Naturally," came the reply. "There will be no evidence of my presence."

"Was there any evidence of a woman having been there?" asked Vunsells.

"Not that I could see," said McCader. "And I did look in every drawer and cupboard."

"What sort of equipment was in the boat?" asked Blue.

"It looked quite sophisticated, considering that from the outside the boat looked pretty dilapidated. Paint faded and peeling in places and windows dirty. Didn't look like the sort of boat you'd take very far. And yet, I feel he didn't just hang around the bay looking at his mags."

"Well," concluded Blue, "that gives us plenty to follow up this afternoon. We won't be able to get back to the shop till tomorrow, and I haven't received anything from the Estonian cops. So, Enver, can you and Arvind follow up Paul Carselaw? And Lena, can you see what you can find out about Ishmael Balfour? I'll go over to the shop and find out how the SOCOs are getting on."

10

A cold rain was falling as he walked to the bookshop. He arrived to find PC Beattie huddled in the doorway trying to keep dry, only partially succeeding, as the shop door was only recessed about a foot from the windows on either side.

"Constable Beattie," began Blue, "I believe you had a conversation with someone earlier this morning who asked what was happening here."

"Yes, er, sir, that's true. It was before you and Sergeant Morgan arrived. I was in the car, and she must have seen it in the lane. She was quite slim, so she was able to get as far as the window. She asked me if something had happened in the bookshop."

"And you told her?"

"Well, yes, I mean, I was pretty vague about it, just said there had been a burglary, and we were still investigating it."

"Did you give any further details?"

"Not really. I mean, all I knew was what that girl in the shop had told me, that someone had been there, stolen some of the more valuable books, and thrown the others around."

"You're aware, constable, that passing precise details of cases under investigation, is contrary to correct police procedure. This is made very clear at your induction into the force, is it not?"

"Well, yes, sir. But…"

"But what?"

"She was very persuasive. It was out before I realised it. I'm sorry, sir."

"Tell me exactly what this woman was like."

"Well, er, she was about my height, I guess, er, but slimmer, as I said, blonde hair, tucked at the back of her head, under a woolly hat. Blue eyes. Very friendly." He smiled at the memory.

Blue realised Beattie had been putty in the woman's hands, and no doubt told her everything he knew. "How was she dressed?"

"Let me think." Blue already knew that thinking wasn't Beattie's strong point. "Er, blue, yes, jeans, oh, and a light blue, or bluish green sweater under a Barbour jacket sort of thing. It was dark brown or black. And a woolly hat with a pom-pom. It was grey, I think. Or maybe light blue."

"Did she tell you her name?"

"No. She said she was a friend of Anna's, who worked in the

shop. She'd seen the police car and wondered if Anna was OK. I was able to reassure her. She thanked me for my help. 'Your police are so wonderful,' she said." Beattie's eyes glazed over as he remembered this sublime moment.

"Did she speak with any sort of accent?"

"She didn't sound local. Could have been from anywhere. I don't know she even had an accent."

"Thank you, constable, I'll need you to make a statement about this incident back at the station. The woman may be relevant to our inquiries. But do remember in future that details of ongoing investigations are not, under any circumstances, to be passed to members of the public. Now excuse me please, I'd like to enter the shop."

Beattie seemed reluctant to move out into the rain to let Blue past; this was understandable given that he had no waterproof garment on. Blue had heard the younger constables saying that the waterproof garments provided as part of the uniform were not cool.

He entered the shop. It was empty; the SOCOs must be at work through the back.

"Hello!" he called. He knew how annoyed the SOCOs got if someone just wandered through to where they were working.

After a couple of minutes, Steve Belford, the SOC team leader emerged from the rear of the shop.

"Hi, Angus. What can I do for you?"

"Hi, Steve, I think you know the answer to that already."

"Where are we? What have we got?"

"Exactly."

"Well, we're finished here in the front shop. Some fingerprints, so we'll have to match those with the staff. We need to eliminate the regular frequenters of the place."

"We took Anna Zeresova's this morning. I'll send you Aino and Paul Carselaw's, as soon as I get back to the station. I can also get Ishmael Balfour's. He's Mrs Carselaw's co-partner, and was in the shop just before Mrs Carselaw went off."

"That would be very useful."

"Once you've done here, I can ask Anna to come in and find out what's missing."

"That should be okay sometime tomorrow. We're not finding very much in the back either. And the first thing you'll want to know is that there's no sign of the lock being forced, either the front door, or the one at the back leading to the green. That doesn't mean it wasn't a skilled burglar, but I think it rules out our local amateurs."

"Looks like it. What about the first door on the left through there? It was locked when we were in this morning."

"Dennis managed to pick it. Do you want to come and have a look?"

"Lead on, Macduff. Just let me put some gloves on."

The previously locked door now lay open. Steve motioned for Blue to go in first, then followed.

They found themselves in a cramped space, about two metres square, which they shared with a spiral staircase.

"Where does it go?" Blue asked.

"Up!" said Steve, echoing the famous line in *Ghostbusters*. "It ends at a door which we're guessing leads into the flat upstairs. That door's locked, too. Dennis is working on it now. We tried ringing the bells on the door to the close between the shops to ask about it; I tried all of the flats, and there was no response. It seems as if none of the flats up there are occupied."

"Could be second homes or holiday lets. I'll find out who lives there. The most obvious reason for the staircase is that at one time the shop-owner lived in the flat. Does it look original?"

"Difficult to tell. It's certainly old. Cast iron, by the look of it. It could have been put in when the place was built, or maybe not too long afterwards."

"Hey guys, we're through!" came a call from the top of the staircase.

"Let's take a look," said Steve. "Come on, Angus. Oh, put some overshoes on first."

They climbed the steep iron stairs. At the top was a doorway, filled by the bulky figure of Dennis Johnston. "Hi guys," he said, "do come in." He squeezed aside for them to enter.

"Wow!" said Steve.

The room they entered was about the size of a bedroom, but, apart from the window overlooking the communal green at the back of the building, and the door in the right hand wall, the walls were entirely covered in bookshelves, from floor to ceiling. And most of the shelves were full of books.

"Reserve stock?" said Blue. He had a quick look round the

shelves. Most of the books were not in English. Perhaps most of the English-language stock was displayed downstairs for the benefit of in-person customers, who in Oban were more likely to be English speakers.

"What do we do now, Angus?" asked Steve.

"Just hold it here for a moment." Blue took out his phone and called Vunsells back at the police station. "Lena, I'm at the bookshop. Through that locked door in the corridor is a staircase to the flat upstairs. Can you call the council and find out who lives in that flat. In fact, find out who lives in all the flats in the building. I'm not sure of the address."

"It's 7 Stairfoot Lane, chief. I'll do it right away."

"Thanks Lena." Blue pocketed his phone. "OK, Steve, let's wait till Lena gets us some information about the place. We don't want to be accused of breaking into anyone's home without authority. We can argue that where we are now is part of the shop, but through that door could well be where somebody lives."

"Dennis," said Steve, "you may as well get back downstairs and give Jill a hand. I'll give you a shout if we need more help up here." Dennis nodded and set off back down to the shop.

Blue looked out the window down into the green at the back. There was no washing out – not surprising since it was raining – and the grass needed a good cut. There was no sign of life – not an abandoned scooter, an old car tyre, or even a tennis ball waiting for a dog. Time stood still.

His phone rang. "Hi, chief, this is Lena. According to the council, none of the flats there are occupied. They're all certified as empty. They're owned by a company called IBB International. Enver's checking them out as we speak. He'll ring once he has something."

"Thanks Lena. OK, Steve, according to the council the place is empty, so I think we can take a look round. After all, whoever trashed the shop may have come in this way."

Blue opened the door which he presumed led to the rest of the flat. It opened into a dim hallway, illuminated only by light coming in from a low window over the main door. Blue found the switch and turned the light on. So the electricity was still connected. The hall was completely empty, its walls painted a dull matt brown. Four other doors opened off it. All were closed.

"Not much sign of life here," he observed. "Let's try this roc

The first door opened into a kitchen, with a win(overlooking the green at the back. "Looks like it was put in in 1960s," said Steve. "Who thought orange was a good colour kitchens? I'll bet the bathroom's in avocado."

"This flat is supposed to be empty," said Blue, gesturing a small Formica-topped table with a single chair pushed under "And I don't think this microwave was installed in the sixties."

Apart from the microwave, and an electric kettle, the counte were bare. Blue drew his finger across one. "No dust," h commented. "Unusual for an empty flat. Have a look in th fridge."

The fridge was below the counter, with cupboards on either side. As Steve opened it, no light came on. Steve knelt to peer inside, "Well, well, lookee here! Some cheese slices. Getting mouldy now. Been here a few days I would think."

"Let's check the other rooms," said Blue, "then I think you'll need to give the place a good going-over. Looks like someone's been here."

The next door led to a narrow bathroom. Steve was right: the suite was avocado, with brown tiles on the walls. There was a toilet roll in the holder, and a small oval bar of white soap by the sink. Above the sink was a mirror-fronted cupboard. Opening it revealed it to be empty.

The next room was a living-room, which faced the lane. By the window was a well-worn wooden table, with a single chair. There was an armchair and an old double-bar electric fire. A cupboard and bookshelf were both empty. "Somebody's been here all right," muttered Steve.

The last door opened into a bedroom. A single folding bed, the sort available in any camping shop, lay against the far wall, bare of any sleeping bag or other covering.

"Oh, shit!" said Steve.

On the bed, face down, lay the body of a man.

He was dressed in jeans and a red and blue check shirt, and had blue socks on his feet, and no shoes. His right arm lay alongside him, the left hung down so that the fingers brushed the pale green carpet.

Steve tiptoed over, knelt down, took the dangling left wrist and

tested for a pulse. Then he felt the man's neck with a couple of fingers. "He's dead all right," he concluded. "Maybe a few days, but I'm no expert. Strangled by the look of it – I can see marks of a thick cord on his neck. No obvious wounds on his back."

"Can you turn his head, so we can see his face?"

"We'll have to photograph him first. I'll call Andy. He won't take long to get here."

"OK," said Blue, "I'd better summon the doc."

He looked round the room before taking out his phone. By the bed stood an old bedside table with a lamp, its drawers empty. Likewise the wardrobe that stood against the rear wall. The bedroom window faced the lane; it was open about two inches at the top. Enough to blow any smells away. There was no obvious piece of evidence lying around.

"More work for us here, I guess," said Steve, as he put his phone away.

"Looks like this guy was living here," observed Blue, "then somebody came to visit, and bumped him off. They tried to clear the place out, but forgot to empty the fridge, and left the soap and toilet paper. Or, on the other hand, maybe someone else was living here, and this one came to visit. And then got bumped off. And the killer then tried to clear the place out and left."

"They've not been away long," said Steve. "There wasn't a lot of mould on the cheese, and it was still the friendly blue variety. The mould, that is. And the smell." He sniffed, as if to demonstrate how it was done. "It doesn't smell like a place that's empty. That tells me whoever was here stayed long enough to warm the flat up and make it feel lived in."

"OK Steve, once the doc's been and the body's gone, get your people up here. See if there's anything that we can use."

"It'll be tomorrow, unless you want us to work into the night."

"No, there's no point in that. I noticed the main door has two pretty solid bolts on the inside, so we can stop anyone getting in. I'll also put a man at the tenement door overnight. But no fuss – there's no point attracting attention at this point."

Andy McGuire was there in ten minutes, and got to work. Five minutes later Dr. Saffraj arrived, and duly certified that the body was indeed dead. He allowed Blue and Steve to turn it over. Just as on the back, there were no obvious wounds in the chest. The doctor's guarded opinion – "purely provisional, you understand"

– on cause of death was, as Steve had suggested, strangulation.

Blue stared at the face. He didn't recognise it. The man was small and wiry, with brown hair cut very short. A pale, thin face, clean-shaven but with a stubble of a few days' growth. Had he stayed longer than he planned, not having his shaving kit with him, before he was killed? Or was the stubble part of his look? Apart from the milky eyes staring at the ceiling, there was nothing remarkable about the face. No scars or blemishes. Forgettable, thought Blue, someone you just wouldn't notice.

He went back downstairs. Jill Henderson reported that there was nothing out of place in the kitchen, toilet or office. There were a few prints, but they'd need to be checked against the regular users.

"What about the safe?" asked Blue. "Any sign that it's been forced?"

"No," responded Dennis. "It's locked at the moment. I had a good look at the lock. It's not been tampered with. That doesn't mean it hasn't been opened, of course. If the burglar knew the combination…" He shrugged.

"OK, thanks," said Blue. "I've said to Steve, there's no need to work late on this, we can start upstairs tomorrow."

"That's good," said Jill. "I wouldn't want to be stuck here in the middle of the night. The whole place is creepy."

Blue was back in the shop when his phone rang. McCader. "Hi Enver, what have you got?"

"IBB International. The main shareholder and company director is Ishmael Balfour. The initials tell us he's not tried to keep his connection to the company a secret."

"So he owns the whole building?"

"Yes. Including the empty shop next to the bookshop. He may have been thinking of expanding."

"I'll ask him. When did he acquire it?"

"Piecemeal over the last six or seven years. Lena can tell you more about that. Hang on a sec."

A few moments later Lena Vunsells came to the phone. "Hi, boss. Yes, I've just been tracking that down. He bought the bookshop and the flat above it from the owner who was renting it to Aino Carselaw in 2015. That may have been part of his partnership arrangement with Aino. In 2016 he acquired the top floor flat. He bought the shop next door in 2017, then in 2018 he got the two flats above that shop. One came on the market when the owner died; with the other, Sandra, that's my contact at the council, says he made the couple in it an offer they couldn't refuse."

"Any idea why he acquired the whole building?"

"Sandra says they think he wanted to turn it into holiday flats. He had some discussions with the planning people, but they didn't get anywhere. So all he did was declare all the flats empty to avoid the council tax."

"OK, Lena, that's useful. Things have become more complicated now. We have a body upstairs. Can the three of you pop round and have a look before they fetch it off to the morgue?"

The ambulance had arrived, though it had to wait in the main street, the lane being too narrow. Blue asked the paramedics to wait until his team had viewed the dead man. They were OK with that. It was not as if he needed urgent treatment.

McCader, Bhardwaj and Vunsells were round in five minutes. Blue felt it was worth them all seeing the corpse where it had been left by the killer.

"Anyone recognise him?" he asked. He didn't expect a positive response, but you never knew, the question was worth asking.

They shook their heads. "Doesn't look local," said McCader. "That pasty complexion reminds me of Eastern Europe. Anything found on him?"

"No," said Blue, "Steve checked all his pockets. Nothing. Labels cut off his shirt and jeans too. Whoever killed him didn't want him easily identified. SOC have already taken prints and samples for DNA analysis. But if he's not UK-based, we may not have much luck. Still, Andy will have taken some head-and-shoulders shots, so someone may recognise him."

"What about Anna?" suggested Vunsells. "He may have come into the shop whilst she was there. And Mr Balfour, he owns the place. The man may be an associate of his."

"And Paul Carselaw," added McCader. "If this guy was working with his wife, he may have been at the flat. Or even on the boat."

"At least we've somewhere to start," concluded Blue. "We can get going on that once we have some pictures. The SOCOs will go over this flat tomorrow. However, now that we know Ishmael

Balfour owns the whole building, I think we need to look at the other flats too."

"We'll need a warrant for that," observed McCader.

"Given we've a body, that won't be an issue. But let's just ask Mr Balfour first. To see how he reacts. We need his prints too, anyway."

"By the way," put in McCader, "what should we do about Carselaw's boat?"

"Nothing for the moment. But we have to confront Mr Carselaw with what we now know about him, and see how he reacts. And show him the dead man. Let's meet again at nine tomorrow."

As the others set off for the police station, Blue decided to check out the Queen Adelaide Hotel, and see if Ishmael Balfour was actually staying there.

The hotel was an Edwardian villa overlooking the north end of the bay, further along the promenade from the Corran Halls and the episcopal cathedral. Blue entered the dim hallway, and pressed the bell on the counter facing him. A woman in dark skirt and jacket appeared from the doorway behind the counter. Her expression was unsmiling but not hostile.

"Good afternoon, sir. How may I help you? Unfortunately there are no vacancies." The accent struck Blue as east European, though he couldn't be more specific.

Blue showed his ID. "Detective Inspector Blue. I wonder if Mr Balfour is here."

The woman's expression did not change. "I'm sorry, sir, I'm afraid Mr Balfour isn't in. May I take a message? He'll see it as soon as he returns."

"Just tell him I called. I'll probably get in touch with him tomorrow. Thank you."

That evening, eating a truffle and mushroom risotto, and sipping a glass of white wine, Blue considered the case. Aino Carselaw's fate had been established, though how and why she came to be lying dead in a meteor crater was still unclear. And the business of her still being married to Kalev Lind was very odd. Paul Carselaw he had begun to pity, but the boat showed another side of him. And where did the burglary at the shop fit in, and the corpse lying on the bed upstairs? Then the large figure of Ishmael Balfour loomed up in his mind. There was still a good way to go before this all made sense.

After the meal, he phoned Alison and brought her up to date.

"Aino Carselaw was up to something," she said. "How do you know she was in Estonia all that fortnight? She could have visited her parents and sister, then cleared off anywhere. And thanks to Schengen she could have gone anywhere in mainland Europe without having to show any ID."

"I'll pass that thought on to the Estonians, and let them worry about it. How's Corrie?"

"Oh, she's fine. But then, dogs don't have a lot to worry about, do they? She looks intelligent but I doubt there's a great deal going on inside her head. That's the advantage of not having language. We'll be back tomorrow. See you then. Love you."

11

Thursday 1 December

When Blue arrived at his office at eight, on a cold and cloudy morning, some of the material from Estonia was waiting for him: six images of the body found in the meteorite crater. One showed the body in the water; little was visible in the murky greenness apart from the swirl of red hair on the surface. Another two showed the body on a stretcher after removal from the water; it was now clear that the woman was fully clothed, wearing jeans and a light-coloured fleece, possibly of brownish colour, and trainers. Her face was also visible. A neat face, thought Blue, with a thin and pointed nose. But, like so many faces drained of life, it seemed very ordinary, all the quirks of expression which would have made it memorable gone. The final three pictures showed her on a slab in the mortuary, naked, presumably prior to the ministrations of the pathologist. One was of the whole corpse: Blue noted how slim she was. The other two were head shots from either side of the face. He compared the images with the picture he had of Aino Carselaw; they looked similar. He would have to show them, or at least some of them, to Mr Carselaw, just to be sure. Not something either of them would enjoy, best done as soon as possible.

The images reminded him to text Andy McGuire and ask when they'd have pictures of the dead man in the flat. Then he checked with the morgue. The post-mortem had been set for ten o'clock.

The team met at nine, Sergeant Morgan being there too. Blue showed them the pictures of the dead woman. "I think we ought to run one or two of them past Mr Carselaw, given that he's only been told about his wife's death, without seeing any of the evidence."

"I'll come along with you," said Sergeant Morgan. "It was my missing persons case."

"OK, Aelwyn, we'll go along after this meeting. Lena, can you call Anna Zeresova, and ask her to come to the shop? The SOCOs have finished in the front-of-counter area, so she can start sorting through the books and work out what's missing. But no mention of the body."

"What about the books upstairs?" asked McCader.

"I don't think Anna is aware of the connection to the upstairs flat. We'll have to check that, of course. But it suggests to me that only Aino Carselaw and Ishmael Balfour made use of it. We'll have to talk with Mr Balfour today."

"What if he turns up at the shop?" asked Bhardwaj.

"He can't be allowed into either the shop or the flat until the SOC team have finished, and I've given him clearance. Lena, can you call him too, at the hotel, and invite him round here for, say two o'clock? He's not a suspect, of course, but we do have some things we need to clear up, and we also need to take his fingerprints."

"What if he tries to put it off, or wants to talk at the hotel?" asked Vunsells.

"Ah, well, that's where you're just following orders. The interview must be at the police station, so that proper privacy measures can be in place, and his fingerprints taken. If he tries to put it off, tell him that he won't get back into the shop until he's been interviewed and fingerprinted. And if he wants to bring a lawyer along, that is, of course, entirely up to him."

"Shall I go to the PM for the dead man?" asked McCader.

"Good idea. Why not take Arvind and Lena with you? Good experience for them. Then go on to the shop. If Lena helps Anna, you and Arvind can take a look at that flat upstairs. Once I get round with the dead man's pictures, we can take Anna up and see what she thinks the stuff there is."

With this the meeting was concluded, and Vunsells sat by the phone in the corner to call the Queen Adelaide Hotel. Blue, apparently checking his notes from the meeting, was pleased to hear that she was perfectly calm, pleasant and yet polite. "… I'm sorry, Mr Balfour, I'm afraid Inspector Blue's diary shows that he's unavailable this morning. But it may be possible to bring your interview forward to, say, 1.30." She twisted in her chair to see how he would react to the proposed time. Blue gave her a thumbs up. She smiled and nodded back, listening to the phone again. "That's very kind of you to consider the pressure you may be putting on Inspector Blue's lunch hour. But I'm afraid meeting him at a restaurant prior to the interview here would not be possible. So, we'll see you here at one-thirty, then? … And it has been a pleasure to talk with you also, sir. Goodbye."

"So it's one-thirty," said Blue. "That's fine. How willing was he to meet, Lena?"

"Oh fine, but preferably right away and at his hotel. He's extremely busy, and every minute matters. On the other hand, I think he really wants to get into that shop, so once he realised you were calling the shots, he agreed on a half-hour gain on the time. Now he can feel he didn't go along with everything you asked."

"Were lawyers mentioned?"

"I made it clear he could if he wanted, but he brushed it aside right away. 'My dear lady,' he said, 'my conversation with Mr Blue is one between gentlemen. I would not wish to sully it with a nit-picking legal insect interrupting at every moment.' So I guess that means he's not bringing one."

By 9.55, Blue and Morgan were outside the flats at Ganavan. Again, Carselaw had to be summoned from his garage. Once they were sitting in his living room, Blue explained that they had received pictures of Aino's body from the Estonian police, and, to confirm the identification, and as a courtesy to himself, they would like to show him a couple. Was he willing to look at them? There was no obligation.

"Yes, of course I'd like to see them. All I've had so far is you telling me she's dead, and that we weren't even married. They won't want me at her funeral, will they? Here's the idiot who thought he was married to her for decades! All right, where are they?"

Blue had brought the picture of Aino on the stretcher by the lake, and the two head shots. Carselaw seized them avidly and laid them on his knees, to quickly look at each in turn. Then he put the stretcher shot on top and studied it for several minutes. Was he remembering other times she'd worn those clothes, or struggling to accept the reality of what he was seeing? "At least she wasn't naked," he muttered to himself. Then he looked equally closely at the other two pictures, as if trying to make his wife come alive again by the power of his concentration.

At length he looked up again, and seemed to notice that there were other people in the room. "Oh! I'm sorry. Was there something else you wanted?"

"I'm sorry, sir," said Sergeant Morgan, "but I have to ask you to confirm that those pictures are of your wife Aino Carselaw."

"Oh, yes. Yes, that's her. Er, may I keep these pictures?"

Morgan looked to Blue. "I'm sorry, Mr Carselaw," he said, "that's not possible, until the investigation is formally closed. After that, I'll see what I can do to get you copies."

Carselaw nodded seriously. "Thank you. Well, was there anything else?"

"Just one small detail, sir," Blue continued. "It seems you were a little inaccurate in giving us your employment status. You haven't been working for X-Syst-X for a while, have you?"

Carselaw looked for a moment as if he were going to protest, but then sighed. "You found out from them, I suppose. All right, it's true. I was sacked for taking stuff home. But I'm not a spy. I was just a workaholic. I told them that but they wouldn't listen."

"The three days every fortnight you claimed to go down to Faslane. What do you actually do during that time?"

"I have a little boat. It's down at the marina at Gallanach Bay. I take it out and just chug around the islands for the three days. Take some booze and a few books and chill out. That's the nice thing about a boat you can sleep in. You can be literally anywhere and nobody bothers you."

"Thanks for clearing that up, Mr Carselaw, we won't take up any more of your time. Oh, just one other thing. I almost forgot. The bookshop was broken into on Tuesday night. We're still examining the scene. I'm afraid I have to ask you what you were doing then?"

"Mourning my wife and my marriage, inspector. With a bottle of whisky. I have very little recollection. I certainly wouldn't have been up to breaking into the shop. I suppose they were after any money there. They'd be out of luck, Aino wasn't that stupid."

"Thank you, sir, that was most helpful," concluded Blue. "We'll leave you in peace now."

Back in the car, Sergeant Morgan turned on the engine, then turned it off again. "Do you know, Angus, I know his wife's dead, and all that brings. But I'm still sure he's not telling us everything. Just my woman's intuition, but there's something. I mean, okay, he IDed the pictures, that can't have been easy. His alibi for Tuesday sounds plausible: having been told his wife was dead, and that she wasn't even his wife, sharing the news with a bottle seems a reasonable thing to do. Maybe it's the boat-trips that don't sound quite right. He calls himself a workaholic, yet drifts off for three days a fortnight to chill out. I don't buy that. Maybe you should have a look at his boat."

"Actually, Aelwyn, we already have. Unofficially, so not a word, please. We did find a book there, but nothing that points to anything definite. However, I agree with you, there's something going on there that we need to pursue. Discreetly. As to the rest, I'm not ruling him out of the bookshop robbery or the murder, just yet. Like you, I don't see him breaking in, but what if he did have a key? He could have taken Aino's and copied it, or she could have given him one."

"Why would she do that?"

"What if there was stuff in the shop that she'd told him to secure if anything happened to her? Perhaps she doesn't trust Balfour. So, as soon as we tell him she's dead, he gets over there, lets himself in and grabs whatever it is, then does a bit of wrecking just to throw us off the scent?"

"I hadn't thought of that. That's why I'm in lost property, not CID. But it does sound rather far-fetched. How does the dead man fit in?"

"That could suggest another scenario. Knowing Aino's dead, Carselaw heads over to the shop to take the most valuable stuff away. He knows about the upstairs flat, goes up to have a look at the books there, and runs into the mystery man. They have a discussion, at the end of which Carselaw kills Mr X, then tidies up the flat as best he can, and gets out. On his way he wrecks the shop a bit, again, to make it look like a burglar or even a couple of hooligans. But, of course, it could be someone else entirely."

12

When they got back to the police station, Blue walked round to the bookshop. PC Beattie was standing at the entrance, stamping his feet to keep warm.

"Morning, constable. A bit chilly, isn't it?"

"You can say that again, sir. I've been here since seven and it's not getting any warmer. Lucky I put my thermals on this morning."

"Very sensible," commented Blue. "Tell me, did Sergeant Graham ask you to keep an eye on the close here as well as the shop?"

"Yes, sir, he made that very clear."

"Good. Has anyone tried to enter the tenement this morning?"

"No sir. Not a soul."

"No further sign of that woman who spoke to you?"

"No, I've kept an eye open for her. Everywhere I've been. But nothing. Maybe she's left town." Beattie sounded disappointed that the magical figure had eluded him.

Once inside, Blue could see that the chaos of the previous day was being converted back into order. Already three sets of shelves were filled with rows of neatly-upstanding spines. On the floor, the random disposition of volumes hastily cast down had been superseded by piles of books perhaps ten or twelve deep, awaiting their turn to be marshalled again on the shelves.

"Good morning, Anna. Are you putting the books back into their original order?"

"Good morning, inspector. Yes. First I put the fallen books onto the shelves in roughly the correct position. Then I start from the beginning and move each book to its exact position."

"Do you have a rough idea, so far, of the extent of what's been taken?"

"It is already clear that the whole contents of the shelves by the counter, where the more valuable books were kept, have been removed. As regards the other shelves, judging by the amount of books on each shelf, I do not think much else has been taken, maybe even nothing. But I will tell you more precisely when I've finished sorting them, and have checked the catalogue."

"What about the books in the room upstairs?"

Anna paused, frowning. "What room upstairs?"

"You've never been through the first door on the left in the corridor?"

"I think you asked me this before. It is always locked. I do not know what is there."

"Through that door, there is a staircase to the flat above, and the first room you would enter is full of books. Perhaps, once you have finished here, I could ask you to have a look at the books upstairs and tell me if they are new or spare stock for the shop."

"That is most interesting. I think it will be clear if the books there are for the shop or not. Whenever you wish to ask, please do so. It is no matter to interrupt the work here."

"Thank you. Do carry on. I'm going to talk with the forensic officers."

In the upstairs flat, he found the SOC team fully occupied, having completed their work on the ground floor. In the living room, Dennis Johnston had lifted the rug from the floor, and was testing the floorboards for any movement with a screwdriver.

"Just checking for any secret spaces," he told Blue. "Nothing in the room with all the books, and looks like it's going to be the same here."

Blue wandered through to the kitchen, where he found Steve Belford. "Hi Steve. Anything?"

"Some prints and a few hairs, especially in the bathroom. But nothing we can identify until we've checked with the files and the lab. Somebody took quite a bit of trouble to get the place clean. Looks like the only thing they forgot was the stuff in the fridge."

"How long do you reckon you'll be here?"

"I think we'll be done by the end of the day."

"Is it OK if Ms Zeresova comes up to look at the books through there?"

"That's fine. There's nothing there. Except books. Nothing inserted in the books, as far as we know, but we only flicked through a few, so you might want your people to do that."

Blue went back downstairs and asked Anna to come up. Blue led the way, so that he could see Anna's reaction when she reached the room.

She stood wide-eyed. "So many books!"

"Have a good look at them," said Blue, "then tell me what you think."

Anna looked carefully around the shelves, occasionally taking a book off a shelf and glancing inside. After about five minutes she turned back to Blue. "Most of these are books which we could sell in the shop. But there is a whole wall over there which are not relevant to us; they are mostly in Italian or French."

"Could they be books waiting to be delivered to another bookshop?"

"That is possible. I do not know."

"Are any of these ones valuable?"

"No. Like most of the books downstairs, few of them would sell for more than a hundred pounds, and many for much less. They are mostly academic books discarded by libraries. None would be suitable for the glass-fronted case by the counter."

Blue thanked Anna and she returned downstairs. There was little more that he could do in the shop, so he set off back to the police station, to work on his report and then get some lunch.

But first he visited the work room, where he found McCader, Bhardwaj and Vunsells sitting round the central table, steaming mugs in front of them, and an open box of doughnuts.

"How was the PM?" he asked.

"Nothing unexpected," answered McCader. "He was strangled all right. From the marks on his neck it looks like some sort of garrotte was used. Put round the neck, then tightened by turning a lever or key. So it didn't require a lot of strength."

"That suggests to me he must have been asleep or unconscious when it happened. Unless he was involved in some weird sex thing."

"There's no evidence of that. But yes, the pathologist reckons he was unconscious, probably drugged. She's taken samples to check that out. Hopefully we'll have the results tomorrow. No other wounds on the body. Stomach contents indicate his last meal was a cheeseburger. And some pickled onions. The big yellow ones, not the little white ones."

"What about the clothes? Any pointers there?"

"Outer clothing had the tabs cut off. And his T-shirt. But not his underpants. Label there in Cyrillic characters. Just a brand name. Could be Russian, Ukrainian, Serbian, Bulgarian. I'll try to track it down. At least it might show us which country he came from. But that, and the onions, suggests Eastern Europe to me."

"Interesting. Another dimension opening up." He reported the conversation with Paul Carselaw. "Both Aelwyn and I feel he's not telling us everything," he concluded.

"Is it worth searching his flat?" suggested McCader.

"That's a difficult one, Enver. I doubt anything worth seeing will be in the flat. He's pretty careful. And it will tell him he's a suspect. Let's come back to that tomorrow morning. I'd like to hear what Ishmael Balfour has to say before we make any further moves. Enver and Arvind, can you dig a bit further into Mr Balfour and his business interests? Lena, can you go along to the bookshop and see how Anna's getting on? I'll come over after I've talked with Mr Balfour."

Blue thought of asking McCader to join him for the meeting with Balfour, but decided that McCader's enigmatic presence would make Balfour too suspicious to say much. A woman would be more likely to relax him. Luckily Aelwyn Morgan was in, and happy to come along.

At half-past one on the dot, Ishmael Balfour was ushered into the upstairs interview room. Dressed immaculately in a grey suit, he carried over his left arm an expensive cashmere overcoat.

He greeted Blue like an old friend, extending his right hand to shake. "Ah, Inspector Blue. Such a pleasure to meet you once again. I do hope we shall make some progress with this matter. And this is your colleague? I am most gratified to meet you, madame. You are also an inspector, I take it. Or perhaps a superintendent even, in the uniformed branch, as I believe they term it."

"This is Sergeant Morgan," Blue introduced her. "She is our missing persons specialist."

Balfour bowed to the sergeant. "I'm privileged to meet you, sergeant. I offer to any colleague worthy of joining Inspector Blue the same respect I offer him. It is, I'm afraid, these days so rare to meet police officials to whom one may extend such a level of respect. And believe me, I have met many in the course of my travels."

Blue offered tea or coffee. "On this occasion, inspector, I feel it would be discourteous to refuse. As you know, I am normally quite particular about what I imbibe, but out in the world, one must sometimes be more pragmatic, or more open. For instance, I don't know if you've ever been to the tea-house near the top of the Varzob Gorge, close enough to the Himalayas – you might call Tajikistan the foothills – to savour their supreme *chai.* Made with a combination of spices I wouldn't have believed could come together with such a profound effect."

"I'll make the tea, then," said the sergeant, and slipped into the kitchen.

Blue offered the visitor a seat. "Thank you for coming in, Mr Balfour. I should tell you that Ms Zeresova is taking stock of what remains in the shop, to identify what's missing. Our Scene of Crime team will be finished there later today, and tomorrow you would be welcome to come round then and give us your impression. Ah, here comes the tea."

Sergeant Morgan brought in the tray with three mugs of black tea, a box of sugar cubes, a jug of milk, and a well-used biscuit tin with a stag on the lid. Balfour took milk and two sugar cubes. "Sugar cubes. How civilised. Do you know, sometimes I go to a meeting and they don't even offer me sugar, or try to palm off some chemical imitation on me. And biscuits, too. I do love a biscuit."

Blue opened the tin. He hadn't looked in advance and didn't know what was in there. Some plain digestives, but also a few of what looked like digestives completely coated in milk chocolate.

"One of these will be fine," said Balfour. "A biscuit isn't complete without chocolate, don't you think? Swiss is of course superior, but this will do. I imagine your budget is limited. So, how may I help you? It is always my habit to assist the forces of law and order in whatever way I am able."

"Thank you," responded Blue. "I have some questions regarding the break-in at the bookshop."

"I'm not sure what I can add to what I've already told you, inspector."

"I believe you own the building which includes the bookshop."

Balfour smiled. "Ah, I see my confidence in your abilities is not misplaced, inspector."

"Can I ask why?"

"Of course you can. Seeing that Oban is one of the few places of true beauty in this world, I considered it both useful and beneficial to own property here. My plan was to have an apartment for my own use, and three other flats which would be rented out, perhaps to tourists. The empty shop I would convert into a cafeteria. Sadly, the local authorities did not appreciate my vision. I wished also to install an elevator. They did not agree. They also felt the lack of parking in the lane would add to congestion, and the flats should therefore be rented on a long-term basis to local inhabitants who did not possess motor vehicles. Now I'm a businessman, Mr Blue, and 'long-term' is not a word in my vocabulary. One must be ready to move very quickly if necessary. Ah, dear lady" – he turned to Sergeant Morgan – "I see you raise your eyebrows. Most elegant eyebrows I should add. Perhaps you're thinking, books, that doesn't sound like a very frenzied sort of business. But believe me, in any business, readiness is all."

"Yet you still own the building," commented Blue. "Isn't that tying up a lot of your assets?"

"I'm not in Oban often, but I still cherish the hope of having a modest pied-à-terre here. Alas, other things have intervened, and it has not yet come to pass."

"So the four flats are currently empty and unused?"

"You've expressed it very concisely. Empty and unused."

"Except the one above the shop."

"I beg your pardon?"

"There is a staircase from the shop to the flat immediately above. There is a large amount of book stock there, and signs that it has been lived in recently. Can you explain that?"

"Ah. Of course. It is so long since I've been there. Yes, I admit to you that I have stored there some small fragment of my total stock. Some will go downstairs, others await transit to one of my other establishments. But I can assure you that nobody has been living in that flat."

"Are you the only person with a key to the flat?"

"Naturally Mrs Carselaw also has access. She is aware of the stock stored there."

"And Miss Zeresova?"

"She does not have access. Only Mrs Carselaw and I have keys."

"What about the other flats? Do you have stock in them too?"

"No. Not at all. They are completely empty. You are most welcome to inspect them."

"Thank you for your co-operation, Mr Balfour. We would like to do that, just to be reassured that they have no link to the robbery. Now let's move on to the bookshop itself. Was it doing well?"

"As well as can be expected. Perhaps not as well as one might hope."

"Who is the woman who spoke to the constable at the shop and reported the robbery to you?"

Balfour was not expecting this question. "I'm not sure to whom you are referring."

"Please Mr Balfour. A woman extracted information from one of our officers, and passed it on to you. How else would you have known about the robbery?"

Balfour took a long sip of his tea. "Mostly Kenyan, I think. But drinkable." He paused as if working out what to say next. Blue waited.

He put his mug down. "Very well, sir. I must confide a little in you. This shop has been, shall we say, a little problematic. I don't wish to make any accusations, but I felt things were not quite going as they should. It's difficult to explain. Let me say only that I suspected that Mrs Carselaw might be doing some business in her own account. Buying and selling books without passing them through the accounts of the shop. Operating a little shop of her own on the side, you might say. Naturally Ms Zeresova is not aware of my concerns, and I do not suspect her of any involvement."

"Are we talking small or large amounts of books and money?"

"Now that is something I cannot tell you. Yet. There are, shall we say, inconsistencies in our records. Items in the catalogue I do not recognise. Mention of clients whose alias I do not know. You may imagine that I requested an explanation of these inconsistencies from Mrs Carselaw, and she has attributed them to minor errors of administration. But I am all too aware of the fallibility of my fellow mortals. That is why I brought in Elsa Maarksen. She is the lady who spoke to your officer. She is an inquiry agent who specialises in book-related matters."

"In your employ?"

"At the moment, yes."

"And has she reached any conclusions?"

"Her inquiries are as yet at an early stage."

"Nevertheless, we would, as you can imagine, wish to hear that from her own lips."

"And wonderful lips they are," sighed Balfour. "Oh, I'm so sorry sergeant, that was a most improper remark to make in front of a lady. Please accept my sincerest apologies."

"Accepted," said Morgan. "But the inspector is right, we need to talk with Ms Maarksen. Could it be possible that Mrs Carselaw's disappearance has anything to do with your inquiries?"

"Everything is possible, dear lady. But far be it from me to insert myself into the mind of Mrs Carselaw. Being always an optimist, I expect only the best of people."

"Yet you hired an investigator to look into her affairs."

"And I shall be most disappointed if anything negative is revealed. Yet I shall be obliged to act if such be the case, if only to maintain my reputation as an honest and upright man of business. Reputation is so important in business, you know."

"We will need to speak to Ms Maarksen," put in Blue. "Where can we find her?"

"As to where she is at this moment, I know not. However, I can pass on a message to her suggesting she make an appointment to see you."

"I've a better idea. You give us her contact details, and we'll call her direct."

"That is most difficult. Without the lady's permission, I would be reluctant to pass such details on to you. I'm so sorry."

Blue sighed. "This is a murder investigation, Mr Balfour. Under the circumstances, I can insist that you hand over Ms Maarksen's contact details."

Balfour looked genuinely surprised. "Murder? But who has been murdered?"

"The Estonian police have reason to believe a body discovered there is that of Mrs Carselaw."

Balfour was silent, and frowned, sipping again at his tea.

"Had your investigator not apprised you of this, Mr Balfour?"

Balfour said nothing, but dug a podgy finger and thumb into his waistcoat pocket and pulled out a business card. He placed it on the table in front of Blue. "Please copy the details and return the card. I regret that I only have one copy."

Sergeant Morgan pulled the card over towards herself, at the end of the table, pulled out her phone, and photographed both sides. Then she slid the card back to Blue, who picked it up and looked at both sides carefully, then photographed the front, before handing it back to Balfour.

"EMK investigations. Thank you, Mr Balfour. That's most helpful. There is one other service you may perform for us. We require a copy of your fingerprints."

"This is most inconvenient at this moment. I must go to a meeting, and with the inky fingers that would not be possible. Perhaps I could come back later in the week and..."

"I'm sorry, Mr Balfour, I must insist."

"And if I refuse?"

"Refusal is not an option. If you refuse to co-operate, we may feel obliged to use a certain amount of compulsion, appropriate to the circumstances."

Balfour smiled. "You reveal a vein of steel, inspector. I admire a man who is not afraid to use force when all else fails. Very well. You have your fingerprinting kit here?"

"No, not here. Sergeant Morgan will conduct you to our forensics department where your prints will be taken. You will be offered a state-of-the-art hand-cleaning product to remove all traces of the ink. Then you may proceed to your meeting. May I express my thanks to you for coming in today."

Blue stood up to indicate that the interview was over. Balfour pushed his bulk slowly up from his seat and shook hands with him. "A pleasure, inspector, indeed, a pleasure." He turned to the door, which Sergeant Morgan was opening, then paused. "Oh. When may I come into the shop?"

"As I said, sometime tomorrow. I'll give you a call at your hotel as soon as it's possible."

"Thank you. Just one question, inspector. Where was Mrs Carselaw's body found?"

"I'm sorry, I think you'll understand that I can't tell you that at the moment."

"Yes, I thought so. Very sad. The poor lady. Well, I hope to see you tomorrow, inspector. I may say it's my privilege to deal with you. So many other policemen are such, how shall I say, little people. People of no knowledge or imagination. So sad." He turned and headed for the door. Sergeant Morgan followed him out.

As soon as he'd gone, Blue took out his phone and typed in the mobile number given on Ms Maarksen's card.

On the third ring it was answered. "EMK investigations."

"Ms Maarksen?"

"Who wants to know?"

"This is Detective Inspector Blue, Oban Police Station. I'm investigating the break-in at Eastwards Books here in Oban, and the disappearance of Mrs Aino Carselaw. I've been speaking to Mr Balfour, and he has suggested I talk with you."

"Sadly, I'm afraid I'm not in Scotland right now. But I've been informed that Mrs Carselaw, whom I was investigating, has been found dead. Can you tell me anything about it?"

"I'm sorry. It's not my case. Mrs Carselaw's death is a matter for the Estonian police."

"Well, Mr Blue, you can hardly expect me to say much if you're not going to tell me anything."

"I can see your point, Ms Maarksen. But I'm only interested in Mrs Carselaw's activities here in Scotland, in connection with Eastwards Books."

Blue was thinking about her accent. He couldn't quite place it. It sounded Scandinavian, or maybe Dutch, with a hint of American or Canadian thrown in.

"Am I a suspect?"

"I'm sorry?"

"For the break-in? Do you think I had something to do with it?"

"Did you?"

"No. Not at all. I'm on the same side as you, inspector. Generally speaking. I'm paid to solve crimes, not commit them."

"Do you have any suspicions as to who might have broken into the shop?"

"That's something I'd rather not discuss on the phone. But once I'm back in Scotland I'll get in touch and we could share what we have. Now I must go. Goodbye inspector."

And before Blue could say a word, the phone went dead.

13

Blue dropped into the work room to find McCader and Bhardwaj working at the PCs.

"Anything useful come up?" he asked them.

"Mr Balfour has a complex web of businesses," reported McCader. "Mostly connected with the book trade. Eleven bookshops, in nine different countries, but all dealing with rare or niche books. Their credentials seem impeccable. Everything open and above board. His headquarters is in Bratislava – most of his companies are registered there. That fits in with his nationality; I suspect investing in Slovakia was part of the deal for getting residence and a passport."

"Any idea where he was actually born?"

"Not so far. He seems to have covered up his earlier life pretty effectively. We could send his fingerprints to Interpol, but I suspect there won't be a match."

"I'm sure you're right. Well, keep digging, something else might turn up. Right, Arvind, let's go round to the bookshop now. We'll need to check out those books in the room upstairs, and see if there's anything in any of them that might be useful."

Ten minutes later they reached the bookshop. PC Beattie was still stamping his feet at the entrance.

"Anybody show any interest in the shop or the close?" Blue asked.

"No, sir, not a soul. Please sir, any chance of a cup of something hot? I'm freezing here."

Blue turned to Bhardwaj. "Arvind, you're well wrapped-up. Take over from PC Beattie here for half an hour. Beattie, go and get a cup of something, at a café or back at the station. But be back here in thirty minutes. Thirty minutes, got that?"

"Yes, sir. Thank you. Don't worry, I'll be back inside thirty." And Beattie scurried off down the lane and disappeared.

Inside the shop he found Vunsells reading out the titles of books while Anna checked them on a laptop. He asked how they were getting on.

"Very well," replied Anna. "Once each book has been checked with the catalogue, I can print a list of those that are missing. Lena here has been most helpful. The work goes twice as quickly! I think we are finished in less than an hour."

"I'm glad to hear that, Anna. You look very much at home with the books, Lena. Maybe you should have been a librarian."

"Rather than a detective?" said Vunsells with a smile.

"No. You'll make a very good detective. It's just that you seem at home with books."

"Strange you should say that, chief. In fact I did work in a library for a while. Even thought about making a career out of it. Then chose a riskier option. But I still have a soft spot for books."

Blue left them to it and went through the door behind the counter. Before he could reach the staircase, Jill Henderson appeared from the kitchen. "Fancy a coffee, boss? Kettle's just boiled. I don't think the late Mrs Carselaw will mind us using up her catering supplies."

Steve Belford and Dennis Johnston were already in the kitchen, with mugs of coffee, and an open tin on the counter. Blue accepted a mug of coffee and a piece of choc chip shortbread. "I'm guessing you've finished the examination," he said, "otherwise you'd have to sift through all these shortbread crumbs."

"That's Dennis," said Jill. "Always a messy eater. Not always in control of his teeth, he says."

Dennis tried to protest, but only succeeded in mumbling incoherently whilst scattering more crumbs. After a slug of coffee he managed to speak. "Look guys, I can't help it if I have a partial denture. Blame it on my parents giving me too many sweeties as a child. False teeth aren't the same as your own. Harder to control, especially with crumbly stuff."

"Rachel should stop you eating biscuits," said Jill.

"Well, she does, usually. Only, if she's out, and there's a packet in the house... And you need biscuits, don't you, if you have children around? I mean, they need snacks, to keep them going. I read an article that said you need a certain carbohydrate input, or your brain runs out of steam."

"Bullshit!" was Jill's riposte.

"Okay, people," put in Steve, "the boss is here, let's behave ourselves. Yes, chief, we're done here. We could spend another week looking for minute organic fragments, but I don't think it would add much to what we've already got. So your team are free to poke around wherever they want."

At this point Bhardwaj arrived, reported that Beattie had returned, and accepted a coffee.

Twenty minutes later Vunsells came through to tell them that Anna had finished the search and was now printing out the results. She accepted a coffee too, and a shortbread finger.

Blue went through to the shop. Anna was taking a thin stack of paper from the laser printer beneath the counter. She counted the sheets – there were three, printed on both sides – and stapled them together at the top left hand corner. She handed the copy to Blue.

"I will print out another copy, to keep in the office, and email it also to Mr Balfour."

"Good idea. So, what does the search tell us?"

"All the books from the glass-fronted shelves have gone. This is understandable, as they are more valuable. There were thirty-one altogether. I do not believe anything else is missing."

Blue thanked Anna for her help and went back to the kitchen, collecting Vunsells and Bhardwaj, and leading them up the spiral staircase and into the book-lined room. "Here we are. All you have to do is flick through each book and shout if anything falls out. And then have a look behind the books, in case there's anything tucked behind them. I doubt there's anything, but it's best to be sure. Tedious, but necessary, like a lot of police work." He left them to it and returned to the station.

14

Back at the station, Blue began to update his report. After ten minutes the phone rang. Katie at reception. "Inspector Blue, I've a call from Estonia for you. They called at three, and then again at half past. Someone called Tark. Says she's a lawyer. Do you want to take the call?"

"Yes, please. Put her on."

"Inspector Blue?" A woman. A voice that struck Blue as cold and hard.

"Yes, I'm Inspector Blue. Who am I speaking to?"

"My name is Margarete Tark. I am an attorney with the firm of Hausmann and Arbuus of Tallinn. Our client in this matter is a *Härra* Lind."

"Kalev Lind?"

"The same. As I am sure you know, his wife, Aino Lind, also known in the UK as Aino Carselaw, had an interest in a business enterprise known as Eastwards Books. Mr Lind, as his wife's next of kin, will of course inherit her share in this business. I am contacting you to inform you that the recent robbery at the premises of Eastwards Books is thus a matter of interest to Mr Lind."

"Thank you for letting me know, Ms Tark. I will bear that in mind."

"I've not finished, inspector. The main purpose of my call is to inform you that Mr Lind wishes to make a statement in relation to the robbery."

"Does Mr Lind know something about the robbery?"

"Not in the specific sense that you may be implying. He does not know who carried it out or commissioned it. However, he wishes to offer some background to the investigation, which he is sure will be of use to you."

"What kind of background?"

"We have prepared a statement on behalf of Mr Lind, which we will forward to you. Mr Lind has approved the wording and is willing to sign a paper copy if such is required."

"What information is Mr Lind offering that we don't already have?"

"He feels he can shed light on some of the individuals involved. He may know more about these individuals than you are currently aware of. You will appreciate that is why we have prepared a legally safe statement."

"Thank you for your clarification. My answer is no thank you."

"I beg your pardon?"

"No, thank you. I am not interested in Mr Lind's feelings and opinions. However, if Mr Lind possesses factual information which is relevant to the case, I will be happy to interview him, over a Zoom link. At such an interview he would be welcome to have a lawyer present. Perhaps you could convey what I've said to Mr Lind, and let me know whether he is willing to be interviewed. I am happy to arrange a time that is convenient for him."

"This is most irregular."

"Not in the least. Investigations are sometimes plagued by individuals only peripherally connected to the case, but who wish to input their own opinions. A request for an official interview usually terminates their desire to be involved. Thank you for contacting me, Ms Tark. Please let me know what Mr Lind decides to do. Have a good day."

"Yes. You also." And with a cold goodbye the line was cut.

Blue was aware that Kalev Lind was closer to the case than some of the crackpots who might denounce a suspect as a confidence trickster, a Russian spy, or a shape-shifting alien. And it would have been interesting to see what he had to say in his statement. He clearly would have opinions about his late wife, but also perhaps about others, such as Paul Carselaw or Ishmael Balfour. But it was clear to Blue that Kalev Lind had things he wanted to say; why else go to the trouble of getting some lawyers to put together a statement? Refusing the statement would therefore not be likely to put him off. And an interview would be much more useful, because it meant the emphasis would be on the questions Blue wanted to ask, rather than the opinions Lind wanted to air. At the end of it, he might be none the wiser. But he had to admit, it would be rather interesting to meet, and question, Aino Carselaw's first, and, legally-speaking, only husband.

If his concern were related to ownership of the shop and its stock, the figures he would be interested in would be his wife and Ishmael Balfour. He doubted Ms Tark's assumption that Lind would inherit all of Aino's share in the business. Paul Carselaw, having lived as Aino's partner for thirty years, would have a very strong claim under Scots Law.

But what if Balfour were the target? Revealing something criminal about Balfour's dealings with Aino would change things. Whether this would enable Lind to get a bigger share of the assets was an issue for the lawyers, not the police. But that could give Balfour a motive for the robbery. Or even link him to Aino Carselaw-Lind's death. Of course, there was a risk that Lind would simply go off in a huff, but Blue's gut feeling was that he really wanted to say his piece.

By five Vunsells and Bhardwaj were back, their rummage through the upstairs book stock having delivered nothing of value, apart from a five-Euro note which had apparently been used as a bookmark. However, there was now plenty on the to-do list for the next day. Blue asked Vunsells to contact Anna again to find out if Mr Lind had ever visited the shop. McCader's attempts to find out about Ishmael Balfour's pre-Balfour life had come to nothing; Blue asked him to switch his attention to Elsa Maarksen. There was more work required on the dead man in the shop. Photographs of the body would be available in the morning, and these would have to be taken to the railway station, and any other likely point through which he may have passed. He'd also have to inform the Estonian police, and see if they recognised him, or could do anything at their end to identify him.

He was back home at six fifteen, and at six forty-five, Alison and Corrie arrived. Corrie bounded up to say hello, and needed some fussing before he could greet Alison. That evening they went to eat at the Greek restaurant in Connel. Roast goat with potatoes, sautéd aubergines and Greek yogurt. And a bottle of retsina, not Blue's favourite wine, but every so often, and with the right dish, it worked.

And after establishing that they couldn't be overheard – there was no-one else in the restaurant, and Costas was the soul of discretion – they talked about the case.

"It's bigger than it seems, I think," was Alison's opinion. "What's the point in roughing up a bookshop, unless there's something else behind it? Let's face it, there are plenty of shops in Oban that are well worth robbing. The distillery visitor centre, that shop that sells binoculars and telescopes, the jewellery places. You only rob a second hand book shop if you know what's there and where you can get a good price for it. So for me it's a move in a bigger game. Maybe somebody's putting pressure on Ishmael Balfour. They've killed his partner, and now they're after him. I would say he's the key to it all. He knows more than he's saying."

"I wouldn't disagree with that. He says he's doesn't touch stolen books. But even if that's true, there may be a level of action higher up where he is playing some sort of game."

"There does seem to be somebody out there whom you've not got near yet. What about this Elsa Maarksen? She may know more about what's going on at the next level."

Baklava and Greek coffee completed the meal. Leaving the restaurant, they noticed it had been snowing. Perhaps only half an inch, but enough that they had to hold onto each other a little bit tighter.

15

Friday 2 December

Blue was in his office at eight. Slightly later than usual, but then, it wasn't easy to leave his bed when Alison was there.

An email awaited him, with several photos of the dead man, taken at the morgue. Blue was impressed; in a couple of the head shots the man looked alive, with open eyes giving him a rather surprised expression. There was another email, from Margarete Tark. It informed him that *Härra* Lind would be willing to attend a Zoom call with *Komissar* Blue that morning, at eleven o'clock Tallinn time. A Zoom link was attached to the message. That would be 9am in Oban, so there wasn't much time. He guessed that was deliberate. He went up to the meeting room; Lena Vunsells was already there, on her phone.

She finished the call. "I was speaking to Anna. She says she's never heard of Kalev Lind, and can't remember Mrs Carselaw speaking of anyone of that name. It doesn't mean he's not been there, of course, but if so he must have done it very discreetly. I can call the airport and see if a Kalev Lind has flown in or out over the last few months."

"Yes, do that. But first I need you to sit in on a Zoom interview. With Mr Lind. At nine. We'll do it from here; that way the others can listen in too, as long as they keep quiet."

McCader was in by quarter past, and Bhardwaj at half past. Blue explained what was happening.

"One thing I'd advise," suggested McCader. "Get a link from our IT people and send it to them. That way you control the call. You can set it to record the whole interview. And stop them muting you when they want to, to delay the questions they don't like. Why don't I go and fix it with IT?"

Blue agreed, and they arranged the room so that McCader and Bhardwaj were well out of sight of the camera on the PC. Blue knew that McCader could remain silent for as long as required, but he wasn't so sure about Bhardwaj.

Bhardwaj was also aware of his limitations. "Look, boss, I'm bound to cough or sneeze, or shout if I discover something. So why don't I go down to the archive and see what I can find out about Ms Maarksen and her company? I'm sure Anjana will be able to point me in the right direction." The archive wasn't just a library and a storehouse of old cases; it was also an information hub. Virtually anything in the public domain, and plenty that wasn't, could be explored there. The new librarian, Anjana Rehan, a rather attractive twenty-something-year-old, was also very on-the-ball.

"As long as it's relevant," smiled Vunsells.

Bhardwaj blushed and cleared his throat. "I'd better get over there now." And he was off.

McCader was soon back with the link, which Blue emailed to Ms Tark, pointing out that police interviews on Zoom must be controlled from the police end, in order to avoid interference with the recording of the interview, which was also obligatory.

He wondered whether the lawyer would reject this proposal, and could imagine a tense conversation going on in Tallinn. Ten minutes later a curt response indicated that the conditions set by *Komissar* Blue would be accepted, although with reluctance, as they seemed to indicate that her client was a suspect, rather than an interested party offering information and possible insights.

At nine sharp the link was activated, and in less than a minute the connection was made. The image from Tallinn showed two people sitting at a desk. Behind them was a blank wall with a picture of a sailing ship at sea. The one on the viewer's left was a woman, perhaps in her forties, with brown hair, wearing a smart beige suit and an icy expression; the other, on the viewer's right, was an older man, tall, with iron grey hair and a neatly-trimmed moustache.

Blue welcomed them, and introduced himself and DC Vunsells. He made it clear that the interview would be recorded; this was normal procedure and the interview would not be possible otherwise. He hoped this would be acceptable.

The woman spoke first, introducing herself as Margarete Tark and the man next to her as Kalev Lind. The man nodded and smiled as he was introduced, although the smile seemed to Blue to be the practised and meaningless smile of the man who attends many meetings.

"Before we start," she went on, "I must express my client's dissatisfaction with the implication that he is a suspect in this case, that is, of the robbery of the bookshop. I must stress that he has offered of his own free will to talk with you, purely in order to assist with your investigation."

"Thank you, Ms Tark," replied Blue. "I have never implied that Mr Lind is suspected of any crime. The conditions set are those pertaining to any interview which we conduct. I look forward to hearing what Mr Lind has to say, and hope that it will be helpful to our investigation."

The lawyer nodded. "I understand. But I must ask you, *Härra Komissar,* to use more simple language in order that your meaning is clear to *Härra* Lind."

"Yes, of course."

"*Härra* Lind will now read his statement," said the lawyer, and Lind picked up a sheet of A4 paper and cleared his throat.

"I'm sorry," said Blue, "we must commence the interview in the form set out in our rules. I first state that the date is the second of December, and the time 9.05 UK time. Those present for this interview are DCI Blue and DC Vunsells in Oban Police Station, and Ms Tark and Mr Lind in Tallinn, Estonia. This interview will be recorded, and a certified copy of the recording will be made available to Mr Lind and Ms Tark. Please indicate that you agree to the recording. If you do not agree, the interview will stop and any recording that has taken place so far will be deleted."

"Yes," said the lawyer, "we agree. Mr Lind will now read his statement."

"This is an official interview," said Blue. "I will ask Mr Lind questions which will enable him to give us information which is relevant to our investigation. When there are no further questions, if he wishes to provide further information, he may then make a statement."

"This is totally unacceptable!" declared Ms Tark. "This procedure amounts to harassment of my client. I demand that he read his statement forthwith."

After a moment of silence, Lind's mute sign came on, and he touched Ms Tark's arm. Her mute signal came on too, and then the image from Tallinn was replaced by a photo of a snow-covered square with the closely packed frontages of mediaeval buildings around it. Blue muted himself and Vunsells. "Let's wait and see what happens."

Five minutes later, the live image reappeared, the mutes came off, and Ms Tark spoke. "Very well. *Härra* Lind agrees to this procedure. But he reserves the right to also send a written statement containing any additional information he considers to be relevant."

"Thank you," said Blue. "We will now begin. Mr Lind, can you tell us when you first met Aino Kuusk?"

"Why is this necessary?" asked the lawyer. "It is not related to current events."

"We simply wish to establish key background facts. Mr Lind?"

Lind leaned forward, as if speaking into a microphone. "Aino and I met when we were students at the University of Tartu. The year we met was 1985. We married the next year, 1986."

"Thank you. And you had one child?"

"Yes, Tiina was born in 1987." Lind smiled at the memory.

"But you divorced in 1988?"

"No, that is not correct. There was no divorce. We remained husband and wife up to the moment of my wife's death."

"Is that clear?" echoed the lawyer.

"Thank you, it is very clear. But what puzzles me, Mr Lind, is why you agreed to your wife moving to the UK, taking with her false divorce papers; then going through a legal ceremony of marriage with Mr Carselaw; and for the next thirty-two years living with him as his wife. It is not easy for us to understand the nature of your marital relationship in view of these facts."

The Tallinn Square reappeared. Three minutes later, the live image was back. Lind leaned forward again. "I understand that it may appear strange. I try to explain. In the late 1980s, the power of the Soviet state weakened. Estonia was the most westernised part of the Soviet Union, and more things became possible for us as rules weakened or were ignored. These were exciting times, and we saw more possibilities for our lives. Aino and I realised that, although we loved each other very much, our life-aims were different. Aino wished to see the world. I was happier to stay at home in Estonia, and develop my legal career. We had many talks about what to do. We agreed on a plan. We would separate and live our own lives, but always be there to help each other. We would meet up regularly. I agreed that Aino would go to England to improve her English. Then she would decide where to go after that."

"Were you surprised when she got married to Mr Carselaw?"

"Yes. It was a great surprise to me. She only told me afterwards, in the spring of 1991, when we met here in Tallinn. We spent a wonderful two weeks together, and during this time she told me all about the courtship and the marriage and the false papers. She told me that she had got false papers of divorce only in order to enter a form of marriage if she wished. She had not thought this would happen so soon."

"How did she get the false papers?"

"You must understand that during these times all sorts of, ah, falsifications, were possible."

"How did you feel about the marriage to Mr Carselaw?"

"This question is not relevant!" snapped Ms Tark. "Confine yourself to facts, *Härra Komissar*!"

"Were you happy that your wife had married another man?"

"This question is..." began the lawyer again, but Lind waved her objection away.

"We had decided that our lives would be separate. The relationship with Mr Carselaw was her decision. I respected it. This is the strength of our relationship. We respect each other."

"And you, on your side have also had relationships of your own?"

"Yes. But I do not think that is relevant."

"I'm sorry. Did you ever meet Mr Carselaw?"

Lind smiled, almost laughed. "Yes, I did, only one time. Perhaps ten years ago, I don't remember the date. He came to Estonia with Aino for a week. The situation with Aino's family was not easy. I had spoken with her parents and her sister. Her parents are old and truly believed that Aino and I were divorced. Maarja, her sister was a different matter; she is intelligent and would ask questions. Therefore I spoke to her in confidence, and explained the true state of affairs. She understood completely. It was with her assistance that I met him. They were staying with Maarja for a few days, so she invited me round to meet them, posing as a cousin of Aino. Maarja had asked for Aino's approval for this, so only Mr Carselaw did not know who I really was."

"What did you make of, I mean, what was your opinion of Mr Carselaw?"

"Again, this is not relevant. But I will answer. He amused me. He is, as you would say, a geek. A pedant. He has the sense of humour of a tortoise. And a big opinion of himself. I wondered why Aino had chosen him. For a strong difference to myself. Or to obtain UK residence. Who knows?"

"Did you ask her?"

"Oh yes. But she would say nothing, only that I should respect her decision. We men are the last to see what goes on inside our wives' heads. Don't you agree?"

"I would hesitate to comment. Thank you for your input, Mr Lind. Not having met your wife, it's most helpful to have your insights." Lind leaned back, looked pleased with himself, moved his hand in a deprecating gesture. "So," continued Blue, "let's move on. Why do you think Aino got involved in bookshops?"

"Aino was always a reader, from early childhood, she told me. Much more than me. She was always happy to talk about books. With a husband like Carselaw, she had much time to read. When there was a chance to work, without payment, at the shop in Helensburgh, she did not hesitate. She enjoyed it very much. After some time she became the manager. She changed the business of the shop so that more books were sold than the other rubbish that was donated to them. So when they moved to Oban, she set up a shop, not for charity but as a business. And to sell only books."

"How did her husband, I'm sorry, I mean Mr Carselaw, see her business?"

"Bah! He was more interested in playing with his trains than Aino's happiness. He just shrugged, she said, and said she could do what she wanted. But he wanted to know how much money it would make. You see, Aino had a sound business sense. Her plan for the shop was developed well. I gave her some advice myself. We worked on it together."

"Did you advise her to work with Ishmael Balfour?"

"No! I advised her to keep away from him. But she thought only of the financial support he could provide, and the stock he could supply. It would enable her to establish a specialist shop, selling across Europe and beyond. He was a clever seducer. In business matters only, of course."

"You thought he would cheat Aino?"

"I knew it! I enquired into his affairs. I discovered that he had tentacles in many pies, as you would say, and all of them sticky. When he began to buy the building where the shop is located, I knew that he was involved in some other business. Much bigger than a bookshop. I told Aino to be careful in her dealings with him. But at that time I had nothing firm. Only suspicions."

"And have you since learned any more about him?"

"Yes. This is what I wish to tell you. I believe he is involved in a network of criminal activities across the whole of Europe. Many of his businesses are based in Slovakia, a hotbed of crime. Also the origin of his wealth is very mysterious."

"Do you know where he comes from? His early history?"

"No-one does. It is hidden well. But I have clues that he is Romanian, or perhaps Moldovan. I have heard it said that he wished to become president of Moldova, but was expelled by those who knew him well. Now he pretends to be from elsewhere. I believe he made much money after the fall of the Soviet Union. He bought state enterprises at low prices, then sold them to multinational corporations who wished to become established in Eastern Europe."

"You have evidence of this?"

Lind shrugged. "People like Balfour do not leave evidence behind them."

"So what do you think his role in the robbery of the bookshop is?"

"I will say to you first that I believe he is responsible for the murder of my wife. Yes, I know that it is not your investigation. But that is what I think. She found out about his operations, and she was silenced! The robbery at the bookshop, it is a pantomime to cover up his own thefts."

"Have you shared your suspicions with the Estonian police?"

"Yes. But they do not try hard to discover the truth about Aino's death. It is easier to find some local culprit than to admit that it is the work of an international criminal."

"Is there anything else you'd like to tell me?"

"No. I have said the things I wanted to say to you. I hope what I have said is useful to you."

"Thank you, Mr Lind. We appreciate your willingness to help us. We will take careful consideration of everything you have told us. And if you do have any evidence relating to this matter, please inform us."

The lawyer leaned forward. "You will send to us a copy of this recording?"

"Yes. You should get that later today. It will not be edited in any way. Please do not edit your copy. Oh, there is one other thing. Do you know this man?" He put the head shot of the dead man onto Lind's screen, leaving the image from Tallinn visible on his own.

He saw Lind's eyes bulge and his mouth drop slightly, then his faint smile returned. "I do not know him. Who is he?"

"Someone we are interested in."

Lind held the smile and tapped the lawyer's arm twice with a finger. She leaned forward. "Thank you, *Härra Komissar.* If Mr Lind has more to tell you, we will contact you again. Goodbye."

And the picture from Tallinn was gone.

Blue asked Vunsells and McCader what they thought of Lind's contribution.

Vunsells began. "His relationship with Aino still seems very odd to me. If they wanted separate lives, why not just get the divorce in Estonia? That doesn't stop them keeping in touch. I don't think he's telling us everything about their relationship. What if he didn't want to separate, and refused a divorce, so Aino simply left him and came over here?"

"Even if he objected," put in McCader, "it would still have been possible for her to get a legal divorce – it was pretty easy during the Soviet era."

"Unless his position in the legal system enabled Lind to prevent it," countered Vunsells, "or at least make it difficult enough for her, so that she gave up and got the forgery instead. It seems to me Lind wanted the relationship more than Aino. It sounded to me that he didn't want them to be just good friends. And he certainly didn't think much of Paul Carselaw."

"I wondered what happened during the times she was over in Estonia," said McCader.

"I'll talk to *Komissar* Kõnekas about it," added Blue. "We'll also have to look at Balfour a bit harder. Lind gave us a few hints, but nothing very definite, nothing that could count as evidence. Nevertheless, we can't ignore what he's said."

"He knew the dead man," said Vunsells. "His reaction was pretty clear. Could the dead man have been working for him?"

"Another complication," concluded Blue. "Lena, can you phone down to the archive and ask Arvind to come back up?"

In a few minutes Bhardwaj returned, reporting that EMK Investigations was a legitimate company registered in Austria, its business described as 'consultancy relating to bibliographic matters.' The CEO was indeed Elsa Maarksen. There was no website or social media presence. Blue guessed that even the business card with contact details was hard to come by. Perhaps Ms Maarksen gained new business entirely by recommendation. Not a bad position to be in.

He asked Vunsells and Bhardwaj to take the picture of the dead man round the town, to places where someone might recognise him. Then he emailed the images to *Komissar* Kõnekas, explained how they'd found him, and asking if the Estonian police could identify him. He mentioned the interview with Kalev Lind, and suggested they have a Zoom meeting to bring each other up-to-date. He also emailed Ishmael Balfour, inviting him to inspect the shop, suggesting they meet there at eleven. A reply within minutes confirmed the arrangement.

16

At ten to eleven he set off in icy rain, arriving at the bookshop to find Balfour waiting under a large umbrella, watched suspiciously by PC Beattie from the shelter of the shop doorway.

Beattie saluted Blue smartly, for Balfour's benefit no doubt, and made a great show of opening the door to him. "What about this gentleman?" he said to Blue, nodding towards Balfour.

"Yes, he can come in too. Good work, constable. Let me know if anyone else wants in."

Once inside, with the door shut, Blue greeted Balfour. "Thanks for coming along, Mr Balfour. Our Scene of Crime officers have finished here, for the moment at least. The bookshop has been tidied up, and we have a list of what's missing, compiled by Ms Zeresova yesterday." Blue handed Balfour a copy of the list. "Perhaps you could have a look and tell me what you think."

Balfour studied the list for five minutes, then nodded. "May I keep this list?"

"Yes, of course."

"I must compliment Ms Zeresova. She has done a very good job here. She indicates that all the books taken were from the glass-fronted cabinet where the more valuable volumes are presented. This makes eminent sense to a book thief, and would seem to indicate that the purloining of these works was the objective of the exercise."

"Can I ask you if anything has been taken from the safe in the office?"

"Of course. Please, inspector, come with me and we will see."

He led Blue through to the office, and, with some difficulty, crouched in front of the safe, which sat on the floor in the corner, and was about four feet high. "Can I ask you to stand back a little, inspector?" he asked. "I'd rather you didn't see the combination. As I said, we occasionally keep very precious volumes there, so it is essential to be able to control access."

Blue stepped back a couple of paces. "Do you know what should be inside?"

"Not necessarily. Books that are too valuable to be displayed. There would be very few of those. I would have to check the Special Catalogue, as such volumes would not be included on the Normal Catalogue. There should also be in the safe the list of clients and their pseudonyms. Only Mrs Carselaw and myself have access to this list."

Balfour's face was serious, as he turned down the brass lever and swung the door of the safe open. "Come, inspector, see for yourself."

Blue knelt by him, catching a waft of sweet-smelling cologne, and stared into the safe. It was empty, apart from a folded sheet of paper. Balfour frowned. "Hmm. No books at all. That is unusual."

"So, what does that mean?" asked Blue.

"It is unusual for there to be no books there, but not impossible. There are times when there is no such stock on the premises. But the client list is still there, I take it. May I check?"

"Just a moment." Blue put on a pair of blue nitrile gloves, reached into the safe, and lifted the sheet out by one corner. He opened it out gently, holding the edges. It seemed to Blue to have two columns of names on either side of the sheet. He held it up in front of Balfour. "Please, have a look. But don't touch it. It will need to be checked for fingerprints. The burglar may have got into the safe, and taken it out to look at, or even to photograph it. I'm afraid I'll have to keep it for the moment. Can you confirm that that is your client list?"

"Yes, this is the list," said Balfour, "but it is of extreme confidentiality. I do not believe anyone has been in the safe, so it is not relevant to you."

"I'm sorry, but it is possible the burglar has been in the safe. What if he had somehow obtained the combination? I'll have to retain it as possible evidence. I'll place it carefully in an evidence bag, and it will be kept secure. There is a protocol for sensitive items which I will flag on the bag." Blue extracted an evidence bag from his pocket, placed the list inside, and sealed it. He wrote a number on the top right hand corner of the bag, and entered the number and the details of the bag's contents into his note book.

"Don't worry, Mr Balfour, this will be returned to you as soon as we have finished with it."

"Excuse me, inspector. As the owner of the building, I would like to withdraw any notification of the burglary to the police. This was not a casual robbery of opportunity, but a targeted exercise by a professional. Such a person will be well away from here by now, certainly out of this country. You will waste a lot of time and energy, and discover nothing."

"Weren't the books taken valuable?"

"The catalogue price would suggest so, but the total sum paid by us to obtain them was much smaller. We are not greatly out of pocket by their loss. And I would prefer to reopen the shop as soon as possible."

"I'm sorry, Mr Balfour. It's too late for that. This is a murder investigation."

"Murder, how so? Please explain yourself, inspector."

Blue took out the folded head shot of the dead man, unfolded it and held it in front of Balfour. "Do you know this man?"

Balfour frowned, and one eye twitched. He took the sheet over to the window and peered at it more closely. Was this to cover a recognition, wondered Blue, or simply the actions of a short-sighted individual.

Balfour returned the picture. "No, indeed. The gentleman is unknown to me. Is he from Eastern Europe? To my mind, there's a Slavic cast to his features. But how is he connected to the robbery?"

"His body was found upstairs, in the flat above the shop. The flat is now a crime scene, and as such I can't allow any further access to either. I'm afraid your reopening will have to wait."

"For how long?"

"How long is a piece of string, Mr Balfour? Until we are sure we have removed every piece of evidence that is relevant to either the robbery or the murder."

"May I ask how this man, whom I can assure you I've never seen before in my life, was killed? And how you think he came to be in the apartment?"

"As to the first, that information is confidential, as part of our investigation. As to the second, perhaps you could tell me how he came to be in a flat owned by yourself."

"Ah. You asked me yesterday if the flat was lived in. Now I know why. But I can assure you that I know nothing at all about it. I would certainly not allow someone whom I've never seen before, and who, frankly, does not look like my type of person, to use that apartment. I can only surmise that Mrs Carselaw allowed this unwholesome stranger into the flat. Perhaps before she left for Estonia. Was he living there?"

"Not necessarily. But either someone let him in, or he broke in. We have no evidence so far of a break-in. Tell me, did anyone else apart from yourself and Mrs Carselaw have keys to the flat?"

"Mrs Carselaw had only a key to the door from the shop into the book storeroom. However, I grant that from there she could have made her way to the rest of the flat. I can assure you that I have certainly not given keys to anyone. Apart from the factoring agency here who are responsible for repair and maintenance of the building. Stokes and Company, in George Street."

"Thank you. We'll check with them."

"But as to whether Mrs Carselaw may have copied her key and distributed it to friends or associates, sadly I cannot give you any guarantee of her probity."

"One other thing. We will have to search and examine the other flats in the building, to make sure there is no sign of occupation or other evidence there. Yesterday you said you had no objection to this. Perhaps therefore you could lend us the keys, or authorise Stokes and Co. to do so."

"Can I be sure the apartments will be treated with respect? They have been tastefully upgraded, and I would not wish them to be trampled underfoot by persons such as the one outside the shop."

"Don't worry. The only people in there will be trained Scene of Crime officers. They will be extremely careful."

"Very well. I will contact the factors and authorise the issuance of keys. I would give you my own, but I do not make a habit of having them on my person."

"Thank you. Can you tell me when was the last time you were in those flats?"

"Some months ago. I'll have to check the exact date. At present I have no cause to visit them."

"And the flat above the shop?"

"As I said at our earlier meeting, I was at the shop to meet Mrs Carselaw the day before she left for Estonia. We went up to the store room then, but neither of us entered the rest of the flat, at least not while I was there. I'm afraid that is all I know."

"Coming back to the safe, can you check in your special catalogue, and let me know if there should be anything in there now?"

"Certainly. The special catalogue is not accessible from the laptop here in the shop. I will have to return to my hotel, to use my own laptop. I'll email you as soon as I've checked."

"Thank you, Mr Balfour. The building will be kept locked and guarded until we are finished. I will let you know as soon as you can regain access. Perhaps we could walk together to Stokes and Co. and get those keys; that would speed things up, wouldn't it?"

Having got the keys to the flats from Stokes and Co., Blue returned to Stairfoot Lane. He visited each of the flats, and had a brief look round, being careful to touch as little as possible. They did seem to be, as Balfour had said, unlived-in since being redecorated. The fixtures seemed pristine and on the beds the mattresses were bare. The electric kettles and toasters were still in their boxes. There was no evidence of anyone having used them. Nevertheless, Blue thought, I'll have to get the SOCs over to check them out, just in case.

17

Back at the station, he found an email awaiting him from Sergeant Morgan: 'Hi Angus, I got the email below at 11.00 this morning.' Below was a forwarded email; the sender was Paul Carselaw: 'Dear Sergeant Morgan, I have decided to go out to Estonia and see what I can find out for myself. Thank you for your help. Best wishes, Paul Carselaw.' He emailed the sergeant to thank her.

There was also an email from *Komissar* Kõnekas: 'Very busy. Can we talk Monday, 0800 UK time?' This was disappointing, as he'd have to wait through the weekend.

He emailed the lab at Gartcosh, asking them to send the results of the DNA examination on the dead man to him as soon as possible, stressing that this was a murder inquiry. Then Superintendent Campbell, asking for a meeting. He got a rapid response: 2 pm that afternoon.

He needed some fresh air, and left the building. The rain had ceased, but heavy cloud still hung over the town. He headed for the organic café by the ferry terminal, bought an egg and shallot sandwich and a coffee, and went into the ferry terminal, climbing the stairs to the waiting area, where he could relax and have his lunch. There were no ferries due to leave, so very few people were there, and there was a peace about the place that enabled him to think as he ate.

He asked himself why Carselaw had gone to Estonia. Perhaps he wanted to talk to the family of the woman he'd known as his wife, and share his grief. Maybe he wanted to see her body, to bid farewell in person, say a last goodbye. Carselaw had not struck Blue as very emotional, but perhaps hidden channels ran deep within him, and he needed an appropriate act of closure.

Or was it something more down-to-earth? More prosaic. Did he want to find out what his wife had been doing in Estonia in the days leading up to her death? Or yet something else?

Carselaw had always said he didn't know anything about his wife's business. But what if that weren't true? What if he'd been party to it, or even part of it? The book in his boat might suggest that; had he been moving consignments of books around in the boat? Meeting anonymous boats out among the islands somewhere for clandestine cargoes of books to be heaved from one deck to another? But that didn't seem to make a lot of sense:

books weren't drugs, after all. There wasn't much point in secretly moving second-hand books around, when you could put them in the boot of a car or send them by post. Was there more to the book trade than Blue realised? Perhaps Carselaw knew something that was sending him to Estonia?

At two he was knocking on the Super's door. The friendly voice called him in. The familiar odour of good coffee assailed his nostrils.

"Do sit down, Angus. Coffee?"

"Thanks, chief. That would be good."

The espressos made and duly sipped, the Super began: "Well now, Angus, how's this bookshop business coming on?"

Blue outlined the case from the beginning, mentioning all the players involved, including the dead and so far nameless putative Russian.

"Interesting," mused Campbell. "How important do you think the Estonian connection is?"

"Difficult to tell, right now. But I think this dead man shows there's an international dimension. And working with the Estonians will be helpful."

"Yes, I think you're right. But we have to be careful. As soon as we mention any country outwith the UK, that sends up big red warning signs that we're going to spend lots of money. And given our present underfunding, shortage of funds is the perfect excuse to limit any foreign liaison."

"I'm not sure what you're implying, sir."

"In the good old days I'd simply have put you on a plane to Tallinn to talk to the cops there face-to-face. That's always the best way. Now that sort of request has to go through a swathe of red tape, and would only be approved if: a] it was a very high-profile case; and b] you can't do the face-to-face stuff on Zoom or some similar medium. This case is not exactly high-profile. Mrs Carselaw's murder is a matter for the Estonians to sort out. We know she's dead, and that ties up our missing-person case. If Mr Carselaw wishes to go to Estonia to snoop around, that's his business, not ours. A break-in at a shop isn't cause for big expenditure. Some of the folk higher up are saying we should give a robbery two days' work, then let the insurance company deal with it."

"What about the dead man at the shop?"

"That's more interesting. We need to identify him. But if he's foreign, there are those who'd just say it's some sort of gang thing or spat between criminals, and we shouldn't be wasting time on it. Don't mention it to the press, and nobody gets worried about it. To some at HQ it's more about impression management than solving crimes."

"That sounds like ACC Clegg."

"Our PR chief? Yes, she's one of them. Anyway, let's see what turns up the next few days."

He spent the next two hours on his report, interrupted only by a phone call from Ishmael Balfour.

"Inspector! How I do value our conversations. But this alas must be a brief interaction, as business matters demand my immediate attention. However, as promised, I have checked the special catalogue for Eastwards Books. And I can confirm that on this occasion there were no books of specially high value in the office safe. That does sometimes happen, as the stock flow in this business can be quite unpredictable, so it's not a cause for concern."

Blue thanked him and returned to his report.

At half past four he went up to the work room. The atmosphere was listless. They seemed to be making little progress. Blue told them that since the case was not seen as high priority, there was no need to be in over the weekend. On Monday they would all be back refreshed and ready to hit the case again. And the meeting with *Komissar* Kõnekas might break the logjam and give them some leads. He wished them a good weekend.

Before going home himself, Blue made sure he'd emailed to *Komissar* Kõnekas all the information he had on the cases of Aino Carselaw's disappearance, the bookshop break-in and the dead man in the flat above. This included all the forensic data, including the dead man's fingerprints and the DNA analyses. He hoped something in there would spark a positive response from Kõnekas and enable him to make progress in Oban.

As Blue neared the house, and saw Alison's green Fiat parked outside, he relaxed. As he got out of his car the front door opened, and Corrie rushed out to greet him. Welcome to the weekend!

They didn't go out that evening. Pan-fried sea bass and shallots, with boiled potatoes and broccoli, and a home-made garlic sauce, would do very nicely, along with a fresh German Riesling. Blue had however to admit he'd got the tiramisu that followed at the supermarket in Oban.

Over the meal he shared what had happened that day.

"It seems to me the answer's in Estonia," commented Alison, "so you need to work closely with Inspector Kõnekas. Give him everything you've got, and see if he'll reciprocate."

"I'm certainly trying to do that."

"Then there's that private eye, or whatever she is. I'm sure she'll know more, especially if the whole thing is about the book trade."

"You're right, Alison. As usual. I've got a Zoom session with Kõnekas first thing Monday morning. Then I'll get back to Ms Maarksen. Now we've got the whole weekend to ourselves. Let's enjoy it."

18

Saturday 3 December

On Saturday morning they saw there'd been some snow during the night, but less than an inch, and already the cars were reducing it to slush on the roads. The heavy cloud still lay above them, having acquired that puffiness which suggested more snow to come. But it wasn't yet snowing, so there was an opportunity to get out for the day, and give Corrie a good long walk.

They left Alison's car at Port Appin and took the little passenger ferry across to the northern tip of the island of Lismore, then walked along the coastal path down the western side of the island as far as Port Ramsay, then followed the road across the island, and turned north again to walk up the east coast. The western stretch, rising above the coast itself, offered views across Loch Linnhe to the hills of Mull, whilst the eastern leg enabled them to see the Isle of Eriska and the Appin coast. Returning on the ferry, they enjoyed a late lunch at the Old Inn at Portnacroish, and a leisurely drive back to Connel. Alison was conscious that other drivers might be in a greater hurry, and happy to signal them to overtake her. She knew from Blue that many of the vehicle collisions in this area, especially in the summer, were caused by the frustration of drivers stuck behind tourists driving at thirty-five miles per hour on a road where the limit was sixty, and tempted to take chances on stretches that were too short.

Sunday 4 December

It started snowing again that evening, and on Sunday morning there was another inch. Blue and Alison walked to St Oran's church for the morning service. Blue didn't go to the church regularly, but did go often enough to be recognised by the minister and by regular attenders. He wasn't in any sense a religious fanatic or fundamentalist, but his Christianity gave him a sense of justice based on a moral code. He believed that people have free will, and can choose to do good or evil. And he did believe that evil was real – he had met enough people in his police career whom he recognised were truly evil individuals, mostly men, whose malice towards their fellow human beings was palpable. He knew that being to any extent religious was regarded with suspicion by some members of the police service, either because they thought he would have fanatical views, or because he would be too honest to take part in corrupt or illegal activities carried out by police officers. His colleagues in Oban regarded him primarily as a competent and reliable police officer, albeit one with an unusually intellectual turn of mind.

Alison was more of an agnostic, but happy to go with Blue to the church, to be immersed in the atmosphere. She relished the calmness and the sense of the spiritual. She believed firmly that there was a spiritual dimension, but just wasn't sure quite what it was. There were places where she felt closer to this other world, including many religious sites of the past as well as the present, and not only Christian ones. She also knew that many people who would never describe themselves as religious nevertheless had a longing for a spiritual aspect to their lives and an awareness that there was more to many things than met the eye.

After the service, there was coffee and biscuits and a chance to chat with others. The minister, Rev. Bryce Jamieson, a slim man, perhaps around fifty, though he looked younger and clearly kept himself very fit, approached them. "Mr Blue, and Dr Hendrickx. Good to see you again. Tell me, do you happen to know anything about the break-in at Eastwards Books? I go in there occasionally. Last time I was in they had a Geneva Bible, printed in Amsterdam in 1665."

"The translation that came before the King James Version? With all the notes and maps?"

"You know your bibles, inspector. You could call it the first study bible. Though the last thing King James wanted was people studying the Bible. He wasn't keen on people thinking for themselves, and just wanted them to listen to it being read out. Hence the Authorised Version. That was 1611, but lots of people preferred the Geneva Bible, so it was imported from Holland, right up to the end of the seventeenth century."

"I'm guessing it was in the glass-fronted cabinet?"

"Yes, that's right. It was very tempting to mortgage the Manse and buy it." He remembered his original query. "Was that one stolen?"

"Sorry, I can't comment on that. Ongoing investigation. Do we need to search the Manse?"

Mr Jamieson smiled. "Sadly, no. Still, I do hope the stolen stuff is recovered. Anna, she's the young woman who works there, comes to the church now and then. She's Ukrainian, you know. Very pleasant and polite. It's awful what's happening over there. Anyway, can I get you another cup of coffee?"

Back home, it was time for lunch. It didn't take long to chop up a boiled egg with mayonnaise and a dash of aioli, then open a couple of brioche rolls, butter them (strictly speaking, lighter-spread-incorporating-butter them), add a layer of smoked salmon, then the egg mayo, and add some salad leaves and a sprinkling of pepper and herbs, *et voilà!* Tasty and healthy, mostly. And coffee and home-made shortbread to finish off.

"So what would you like to do this afternoon?" Blue asked Alison.

"Well, I was thinking of a walk round Gallanach Bay. Have a look at the marina perhaps."

He smiled. "The marina, eh? Anything in particular?"

"I'm rather curious to see what Paul Carselaw's boat looks like."

"The *Jolly Mermaid.* Well, that sounds as good a plan as any."

They took the narrow road down the coast, past the little ferry that crossed the strait to Kerrera, and on past the caravan park, until they reached the car park at the marina. Not one of the biggest by any means, but picturesquely placed in a small bay opposite the bottom end of Kerrera.

"Don't worry," said Alison to Corrie, "Your walk comes first." And for the next hour they took Corrie for a walk round the bay. There was more snow lying here. Corrie stared at the footprints of other dogs, as if puzzling what animals had made them. Or perhaps not thinking of very much, merely distracted by the shapes in the unusual white carpet. Back at the car park, they left Corrie in the car, in case there were rules about dogs at the marina, and headed for a small brick building with a flat concrete roof which looked like the office.

The door was open. A dark-haired woman, perhaps in her early forties, was sitting at a laptop, looking at pictures of shoes. She hastily closed the laptop as she realised someone had come in. "Oh, er, sorry, I was busy. How can I help you?"

Blue showed his ID. "Hi. I'm Detective Inspector Blue. This is my colleague, Dr Hendrickx. Would you be Emma McIntyre?" The woman nodded. "I think a couple of my colleagues were here earlier in the week asking you about a boat owned by a Mr Carselaw."

"Oh yes, I remember. I pointed it out to them. The *Jolly Mermaid.* Bit of a daft name for a small cabin cruiser. But that was the name old Jack McDade gave it. Mr Carselaw bought it after Jack died. That was in 2014. Jack's widow wasn't interested in keeping it."

"Can you point it out to us? We just need an idea of what it looks like."

"No problem. Come on, I'll show you." She led them out of the office and onto one of the floating pontoons alongside which the boats were moored. "It's usual mooring is just along here."

But before they'd reached the end she stopped. "Oh. It's not there. That's her usual berth there, but no sign of the *Jolly Mermaid.*"

"That's odd," said Blue, "she should be there. Mr Carselaw is out of the country at the moment. Do you remember when you last saw her?"

"I'm sorry. The last time was when your colleagues were here. When was that? Tuesday or Wednesday, I think."

"Yes, it was Wednesday. Tell me, is there any way you can locate her? Do the boats have radio beacons, or anything like that?"

"Ah. You mean AIS, the Automatic Identification System. A transceiver on a ship enables its position to be plotted, the signal is picked by satellites or terrestrial receivers. There are now some very neat apps that enable you to spot ships anywhere in the world."

"Would that help with the *Jolly Mermaid*?"

"Sadly, no. It's only ships over 300 tonnes that have to have the AIS transceivers. Even then, they can switch them off when they don't want to be located. For instance, last month a Russian trawler in the Bay of Biscay..."

"I'm sorry to interrupt," cut in Blue, "but does that mean we've no way of knowing where the *Jolly Mermaid* has gone?"

"Yes, I'm afraid so. Though I doubt she'll be far away. These boats are only designed for coastal or inland waters."

"But if she was last seen on Wednesday, and left not long after that, she could be a long way away by now."

"It's possible. But most of the boats here don't go very far. For one thing, if you go somewhere else you have to pay a mooring fee. Though we do have a few who travel a bit more widely, especially in the summer."

"Could he have gone abroad?" asked Alison.

"It would take him a very long time, hugging the coast. These boats are not built for open seas. A cabin cruiser like the *Jolly Mermaid* would be very unsafe out in the Atlantic or the North Sea."

"Out of their depth?"

She laughed "Exactly."

"Just one other thing," said Blue, "Could you show us a cabin cruiser the same type and size as the *Jolly Mermaid*? Just so as we can picture what she looks like."

Ms McIntyre looked around the marina, before nodding, and leading them onto another pontoon. "There we are. It's similar to that one. The cockpit's aft, and the cabin's down inside at the fore. A neat little boat, about seven metres long, I'd say. Twenty feet or so."

"What sort of facilities does it have?" asked Alison. "If you wanted to go away for a few days."

"The bench seating either side of the cabin converts to two single beds, or in some models a double. There's a galley with a hob, fridge, microwave, and a small toilet with washbasin. The cockpit area can take a couple of reclining chairs. A bit tight for a family, but fine for a couple. And it has a petrol engine."

"Easy to drive?"

"Not too complicated. You don't need to pass a test to sail her, but we'd encourage a beginner to take a training course. Just so they don't do anything too stupid. And you have to have insurance."

"How much would a boat like this cost?" asked Blue,

"Obviously that depends on age, condition and so on. But you could get a reasonable second hand one for twenty thousand. If you want a new one, that's a different ball game."

"How old is the *Jolly Mermaid*?"

"She's a good few years old. I'm not sure exactly, I'd have to look it up. It should be on our register."

Back in the office, she consulted her laptop. "Here we are. Built in Poole in 1996. So still some years in her. I don't have a record of how much Mr Carselaw paid for her."

"Thank you, Ms McIntyre, you've been most helpful. One final request. Here's my card. Can you contact me as soon as the *Jolly Mermaid* reappears?"

"Of course. No problem. But if you want to find her before that, I'd suggest contacting other marinas on the west coast. I'd be surprised if she's gone any further."

Back at the car, they took Corrie for another walk along the shore out to a point where they could look west past the tip of Kerrera and out towards the solid bulk of Mull. And with no-one about, they could speak freely about what they'd seen at the marina.

"I thought Paul Carselaw had gone to Estonia," said Alison.

"That's what he said in his email."

"Could he have sailed the boat to Estonia?"

"From what Emma said that looks very unlikely – he'd have to hug the coasts and goodness knows how long that would take."

"What if he has gone to Estonia, as he said, and someone else took the boat? Either someone who knows him, or a thief?"

"That's also possible. I'm sure there's a thriving market for stolen boats. An astute thief could have watched the boat and worked out when he used it regularly. I'll have to check with the police in Estonia on Monday, to see whether he arrived there."

"What about the boat?"

"I'll get someone to phone round the marinas on the west coast, as Emma suggested. We need to find it, whether Carselaw's with it or not."

"Could he have been responsible for the robbery at the bookshop?"

"It's possible. But why?"

"What if they had a major falling out, and he wanted revenge? Maybe he found out something about her meetings with Lind in Estonia. Surely he must have wondered what she got up to on all those visits without him. Although I have to say, men can be remarkably stupid."

"He does seem very devoted to his model railway."

"Say no more."

Sunday evening was spent in relaxed mode. A meal prepared by

Blue: a roasted duck, along with roast potatoes and parsnips, and a creamy orange and herb sauce, along with a nice bottle of Romanian red wine, followed by a home-made chocolate mousse with port-infused cream. And an evening reading in front of the electric stove which gave a very good impression of having flames inside. Corrie lay in front of it and gently snored her satisfaction. Blue liked reading crime novels from earlier eras; he was reading *Black Money*, by Ross Macdonald, the heir of Dashiell Hammett and Raymond Chandler. Alison preferred historical fiction, but on this occasion she had downloaded a short history of Estonia onto her Kindle. She didn't know much about the country, and felt she needed to know more, if that's where the mainsprings of Blue's case were to be found.

19

Monday 5 December

They were up early, as Blue needed to be in his office by eight for his meeting with *Komissar* Kõnekas. Alison was happy to be off early too, as she wanted to get back to her flat to change before going to work. She promised to be back on Thursday, and as usual Corrie went with her.

At eight, the Estonian officer was in the Zoom waiting room, and Blue let him into the meeting. Now he saw, on the screen, *Komissar* Kõnekas for the first time. He was not quite what Blue had expected. From the voice he had somehow expected a big man; but Kõnekas, or at least the head and shoulders that he could see, was thin, and did not look particularly tall. And he was smiling. "*Tere*, *Komissar* Blue! It's good to see you at last."

"And you, inspector. *Tere!* Did you receive the materials I sent last week?"

"Thank you, I did. Some very interesting items there. One I can help you with immediately. The body you found in the apartment above the book-store. I can identify him for you."

"Great! Fire away, please." Blue grabbed a pen and flipped open a notepad.

"His name is Boris Drekhkov. An Estonian resident of Russian origin. Lives in Tallinn, not far from the harbour. Criminal record for minor offences, mainly smuggling. I'm interested that you found him in Scotland."

"Is he some sort of courier?'

"Yes, that's the word. A courier. His role in the criminal universe is to take things from A to B. His main routes are in and out of Russia. As a Russian in Estonia, he may have both Russian and Estonian passports. The Estonian would be the hardest to get: he'd have to be able to speak Estonian. But that would enable him to travel in and out of Russia without any visa requirements, and also to anywhere in the EU, and plenty other places, without any trouble."

"What sort of stuff are we talking about?"

"Could be anything, though we don't think he carries drugs. A car stolen in Germany, given a makeover in Poland, then driven into Russia for sale. Or some electrical component that the

Americans won't sell to the Russians; label the crates as cuckoo clocks and he'll drive a van load into Russia. And so on. The other way, it's often stuff stolen from state institutions, including museums. Or stuff that's come into Russia from Central Asia, and is heading west, to Europe or the US. The US especially – that's where the private collectors with the most money are. But Boris Drekhkov wouldn't go that far. Not usually even as far as Scotland. I can only guess that it was a valuable object or an important message he was carrying."

"How could we find out what he was carrying, or who employed him?"

"We will make enquiries here, and get back to you."

"That would be useful. By the way, can you tell me anything about Aino Lind's death?"

"We are still investigating. It seems she was last seen on Sunday 13th November, when she left her parents' house in Tartu that morning. She told them she was meeting a friend in Valga. But the parents are old, and can't remember the friend's name. The last her sister saw of her was on Friday 11th November when she left for Tartu to visit her parents."

"So the text Mr Carselaw received on the 17th saying she was at her sister's was not correct?"

"Exactly. Wherever she was, it was not at her sister's. The sister was expecting her back on Saturday 19th, to spend a couple of days with her before returning to the UK, but she never turned up. So the last time she was seen alive was, as I said on Sunday 13th November."

"Wasn't the sister worried when she didn't show?"

"She says it happened quite often. *Proua* Lind would often change her plans at the last minute."

"Does the sister know anything about her movements during that fortnight, or why she would go to Saaremaa?"

"No. And it's been hard to talk to her. She's been out of Estonia since the 22nd, advising the team building a water-supply and drainage system for a charity organisation in Eritrea. She's the only expert they've got, and they can't find a replacement, so she can't come back yet. Even talking to her has been difficult. The project is many kilometres from the nearest town. She was going to go with *Proua* Lind to the airport on the 22nd, and fly with her as far as Amsterdam, where they would catch their different onward flights. But she wasn't on the flight from Tallinn. The sister kept an eye open for her at Schiphol, but did not encounter her."

"What about Mr Lind? Wasn't she going to meet him at some point?"

"*Härra* Lind says he had arranged to meet her in Tallinn on the thirteenth. But she never turned up. He tried phoning and texting but got no response."

"Wasn't he worried about that?"

"Yes, he was. But he got a text on the 18th from her apologising, saying that an urgent business matter had come up, and that she'd also forgotten to take her phone charger with her, and the battery had run down, so she couldn't contact him earlier."

"But she had texted Paul Carselaw on the 15th and the 17th, as well as the 18th."

"Yes. She said that she'd get to *Härra* Lind's place as soon as she could, once the business was sorted out. But he says she never showed up."

"So we've no idea where she went after the 13th. Could she have left the country?"

"Very easily. Thanks to the Schengen Agreement, our frontiers with other EU states are open. For instance, you can go to Valga and simply walk into Latvia. There is only a post stuck in the ground indicating where the border is. She could be anywhere in the world by now."

"Do you trust Mr Lind's version of events?"

Kõnekas laughed. "Mr Lind is a very shifty character. We suspect he is involved in various illegal activities. But we have no evidence yet that he is lying. Or that he tells the truth."

"What about Ishmael Balfour? Have you come across him in Estonia?"

"No, we are not familiar with him."

"Mr Lind asked for a Zoom meeting with me. That was on Friday. His main aim it seems was to cast suspicion on Mr Balfour. But he did confirm some of the details of his relationship with his wife. We didn't talk about her disappearance. He thinks associates or employees of Mr Balfour are responsible for her death. I'll send you the file as soon as it's been processed."

"Thank you."

"There is one thing. Mr Lind recognised the picture of Boris

Drekhkov, although he didn't admit it. You could read it on his face."

"That is most interesting. I look forward to watching the interview."

He met the team in the meeting room at nine, with Sergeant Morgan sitting in too. The mood was upbeat; refreshed by the weekend, there was a feeling that this week would be decisive. Blue brought them up to date on his talk with his Estonian colleague. "At least we now know the name and profession of the dead man," he concluded, "though we're still in the dark about what he was doing here."

"He was found in the flat owned by Ishmael Balfour," said Vunsells. "That does seem to point to him. And if what Mr Lind said is true ..."

"We should pull in Balfour for questioning," Bhardwaj concluded for her.

"That probably wouldn't get us anywhere," responded Blue. "Mr Balfour is not stupid. He knows we have nothing linking him either to the bookshop robbery or to the dead man. And Lind provided no evidence to back up his claims."

"Balfour seems to think Aino Carselaw was up to something," put in Morgan. "Perhaps the dead man was working for her."

"There are still plenty of unanswered questions," said Blue, "and here's another twist that I should share with you all. Alison and I went down to the marina at Gallanach Bay yesterday afternoon. Paul Carselaw's boat has gone."

"But he's in Estonia!" said Bhardwaj. "Somebody must have pinched it."

"Do we really know for sure that he's in Estonia?" asked Vunsells. "What if that was just a blind, and he's up to something here?"

"There are two things we need to find out," said Blue. "One, where Carselaw is, and two, where his boat is. They may, or may not, both be in the same place. Arvind, can you find out whether Carselaw has flown to Estonia, or gone anywhere else for that matter? Lena, can you phone round all the marinas you can find, and see if the *Jolly Mermaid* is there? Enver, can you contact Europol and see what they've got on Mr Balfour? And Mr Lind, too, while you're at it. As I said earlier, Lind recognised

Drekhkov. Anything else?"

McCader raised a finger. "Yes, chief. What Lind says about his relationship with Aino is interesting, but I don't believe it. There's another explanation. Espionage."

"Spying!" exclaimed Bhardwaj.

"You could say that. Here's my suggestion. Lind and Aino were both members of the KGB. Lind was Aino's controller. She was sent to the UK specifically to make contact with someone working in the Naval Dockyards at Plymouth. Paul Carselaw was identified as a target. A single man, geeky, not good with women."

"So her meeting with Paul was set up?" asked Morgan.

"That's what I'm proposing. And he fell for it. And her."

"No wonder they got married so soon afterwards. But she must have had some feelings for him. They were married, I mean, together, for years."

"Maybe she just got used to him," suggested Vunsells.

"How would the fall of the Soviet system have affected things? Would she have gone on spying after that?" asked Blue.

"I would think so, if my theory is correct, that is. After the Soviet collapse, the KGB was succeeded in the Russian Federation by the FSB, who inherited most of the networks set up by the KGB. After all, we're talking about the same people still running the show, with a different set of initials."

"But then in 1991 Estonia became independent. Wouldn't that have given Aino some cause for thought?"

"Possibly. But people whom the KGB had used were vulnerable. The FSB knew too much about them. Lind and Aino wouldn't have been very popular in Estonia had they been revealed as KGB agents, and Aino would certainly have been arrested here for spying and faced a long jail term. So the spymasters could 'persuade' their agents, even if they weren't Russians, to remain in service."

"Blackmail!" added Bhardwaj.

"So you think she was still working for the Russians when Carselaw got the job at Faslane?" asked Blue.

"It would seem likely. He was bringing stuff home, and she no doubt copied or summarised it and sent the information to Lind, who in turn passed it to Moscow."

"But Carselaw got sacked in 2013."

"Yes. They told me they didn't think he was a spy, and I can believe that. He's not subtle enough, he'd soon give himself away."

"Are you saying he didn't know his wife was copying all the documents he took home?" asked Vunsells, "That doesn't seem very probable. Is he that naive?"

"She could have encouraged him to bring stuff home," suggested Morgan, "if he was already prone to doing it. And then sent him to play with his trains, and copied the stuff then. Maybe he did suspect, or maybe he knew."

"We certainly need to talk to him again."

"What would happen when Carselaw got the sack?" asked Bhardwaj. "I mean, to Aino's spy work. She wouldn't be able to get any more information."

"A good point, Arvind," continued McCader. "Without her source, Aino wouldn't have been much use to the FSB. I would think at that point they would have stopped paying her and told her her spying days were over. After all, she would be hard to move to another assignment. Easier just to let her go and save a few roubles."

"And the Carselaws move to Oban and live happily ever after?" asked Vunsells. "Did she get into the book trade to start earning?"

"Looks that way. Or it may have been Lind who directed her that way. Maybe they terminated his employment too, so he needed a new business. But remember, this is all just a theory."

"Though it does sound plausible," commented Blue. "Thanks, Enver. It makes it all the more necessary that we catch up with Paul Carselaw. The disappearance of the boat does suggest that the email about Estonia was a blind."

"Where would he go if it wasn't to Estonia?" asked Bhardwaj. "Has he connections with anywhere else?"

"Good question," said Blue. "We need to do some checking. Let me know as soon as you've got something. Otherwise let's meet again at twelve."

In his office, Blue checked his email. The recording of the interview with Kalev Lind was waiting there, along with a message informing him that a transcript would be ready sometime that afternoon. He emailed the recording to *Komissar* Kõnekas, then called the number for EMK Investigations. There was no response. He got down to updating his report.

Half an hour later the phone rang. Bhardwaj. "I checked

Glasgow and Edinburgh airports. Carselaw hasn't passed through them, and he's not booked on any flight for the rest of this week, either outward or returning."

"Thanks. Can you check Newcastle, Manchester and Aberdeen, in case he went a bit further?"

"What about London?"

"That'll take a while. I think if he were going to go from one of the London airports, he'd fly down there from Glasgow. No, just concentrate on those three."

At 11.30 his phone rang again. "Inspector Blue? This is Elsa Maarksen. I noticed your call. I've just arrived in Glasgow, and am flying on to Oban at 13.00. Perhaps we could meet later today?"

"I could meet you at Oban Airport, and drive you into Oban, if that helps."

"Thank you, but I have a hire car booked at the airport. Wait, is there a café there?"

"Yes, there was a small one, last time I was there."

"Do you mind meeting me there? I'll explain why when I see you. I'm quite good at spotting policemen, so I don't need to ask you to wear a blue carnation and carry a copy of *The Times*."

"OK. I'll be there for half past one, and wait for you."

At twelve they reassembled in the work room, apart from Morgan, who had to deal with a three-legged dog found wandering in the car park at the hospital.

Bhardwaj reported that he had found no trace of Carselaw moving through Manchester, Newcastle or Aberdeen airports.

"I suppose he could have taken a ferry and a train to Estonia," commented Blue, "but flying is quickest, and probably cheaper too. It is looking like he never went to Estonia. Lena, where are we with the marinas?"

"Nothing so far, chief. I hadn't realised how many of them there are. And varied in size too, some very big, like the ones at Tayvallich or Inverkip, and others a lot smaller, with just a couple of pontoons. And nearly every island has one. However, the people there have been really helpful. And I've still a good few to go before I've completed the west coast of Scotland. I suppose he could have gone to the Isle of Man or Ireland too."

"OK. Keep on looking. Enver, anything on Lind?"

"Europol have nothing specific on him, although they note him as a 'person of interest.' They don't say why, so it could mean anything. However, I managed to talk to someone at GCHQ in Cheltenham, and he was more helpful. Off the record, of course." He looked questioningly at Blue.

"Absolutely. Remember, everyone, you never heard this." Bhardwaj and Vunsells nodded.

"They have a file on Lind," began McCader. "He's listed as quote, 'probable KGB' in the Soviet days. After the Soviet Union fell to pieces he set up in practice as a lawyer in Tallinn. However, our friends suspect he continued working for the FSB, although now more discreetly. As an Estonian working for the Russians he'd certainly be seen as a traitor in his home country. References to him in the file thin out after that, and there was nothing after 2010. So they're very grateful for our information on Paul Carselaw and his sacking in 2013. That fits in with what I suspected. But they don't know what he's involved in now. If it's merely criminal, as they said, they'd not be interested."

"Thanks Enver. Right. We've now got four events that seem to me to be linked: Aino's disappearance and death, the robbery and the body at the bookshop, and now the disappearance of Paul Carselaw and his boat. We just have to join them all together! Let's reassemble at 4.30."

20

After a quick lunch in the canteen, Blue headed back to Connel and over the bridge to Oban's airport in North Connel, overlooking Ardmucknish Bay. The terminal one might describe as 'bijou,' not large, but perfectly formed. He was disappointed to find that the café was no longer there. "But there's a self-serve coffee-and-biscuit station there in that corner. Just put the money in the box," explained the helpful airport employee on his way out to take the fire truck onto the perimeter ready for the incoming Glasgow flight. Soon the airport administrator, Mairi Hayter, appeared from her office, to greet the arriving passengers, and Gary Stenhouse, the young man who operated the car-hire desk. They both recognised Blue from an earlier investigation which had involved several visits to the airport; Mairi greeted him effusively whilst Gary merely nodded and busied himself at his desk.

"What happened to the café?" Blue asked Mairi.

"Ach, there just weren't enough folks to keep it going. Too few flights. And short ones, so there's no hanging around before or after. So we replaced it with the self-serve machine, and the box of biscuits. The only positive point is that the coffee's cheaper; you just put two pounds in the box and help yourself."

Blue settled himself in a comfortable chair in the tiny waiting area, with a view out onto the runway. This wasn't exactly a bustling transport hub. There were just three flights out and three in that day. Most of the flights were to the islands, the Glasgow flight the only other.

At two o'clock on the dot the small yellow plane landed, and eight passengers climbed down the steps and walked the fifty yards to the terminal building. Most of them walked straight through the building and out into the car park. Only two stopped to wait for luggage: an old lady leaning on a stick, and another woman, perhaps in her forties, slim, smart and with blonde hair drawn into a chignon. She matched the description given by PC Beattie, and also that given by Anna Zeresova of the woman who had come into the shop. Not as tall as the impression PC Beattie had given, but then she'd been stooping when she spoke to him in the car. Perhaps older than they had suggested. And she gave a general impression of fitness – she probably spent an hour on an exercise bike every morning before breakfast. Wearing a dark blue waterproof jacket over a grey woollen jumper, jeans, and expensive trainers. He approached her.

"Ms Maarksen?"

"Ah, Inspector Blue, I presume. Pleased to meet you." She smiled politely and shook his hand.

Just then the two suitcases were delivered by the man whom Blue had seen earlier driving the fire truck. Elsa Maarksen wheeled hers over to a chair opposite the one Blue had been sitting in, and where he'd left his jacket. Blue offered to help the old lady, and carried her case out into the car park, just as a blue BMW drew up. A man jumped out. "Hi Mum, sorry we're late." He turned to Blue, "Thanks mate, we'll take it from here." He thrust a £2 coin into his hand, then grabbed the case and made for the rear of his car. Blue shook his head and returned to the waiting room. Ms Maarksen was by the car-hire desk, signing a paper. He sat down to wait for her.

She was back in a couple of minutes. "I'm afraid this has replaced the café," said Blue, indicating the coffee machine and box of individually wrapped biscuits. He dropped the two pounds into the box and added two more. "What can I get you? Black coffee, white coffee, or espresso? Sugar sachets in the bowl. The biscuits are oat crumble, ginger crumble or hazelnut crumble."

"A plain espresso will do me. And no biscuit. I've just been on three flights so I've had enough biscuits for a month."

Blue got two espressos, added sugar to his, then put them on the low table by the window, and fetched himself an oat crumble biscuit. He noted that both Mairi and Gary had disappeared.

"Well, Ms Maarksen, we're pretty much alone here now. I'm guessing that was why you wanted to meet me here, rather than at the police station."

"Yes. As a private enquiry agent, it's not good for me to be seen talking with the police. It has a negative effect on my clients' assurance of my confidentiality."

"I understand. How did you get into this business?"

"I was born and brought up in Denmark. I studied literature at the University of Copenhagen. Then I went to the US, and got a Master's in Librarianship at the University of Chicago. Then a PhD at Princeton, looking at the relationship between archives and politics. After that I worked in the library at Princeton. For two years I was seconded to UNESCO's Cultural Crime Unit, in Boston. That was really interesting. Now I'm a freelance investigator, based in Salzburg, Austria, but my work takes me all over the place."

"Salzburg? Any reason for being based there?"

"I like it. If you're travelling all over the world, it's good to have some place nice to come home to. I must say Oban's very nice too. But rather out of the way for world travel."

"So working for the Cultural Crime Unit pushed you in the investigative direction?"

"Exactly. There are two aspects to the Unit's work, theft and destruction. Theft includes looting by governments and stealing by individuals."

"And destruction?"

"Destruction is usually caused by governments. The motive is normally political: to eliminate the works of a particular individual considered an enemy of the state, or to wipe out the entire culture of a nation or a racial or religious group. In extreme cases the people are wiped out too."

"I can think of examples. But that's a very wide remit."

"My specialism is book theft."

"Is there a lot of it about?"

"You'd be surprised."

"Why are you telling me this?"

"I know something about you, Mr Blue. I do my homework. I know you are a dedicated and honest police officer, and that you are not simply a tool of your superiors. I am telling you about myself so that you may trust me. I would like us to work together on this case."

"You propose an exchange of information?"

"Yes, that is so."

"You'll be aware that the police position is, and must be, you tell us what you know first."

"Yes, I am. Let me say first, that there's a lot of money in books. More than you'd think. I mean, not in most of the stuff in Eastwards Books. One of them could fetch up to a hundred pounds, maybe even a few hundred, that is, if the right person comes across it. But the books I'm concerned with are worth a lot more. An awful lot more."

"Why are they worth so much?"

She laughed. "I could give you a two-hour lecture on that. But the simple answer is twofold. First, there are a lot of very rare books out there, which are valuable because of the unique chunks of our culture they preserve, or because of their historical significance. There are both libraries and private collectors who want to possess these volumes. And second, in recent years books have also become an investment target, both for wealthy individuals, and financial institutions looking for assets which will safely accumulate in value. But the fact that they're worth so much means there are also persons out there who want to acquire them in non-legitimate ways."

"I see. Let's focus then on what you're looking at here."

"Robberies of specialist bookstores are not common, but do occur often enough for patterns to emerge. This one is unusual, because of two things. I should say, two people. The part-owner of the shop, Mrs Carselaw, found dead in Estonia. And the gentleman found in the apartment above the shop."

"You're very well-informed."

She smiled. "Four months ago I was approached by Mr Balfour, whom you know, to obtain my services. At that time, I was engaged in another investigation and couldn't oblige him. However, he was willing to wait until I was available – I have a good reputation as an investigator – which was about six weeks ago. His concern was that Mrs Carselaw was running her own business on the side, which he regarded as outwith the terms of their agreement."

"Forgive me for saying so, but that seems like small beer for an international investigator like yourself."

"Hah! You flatter me, inspector. In fact, there is more to this case than meets the eye."

"Tell me about it."

"When I began to look into Mrs Carselaw's activities, the first thing I noticed was the frequent trips to Estonia. That was fortuitous – I do like an international connection, it makes a job so much more interesting. I wondered why she travelled there so often."

"And you went out there?"

"Eventually, yes. I came over here first, to see what was going on. I posed as a buyer for an anonymous collector, and contacted Mrs Carselaw by email. She drew my attention to the website, but also mentioned that there were other possibilities, depending on my areas of interest. I gave a veiled hint that I wasn't too squeamish about the provenance of the books on sale."

"So Mrs Carselaw was selling, under the counter, as it were, stolen books?"

"Stolen is not a very helpful term here; it can mean many things. Books move around in many ways, and it's often governments who are responsible for some of the worst situations. You'll be aware of the controversy over the Elgin Marbles, seized by British collectors with government support. Or the ransacking of the Baghdad Museum after the American occupation in 2003, a cultural crime that was also carried out with the connivance of the occupying power. Indeed, on that occasion many of the finest artefacts were chosen to order for American private collectors. Just like museums, libraries and archives are targets for looters in the aftermath of war, whether they are private individuals or functionaries of the occupying power. For governments, they become legitimate booty, to be awarded to libraries and collectors back home. For terrorists, they are an asset that can be sold to buy weapons, explosives, or whatever. And any political instability, in any country, can lead to opportunities for the theft of state assets."

"And Mrs Carselaw had access to such material?"

"It seemed so. The first volume she offered me was a 300-year-old bible from a Coptic Church in Egypt. I discovered later that the church had been seized by an Islamic mob, some of whom had taken the church's books before setting the building on fire. We're now seeing more Christian and Jewish books sourced from areas in which extremist Islamic groups are operating. The militants sell them to fund their activities or buy arms. But it may also be that professional thieves are infiltrating these groups, maybe even instigating attacks on book- or antiquity-rich targets."

"Did you buy it?"

"No. I told her that wasn't the sort of stuff I was interested in, and asked what else she had. Of course, then she got more cagey and asked exactly what I was interested in. Knowing what the shop specialised in, I suggested Eastern Europe. My guess was that to shelter under the shop umbrella, she'd focus on items within the same range that the shop held."

"But items obtained through more unorthodox channels?"

"Both she and Ishmael acquire their more valuable stock by

legitimate means, the most likely being the auctioning off of collections, when the collector finds himself short of money, or when he – and it's usually he – dies. Ishmael is on the level, and sticks to legitimate sources. Most of the time. Occasionally something will slip into his hands from a more fuzzy point of origin. But I soon began to suspect that Mrs Carselaw was routinely acquiring stolen books."

"From anywhere in particular?"

"Eastern Europe. The most culturally disruptive events in Europe since 1945 have been the breakup of the Soviet Union and the collapse of Yugoslavia. In Yugoslavia of course there was actual warfare. In the former soviet countries there was a period of chaos after the collapse of the Soviet Union, during which there was little control over state assets. Men who'd become rich through corruption within the system were now well-placed to buy up profitable assets, often working closely with the politicians who'd now gained power."

"And that could include cultural assets?"

"Exactly. Mrs Carselaw then offered me a book that I was able to source with some certainty, a volume of the Book of Job with the Hebrew text and Polish translation, printed in Warsaw in 1738. With finance provided by Mr Balfour, I bought it. It was posted from the bookstore to me, or at least to the name I had assumed for the purpose, at an apartment in Milan owned by Mr Balfour."

"Mr Balfour owns quite a lot of property."

"I believe so. The point is, I could trace this book. It was purchased by the University of Wroclaw in 1742, and remained there until 1940..."

"When the Nazis arrived."

"Yes. The Nazi goal was to reduce the Polish people to peasant farmers and labourers in factories. Polish culture or education had no place in the scheme. The university library was boxed up and shipped off to the Fatherland, for distribution to German universities and research institutions."

"This one was in Hebrew. Wouldn't they have destroyed it?"

"You might think so. Books in Hebrew wouldn't have been handed out to universities. But they were not destroyed. They were sent to special institutions set up for the so-called 'study of the debased culture of the Jews,' run by agencies of the Nazi party.

The book I bought was stored in a warehouse in Rostock, on the Baltic coast, but was never moved on. Now fast-forward to 1945, and the Russians arrive, moving through eastern Germany very rapidly, taking Rostock on 2 May. So now the books are seized by the Russians. And guess where they go now."

"Russia?"

"Of course. But this is where it gets a bit murky, as we don't have much access to the historical catalogues of the Russian libraries. The book disappears into the darkness of the Soviet system. Now fast forward again to 1991. The Soviet Union collapses, and during the chaos and uncertainty of the first few years of post-soviet Russia, plenty of cultural artefacts, including books, find their way into private hands. Someone acquired that book, buying it or stealing it from a library, then shipped it for sale to a dealer in the West. And now it comes to Mrs Carselaw's attention."

"How would that have happened?"

"She will have developed contacts with a middleman who facilitates the movement of books out of the former Soviet bloc. He offers it to her, maybe to others too."

"How do you know about the book's movements?"

"There is a coat of arms of the University of Wroclaw on the half title page, sorry, that's the page preceding the title page. At the back there is a rubber stamp of the Institute for Hebrew Studies of the Nazi Party's Cultural Foundation. Below that is another stamp, of the Reparations Administration of the USSR; it's dated August 1945. There's no further clue to the book's sojourn in Russia. But what the book told me about was Mrs Carselaw's involvement in the stolen book trade. Purchasing one book naturally led to more offers, which confirmed my hypothesis."

"How did you keep in contact with Mrs Carselaw?"

"An encrypted email address whose passwords changed every 24 hours."

"When was the last you heard from her?"

"About three weeks ago. There was an announcement, I assume to all her clients, that she was in the process of acquiring more books, and her business would be suspended for the next two weeks. Then it would resume."

"And did it resume?"

"No. So I came over here to see what was going on. I arrived just three days ago, and went to the shop as soon as I could. I asked the girl in the shop if I could speak with the owner, and was told she was in Estonia and currently unobtainable. The next day I heard from your very co-operative officer about the break-in."

"And Mr Balfour is aware of all you've just told me?"

"Oh yes. There's nothing I've told you that I need to keep from him. And he keeps me informed too, for instance, about the body in the apartment."

"How does he feel about what Mrs Carselaw is doing?"

"He is, shall we say, disappointed by Mrs Carselaw's activities, and does not wish his own reputation to be besmirched by the activities of a business partner. But he is not a murderer. His solution to the problem, were Mrs Carselaw still alive, would be a business one. He would end the partnership, remove his assets from the business, and ensure that other respectable members of the book trade would be made aware of her actions."

"Do you have any idea who might want to kill Mrs Carselaw?"

"No. Perhaps she has cheated one of the middlemen, or maybe not paid money she owed. When money is not paid, the debt can be farmed out to people who are much, much nastier than the book thieves or the middlemen."

"So how does Estonia fit into all this?"

"Estonia is right next door to Russia. I suspect it's not too hard to move stuff across the border. That would be one route by which books stolen in Russia find their way to the west."

"What about Kalev Lind? Where does he fit in?"

"Mrs Carselaw went out to Estonia regularly to meet him. My suspicion is that he is one of the middlemen she deals with, probably the principal one. He has made a number of trips into Russia and the Soviet successor states over the last few years. Some of these states are notorious for corruption. But imagine, you are a library director earning a pittance, and someone offers what is for you a fortune, simply to enable a few volumes to vanish from the shelves. You don't even have to steal them yourself; merely leave the side door unlocked one evening as you leave. It's very tempting."

"Is Lind collecting stuff on these trips?"

"No. He'll be too clever for that. He would be looking to see what's available, and arranging the deal. He may even have a wish-list from rich collectors. He will then return home, and a few weeks later the books will disappear. There may be a robbery, which remains unsolved. Or, if they are in a store-room rather than on the open shelves, the theft may not be noticed until someone wants to consult the book, which may be months or even years later. Or never, especially if the book can be quietly erased from the catalogue. After the robbery, the thieves will pass the books on to a courier who will smuggle them back to Estonia. Other couriers will then distribute to outlets in Western Europe or the US."

"Is it easy to take stuff from Russia into Estonia?"

"It depends who you are. You or me, we will be searched at the border post. But the couriers may be waved through by officials whom they have bribed. And, apart from the official border crossing points, there are plenty of routes available. A small boat can easily cross Lake Peipus at night undetected by the Russian or Estonian border patrols. At the southern end of the lake there are marshes, but there are safe paths across the border for those who know them."

"Do you think Mr Balfour may have bought items from Lind?"

"It's possible. But not my business."

"What about the dead man found in the flat above the shop?"

"He may have been a courier for Lind, or another middleman. But it is unusual that a courier is killed. They are useful to the business, so there is no point in killing them."

"Could it be like gang warfare, members of one gang killing the couriers of the other to drive them out of business? Or away from what they think is their patch?"

"I don't believe so. These gangs have not yet invaded the book trade. There is still more money in drugs and people-trafficking. Now, I am answering a lot of questions. What can you tell me?"

"Actually, very little. The dead man in the shop was Boris Drekhkov, a Russian resident in Estonia. The Estonian police tell us he was, as you suggest, a courier. But they don't know any more. Until the robbery our main focus was on finding Mrs Carselaw, and we'd not made a lot of progress there when the Estonian police reported her death to us. Mr Lind has been in touch, but apart from pointing a finger at Mr Balfour, had nothing concrete to offer. But if you have any specific questions, I'll try to answer them." Blue didn't mention the KGB connection – that information had been obtained through confidential channels.

"Perhaps I could visit the bookstore and have a look around myself."

"I don't see why not. When were you thinking of?"

"Can I meet you there? I'll take my car to my hotel – it's the Alexandra, on the front, near the Corran Hall – and then walk round. Can we meet there in, say ..." – she glanced at her watch – "in an hour, at three forty-five?"

"No problem."

21

Having left his car at the police station, Blue walked round to the bookshop.

Inside the shop, he noticed that everything was back to what it had been before the break-in. Almost. Apart from the glass-fronted cabinet next to the counter, which now stood empty. Anna was sitting behind the counter with a mug of something steaming; she stood up on seeing him come in.

"Hello, Anna. I see things are getting back to normal here."

"Yes. I am very relieved. I hope all the trouble is over."

"The shop is still open?"

"Yes. Mr Balfour has decided the business will carry on. He has made me now the manager."

"I'm pleased to hear that. I think you know what you're doing and do an excellent job."

"Thank you. Is there anything I can do for you?"

"A cup of coffee would be nice. I'm waiting for someone who wants a look round."

Anna knew not to ask too many questions and went to get the coffee. Blue looked at the books on the shelves. A few minutes later Anna returned and gave him a mug of coffee. He had just thanked her when the bell over the door tinkled, and Elsa Maarksen entered.

Anna looked at her, and frowned.

"Anna," said Blue, "I think you recognise Ms Maarksen here as having been in the shop on Tuesday afternoon."

"Yes, inspector, that is the woman who came in. I'm sure of it."

Ms Maarksen held out her hand to Anna. "Pleased to meet you, Anna. I'm Elsa Maarksen. I'm a private eye!"

Anna shook her hand. "I have never met a private eye before. Only read of them in books."

"I am just like them, except that I don't get into so many fights. Anna, may I have a quick look around here?"

"Of course. Oh, would you like a coffee?"

"How kind of you to offer. No thank you, I've been on three aeroplanes today and drunk more than enough coffee. None of it very good."

"What about tea? I have some nice chai."

"That sounds excellent. Yes please."

Ms Maarksen glanced at each shelf. Then she looked at the empty glass-fronted cabinet and nodded. "Hmm. I guess most of the stuff stolen was in here."

"Yes," said Blue. "Would you like to see the list of what's missing?"

"That would be very helpful, thank you. By the way, please, I am Elsa."

"Angus." He gave her a copy of the list. She ran her eye down it. "Yes. Worth keeping under lock and key, but nothing that stands out as a target. Were there others kept in a safe?"

Anna returned with a mug of spiced tea.

"There is a safe in the office," said Blue. "Mr Balfour opened it for me. There were no books in it, only a few papers. I asked him if anything was missing. He said no, there wasn't."

"That is odd," Elsa said to them. "It surprises me there were no books in the shop of sufficient value to be stored there."

"The most expensive books are listed in the special catalogue which only Mrs Carselaw and Mr Balfour have access to," said Anna. "These books I do not sell; that was done by Mrs Carselaw. I assumed they are in the safe. Maybe there is another safe somewhere else, away from the shop."

"That's possible," said Elsa. "Angus, can you show me the upstairs flat? Mr Balfour told me about it."

Blue led her up the spiral staircase to the flat. She looked at the books on the shelves there. "Hmm. Nothing of particular value here. Have you searched the flat?"

"Yes. Nothing. No secret hiding places either. Just a dead body."

"Here's the problem, Angus. A man is not killed if there is nothing valuable involved. The books taken from the shop would fetch maybe six or seven thousand euros, if the right buyers came along. And given that they will be reported stolen, the open market is less easy, and that makes the process of selling them more complicated, and will certainly depress the prices. Perhaps the thief will get four or five thousand, maybe less. That's fine for a routine robbery. But the dead man here means this is not routine. If Drekhkov heard the robber and came down to see what was going on, and was killed there in the shop in panic by the thief, that would be understandable. But he is strangled, perhaps after being drugged. And it happens up here, a place a routine thief would be unaware of. No, there is something more.

Something much more valuable. Mrs Carselaw must have had some more valuable books hidden somewhere. If not in the shop or the apartment above, maybe her own apartment. Or some other place we don't know about yet."

"Have you anything in mind for this 'something?'" asked Blue.

"My guess is a small number of very valuable books. Codices or incunabula. But each one very valuable indeed."

"Codices are written manuscripts, aren't they?"

"Yes. A codex is a handwritten manuscript, or collection of manuscripts, bound into a book. In contrast to a scroll, which is a continuous roll of parchment or papyrus wrapped around a wooden roller. The pages are known as leaves or folios. Codices are rare because each one is unique, and because they date from the middle ages or earlier. Nowadays they can be worth tens of millions of euros. For example, the so-called Codex Sassoon, a text of the Hebrew Bible dated to the tenth century, was sold recently in New York for thirty-eight million dollars."

"That's a lot of money."

"Quite. And the value of the best codices, like the Book of Kells, is incalculable."

"What about incunabula? They're early printed books, aren't they? Published before 1500."

"You're obviously a book-lover, Mr Blue. The print runs for these were very small, and they are now also rare and thus much prized by collectors. Although there may be multiple copies still in existence, some are rendered unique by the marginal notes added by early owners. Writing your own notes in books was quite common in the early days of printing. So you can see, even a small collection of codices and incunabula could be worth many millions."

"Where might Aino Carselaw get these from?"

"As I said before, Kalev Lind has been travelling in the former Soviet states during the last year. I suspect he found them there. No doubt librarians or museum directors were offered what would seem large sums of money for them. But small compared to what they would fetch in the West." She smiled. "Rather like the early days of book-hunting, when a hunter would offer the abbot of a decrepit monastery in Italy or Spain a pittance for a valuable manuscript, and sell it for thousands of ducats to a wealthy collector."

"So Lind would arrange the deal, the money would follow, and a courier would fetch the books out to Estonia. Then they'd be brought over here."

"You learn well, Angus. That is most likely scenario. My suspicion is that there is a consignment of very valuable books somewhere. Somewhere around here."

"Could Mr Balfour be hiding them?"

"He told me all the most valuable books would be in the safe. He could, of course, have spirited them away, then arranged for the robbery as a distraction. Not likely in my opinion, but nevertheless possible."

"There's also a boat, owned by Mrs Carselaw's husband. Sergeant McCader had a brief look around inside, but didn't see a safe."

"A boat is not a safe place. It's too easy to steal, then take somewhere quiet and blow the safe."

"Hmm. That's what may have happened. The boat has disappeared."

"I'd still be surprised if you find an empty safe in it. I think the Carselaws' apartment would be the first place to check."

"We're working on that."

"Will you tell me what you find?"

"Certainly. Do keep in touch."

As soon as he got back to the station, Blue contacted the procurator fiscal, requesting a warrant to search the Carselaws' flat, citing the possible presence of stolen goods, in this case, books and the suspicious disappearance of Paul Carselaw as reasons. He added a similar request to search Paul Carselaw's boat.

The team assembled at 4.30.

Bhardwaj had had no more luck with the airports regarding Paul Carselaw, but did have something positive. He'd spoken to the KLM desk at Schiphol, and persuaded the woman there to look at people with Slavic names travelling to Glasgow or Edinburgh. She had found a serious possibility: a man named Pavel Dreshkov travelled on a flight from Amsterdam to Glasgow on Tuesday 29th November. He was due to return on Thursday December 1st, but had not turned up for his flight, and had not attempted to rebook. He had come from Tallinn to Amsterdam, and would have returned there. He was travelling on a Latvian passport. It wasn't definite, but Dreshkov and Drekhkov were too similar for it not to arouse suspicion.

Bhardwaj had then contacted Glasgow Airport to see if any CCTV footage was available which might capture Dreshkov there on the 29th. They were in luck. Security staff at the airport had watched the footage from the gate where the flight had arrived, and emailed it to Bhardwaj. They all watched it. And there he was, the dead man living once again, exiting the gate with his head down. But he glanced up once, to look for the signs to baggage reclaim. It was Drekhkov, there could be no doubt. One more tiny piece of the jigsaw in place.

Vunsells had not been idle either. She had been checking the smaller marinas – some hardly meriting the name – on the west coast, and, not long before the meeting, had struck lucky.

"The *Jolly Mermaid* is currently moored at the Kyles of Bute marina, on the Isle of Bute," she announced. "According to the manager there, the mooring was booked online by Paul Carselaw, and the fee paid using a credit card in that name. The boat arrived on Thursday 1st December, about 6 pm, and was booked in for a week, so the fact that it's still there has aroused no suspicion. The manager hasn't seen anyone moving on the boat. He'd assumed the long booking was because the boat owner was visiting friends or relatives on Bute, and might not be back for a few days. It's a small marina, but there are vacant moorings during the winter, as quite a few people have their boats taken out of the water for the colder months."

"Right," said Blue. "Before coming here I contacted the fiscal to get search warrants for the Carselaws' flat and the *Jolly Mermaid*. Hopefully the warrants will arrive tomorrow morning. Then we can hit the flat and the boat at about the same time."

"Wow!" exclaimed Bhardwaj. "A simultaneous hit. Just like a movie. Will we find drugs or corpses?"

"Hopefully, neither. Paul Carselaw or some stolen books would be useful. And while we're on that subject, I've been talking with Elsa Maarksen, the private detective hired by Mr Balfour, and she suspects there may be a cache of books much more valuable than the ones we know are missing. This cache may be in the flat, or on Carselaw's boat. Or somewhere else. Or it may not exist. But we should bear in mind that possibility. Anyway, Enver, can you and Lena take the flat? Arvind and I will take the boat. As I said, we'll move as soon as the warrants arrive."

"Should we ask the local cops to watch the boat overnight?" asked Bhardwaj.

"I don't think so. If anyone is in the boat, it might alert them. And if they were going to make off, having got to Bute, they'll have done it by now." Everyone seemed satisfied with that.

"Any other business?" asked Blue.

"Yes," said McCader. "Once Arvind got the possible hit with the airport, I contacted the car-hire people at the airport to see if Drekhkov had hired a car. He hadn't."

"Interesting," commented Blue. "So he wasn't planning on visiting several different places, just one destination. I'm guessing he used public transport. Did he?"

"Scotrail have footage of him from the CCTV on the train from Glasgow to Oban the same day he flew into Glasgow. Seems he took the airport bus into Glasgow, then the train up here. He'd avoid taxis, in case they remembered him."

"Do we know where he stayed?" asked Blue.

"I've sent his picture to all the hotels and other accommodation venues in and near Oban. But he may have stayed at the flat. If he was delivering stuff regularly to Mrs Carselaw, she could have given him a key and let him use it each time he came."

"Good work, all of you," concluded Blue. "Let's leave it there today. We'll meet up tomorrow morning, once the search warrants have arrived."

That evening Blue felt better about the way things were moving. The input from Elsa Maarksen had been useful. He made himself a smoked mackerel and spring onion omelette for tea. After that he phoned Alison to report on the day's achievements. It was quite a long call, even though he left plenty of the detail out. And much of it wasn't about the case at all.

22

Tuesday 6 December

Blue reserved two cars from the pool, then emailed Steve Belford, alerting him to the fact that they were doing two searches, and might require SOCOs at one or the other, or both, depending on what the searches turned up.

The warrants, duly authorised, were delivered by hand at five past ten, and he went up to the work room with them. "OK everybody, we have the warrants. We're good to go. Enver, you and Lena will probably be done before we're even on Bute. I'll call you when we get there. Arvind, I'll meet you in the car park in ten minutes. Let's hope we turn something up."

A grey Astra Estate awaited them in the car park, and Blue asked Bhardwaj to drive. "We'll take the scenic route. Not so quick, but better for the soul, so long as you don't drive us off the road."

They set off just after 10.15, heading south out of Oban on the A816, sometimes alongside sea lochs and at others through the hills between them. They passed by the waters of Loch Melfort, grey and choppy under a louring cloud mass, then turned inland and south. Blue always enjoyed seeing the prehistoric monuments at Kilmartin, stone circles, cup-marked rocks, and standing stones, reminders that people had been here, seeking the spiritual dimension, thousands of years before. He pointed them out to Bhardwaj as they passed.

A few miles later they reached the sign pointing to the rock of Dunadd, a major centre for the ancient Scots early in the Dark Ages. Carrying on south, they passed Lochgilphead, and soon reached the shores of Loch Fyne. They passed Inveraray, catching sight of the castle on their left as they went over the eighteenth-century bridge. Twenty minutes later, almost at the head of the loch, Blue asked Bhardwaj to turn into the car park of a café and garden centre. They enjoyed coffee and a slice each of an excellent home-baked carrot cake.

Then off again, down the eastern shore of Loch Fyne, then inland, still heading south, through wild and empty country, the hillsides darkened by great swathes of forestry. Where the trees reached the road, Blue could see the dark interior, where the tall conifers suffered neither light from the sun nor nutrition from rotting leaves to enrich the barren soil around them. Finally they emerged onto the water's edge again, at Colintraive, and were queueing for the ferry. The vessel resembled a flat platform with a superstructure squeezed around it, and conveyed them, in five minutes sailing, across the Kyles of Bute and onto the island itself. They followed the road south alongside the water, and soon spotted the masts of yachts tied up at a small marina. A short drive took them to a car park. Bhardwaj switched the engine off at twenty past one. Blue called McCader and asked how the search at the flat had fared.

"No-one answered the door, so I had to ask Dennis to come out to pick the locks. Better than beating the door down. Sadly not a lot to report so far. Paul Carselaw seems to have a mania for neatness, which I suppose helps, since every drawer and cupboard has a label saying what's in it. But also for security, so as well as labels, most of them have locks. Dennis has had plenty to do. Lena's going through a filing cabinet at the moment. But nothing significant lying about in plain sight. No sign of any guests having used the spare room recently either. Where are you, chief?"

"Just arrived at the marina. We'll hit the boat next."

A Portakabin housed the marina office, where a man with long grey hair, a white beard, a paunch and a cigarette in his mouth greeted them with a smile and a coughing fit. Blue introduced himself and Bhardwaj and they showed their ID.

The man's smile vanished. "I got nothin' to hide, inspector. Everything here's above board, I swear it." His accent was north of England. "I been clean since I got out, honest I have. Moved away from it all, right up here, middle o' nowhere like. It's a good life here too. They don't pay much but I get by. Whatever some bastard said about me, it ain't true."

"It's not you we're interested in," said Blue, "We don't even know who you are."

The expression changed again. "Oh. Sorry, forget what I said. It's Barry, Barry Stanhope. What can I do for you?" On a sudden thought, he pulled the cigarette from his mouth and tossed it out the cabin door.

"You have a cabin cruiser moored here, the *Jolly Mermaid*?"

"Hang on." Stanhope opened a dog-eared ledger and flicked

the pages. "Oh, aye, so we 'ave. Been 'ere since, er, sorry, can't read my own writing, wait a mo..."

"The first of December?" said Blue. "Last Thursday."

"Yeah. How did you know that?"

"One of my officers phoned yesterday, and was given that information."

"Oh. Monday's my day off, see. That would be Jim took the call. He's the boss. Is it him you want to see?"

"No, we have a warrant to search the *Jolly Mermaid*. And we'd like to do it now."

"You're the boss. I'll take you to her. She's at" – he peered at the page again – "B13. Is it drugs, then?"

"We suspect there is stolen property aboard. I'm afraid I can't be more specific. But I do have to show you the warrant before we go to the boat." He produced a brown envelope from his inside pocket, then extracted from it a single sheet of paper, which he passed to Stanhope. He glanced at it without making any attempt to read, and passed it back.

"Yeah, okay, she's this way." He motioned to the door. He led them onto a pontoon, and half way down pointed to a boat, similar to the one Blue had been shown at Gallanach Bay. "That's her. Don't look like there's anyone in."

"Have you seen anyone on or around her since she arrived?"

"Can't say as I 'ave, now you mention it. Maybe they scarpered as soon as they got 'ere. We've had that afore. A couple of Frenchies brought a boat in – this would be a few years ago, mind – took a couple of suitcases out, and walked straight out to the bus stop. But they 'adn't paid, see, so Jim was onto the coppers in Rothesay, and they picked them up at the pier – they was goin' for the ferry, see – and guess what, them suitcases was full of cocaine. Enough to make the whole of Bute float away. Well, they went down for a long stretch. But after a couple of years they put them on a boat back to France. An' 'ere's a thing, those two Frenchies never got off at the other end, and the bodies was washed up on the French coast two days later. Punished for losing the stuff, eh?"

"Interesting story. Did you know them?"

"What!? No, no, it were nowt to do wi' me, I can tell you. Anyway, here's the boat you was lookin' for. Shall I wait?"

"No thank you, Mr Stanhope. You've been very helpful, but we'll get on with it. Quietly. So please don't mention we're here to anyone. Not just yet."

"Mum's the word, eh? You're the boss. I'll be in the office." As he walked back, Stanhope pulled a cigarette packet out of his pocket.

"He looked a bit nervous, chief," remarked Bhardwaj.

"He certainly did. Right, let's get on board and have a look."

They stepped carefully onto the boat feeling it rocking in the water as they did. The bridge was virtually empty. A single seat fixed to the deck by the steering wheel and other controls. The only other thing there was a folding lounger near the rear of the boat.

"Not much here," said Blue. "Let's get inside. But first, we need something on our hands and feet." He took from the rucksack two pairs of blue nitrile gloves and two sets of plastic overshoes, and they put them on. "Now for the cabin. Door's over there."

To the left of the control area were five stairs leading down to a low door, painted green. Blue tried the handle. "Locked. Looks like we'll need to use some force. Do you agree, constable?"

"Yes, chief, definitely. Shall I barge it?"

"I think that would be difficult. At the bottom of those stairs you won't get any momentum. Let's try this." He produced a large flat-headed screwdriver from his rucksack, stuck it into the gap between the door and its frame, just above the lock, and pushed the other end towards the door. A loud cracking ended in some damage to the door frame and the door opening inward a little. Blue left his rucksack on the deck, and, using the screwdriver pushed the door fully open.

The smell hit them before anything else.

"Bloody hell!" gasped Bhardwaj. "What's that?"

"Rotting flesh, Arvind. Human, I suspect. We'll have to move very carefully, we mustn't disturb anything." They stooped to enter the cabin. In the dim light from the narrow horizontal windows near the low ceiling the body was clearly visible, lying face-down on the threadbare carpet in the centre of the room, between the two cushion-covered benches which functioned at night as beds. Around the head a deep shadow lay on the floor.

Blue flicked on the light switch, and a single bulb at the forward end of the cabin lit up. Not strong, but enough to show that the stain was dried blood. "Must have been a big puddle of blood here. Look, some of it's still sticky."

A fly buzzed past them. "And we're lucky it's so cold, or there would plenty more of these. And maggots galore."

"Mind if I go out for a minute, sir?" gulped Bhardwaj, and without waiting for an answer dashed out the door and up the staircase onto the deck. Blue could hear him retching over the side. He leaned out the doorway and called to Bhardwaj. "No need to come back down, Arvind. Stay there and don't let anyone on board. And don't say anything about this."

He looked back at the body, and then took his phone out and photographed the scene; that would give them a time-stamped image at the point of discovery. Then, holding the phone as a torch, he knelt down to look closer at the head. The face was directly down on the blood-soaked carpet. He used the screwdriver again to lever the head round, just enough to see what he needed.

Paul Carselaw stared blindly at him from milky eyes, beneath a bloodstained brow. And below his chin Blue could see clearly where Carselaw's throat had been cut, and his blood splashed onto one of the benches, then pooled onto the cabin floor.

He'd seen enough. Time for the SOCOs to take over. He clambered back up to the deck, sucking in lungfuls of fresh air. He noticed it was raining, however the bridge was well-covered. Bhardwaj was slumped in the driver's seat.

First he called McCader. "Hi Enver, we've got a body. Paul Carselaw." He heard the intake of breath at the other end. "No need to come down here yet. Keep working on the flat. I'll call you later. I'm going to get the SOCOs down and make contact with the local cops. Arvind and I will stay here tonight. I'll call you later."

His next call was to the SOC team, where he explained to Steve Belford what they'd found.

"OK," said Steve. "Do you want us down right away?"

"If you can. We won't be able to keep the lid on it for long. Tell you what, why don't you and Andy come down now. Andy can take some photos as soon as you get here, and you can make the initial log entry. Then Dennis or Jill can come down tomorrow morning if you need them. There's not a lot of room in the cabin."

Next Blue phoned the police station in Oban and asked to be put through to the Rothesay station. He asked to speak to whoever was in charge. A man's voice, low and slow, and polite.

"Inspector Watts here. How may I help you?"
"This is DI Blue, Oban police. I'm at the Kyles of Bute marina. We were following a lead, and have found a dead man in a boat. Murdered. We'll need some assistance." There was a pause as Inspector Watts took in what Blue had said. Then, just as calm as before, he replied, "Certainly, Inspector. What do you need?"
"Enough people to isolate and guard the crime scene. Our SOC team is on the way, but it'll take them a while to get here."
"We'll be round in fifteen minutes," replied Watts. "See you then." And rang off.
Blue ordered Bhardwaj to guard the boat, and made for the office.
"Found summat?" queried Stanhope, as Blue came in.
"Yes. The local police are on the way. Can you close the gates to the marina once they get here? We need to keep people away from the *Jolly Mermaid*."
Stanhope didn't ask any more questions, just nodded, and shuffled out towards the gates.

Watts was as good as his word, and two police cars swung through the marina gateway before the quarter hour was up. Stanhope closed the gates behind them. The first man out was tall, with waved grey hair and beard, and reminded Blue of the statue he'd seen in Rome of the Emperor Marcus Aurelius on horseback, one hand held up in acknowledgement of the people's cheers.
"Inspector Blue? I'm Graham Watts. I've brought all the manpower we had. Four, plus me. And the kit for sealing off the scene. Will that be enough?"
Blue shook the proffered hand. "Angus Blue. I should think so. It's on a boat, so should be straightforward to contain."
"There's a corpse in there?"
"Yes."
"I'll call the hospital. They'll send someone down to certify it's dead."
"Thank you. There's something else I need to ask."
"I think I can guess. You're quite a way off your patch here, so the local CID will have to be involved. They may even want to take the case."
"Exactly. So who should I call?"
Watts thought for moment. "This is a case you've been

following from Oban?"

"Yes." Blue gave Watts a brief summary of events since Paul Carselaw had reported his wife missing.

"I'd suggest you speak to Chief Inspector Hailstones in Greenock. That's our nearest CID. Hailstones is reasonable. He's also close to retiring and given to caution, so with a bit of luck he might just let you get on with it, and send a sergeant for liaison purposes. If Hailstones is not there, don't let them pass you to Inspector Green, or he'll be out here in minutes. Just promoted inspector, and looking for cases to make his mark, and get himself higher up the tree. In fact, I'll tell you what, I'll phone the chief inspector and then hand over to you. How's that?"

"Great." Blue felt here was a man he could work with, who put the job before the ego, and could size up people well.

Inspector Watts called Greenock, and Blue heard him say, "No, I have to speak to DCI Hailstones. I don't mind waiting, but I'd appreciate it if you could bring him to the phone. It's an important matter which needs his immediate attention." And then, after a while, "Ah, good afternoon, sir, it's Graham Watts here. I've got DI Angus Blue here from Oban. He's CIO on a case that's led him here, and he's found a body... Yes, murdered, throat cut. He'd like our assistance... Yes, of course, he's right here, I'll put him on the line."

And Blue explained again how events had led him to the body at the marina.

"You say the dead man lives in Oban, and the fact that his boat is here is the only thing that links him to Bute?"

"I can't say that for sure yet, sir. But the case is based in Oban. My gut feeling is that Bute was only chosen because it was some way from Oban, and that as soon as the deed was done, the killer made his way off the island as fast as he could."

"All right, here's what I'll do. I'll leave the case with you, rather than claiming it for us, which would only cause complications. But I'll send someone to liaise, so that we're aware of what's going on, and can offer help if local inquiries are necessary." He paused for a moment. "Yes, I'll send over Detective Sergeant Launceston. Right away, as soon as I can find him, that is."

23

There was not a lot to do now. The boat was cordoned off, with a uniformed officer on guard. A doctor arrived from the hospital in Rothesay, and duly pronounced the man dead. He gave a rough estimate of the time since death at four to five days. He explained that the body would have to be taken to Greenock for the post-mortem. A van was on its way from the mortuary.

There would now be some time to wait until the SOCOs arrived, so Inspector Watts drove Blue and Bhardwaj to a café further along the coast, at the village of Port Bannatyne. Over coffee and something to eat – Blue had a freshly baked scone with cream and home-made jam, Bhardwaj a Scotch pie and chips – Blue shared the facts of case with the local man.

"Just as well the chief inspector left it with you," said Inspector Watts. "Too many loose ends for my liking. First I'm thinking whether this Carselaw had any local connection. Bute's not a big island, and most of my people – there are only five as well as me – have been here a while and picked up a lot of what goes on."

"That would be very helpful. One possibility is that the killer was on the boat with Carselaw, killed him, brought the boat here, then left. Another is that the killer was waiting when Carselaw arrived, got on the boat, killed him, and then left. I don't see the killer hanging about on Bute. Unless he lives here. We know the boat came in on the first of December – last Thursday – at about 6pm. I suspect the killer would then have got off the island as fast as he could."

"We'll get the CCTV from the ferries. If we see the same car coming over that afternoon and returning in the evening, we can check it out. Not many people come over for the day at this time of year. There's only one boat that leaves after six on a Thursday evening – that's at five past seven – so we'll have a good look at that one. There's also CCTV in the terminal buildings."

"What if no-one picked him up at the marina?"

"He'd have to get a bus – there's a stop by the drive to the marina – that would get him to Rothesay. He'd make it in time to get the boat."

"So, unless he laid low on the island, he'd be on the 7.05 ferry to Wemyss Bay?"

"Ah, well, there is another option."

"The way we came in, from the ferry at the top of the island. To Colintraive."

"Yes, that's it. With a car he'd be there in no time, and it's only five minutes to cross. And there's a boat every half hour until nine o'clock. The only disadvantage is that it would take longer to get away after that, and there's a lot less traffic, so a single vehicle would be more likely to be remembered by someone who saw it. Whereas once you're off the main ferry at Wemyss Bay, you can soon be on the motorway and away in no time. But we'll check out Rhubodach to Colintraive too, just in case. Let me ask you one other question."

"Fire away."

"Are you thinking Carselaw knew his killer?"

"It does look that way. Carselaw had his throat cut, and fell forwards. There's blood spatter on the bench. And I didn't see any other wounds on the body. That suggests to me that someone came up behind him when he wasn't expecting it and slit his throat. We need to look more closely at Paul Carselaw. His role in the wider case is still unclear. Was he just the geeky husband who maybe shifted stolen books? Or was there another side to him that we haven't seen yet?"

"They might find something at the flat," put in Bhardwaj.

"Yes. Let's hope so. It's a pity we didn't spot the boat had gone sooner. Inspector, can we talk to the people at the marina next, see if anyone saw anything?"

"Of course. It's your case, we're here to help."

"I was just thinking," said Bhardwaj. "What if your second theory is correct, that the killer wasn't on the boat until it got here? Maybe Paul Carselaw came here regularly. What if this is where he was for those three days every fortnight. Meeting a woman, or another model railway buff."

"Good thinking, Arvind," said Blue. "Check it out now. Get Mr Stanhope to look for earlier bookings by Carselaw. Shall we go now?"

Blue and Watts questioned three boat-owners who happened to be around whilst Bhardwaj was in the office. One hadn't been there on the first, and the other two couldn't remember seeing anything.

As they headed for the office, Bhardwaj came out and waved

excitedly to them. "Chief! I've found something. Paul Carselaw was here every fortnight. It's in the book. And Mr Stanhope thinks he saw on one occasion Carselaw going to the boat with a woman. I showed him Aino Carselaw's picture and he said it definitely wasn't her. The one he saw was short and plump with a round face, mousy brown hair in a ponytail, and walked with a slight limp."

"Good work, Arvind," said Blue. "That's very interesting."

"Walks with a slight limp," repeated Inspector Watts. "I'll ask my officers if that description rings any bells with them."

They went back to the marina, where the local officers, two men and two women – the fifth local officer was off duty – were chatting by the *Jolly Mermaid*, having draped police tape all round it, and coned off the pontoon. Inspector Watts introduced Blue, quoted Bhardwaj's description, and asked if it rang any bells. They all stared into space for a while, thinking hard or trying to look like it. The two men eventually shook their heads, but one of the women nodded. "Aye, chief, now that might be Roxanne Skirving."

"Go on, Linda," said Inspector Watts, "tell us more."

"Remember that case in January where that truck driver – he had a load of logs from the plantation – was trying to get back onto Argyle Street?"

"That's the main road along the front and through the town," put in Watts.

"His SatNav had sent him into that car park next to the Co-op where the West Church used to be. This was about four o'clock in the evening, so it was getting dark. He soon realised he was at a dead end and was reversing to get out when the truck hit Roxanne. It wasn't all his fault – the beepers were working, but Roxanne was bending over the back of her car putting her shopping bags in. The glancing blow from the truck's rear – it was moving very slowly – should just have pushed her aside. But there's a lot of potholes in the car park and her foot caught in one and gave her a nasty twist as she fell. Some ligament damage and a broken bone in her ankle. I know all that 'cos I interviewed her. I see her around now and again – she lives in that block of flats opposite the police station – and I always ask her how she's getting on. I think the pain's gone, but not the limp. Mind you, she always looks guilty if I ask her if she's keeping up the exercises from the physiotherapist."

"We should check her out right away," said Blue.

"Tell you what," said Watts, "why don't Linda and I come with you? Since Roxanne knows Linda, she might be more forthcoming. It's PC Linda Baird, by the way."

"I'm happy to let Linda do the talking," said Blue, "we just need to know if she met up with Paul Carselaw here. If she did, then we'll need more detail. Arvind, can you call Sergeant McCader and ask him to look in the flat for any evidence of a relationship with another woman? Letters, photos, anything like that. Then check whether anyone saw a car waiting here on the days Carselaw's boat arrived, or saw him at the bus stop. There are a few houses, so try them too."

Inspector Watts asked two of the local officers to assist Bhardwaj, leaving the second woman constable to guard the boat, then he led Blue and PC Baird to one of the police cars.

Ten minutes later he parked the car outside the police station, on the High Street, which ran from the ferry pier up a long hill, and then on out into the countryside. Across the road Blue could see a block of flats, probably built by the council in the sixties, the concrete walls stained and crumbling.

"Why don't you two talk with Roxanne?" said Watts, as they stood outside the police station. "Three of us might overawe her. And I've plenty to get on with in here."

Roxanne's flat was on the second floor. She opened the door readily enough, only freezing when she saw the uniform. She finally recognised Linda and asked, rather nervously, what they wanted.

"It's no big deal, Roxanne," said Linda. "This is Inspector Blue, from Oban. He's got a case that seems to have some connection here, and it's possible you might know something about. Don't worry, it's not you we're after."

Unless you murdered Paul Carselaw, thought Blue. But he said nothing, only smiled and nodded.

"All right then, yous had better come on in." Roxanne led them into the tiny hallway and then through to the living room, which offered a fine view of the police station across the road. The room was over-warm and stuffy, despite, or maybe because of, the cold and damp outside. The windows were tightly shut; there was probably little ventilation.

Roxanne pointed them to the threadbare sofa, and took the armchair opposite. Almost out of habit, she stared at the fifty-inch TV screen on the wall.

"How's the leg?" asked PC Baird.

"Ach, no bad. It's no painful, but I guess it's always going to be a wee bit off. It disnae bother me too much, really. It's no as if I'm a marathon runner, eh?"

"I'm glad to hear that. The person we're interested in is called Paul Carselaw. Do you happen to know him?"

It was immediately obvious that Roxanne did know him. Her hand flew to her mouth. "What's he done! I hope he's no killed his wife."

"No, no, he's not killed anyone," Linda reassured her. "But he seems to vanish from his home for a few days every fortnight, and it would be very helpful to know where he goes."

"You mean, like, an alibi?"

"Yes, something like that."

"Aye, well, he comes to see me. Every fortnight, here on Tuesday, off on Thursday."

"Are you in a relationship with him?"

She shook her head. "I don't know about that. He's an odd one, right enough. He lost his Mammy at an early age. Killed in some sort of accident when he was just five, he said. I guess you never get over something like that, eh? And I know what you're going to say next. Does he pay me for sex? No's the answer to that, I'm no a whore."

"I know that, Roxanne," said Baird. "How did you meet him?"

Roxanne smiled at the memory. "My Dad's always been into model railways. He was in a club, and they had a big get-together a few years ago, a festival, they called it. In the Pavilion here, in the main hall. Lots of model railways set up, it was quite impressive. For me, once you've seen a wee train goin round the track a couple of times it gets boring. But if it keeps men off the streets then it's no a bad thing, eh? Anyway, they had the tables out down the side of the hall, where you can see the water, and me and Mum were sat there havin a coffee, when Dad comes back to the table with this geeky-looking guy."

"What did you think of him?"

"I have to say, I thought he was a wee bit odd. He could be quite good-looking, if he got a makeover and smiled a bit more. But he's very intelligent. He seems to know everything. Whatever you ask, he's got an answer for it. Mind, it's not always the right one, but he'd never admit that. He's very proud of his brain. He said he had an IQ of 153; he said that was really high, close to being a genius. I think he was sorry it wasn't higher. Anyway, he told us about his boat, and I said I'd love a trip out in it. He said we could do that the next day. He asked my Mum and Dad if they'd like to come too, but they said no."

"What did they make of him?"

"They thought he must be a professor somewhere. My Dad said his knowledge of 00 gauge was more comprehensive than anyone he knew. He knew all about computers too, and this was just when the model train guys were all talkin about gettin the computer to control the trains. Paul writes programs for them to use. He's very clever that way, you know, with computers."

"What about your Mum?"

"Oh, she thought he was a geek, but she liked how well-spoken he was. 'He's a cut above us, Roxanne,' she said to me once. But she also wanted me to meet up with someone. I mean, I was thirty-one then. He's quite a bit older, but he looks younger than his age."

"Did he mention that he was married?"

"No. Not at first. He was quite clever that way. He doesn't wear a ring, and there was no sign of another woman on the boat. And I've never seen his place in Oban. Eventually he had to admit it. It was soon clear he only wants to see me for a few days every fortnight. I mean, it's nice bein on the boat, out on the water, and we go to some nice places in it – Ayr and Girvan, and Arran."

"Sorry to ask this, but do you sleep with him?"

"Once or twice, to begin with. But it was no fun. I don't think he's really interested in that. With women, I mean. I think he's gay but won't admit it to himself. He'd be a lot happier if he did, I think. I soon realised we'd never be married, especially after I found out about his wife. But there's no-one else, and it's nice to get out every couple of weeks."

"How did you find out about his wife?"

"He had a wee bit too much to drink one evening – he doesna hold the alcohol well – and he started talking about this person called Aino. What sort of name is that? It took me a while to realise that it was female, then the penny dropped. He admitted it right away. He said she kept going off somewhere, the country she came from, and he thought she had a lover there. He got quite maudlin, but it was all about him. He doesn't take a lot of notice of other people."

"When he comes over, do you meet him, or does he come here?"

"Oh, I drive over and meet him. The car's really my Dad's, but he's too old to drive, so he gave it to me. It's quite old now, but does me fine. I go to the marina and wait in the car; he emails me the time he'll be arriving, it's usually about half past eleven. Then we go to the café at Ettrick Bay for lunch, and look at the map and decide where to go in the boat. Well, it's usually me that decides where I'd like to go, sometimes he'll say it's too far, like the Isle of Man, but I've a good idea of how far he'll go now, so there's usually no problem. And after lunch off we go. Now and then he even lets me steer the boat."

"Does he ever give you things, or ask you to look after things for him?"

"Like packages of drugs, eh? No, nothing like that. He's no even very good at givin me things. He's quite mean wi his money. Or maybe giving gifts is not in his nature. He pays for meals now without quibbling."

"What about books?" asked Blue.

"I read an awful lot. They've a great library here. Once or twice Paul lent me a book to read, old ones that he got from his wife's shop. She has a second-hand bookshop, but it's only for rare books, he says, so I have to hand them back when I've read them. You know, Sir Walter Scott and stuff like that. Those old books can take some getting used to, especially as quite often the story doesn't start till you're a hundred pages in. But they're good stories. And you can imagine people in the old days, how they talked and so on."

"What was the last one he lent you?"

"That was *The Scottish Chiefs*. All about William Wallace and his pal Andrew Moray. I liked Moray, but he got killed, with an arrow, in one of the battles. Last time I saw Paul, I gave it back. He said it was quite valuable, a first edition. Warned me no to spill ma tea on it!"

"Thanks, Roxanne. That's useful." Blue nodded to Baird to resume her questioning.

"Is Paul coming over this week?" she asked.

"No. I got an email on Saturday saying he couldn't make it, he had some repairs to do on his train set. Honestly, what kind of man turns down a woman for a train set? Otherwise we'd be off somewhere right now. I was planning a wee trip round Ailsa Craig."

"Has he emailed you since then?"

"Yes, I got another message on Sunday. Just 'How are you?' and a couple of X's. That's very unusual for Paul. The X's I mean. Maybe he's missing me."

"Has he told you his wife's gone missing?"

"No. What's happened to her? Has she left him? To be honest, I wouldn't blame her. He's okay for a couple of days, but I can't think what it would be like being married to him. Who knows what'll happen now, if she has gone. He may even ask me. I'm not sure what I'd do."

"When was the last time you saw him?"

"Three or so weeks ago. It would be, let me see, the fifteenth. He was going to come on the 29th, but said he had a meeting of the model railway club committee, so wasn't available. And then this week's off too. I wonder if he's had enough of me. Tell me what's goin on, Linda. You wouldn't have a detective inspector here if it wasn't something bad."

"Just one more thing. Can you remember what you did last Thursday evening?"

"Oh, that's the craft club. We meet in the Baptist Church hall, at six, it's just opposite the castle. We're doing weaving at the moment. They've got these looms, and it's amazing what you can do. I got there early, at quarter to, and wasn't away till it finished at nine. I made a wee scene, with waves and a pier. But why are you asking that? Paul's in real trouble, isn't he?"

Baird looked at Blue, who nodded. "Roxanne," she said quietly, "I'm afraid I have some very bad news for you. Paul Carselaw is dead."

Roxanne didn't respond at first. Then, "How odd," she muttered. "As soon as you came in, I thought, he's dead. I dismissed that thought. You would, wouldn't you? That someone you know is dead. I think I know him better than most people. He's himself with me. But what's that? A poor man lost even to himself." A tear rolled down her cheek, and she wiped it away. "I'll miss him. I suppose I thought I could cure him, make him more himself. But would I lose him then? He gets angry when I don't understand something he's saying, or when I disagree with him. So angry I sometimes get scared. Not that he's ever violent. Excuse me." She jumped up from the armchair and hurried out of the room. A door slammed. Behind it they heard an awful cry.

"I'll stay with her," said PC Baird.

"Thank you, Linda," said Blue. "You did really well." He squeezed her arm, and got up.

"Should I bring her over to the station to make a statement?"

"Not this evening. Maybe in the morning. By then we'll maybe know a bit more, and be able to focus just on what she can say that's relevant to the case."

"What if she asks how he died?"

"Just say we're still investigating. We'll tell her tomorrow."

Outside the police station, Blue turned the ringer on again on his phone. He saw a missed call from McCader, and called him. "What have you got, Enver?"

"Hi Chief, Arvind phoned and put us in the picture. We're still searching the house, but we've already found some letters signed 'R' with three X's. That could be the woman you've identified there. They talk about trips they've been on in his boat."

"That does sound like her. Photograph a couple and email them to me. It should confirm what she told us."

"Could she have killed him?"

"It's possible. But I don't think so. We've just questioned her, and she's given us a lot. I don't think she's hiding anything." The last cry he'd heard from Roxanne still haunted him. A part of her life torn away. Even if it was a bit she wasn't sure about.

"Chief, you still there?"

"Yes, sorry. Anything else?"

"It's weird, but there's very little evidence of Aino's existence here. As if he's been trying to wipe out the memory of her. Apart from a few pictures taken years ago, there's nothing of hers left."

"OK. Arvind and I will stay here till tomorrow at least. I'll let you know then what's happening and when we'll be back. Give me a call if anything else turns up."

He reported the conversation with Roxanne to Inspector Watts, and the two of them returned to the marina. Here they found that

Steve Belford and Andrew McGuire had arrived from Oban. They could see bright light shining from the small cabin windows. A refrigerated van had also arrived from the mortuary in Greenock.

Detective Sergeant Launceston from Greenock CID had come over on the same ferry as the mortuary and the SOC vans, a tall, cadaverous individual with thinning grey hair and a drooping grey moustache. The ill-fitting dark green suit seemed to hang from his limbs as if there were very little inside it. But his voice was a deep comforting baritone. He shook hands with Watts and Blue, and listened to Blue giving another summary of the case. "Aye, we don't get a murder on Bute very often. Although, strictly speaking, this one wasn't exactly on the island, was it?" He went on to explain that he'd already contacted the pathologist, and the post-mortem would be held the following morning at the Inverclyde Royal Hospital in Greenock, at twelve noon.

"Thank you, sergeant," said Blue. "I'll come over myself to see what the pathologist tells us."

"Did your talk with this girl sort things out?" the sergeant asked.

"It was very useful. But I don't think she killed him. We'll see what turns up tomorrow."

Launceston nodded. "Right you are, sir. I'll get back to Greenock and report to the chief inspector. Can I say you'll update me tomorrow when you come over for the PM?"

"Yes, that's perfect. I'll see you then."

The sergeant headed back to his car to make for the next ferry back to Wemyss Bay.

It was already getting dark, and Blue didn't see there was more they could do that day by way of investigation. Given that the key events had all happened a few days previously, there was no pressure to do things that evening. He had the whole night to think about it, and would be fresher in the morning. Inspector Watts told him he'd arranged accommodation at the Victoria Hotel. "Usually packed in the summer, but this being the off season, there's room. And the food's good too."

The local officers were released until the morning, apart from one of the men who would stand guard on the boat overnight. Steve Belford explained that they'd need maybe another half-hour, then the body could be removed. "Can I make a suggestion, Angus? Once the corpse has gone, we don't need to look at the boat till the morning, when we photograph it in daylight and check the pontoon for any footprints or other traces. I've been talking to Mr Stanhope, and the marina can hire us a trailer and lift the boat onto it once we're done in the morning. We can then tow it behind our van back to Oban. Then we can have a good look at it there." Inspector Watts didn't object to that, so Blue gave Steve the OK.

Inspector Watts chatted to Blue and Bhardwaj until Steve re-emerged to say they were done for the evening. He proposed that he and Andrew would remain overnight on Bute. Blue okayed it, and Inspector Watts phoned the Victoria to book them in. The mortuary attendants now went in and removed the body on a stretcher to the van. Then they too were off to the ferry. Blue and Bhardwaj in their car, the SOCOs in their white van, and Inspector Watts in a marked police car, all headed for Rothesay. The Oban officers checked into the hotel, and Blue went up to his room for a wash. He called Alison to explain what had happened.

"Interesting," said Alison. "Looks like someone emailed the girl pretending to be Carselaw, so that she wouldn't go to the marina today. Presumably took his phone after they'd killed him. But the boat's been there since before the weekend. Why did he come over then?"

"What if the killer pretended to be Roxanne and invited him? He could have emailed Paul, claiming to be her, saying there was a problem with her email and she'd got a new one, and he would then reply to the fake one. As soon as Carselaw arrives at the marina, he goes on board and kills him, then takes his phone and uses it to text Roxanne."

"As you say, the way he was killed suggests he knew the killer. So he can't have been surprised when they turned up instead of Roxanne. They'd still have to explain their arrival to him."

"It comes back to someone Carselaw knew," concluded Blue. "A friend or acquaintance. Anyway, how's Corrie?"

Later that evening Inspector Watts, now out of uniform, joined them for a meal at the Esplanade, a restaurant overlooking the pier. "Where the locals eat!" proclaimed the sign over the door. They knew that in public places you don't talk about police work, and had a relaxed evening.

24

Wednesday 7th December

Blue, Bhardwaj and the SOCOs met again at breakfast, and wasted no time checking out and heading for the police station, now visible in daylight. A late-twentieth-century erection that looked like it had been made from parts borrowed from a high-rise block: rendered concrete panels, blue plastic panels, and windows. Inspector Watts greeted them and reported that the officer guarding the boat had been relieved. The SOCOs set off for the marina, whilst Blue, Bhardwaj, Baird and Inspector Watts walked down to the ferry terminal. Bhardwaj had a folder of photos which he showed to the staff, but drew no positive responses. Watts asked for CCTV footage from the last week, from the terminal and from the ferries, and from the terminal at Wemyss Bay. Bhardwaj and Baird were given the task of searching through all the footage once it had arrived.

They all returned to the police station. Blue phoned McCader.

"Got something very interesting, chief. We finished searching the flat yesterday evening and got on to the garage this morning. The space is eighteen by nine feet. The train set is on a chipboard bed twelve feet long by five wide. That enables the operator to reach with a hand any part of the track. The chipboard rests on two long cupboards with drawers down each side, leaving about six inches of overhang. That's where Carselaw stored all his parts and spares. At each end there's a set of bookshelves, with various train books and mags and boxes on them. But here's the thing: the one at the inner end is on low wheels, and when you remove the screws linking each side with the cupboard beyond, and pull it out, guess what's hidden behind it?"

"A body?"

"A safe."

"And what's inside?"

"We don't know yet. Dennis is currently having a go at it. But we may have to get an expert in."

"Blow it if you have to. I'm not *au fait* with model train enthusiasts, but my guess is that they don't keep their engines in a safe. A locked cupboard perhaps, but a safe is a big step further, particularly if it's hidden behind a bookshelf. You'd have to have some very valuable engines for that. Let me know as soon as you get into it."

Blue didn't want to be late for the post-mortem, so he got the ten o'clock ferry to Wemyss Bay, and the 10.55 train to Glasgow. He got off the train at Branchton, as Sergeant Launceston had advised; from the platform he could see the dark brown slab of the hospital on top of the next rise. He was there in ten minutes, and realised he was half an hour early. He spent that with a cup of coffee and a chocolate brownie in the ground floor café run by volunteers. After ten minutes he was joined by DS Launceston, carrying a cup of tea and an iced doughnut. "Anything more to report, sir?" he asked. "For the chief inspector, like."

"The SOCOs are at work, and they'll take the boat off to Oban once they're done. I've got some people looking at CCTV footage. Trouble is, we don't know what to look for yet."

"Aye, it's a tricky one all right." DS Launceston glanced at his watch. "Ah well, we'd better get down. Doctor Kelling hates to be kept waiting."

The sergeant led Blue along corridors and down stairs and along more corridors to a bleak waiting room in the basement. They were there just before twelve, and as the hands of the clock on the wall aligned themselves exactly to the vertical, Doctor Kelling entered from a door at the rear of the room. A thin, but not tall, bird-like man with a large beak-like nose, and eyes that seemed to stare through you. "Why didn't you put those on, eh?" He gestured to a row of white lab coats on hooks. "I don't have time to waste. And gloves too. You're bound to touch something."

The body lay, awaiting their attention, on a steel topped table. A technician waited a few paces away. Doctor Kelling switched on a voice recorder, gave the date, time, his name and that of the body, then pointed the device at Blue and Launceston. "Introduce yourselves!" he commanded.

"Detective Inspector Blue, Oban police station."

"Detective Sergeant Launceston, Greenock police station."

"You two look experienced, so I don't need to tell you where the sick bags are. Here's Mr Carselaw. I can confirm he's quite dead. Nasty looking incision in his neck. Probable cause of death."

Twenty minutes later they were back in the waiting room, waiting for Doctor Kelling to save the voice file, and supervise the blood and other samples. Fifteen minutes later he joined them.

"No need to ask me. Cause of death was a cut in the throat, which led the unfortunate Mr Carselaw to bleed to death fairly rapidly, probably creating quite a mess on the carpet and furniture around him. There's a bump on his head, but it's not serious, probably hit something as he fell. No other recent injuries or wounds on the body. Was he drugged at the time? Can't tell you that till I get the bloods back. Time of death, approximately four days ago, plus or minus one, depending on environmental conditions of the location of the body."

"Direction of the cut?" asked Blue.

"Left to right. His left to right, that is. Shape of the cut suggests probably done from behind."

"How much effort would it need?"

"Not a lot. Edges of cut suggest very sharp blade. Kitchen knife maybe."

"Anything else you think worth commenting on?"

"Very good teeth for a man his age. Fairly fit. Though quite a drinker, too. Sergeant, I'll send you the test results as usual. Good day gentlemen." And he was gone.

Sergeant Launceston led Blue to a black Astra in the hospital car park. They drove down the hill to the main road, and were parked at Wemyss Bay station in ten minutes. The next ferry was at five past one, in eleven minutes. "We'll leave the car here," said the sergeant. "Boss doesn't like us taking it over on the ferry if we're only going to Rothesay. Cost-savings."

They walked down the long bright Victorian covered way leading to the ticket office, and then onto the *Bute* in time for departure. Coronation chicken sandwiches, coffee and a fruit slice constituted lunch for Blue, whilst Launceston preferred BLT and a doughnut with caramel icing. The sergeant must have a rapid metabolism, thought Blue. Or a tapeworm.

As usual in a public place, their conversation touched upon nothing significant. At one forty the *Bute* pulled alongside the ugly structure which had replaced the wooden gangways of old, and they were back on the island.

At the police station, Inspector Watts asked how the PM had gone. Blue gave him a summary of the results, and asked what was happening there.

"Linda and DC Bhardwaj have been staring at CCTV footage since you left. I told them to take a break at one. They should be back soon. I don't think they've anything to report so far."

"Did the SOCOs get off the island?" Blue asked.

"Yes, they were on the ferry at eleven. They'll be going back using the main roads, with that trailer behind them. It didn't look like the newest one they have at the marina."

"Did Roxanne come in to give her statement?"

"Yes. Have a look at it and tell me what you think."

Quarter of an hour later Blue had the statement. It didn't add anything significant to what she'd said the previous day, but now they had it in writing. Watts told him to keep the copy; he'd retain the signed top copy, as protocol required, but would forward it to the fiscal in Oban if it were needed.

Ten minutes later, Blue was just relaxing with a cup of coffee in Inspector Watts' office upstairs, the inspector himself having gone home for lunch, when Bhardwaj came up. "Boss, we've got something that might be important. Can you have a look, see what you think?"

Down at the viewing room, Baird gave up her seat to Blue, and Bhardwaj ran the relevant footage. "This is from the 7.05pm boat from Rothesay to Wemyss Bay on Thursday the first. The camera is in the foyer area in the centre of the boat, facing the coffee and snack shop. In a few seconds someone comes out of the shop with a cup and a packet of sandwiches. See what you think."

Blue could see a figure at the coffee shop till, handing over money. Then they turned and came out, holding the drink in one hand and the sandwich packet in the other, heading for a point to the right of the camera, where he remembered the milk and sugar and stirrers were, and maybe to the seating area beyond.

He watched the film a second time. The black and white image was grainy, but he saw what they'd seen. "What do you think, Arvind?" he asked Bhardwaj.

"It looks awfully like Aino Carselaw, boss. OK, the hair is short and black, and she's wearing glasses, but there's certainly a strong resemblance in the face." Bhardwaj pointed to the photo of Mrs Carselaw her husband had given them several days previously.

Blue couldn't disagree. "You may be right. There is a resemblance."

"If she weren't dead, it could be her," said Bhardwaj.

"And she's had a wee makeover," added Baird.

"That's right," agreed Bhardwaj. "Cut the hair short, dye it black, and get a pair of specs."

"Have you got her on any other footage?"

"Yes, there's another shot when she's heading for the gangway, but it's not as good as this one."

"Okay. I'll get back to *Komissar* Kõnekas and see if he's done a check with the DNA data we sent. If he has, then it's just someone who looks like Aino. But we won't rule out the other possibility yet. Look at the footage from the walkway at the Wemyss Bay end. If she got on as a foot passenger, she may be heading for the station to get the train to Glasgow. Or she may have a car parked there."

"Sir," said Baird, "if the killer didn't have a car on the island, they'd have to get the bus from the marina to the pier. There's a camera on the pier that should show people getting off the bus there. We could check that one too."

"Make it so!" said Blue. "I'll call Estonia now."

He returned to Watts' office, and called the number *Komissar* Kõnekas had given him. It was now 3pm, that would be five in Estonia. He hoped Kõnekas wasn't one of those officers who were out the door dead on closing time.

He wasn't.

"*Tere*, *Komissar* Blue. You are making progress?"

"*Tere*, *Komissar* Kõnekas. Yes. We found Paul Carselaw yesterday, murdered in his boat."

"Ah. Do you know who killed him?"

"We're working on it. But I hope you can help me. Have you compared the DNA data I sent for Aino Carselaw, or Lind, with that for the body you found in the Kaali crater?"

"No. Both Kalev Lind, in person, and Mr Carselaw, when you showed him the picture, identified the dead woman as Aino Lind. Do we need more proof?"

"I wonder if you could do that comparison as soon as possible. I would like to be sure the dead person over there is in fact Aino Lind. I can assure you that the data we sent is that of Aino Carselaw. Or Lind."

"Inspector, do you have cause to doubt the identity of *Proua* Lind's body?"

"A possible ID has come up in our investigation, which needs to be confirmed or eliminated."

"Very well." Kõnekas didn't sound convinced. "I will contact the lab now; maybe there are still people there. I'll phone you as soon as it's done." And he rang off.

Inspector Watts came into the room. "I heard you on the phone, and didn't want to disturb you. Sounds like something's come up."

Blue explained what Bhardwaj and Baird had found on the CCTV footage.

"That would certainly turn things upside down. Care for another coffee while we're waiting?"

Half an hour later, *Komissar* Kõnekas was back on the line. Blue put the phone on speaker.

"*Tere, Härra Komissar.* I have news. The profiles do not match. It seems the woman in the crater is not Aino Lind."

"Thanks for getting back to us so quickly, *komissar.* This certainly changes things."

"But why did both Mr Lind and Mr Carselaw identify the dead woman as Aino Lind?"

"That's what we need to find out. Unfortunately we can't ask Mr Carselaw."

"We are lucky we still have the body. *Härra* Lind wanted it released as soon as possible for the funeral, but the procedures had not been completed. He has some serious questions to answer. I will talk with *Härra* Lind. But first I will make an extra check of the dead woman's identity. I will go to Tartu tomorrow morning and show *Proua* Lind's parents some images of the dead woman. It would be helpful if they can state that she is not their daughter."

"Is there a reason why they were not asked to identify the body when it was discovered?"

"Lind asked us not to ask them to view the body. He said they were old and their health was very fragile. He worried that it could kill either of them to see their daughter's corpse. And he was very definite that the dead woman was his wife."

"What about the daughter? Tiina. Wasn't she available for an ID?"

"Yes. But she said she had seen so little of her mother over the years that she could not be sure about the identification. And she was also very upset; Lind had already told her that the dead woman was her mother."

"Could he have done that to influence her identification?"

"It is possible. I will contact you when I have spoken to *Härra* and *Proua* Kuusk."

"Interesting," said Watts. "So if the dead woman in Estonia is not Mrs Carselaw, she could be anywhere. And that could have been her on the boat. What do you think?"

"It's certainly possible. Perhaps even likely. And if it was, the question is, where is she now? And what's she after? I think I should get back up to Oban this afternoon. But I'd like to leave DC Bhardwaj down here to carry on looking at the CCTV footage."

"No problem. I'll look after him. We can get more footage from the mainland, so see where the woman went after the ferry. I'm sure DS Launceston will help there too."

After a short meeting with Bhardwaj, Blue was in the queue for the four o'clock ferry, as the *Argyle* pulled into the pier and tied up. Coffee and a choc chip muffin set him up for the drive back. Crossing the Clyde at the Erskine Bridge, he followed the A82 north by the banks of Loch Lomond, on to Crianlarich and then Tyndrum, then turned left onto the Oban road. He passed by Loch Awe and through the Pass of Brander, then Dalmally and at last was at Connel.

By the time he opened his front door, it was nearly eight, and he was tired out. No time for a gourmet meal now; but he had some leftover roast duck in the fridge, so a duck korma with microwave rice was soon on the table, along with a glass of Czech lager. And a glass of whisky later as he sat in front of the fire. He didn't want to speculate until he'd heard from Estonia the next day, so tried not to think about it.

But he did phone Alison to bring her up to date.

"That would be a turn up for the books!" she said. "Now let's talk about something else. And I suggest you have a nice hot bath tonight."

Which he did.

25

Thursday 8 December

The day dawned cold and clear; frost on the ground and the trees all white. And ice underfoot. Blue drove carefully, and was relieved to find the steep hill running down into Oban had been gritted.

He was at his desk by seven thirty. That would be nine thirty in Estonia, too early for news from there. He emailed McCader and Vunsells to be ready for a meeting at nine. He invited Sergeant Morgan too; Aino Carselaw had been her missing person case.

At quarter to nine the call came.

"*Tere*, Inspector! We have results. I am in our office in Tartu now. I visited Aino Lind's parents. They are old, both over eighty years, but do not seem so frail as *Härra* Lind suggests. The father was not sure about the images; his eyesight is not good. But the mother was very definite. That it was not Aino. So it is now clear that the body in the Kaali crater is not Aino Lind."

"Thank you. It may be that Aino has been here in Scotland. If that is the case, it's possible that she killed Paul Carselaw. Good luck with finding who the dead woman really is. I'll keep in touch."

The next call was to Bhardwaj to confirm that Aino Carselaw/Lind was not dead, and could have been the person on the boat. "Well done, Arvind. It's a breakthrough, though where we'll break through to is not clear right now. As I said yesterday, see if you can track her on from Wemyss Bay. We need to know where she's headed."

"Will do, boss. I'm ready to roll!"

He next phoned Inspector Watts and then Sergeant Launceston, to pass on the news. They were both keen to offer whatever help they could.

When he went up to the workroom at nine, McCader, Vunsells and Sergeant Morgan were already there, coffees steaming in front of them. Vunsells pushed the extra one over to Blue. "Mocha, just like you like it, boss!"

As they could see Blue was ready, a hush descended. "The first thing I have to tell you is that it's clear now that the corpse found in the crater lake in Estonia was not Aino Carselaw. The DNA comparison has been backed up by Aino's mother." He gave them a few moments to digest this, then went on, "So in the absence of evidence to the contrary, we must presume Aino is still alive. This opens up the possibility that she was on Bute and may have killed Paul Carselaw. Forensics will examine the boat, and Arvind is still on Bute, trying to track the person who might be her after she got off the island. But if Aino is here in Scotland, when did she arrive, and where's she been?"

"Here in Oban," said McCader, emphatically. "This is where her interests are. I'd say she went over to Estonia and met Lind. He says he never saw her but I think he's lying, and she and Lind are in this together, whatever 'this' is. I'd say they conspired to murder the woman found in the crater. Lind finds someone, maybe in Russia, who looks like Aino. Offers her a job in the west, brings her over, gets her at her ease, and kills her. Then they dump the body in the crater lake to make sure it'll soon be found. But only after Aino's sister has gone off to Eritrea. Then Lind identifies the body as Aino before anyone else can, confuses the daughter, and dissuades the police from asking the parents. Meanwhile Aino comes back here, and keeps under the radar."

"The fact that both Lind and Paul Carselaw IDed the body as Aino shows the placing of the dead woman in the crater is part of all this," added Blue.

"Could she have stayed with Paul Carselaw?" asked Vunsells. "That would explain why he confirmed the picture of the dead woman as Aino. If he already knew she was here. And he was in on whatever she was up to."

"That's possible," put in Sergeant Morgan, "but my feeling is that when he saw the pictures he was surprised. It wasn't what he'd expected, because it wasn't Aino. He hid it very quickly. But he only realised then that Aino was still alive. So I don't think she was staying with him. She would avoid hotels. Even with fake papers, there would always be the risk that someone would find her. And a B&B would add the risk that the proprietors would remember her."

"Where would you suggest, Aelwyn?" asked Blue.

"I would say a caravan site. There are plenty round here, and you can usually manage to hire a caravan or a lodge for a week or two, especially at this time of year. You can do your own thing and nobody bothers you."

"We'd need to check them out, discreetly, in case she's still there."

"I can do that, in plain clothes. I know most of the managers – I regularly check them for folk who've gone missing. Quite often they just want to get away from family or partner for a week or two, but don't want to leave the area."

"That sounds good. Let's come back to the question Enver raised. Why would Aino come back here? What unfinished business might she have had?"

"To rob the bookshop?" suggested Vunsells. "The books from the glass-fronted case would fetch a few thousand pounds. Though why she would wreck the place doesn't make a lot of sense. All she had to do was take the books."

"It seems an awful lot of trouble," said Blue, "just for a few thousand pounds worth of books. Faking her death, killing Drekhkov, and now perhaps Carselaw too. I'm sure there's more to it. I'm inclined to agree with Ms Maarksen that there's something more at stake. Maybe a consignment of extremely valuable books. If they're worth millions, that would raise the game to a new level."

"The safe under Carselaw's railway," said McCader. "When we got it open there was nothing inside. Perhaps something *had* been in it, and either Aino or Paul Carselaw removed it. Then there's the empty safe at the office. What if this consignment had been there too at some point?"

"That suggests Balfour knows more than he's telling us," commented Blue.

"Wait a minute," put in Vunsells. "If Aino was going to disappear in Estonia, why not collect the consignment there? Why get it sent all the way over here?"

"Money," said McCader. "What if the money they needed to buy the books was being sourced here? Let's say Lind doesn't have the money it takes to buy them, so Aino negotiates a loan over here, or offers a part-share in the deal to someone else. Maybe even the major share. Then the goods have to be delivered here so that the investor can see what they got for their money."

"So who's the investor?" asked Vunsells.

"The empty safes could suggest either Paul Carselaw or Ishmael Balfour. Though it could be someone else we don't know about. We can check Carselaw's bank records, but I don't see him having huge wealth hidden away. If he did, I suspect he'd have bought a bigger boat, and rented a warehouse for his train set. Perhaps he was involved with Aino in her dodgy book dealings, and that's why he had the safe. Then Aino could store stuff there she didn't want seen in the office."

"Balfour could be the investor," said Blue. "He was surprised when he found the office safe was empty, though he hid it well. If he thought the consignment was there, that would explain his surprise. And he would realise that only one person could have got into the safe to remove it. Aino."

"Who had double-crossed him," added Vunsells. "Taken his money and cleared off with the goods. If Balfour was the investor, that is."

"Right," said Blue, "that's giving us the following story. Lind makes a deal in Russia or further east for a consignment of very valuable books. But he doesn't have enough funds, so Aino gets someone else to come in on the deal. Let's say that it's Balfour. He's already in the book trade, so he sees the value of the consignment. He's usually honest, but this deal is too good to pass on. So he agrees, and transfers the funds to Aino. But he wants to see the goods. So the shipment is brought here, and, some time before she leaves for Estonia, she shows it to him. He sees that it's safely stored in the safe in the bookshop."

"So why didn't she take it when she went to Estonia?" asked Vunsells.

"Good question, Lena. Perhaps Balfour had said he would check on it regularly. If that happened just after she left, he'd be after her before she managed to kill the decoy woman and reinvent herself. So, with her new identity in place, she has to come back for it. She carries out the bookshop break-in as a cover, and takes all the books in the cabinet as well, to make it look like a theft."

"But she'd know that Balfour would realise it was her as soon as he opened the safe," put in Vunsells.

"I suspect her plan was to be off again soon after the robbery. But something got in the way. Or someone. Paul Carselaw. What if he finds out about the consignment, and knows it's in the safe in the office? What if he's got the combination, or has forced Aino to give it to him? He's looking forward to the huge profit the stuff will bring him and Aino. But when Aino doesn't contact him from Estonia, he suspects she's double-crossing him."

"He's right!" said Vunsells.

"So he opens the safe, takes the consignment out, and moves it to the safe under his railway. He's not intending to double-cross Aino; he doesn't have the connections to sell the books himself, so he needs her. He just wants to hold her to his share of the deal. He perhaps realises she's left him for good, and maybe isn't bothered about that. But the deal is a different matter. So the stuff is in his safe as insurance, for when she comes back."

"So why does he report her missing to us?"

"I can answer that," put in Sergeant Morgan. "He wants to put pressure on Aino, because he knows we'll contact the police in Estonia. Once they start looking for her, she'll have to move quickly, and come back here to get the consignment."

"Hold it," said Vunsells. "You're saying that when Aino trashed the shop, the consignment had already gone?"

"What if it was in Carselaw's safe by then?" said Blue. "Maybe that's why she trashed the shop, out of sheer annoyance."

"So who killed Boris Drekhkov?" asked Vunsells. "And who was he working for?"

"Drekhkov could only have been working for either Lind or Balfour," Blue continued. "Here's an idea. Lind begins to suspect that after her makeover, Aino will double-cross him. All she has to do is come back here, collect the consignment, and disappear, probably to another continent where she can sell the stuff. So he sends Drekhkov over to check out what's happening."

"Why not come himself?"

"Maybe he thinks that's too risky. He doesn't know how dangerous Balfour might be. Or he's too busy with other deals. And he trusts Drekhkov. He tells Aino Drekhkov's coming, and she lets him into the flat. She assures him she's collected the goods and is going to bring them back to Estonia as planned. She gets on the right side of him. Maybe they have a meal in the flat, she plies him with wine, or vodka, drugs him and strangles him. Then robs and trashes the shop."

"But does she know at this point that the consignment is no longer in the safe?"

"I would guess so. She daren't tell Drekhkov this, or he'll tell Lind, who'll conclude, correctly, that she's cheating him."

"And if she thinks Paul Carselaw has the stuff," said Vunsells, "she'll think he can be dealt with."

"But she's underestimated him," said Blue. "She confronts him at the flat, sweet-talks him too, swears that she always meant to come back, that it's her and Paul who'll go to San Francisco or Singapore or wherever, and get millions for the books. He's not going to leave her alone in the flat, so she says she'll be back in a couple of days once she's made arrangements for them to travel. She says she trusts him to look after the consignment. She comes back a couple of days later with a bottle of wine and some powders. He's going to go the way of Drekhkov. But he's not there, and the safe is empty. She goes to the marina and sees the boat has gone, with, she guesses, Paul and the consignment on board."

"To Bute?" asked Vunsells.

"Yes. Let's say Aino knows about Roxanne. Maybe she's seen letters from Roxanne at the flat, and found her email address. She wonders if Paul's double-crossing her, and is going to run off with Roxanne and the goods. So, pretending to be Paul, she emails Roxanne to put her off in case Paul has already arranged to meet her. Then she phones Paul, says she knows where he's going, maybe even threatens to kill Roxanne if Paul doesn't share the goods with her. That would still net him millions. He thinks that's OK, even fair, so agrees to meet her on Bute and split the goods. He tells her when he'll arrive, and she meets him on the boat, exuding charm. Maybe she even brings the bottle of wine, intending to drug and strangle him. But he's suspicious, wants to stick to business. So as soon as he turns his back to her, she comes up behind and cuts his throat. Then grabs the books and heads for the ferry."

"That's a pretty convincing story," commented Sergeant Morgan.

"But right now that's all it is. We need a lot more evidence. And the story may turn out to be altogether different. For instance, though the story includes Ishmael Balfour, we don't know what he's been doing since the robbery. And Drekhkov is still a bit of a mystery. He could easily be working for Balfour, and keeping an eye on the shop for him. If Balfour realised Aino had taken the consignment, he'd know also that she was still alive, that the body in the crater was not her. So what does he do then? And the biggest question is the present whereabouts of Aino Carselaw. If

Carselaw had the consignment in his boat, and she took it from him on Bute, her most obvious move would be to leave everyone in the lurch and clear off immediately for foreign parts."

"The obvious thing to do," said McCader, "would be to go straight to Glasgow Airport, and get a flight out, to Heathrow or Amsterdam, or anywhere she could get an onward flight to a bolt-hole far, far away. Then after a few months get the books discreetly onto the underground market, collect the money and vanish again, this time as a very rich woman."

"If that's what's happened," said Blue, "then we're too late. The bird has flown. So the first thing we need to find out is whether Aino has gone or is still here. Lena, can you go with Aelwyn to check the caravan sites? Just in case Aino is still there."

"Will do," replied Vunsells.

"Arvind's working on Aino's movements at the Bute end, but we need the bigger picture. Enver, can you send her picture to the airports, see if anyone can recognise it, especially on flights to or from Amsterdam, Heathrow or Estonia." McCader gave a thumbs-up.

"Thank you. OK, everyone," concluded Blue, "we've certainly moved on. We've a narrative that might not be completely right, but it gives us a direction for the investigation. Plus we now have a clear suspect for at least one crime. That's more than we had before. Let's meet again at four."

26

Just before eleven, Bhardwaj phoned. "Progress, chief. We've got Aino on the four o'clock boat from Wemyss Bay to Rothesay. Then we've a shot of her later at the bus stop opposite the pier, waiting for the bus that goes past the marina. Linda, sorry, PC Baird, is tracking down the driver of the bus, to give us a positive sighting and hopefully confirm that she got off at the marina. That would have got her there in good time, if the *Jolly Mermaid* didn't arrive till around six."

"Good work. What else have you got?"

"Thanks to Sergeant Launceston, we've got footage of her with other foot passengers coming up the covered section at Wemyss Bay pier, at 7.40pm. Then a few minutes later she's in the station car park getting into a metallic grey Toyota Yaris."

"Did you get the number?"

"Unfortunately she'd parked the car behind a stone column, so the camera couldn't pick it up. However. the sergeant's getting onto Traffic Division, to see if the cameras in Greenock or on the M8 have picked her up, even if we end up with several Yarises to chase up. The trouble is, we don't know whether she turned left or right out of the station car park, so instead of making for Greenock and the M8 she could have driven south towards Largs and Ardrossan and Ayr. But I'm sure we'll find her. What would you like me to do next?"

"Get over to Greenock and give Sergeant Launceston a hand. People always concentrate more when you're sitting next to them. As soon as you've got something, get back to me, and we'll start looking if it seems she came up this way. Take your stuff with you, in case you have to come straight back."

He emailed the description of the car to Vunsells and McCader, then got back to his report.

At twelve he went up to the workroom. Only McCader was there. "Sorry, boss, nothing to report so far. We really need to know what name she was using. I sent the images we have to the airports, but a name will make all the difference."

Blue took a break for lunch, buying a sandwich and coffee to take out at the café by the ferry terminal, and going up to Pulpit Hill. The weak sun had failed to take the frost off the trees, but the roads and paths had been gritted that morning, so he was able to get there safely, and the view made the effort worth it. Below him lay the white rooftops of the town; then the cold grey waters of the harbour, heavy and sullen, and Loch Linnhe beyond, and then the snow-clad hills of Mull in the distance. Even Kerrera, stretching away to his left, had a dusting of snow, lingering white on its central ridge. The cold air cleared his mind, and helped him relax.

He'd just finished his lunch when his phone rang. "Hi, chief, Lena here. Bingo!"

"OK, Lena, fire away."

"We're at a small site, on the shore of Loch Creran, before you get to the bridge at Dallachulish. Ten static caravans and six lodges. All available for hire. The owner, that's a Mr William Forster, remembers her. She turned up on the evening of Monday 28th November and asked if there were any caravans available for hire. November's not exactly a peak month, so in fact most of them were available. She booked for a fortnight, till the 12th December and paid in cash. She gave her name as Sarah Wainfleet, and an address in Southampton. And no, he didn't check her documents. He reckons she had a small grey car. He couldn't place her accent so he asked her about it. She said her mother was Danish. Mr Forster thought she spoke very carefully and formally. He asked her what she was doing up there, she said she had some work in the area. It was clear to him she wasn't going to say any more. He couldn't tell us anything about her movements; his office is at the back of the farm complex on the other side of the road, so he can't see what's happening at the caravans. He never saw her after that. Every time he checked the site – usually around two in the afternoon – her car wasn't there and there was no sign of life in the van. He suspected she was an estate agent working for people in England who wanted a second home in scenic Scotland, and she was off scouting out properties."

"That's very useful. She wasn't by any chance there?"

"No such luck. We asked if we could look inside her van, but he was reluctant, said it would be better if we got a warrant. Ms Wainfleet looked like she knew what she was doing and he didn't want to cause her any trouble, just in case she was a lawyer of some sort. He said we could look in the windows, but all the blinds were down, so that wasn't much use."

"I'm sure we can get a warrant tomorrow, and we'll search it then. Even if she's already skipped the country, there may be something left behind. Oh, did Mr Forster record her car registration?"

"Yes. At least he asked her what it was, and she gave him a number. He didn't check it with the car though, so she could have just made it up."

"We'll run it through the DVLA database just the same." Blue jotted down the number as Vunsells read it out.

"What do you want us to do now, chief? Should we put a watch on the place, in case she does come back? We could easily hire one of the other vans and keep hers under observation."

"I think that's a good idea. How are the caravans arranged?"

"In a rough semicircle following the line of the bay. They all have the main window facing the water. That means it would be quite easy to observe her caravan from any of the others."

"OK. Can you put Sergeant Morgan on the line?"

"The call's on speaker. She's just here."

"Hi Angus," came Morgan's Welsh lilt. "Shall I talk to Mr Forster? I know him, he'll be discreet. Don't worry, we won't get the one right next door to hers. Hers is at one edge of the semicircle, so I'll go for one further along. Lena and I can do it. Two women enjoying a few days in a caravan will look plausible, and one of us will always be awake."

"Lena, are you up for doing the surveillance?"

"Absolutely, chief!"

"Right. Once you've booked the caravan, and got the keys, get home and pick up some stuff for overnight. For a few days. Then come on here and we'll get you some binoculars and a couple of other useful bits and pieces. Then you can get back there. But come and see me before you go."

The pieces of the jigsaw were coming together.

Back in his office, he accessed the DVLA database, and typed in the registration number Aino had given the site owner. It came back as a green transit van owned by a firm of plumbers in Accrington. That didn't surprise him, but it was a disappointment. He emailed Bhardwaj and McCader to tell them about the caravan site. Then he filled in the Surveillance Request Form, and took it up to Superintendent Campbell's office. As he expected, the Super welcomed the interruption to his tedious administrative duties, offered Blue coffee, and asked for an update on the case.

"That's good," he commented, "you're clearly making progress. Identifying Aino Carselaw has turned the case on its head, but also made the whole thing more intelligible. Yes, by all means do the surveillance. It wouldn't surprise me if she's already flown the coop and is sunning herself in some distant part of the world. But you never know. If you've got the form there, I'll sign it. Do you think Vunsells is OK for it?"

"I think so. She's intelligent and sensible; I don't think she'll do anything daft. But I'll have a word with her before she goes."

"Good, good. It'll be useful experience for her. Do keep me updated."

At twenty past two Morgan and Vunsells reported back. Morgan was wearing dark green jogging pants, a brown fleece and black Barbour jacket, and carried a holdall. Vunsells had changed into jeans and a purple waterproof jacket over a red jumper, and had a rucksack on her back.

"You two look just the part!" said Blue. "Now, here's a list of a few items you'll need. Binoculars, digital recorder and long range mike, powerful torch, night vision goggles, etc. Get down to stores and they'll give you them. You'll have to sign for them and give the case number and me as CIO. Then get a car and head over to the caravan."

"Do we get firearms?" asked Vunsells. "In case things turn nasty."

"No, I'm afraid not. This is surveillance only, so do *not* get involved in anything you might see. Call me immediately if anything happens. If you witness anything that requires emergency services, call them first."

"Should we just lurk in the caravan all the time?"

"You don't have to be in it all the time, but don't leave the site. You can potter about, hang the odd clothing item over the balustrade round the decking, even put out a chair there and read a book. Have coffee and chat. If it's sunny, that is, otherwise it may look suspicious. Set up a surveillance log on your PDAs and whoever's awake can put an update in approximately every half hour."

"What do we do during the night?"

"It'll look odd if your lights are on all night, so turn them off sometime between eleven and midnight. But keep observing her caravan regularly, even if it looks like there's no-one there. You can station yourself in a chair in a window, but walk around regularly, to keep awake. I can assure you that it will get very boring."

"What if something happens?"

"As I said, phone me immediately and report it. Don't make any attempt to intervene in anything unless I give you a specific order to do so. If any intervention is needed, I'll send people, and you wait for them to arrive. Oh, and on your way over there don't forget to stop at a shop and get yourselves something to eat and drink. Remember to keep the receipts. OK, anything else?"

"I don't think so," said Morgan. She pulled two keys on a ring from her pocket. "Two keys for the caravan door." She took one off the ring and handed it to Vunsells. "Mr Forster has spares in case something happens to us. We'll get off then. See you later."

"Good luck," said Blue. "I'll be in touch sometime tomorrow if nothing happens overnight."

At ten to three the next call came. Bhardwaj. "Results, chief! The cameras caught five Yarises on the M8 between Greenock and the Erskine Bridge in the hour after the ferry got in to Wemyss Bay. We ran them all through DVLA and got what looked like a hit. One of them was owned by a car rental operation in Paisley."

"At Glasgow Airport?"

"No. In the town. Small place behind a garage. 'Ron's Rentals.' Sergeant Launceston reckons, if that was the one she was driving, she'd have got a bus from the airport into Paisley then rented the car there. So that if we approached the airport rental desks, they wouldn't know her."

"That sounds plausible. What did Ron have to say?"

"We've just come out of his place now. He claimed to be very forgetful, and couldn't remember any woman coming in to rent a car, but Sergeant Launceston had a few words with him and his memory came back. He even remembered where he kept his records. And he IDed Aino's picture. He has photos of her passport and driving licence. I'll email them right away."

"So what name is she using?"

"Anneka Ländemann. Finnish passport and driving licence.

Address in Turku, Finland."

"Excellent. Can you put the sergeant on the line?"

After a pause, the sergeant's slow drawl greeted Blue. "Good afternoon, inspector. I hope that the information the lad and I have got is useful."

"Very much so. Tell me, did Ron give any further information about her?"

"Yes, sir, he did. Said she seemed very smart and well-organised. Dressed like she was the boss of some company, everything the best. Hair, makeup, everything just right. He wondered why she'd come to him. She said he'd been recommended. She took the car on a flexible contract, basically for as long as she needed it. He asked her where she was going, but she just said she had various places to visit. She was anxious to get moving and avoided any chitchat. Jumped in the car as soon as she could and was off. Ron asked her if she needed directions anywhere, being from overseas, like. She said no, that was what the SatNav was for. Ron likes to think he's helpful, especially to a woman, so he was a wee bit miffed by that."

"How did she pay?"

"Cash. Ron thought that rather unusual, especially for someone from abroad. They'd usually use a debit card. On the other hand, he'd been done once by someone with a fake card, so he was quite happy with cash. She didn't look the sort who'd robbed a bank, he said. But Ron isn't one who'll ask too many questions. Better not to have the answers, eh?"

"You've encountered him before?"

"Oh yes. Nothing particularly bad. Little things, but they point to an attitude, don't they, those little things. And sometimes they can lead on to bigger things. We keep a friendly eye on him."

"Many thanks for your help, sergeant."

"Well, you're no rid of me yet. We'll get back to the station and get our traffic pals to find this car on the traffic cameras. We should be able to tell you at least whether she crossed the Erskine Bridge. I'll get the laddie to phone you as soon as we have something useful."

Blue called McCader and gave him the name Aino now seemed to be using.

"Thanks, chief. That's very useful. Interesting that she didn't use that ID at the caravan site. But it makes sense. No obvious connections that can be traced. However, unless she's got another fake passport, she'll have to use that one when she's travelling."

And indeed, at half past three, McCader phoned back. "Hi chief. We've got her! Arrived from Amsterdam on Monday 28th November, at 15.23. Used that Finnish passport. No return journey booked, or onward one to somewhere else, not with KLM anyway. I'll check with the others too."

"Excellent. Yes, do that. I'll cancel the four o'clock meeting, since Lena and Aelwyn are doing surveillance and Arvind's still down in Greenock. Let's make it nine tomorrow morning. But let me know as soon as you have anything else."

At half past four, Bhardwaj called again. "Some news from traffic. They've got her coming off the Erskine Bridge and heading north, then at Tyndrum, then Cruachan, and crossing the Connel Bridge, still heading north. But no sign of her at Ballachulish."

"Thanks, Arvind. Looks like she was heading for the caravan site. What are you doing now?"

"Nothing. I was going to ask you what I should do next."

"You've got your stuff with you, haven't you?"

"Yes."

"Good. I think you should get back up here now. Inspector Watts will finish things off on Bute, and DS Launceston will help if we need more information at that end. We now know she came up here after killing Carselaw, so this is where we need to focus our efforts. Can you do that?"

"No problemo, boss. I'm sure Sergeant Launceston will get me to the bus or train station, and I'll take it from there."

"Great. Go for it. Let me know how you're getting on."

McCader had come into Blue's office as he was speaking and waited till he'd ended the call to Bhardwaj. "Something else's come up, chief. One of my contacts at the airport got back to say that Anneka Ländemann is booked on a flight to Dublin on Saturday morning. Clever move; from there she can double back to Europe or, if she prefers, head west across the Atlantic."

"Saturday. That suggests she's still around here somewhere, but she thinks she'll be finished by then. Thanks, Enver, I'll tell Lena to be alert tonight, in case Aino turns up at the caravan."

"There's something else. The KLM desk also got in touch. Kalev Lind arrived at Glasgow Airport this afternoon at 15.23."

"Now that is interesting. Did he get a vehicle?"

"I called the airport car rental desks. He hired a car there, I've got the make and number. A Lexus. He likes travelling in style. His flight was business class too. I've contacted Traffic Division to see if we can track him. I don't see him staying in a caravan, so I'll check the hotels and see if he's booked in anywhere."

"Good work. Things are moving. What if we're right about there being a valuable consignment of books? We're assuming Carselaw had them on the boat, and Aino took them. But remember the pictures from the boat. Aino's just carrying her coffee and sandwich. If it were me, and I had a package worth millions, I wouldn't leave it on my seat on the boat to get a cup of coffee. I'd take it with me, in a rucksack, so that it wasn't out of my sight. I don't think Aino would be that careless as to leave the stuff unattended."

"Unless she didn't have it."

"Exactly. So what if Paul Carselaw tells Aino he'll have the stuff on the boat? Then, when she arrives, he reveals that he doesn't have it with him. Maybe he says it's in the safe under the railway layout. So she kills him and heads back up here to get it. It's the only convincing reason I can think of for her to come back. Plus, if she's just got hold of a few millions' worth of books, the obvious thing to do is clear off right away. But she doesn't do that. *Ergo*, she doesn't have the books."

"But we searched the flat, and they weren't there. The safe was empty."

"Tell me, Enver, how did you leave the place?"

"Just like we found it."

"The safe?"

"Locked and the bookshelves fitted back in front of it."

"We should check the flat again. What if she's been back there, to get the stuff?"

"But it's not there."

"We know that. But I'm not sure she does."

"So she may have gone there after we'd been through the place?"

"That's what I'm suggesting."

"OK, boss, I'll go over there now, and check it out. I can remember exactly how we left it. I'll call you from there."

27

Blue had not heard from Elsa Maarksen. He wasn't sure what to make of her. Was her suggestion of a consignment just a theory, or did she already know it existed? He called her mobile. There was no response, not even an invitation to leave a voicemail. Wherever she was, she wasn't letting on. Or was he getting paranoid? In a case involving so many dodgy characters, it was tempting to assume they were all like that. She could just be driving, or following up an enquiry concerning Ishmael Balfour, or some other business altogether which was not relevant to his case. Nevertheless, she'd said she was going to find Balfour, and Blue didn't think Balfour was the sort of person who dashed hither and thither all day throwing off pursuers.

He called the Queen Adelaide Hotel and asked for Mr Balfour. The female voice on the line, who identified herself as Natasha, would only say that Mr Balfour was not available at present. He didn't blame her – he could after all be anybody. He'd have to go round there himself.

He was just passing the Corran Halls when McCader phoned. "You were right, chief. The flat has been done over, by somebody looking for something. The safe's wide open – looks like he gave her the correct combination. Or she got it off him after he was dead, if he had it written down. But she – if it was her – has turned over everything: cupboards, drawers and wardrobes emptied, washing machine, dishwasher, and freezer left open, contents of the freezer all over the floor. That suggests the safe was empty, and she's had to look elsewhere."

"Right. Call in the SOC team and some uniforms to search for some sign of who was there. We mustn't assume it was her. Any sign of breaking-in, by the way?"

"No. Looks like whoever was there has a key. Or has acquired one."

"OK Enver. I'm heading to the Queen Adelaide Hotel. Once the people arrive there, can you get over here? If Balfour's in, it would be better if we both spoke to him."

The Queen Adelaide Hotel was further along the north side of the bay from the Corran Halls, past the catholic cathedral. It had been built in the 1880s by a wealthy brewer from Glasgow, who sent his family up there every summer whilst he got on with making money. It was built in the best gothic style, with a square tower at each end of the frontage, and an elaborate porch in the centre, complete with rainwater spouts disguised as gargoyles. A cluster of tall stone chimneys sprouted from the centre of a complex cluster of dormered roofs. The place must cost a bomb to maintain, thought Blue. Maybe that was why it was one of the most expensive hotels in town.

The foyer was panelled in dark oak, and smelled of wax polish. The carpets were thick and soundless. At the rear stood the reception counter, also of dark wood, and behind it a young woman sat frowning, focussed on, he presumed, a laptop below the level of the counter.

She looked up as he approached. She was tall, with long blonde hair, not its natural colour, he guessed, and a pale, almost pasty, complexion. And glasses with black plastic frames, which gave her a faux academic look, although when he looked at her eyes he realised they couldn't be very strong. Perhaps for reading, or just for effect.

"Good afternoon, sir," she said, with a marked Slavic accent. "How may I help you?" Her tone suggested helping wasn't her priority right now. Blue suspected he didn't look like the sort of person who would want to take a room there.

"Good afternoon, Natasha." He recognised the voice of the woman he had spoken to on the phone. She looked surprised, her mouth slightly open. "I spoke to you earlier on the phone. Detective Inspector Blue, Oban CID. Here is my identification."

Now Natasha looked wary. "What do you wish, inspector?" she asked politely.

"Just to ask you a few questions, mainly concerning Mr Balfour."

"It is not the policy of the management to give any information concerning our clients to third parties. I am sorry I cannot help you."

"I appreciate the management and your clients' preference for discretion, Natasha, but I am investigating a murder and I do need to ask you some questions."

A door behind her opened and another, older, woman entered: shorter and bulkier, but solid-looking, with hair dyed a dark red, almost black. Blue guessed Natasha had pressed a button behind the counter to summon assistance. "I am the manager. Do you have a problem?" No 'sir' this time, and the voice was outrightly hostile.

Blue identified himself again. "And may I ask your name?"

"My name is Ivana."

"And your surname?" Blue now had his notebook out.

"Volodnikova. Ivana Volodnikova."

"I am investigating a murder, Ms Volodnikova. I must ask some questions about one of your guests, Mr Ishmael Balfour. I hope you and your staff will co-operate with our inquiry. It would be unfortunate if we thought you were not doing so."

"It is our policy not to ask questions of our clients, nor to observe their coming and going. Discretion is at the heart of the Queen Adelaide experience," said the manager, as if repeating a memorised mantra.

At this point the main door behind Blue opened, and he turned to see McCader come in. "Hi, chief. How can I help?"

"Could you persuade Ivana and Natasha here to be a bit more co-operative?"

"No problem." Without speaking McCader took out his ID and showed it to the two women. Then he smiled and began talking rapidly in what Blue assumed was Russian. Whatever he was carefully explaining was clearly enough to thoroughly frighten the two women. Perhaps McCader knew how to sound like the KGB. Or maybe he was just wondering about their visa status.

Ivana turned to Blue. "I am so sorry, *Kommissar*, we did not understand the importance of your visit. Of course we will be most happy to answer any questions you may have."

Blue nodded to McCader, then turned back to the two women. "Thank you. That is most helpful. Perhaps you could first tell me, is Mr Balfour a regular guest here?"

"Yes," said Ivana. "He comes here at least two times each year. He always stays in this hotel. Our guests are most loyal, and always return. They appreciate the privacy."

"And does he always come on his own, or with a wife or other partner?"

"He comes always alone. But there is with him usually a driver or assistant. A Slovak." She said the words as if referring to some unpleasant insect. "His name is Andreij. He does not stay here, but in some lesser lodging. I do not know which one."

"Does Mr Balfour always have the same room?"

"Yes. We try always to give our clients a preferred room. His is the tower room on the right." She gestured to her right, Blue's left as he faced her. "It is very superior room. Extra king size bed with four posts. Armchairs and coffee table. Minibar and safe."

"Is Mr Balfour out at the moment?"

Ivana looked at Natasha and nodded. "Yes," said Natasha.

"Do you know where he's gone?"

"No."

"Or with whom?"

Again Ivana nodded. "A woman," said Natasha. "I don't know her name. Average height, dark hair. I don't think she is Scottish, or even English."

"Did the woman call for him?"

"She came this morning, about ten thirty. She did not give a name, but said she was expected by Mr Balfour. I called Mr Balfour's room to say a woman awaited him. He told me to tell her to wait. She waited about fifteen minutes, looking at her phone. Then Mr Balfour came, and they went out."

"Did they say anything to each other when he came down?"

"He said, 'I'm so glad to see you again, my dear.' She shook his hand, as if she was a business associate, not a lover. Then they went out. I do not know where they were going."

Blue took out his phone, selected one of the CCTV pictures of Aino Carselaw, and showed it to her. "Was this the woman?"

Natasha peered closely at the picture. "Yes. I would say it is her."

"Thank you, Natasha, that was very helpful. Now we would like to look at Mr Balfour's room."

"That is forbidden!" said Ivana. "It is our policy that ..."

McCader laid his hand on her arm and said a few quiet words.

She paled, and nodded. "Yes, on this occasion, I think it will be permitted."

"Just give us the room number," said Blue. "We'll find our own way."

"Just one other thing," added McCader, in English. "If Mr Balfour does come back while we're there, do phone up and let us know."

The room was spacious and gave a feeling of luxury, from the huge four-poster bed, through the richly-textured wallpaper to the heavy drapes framing the window, with its view over the lights of the town, the black lustrous water of the harbour, and the dark bulk of Kerrera, like some gigantic sea creature lying at rest off the shore. By the window were two well upholstered armchairs flanking a dark wood coffee table. On another table by the entrance to the ensuite were tea and coffee-making facilities, and below the table an array of drinks in a glass-fronted minibar.

By the wardrobe stood two black, wheeled travel cases. Opening the wardrobe revealed an array of clothing, and a small safe, big enough to hold a passport and a wad of notes but not much else. Certainly not a selection of rare books. Against the wall opposite the bed stood a desk and chair, again of dark wood. But no revealing papers lay there, nor in the desk drawer.

"He's no fool, is he, boss?" remarked McCader. "Nothing very informative lying about."

"It looks like he's gone out with Aino, doesn't it?"

"It does, chief. But where? And what are they up to?"

"She could be doing a deal with him, to get him off her back. Or maybe he has managed to find the consignment. Perhaps it was his agents who searched the flat."

"Or she's simply going to kill him."

"Yes, that's a possibility too. Let's go."

But before Blue could go anywhere, his phone rang.

"Hi, Angus. Elsa Maarksen here. Sorry I wasn't in touch earlier. This morning Mr Balfour phoned me. He remembered from when he bought the property, that there was mention of a basement below the shop, from a previous building, which had then been sealed. He thought Aino may have found a way into it, and stashed some books down there. He asked me to go to Edinburgh, to the Register Office, to look at the documents recording the original building of the tenements and shops, in the late 1800s. In fact, there is a basement, but it's under the shop next door, which has been empty for a while. I'm on the train now, on my way back."

As he listened, Blue looked out of the window. The setting sun was colouring the sky a fiery red, with some of the clouds glowing orange and other, heavier ones a dull purple.

"Thanks for letting me know. Did Mr Balfour tell you what he was going to do today?"

"No. Why?"

"Looks like he met up with Aino Carselaw this morning."

"What! She is alive? And here?"

"So it seems. I'm sorry to be blunt, but were you aware of that?"
"No, not at all. She was not killed then?"
"No. She is not the dead woman in Estonia. Any idea where he might have gone with her?"
"Hmm. Ishmael Balfour is no fool. It would be a place he knows. Preferably very public and top quality. And he would always have his henchman Andreij with him. He is ex-Czech Special Forces, and always armed. But of course, nothing can be guaranteed one hundred percent."
"Thanks. Oh, by the way, do you have his mobile number?"
"Why not simply ask me?" The voice was behind him. He turned quickly to see Ishmael Balfour standing in the doorway.

28

On Balfour's right stood another man, like McCader, not particularly tall nor well-built, but clearly very fit. However, his key feature was the automatic pointed at McCader, who stood in the corner of the room with his hands up. He jerked the pistol towards Blue. "Turn the phone off! Put it on the table. Then put your hands up!"

Blue complied.

Balfour smiled benignly as he quietly closed the door behind him. "Well now, inspector, this is a surprise. I'm just thinking of having a chat with you, and here you are, waiting for me. How considerate. Oh, by the way, I assume you have a warrant to search my room."

"It was my idea," said McCader. "The inspector came up to see where I was."

"Ah," smiled Balfour. "The ever-loyal subordinate. How touching. But really, Mr Blue, I don't mind at all. Or let me rephrase that; I'd have preferred to conduct you round the room myself, so that you might appreciate its style and comfort. You'll appreciate that I spend many nights away from my home, and I do find it important, even essential, to have an environment which allows one to work, relax and sleep without distraction or interruption. I give you one example: the walls of the bedrooms here are clad with acoustic panels, and even this wallpaper is sound-resistant. It means that no noise will come to this room from its neighbours, and no noise from here will be heard elsewhere. Even a gunshot or two would go completely unnoticed."

"You would be very unwise to shoot us," said Blue calmly. "My colleagues know where we are."

"My dear inspector, I have no intention of shooting you, or your sergeant here. I would indeed commend his loyalty to you. Oh, and I should introduce Andreij here. He is loyal to me, and I value his services. But I think it's now time to dispense with the weaponry. As I said, it's time we had a little chat. Believe me, I have great respect for your knowledge and intellect, inspector, and do therefore enjoy our conversations." He said a few words to Andreij, who put his gun away.

"Threatening citizens with a weapon is a serious crime here," said Blue.

"Didn't I mention that it's only a replica? A very good one, but it only fires a little ball of resin, powered by compressed air. Not enough to kill anyone. Well, no, let me correct that; if Andreij were to put the barrel into your nostril and fire, the ball would penetrate the brain, and undoubtedly cause some damage. It might even be fatal. To my knowledge he has not tried that yet. However, now we're wasting time which could be better occupied. Please take a seat on one of the armchairs by the window, and I'll join you once I've hung up my coat and removed my shoes. But I would wish our talk to be private, therefore I suggest that our subordinates go to the hotel bar and reminisce about their various military pasts. At my expense, of course."

"I'm afraid Sergeant McCader needs to be here to witness our conversation."

"I'm sorry, inspector, but our conversation will be private. A chat between old friends."

"I could invite you to the police station."

"That's true. I would, of course, attend, along with my lawyer. But I fear that then you would discover that my memory can be so bad. This way you will learn a lot more. You will not be able to attribute it to me, but it will certainly be most useful to your investigation. I'm at your disposal."

Andreij waved McCader towards the door. "Come on, buddy. To the bar. We drink to old times!"

McCader glanced at Blue, who nodded briefly, then followed the other man out, closing the door behind him.

As Balfour, now wearing slippers, lowered himself into the other armchair there was a knock at the door. "Room service!" called a voice, which Blue recognised as Natasha's.

"Come in!" called Balfour, and Natasha came in, bearing a tray. She placed at each end of the coffee table between the armchairs an empty shot glass. She smiled at Blue as she put his down, apologetically he thought. Finally she placed a bottle in the middle of the coffee table. It was of dark brown glass, so Blue could not see how full it was.

"Thank you, Natasha," said Balfour, and as the girl left, he turned back to Blue. "That's one of the nice things about this hotel. You don't have to lock your room. There is total security. Except of course when the officers of the law are here. Well, now, enough of that. I notice you were talking to Ms Maarksen on the telephone when we arrived. Tell me, what has she to report?"

Blue hesitated.

"Please, inspector, do not think me simple, or uninformed. Naturally I am aware that Ms Maarksen would be in touch with you. I make it my business to check out fully anyone who works for me, in any capacity. I can even tell you plenty about Natasha, and about Ivana. Did you know that she, Ivana, that is, formerly worked in the Russian Prison Service? How Mr Subanaram, who owns the hotel, manages to get visas for the Russians he employs here, I don't know. Perhaps he doesn't. Anyway, that's not what we're here to talk about. Ms Maarksen's report, please."

"In a moment," replied Blue. "What's the drink?"

"Ah! I'm so glad you asked. A favourite of my own, a herbal liqueur from Slovakia, with hints too of almond and apricot. But we're off the point again. Ms Maarksen. I sent her to Edinburgh to look at the plans for the shop building to see if there were a basement. Did she find it?"

"She reports that there is, but that it's under the shop next door. Was that simply to get her out of the way while you met with Aino Carselaw?"

"Yes and no. Yes, I needed her somewhere else. But this line also needed to be investigated. Two birds with one stone, you might say."

"Quite. Now, why don't you tell me about your meeting with Mrs Carselaw."

"Ah yes. You quizzed the lovely Natasha, and the not-so-lovely Ivana. Let me guess, perhaps you offered them free trips to some place they'd rather not be if they didn't co-operate."

"Now it's you who're drifting from the point," Blue reminded him.

"*Touché, inspector. I do enjoy chatting with you. But I've nothing to hide, despite what my detractors might say.*"

"Would that include Mr Lind?"

"Ah! I do believe that gentleman has been in touch with you. No doubt to deflect interest from himself by accusing me of all sorts of illegal activities. But I ask you, sir, did he offer any proof? Or merely a generous casting of mud, in the hope that some of it will stick."

"I'm afraid I can't comment on what Mr Lind may or may not have said."

"Let me simply say, before I return to the subject of Mrs Carselaw, that my researches have included Mr Lind. Perhaps you'd like to hear what I found out."

"Only if what you tell me is based on sound evidence."

"You're a man after my own heart, Mr Blue, indeed you are. I often think I would have made an excellent detective. But I suspect that a lot of what I would be asked to do would turn out to be not in the least interesting. And the emolument would be far below what I am worth. Still, where was I? Ah yes, Mr Lind. You may wish to know that he once worked for the KGB. I see you raise your eyebrows. Yes, indeed, even before he left the University of Tartu – a most prestigious establishment – he was recruited by them. I have copies of files from the archives in Moscow. He managed a number of agents. One of them was his wife, formerly known as Aino Kuusk. It would not be unreasonable to imagine that her marriage to Mr Carselaw was part of a strategy to obtain information on the design of British naval vessels. Of course, things changed after the demise of the Soviet Union. Under the FSB his role diminished – perhaps non-Russians were regarded as not completely trustworthy – and after a few years he was released from their service.

"Well now, former spies do not look for honest work, and Mr Lind is no exception. He became involved in the smuggling of valuable items out of the former Soviet states – including Russia itself – for sale in the west. I mean of course artworks and other precious objects. Mrs Carselaw was very likely also involved in this trade; her frequent trips to Estonia lend circumstantial support to that conjecture. So you will understand that when I talk of Mrs Carselaw's actions, I am confident that Mr Lind is somewhere in the background.

"And so to the lady herself. As I told you during an earlier conversation, after going into business with her, I discovered that she was also operating a little undercover bookselling of her own. I turned a blind eye at first, whilst my investigations continued. However, before I had made a decision on what to do about it, she approached me with a proposition. She had, she claimed, arranged the purchase of three volumes from a university library in Belarus, which had no further use for them, and needed funds which could be used to develop the institution. The only problem was that the government of that country might not take kindly to the sale."

"What were these volumes?"

"One of them is a handwritten illuminated mediaeval manuscript, bound into a codex. An eleventh century text of the New Testament in Latin, produced by monks at or near Gniezno. That city was once the capital of Poland. The other two are what we in the business call incunabula."

"Books published before AD 1500."

"Ah! You're well-informed. That's what I like about you, inspector, you research your cases as fully as any academic. Indeed, I suspect you would be most successful in an academic career."

"Let's stay focussed. The incunabula?"

"Of course. They were added to the deal to make up a bundle. One is a text of the Pentateuch, in Hebrew and Polish, the other a history of the Teutonic Knights."

"How much do you believe they're worth?"

"Ah. Well, inspector, I'll be honest with you. I don't know. This trio of volumes would fetch a very large sum, a very large sum indeed, even in the rather private market which the manner of their acquisition would necessitate. My investment was nearly a million pounds. Perhaps another half a million was added by Mrs Carselaw, or perhaps Mr Lind. But how much would they fetch? Many times more than that, I can assure you. The Codex alone would be worth many millions of dollars. The other two could fetch a million each from the right purchaser."

"How did you acquire the bundle so cheaply then?"

"In deepest Belarus people, especially in libraries and museums, have little perception of the true value of what they hold. And a million dollars sounds to them like a sum from their wildest dreams. For this amount in Belarus you can obtain almost anything. A house, a car, women, servants, possessions. A man with such wealth could even think of moving to the West. Where such a modest fortune would disappear very quickly!"

"And she came to you because she couldn't fund the whole deal herself?"

"So she told me. Given Mr Lind's worth, I was sceptical. But she assured me she had no connection with Mr Lind, and the sale was entirely of her own devising, through a middleman in Belarus whom she was unwilling to name. You may suspect – it is of course your job to suspect – that my motives in agreeing to help her were entirely mercenary."

"The thought did cross my mind."

"However, it was the provenance of the volumes that persuaded me to become involved in what might be regarded as a shady deal. You see, during World War Two these books had been looted by the German occupiers of Poland from the library of the University of Kraków. They were then sent to Königsberg in East Prussia. In 1945 the Soviets captured the city. As usual with captured cities, Königsberg was expertly looted, and anything of monetary, economic or cultural value sent back to the Soviet Union. These three volumes ended up in an obscure university in Belarus, where they remained ever since. So you see, in facilitating the transfer of these volumes out of Belarus, I would be in effect liberating them. And it would please me greatly were they to be purchased by an institution in Poland, so that they may return to their origins."

"How do you know all this?"

"I demanded descriptions of the books from Mrs Carselaw, and then hired my own investigators to confirm those details and add whatever else they could find out. And I would like them to go to an owner who would respect them and study them, not leave them in a safe or a basement. Things of cultural value should be owned by the world, don't you think, so that we may all have access to them. Not always achievable in practice, I admit, but nevertheless, an ideal to be held in our hearts."

"So you agreed to the deal with Mrs Carselaw. What happened next?"

"I made the money available to Mrs Carselaw, and the books were duly smuggled out of Belarus into Lithuania, and thence to Estonia, from where they were transferred here to Scotland."

"How did that happen?"

"That was not my business, inspector, and Mrs Carselaw would certainly not have revealed that aspect of the transaction to me, even if I had asked."

"So the books arrived here?"

"Yes, around the beginning of November. It was the Sunday before she set off for Estonia when Mrs Carselaw showed them to me. Beautiful pieces, inspector, each one an exquisite work of art. I think a man of your undoubted intellectual capacity would find them as fascinating as I do. Anyway, to cut a long story short, the volumes were placed in the safe at the shop, until they could be moved to a more secure place. To protect them from environmental contamination, they were in a sealed archive box. Mrs Carselaw told me that whilst in Estonia she would explore the possibility of purchasers in Poland, and what price they might offer. When she returned, the plan was that we would then, if necessary, open the sale to a wider range of potential purchasers."

"When did you discover the books had been moved?"

"Only after Mrs Carselaw had disappeared and you asked me to open the safe."

"Why didn't you look at the books again? Even to check they were still there. You must have longed to look through them again."

"Ah, how perceptive you are, inspector. Indeed, the temptation was great. But I resisted. Partly because I am a very busy man, and had much else to do in other places. And partly because I knew that if I began to look at them, I would become addicted. I would want to see them again and again, and in the end I would be unwilling to sell them. I might then have taken them from the safe and spirited them back to Slovakia. And then, of course, Aino and Lind would come after me."

"You thought they might be dangerous?"

"Oh yes. I recognised very quickly the ruthlessness that is in Aino. It was obvious to me that her marriage to Carselaw was a sham, on her part at least."

"When do you think the books were moved?"

"It must have been before Mrs Carselaw left for Estonia. Not long after she showed them to me."

"You think she moved them?"

"Who else? Only she and I had the combination for the safe. To my knowledge, that is. Although she could have shared hers with a third party."

"Her husband?"

"Not impossible, but unlikely. As far as I know, she despised him. And I must confess that on that point I do not disagree with her. A pathetic creature."

"So who were you thinking of?"

"Her former husband, Lind. He is her partner in this business. But he was in Estonia at the time, I believe. And she had, as you policemen would say, the motive."

"Which was?"

"Why, isn't it obvious, Mr Blue? To defraud me, of course. Our arrangement was that I would put up a sum to enable the purchase of the books, and I should then receive a substantial proportion of the price which they would later raise. My suspicion is that she intended to abscond with the books and sell them purely for the benefit of Lind and herself."

"So when you opened the safe, you realised that she was not dead?"

"Not quite. I cannot deny that the thought did occur to me. It was possible that she'd removed the books and taken them to Estonia, and been killed there, perhaps by thieves who took them. But I suspected that she was too careful for that to happen. Thus it came as no surprise that the body in the lake was not her. It was the break-in to the shop that convinced me. No-one else had any motive for that. It told me not only that she was still alive, but that she had not taken the books with her to Estonia. She had come back for one thing only, to recover those books."

"So why didn't she take them with her to Estonia?"

"I confess to you, inspector, that I do not know. I can only conjecture that she wished to return under another identity to pick up the books. Perhaps she thought I would not realise it was her and would continue to search here for the books under the belief that she was dead and they remained hidden where she had put them."

"What about the body we found in the flat above the shop? Was he working for you?"

"I'm sorry. I know nothing about him. Ms Maarksen tells me he was a Russian."

"Who do you think employed him?"

"He may have been the courier who brought the books. Or someone sent later by Lind to check that the books had been received. Perhaps, after helping to fake his wife's death and, I presume, assisting her in creating a new identity, he became concerned that she would no longer co-operate with him. Indeed, perhaps that's why she left the books behind. Maybe she told him they hadn't arrived yet, and he sent this man over to check."

"Did you let him into the flat, or give him a key?"

"Most certainly not."

"How do you think he got into the flat then? We found no evidence of the lock being forced or any sign of him having broken in."

"A most relevant question, if I may say so. Perhaps Mr Lind sent the man after Mrs Carselaw had left Estonia in her new guise. Let us say she was already in Oban when he arrived. She met up with him, and invited him to use the flat. Then killed him as soon as she had the opportunity. Then caused havoc in the shop and took a selection of books to throw us off the scent. Quite a clever stroke. I assumed she had then recovered the consignment from wherever it was hidden and made off, either back to Estonia, or to somewhere else where she would meet up again with Lind. You can imagine my surprise when she contacted me this morning."

"Tell me about that."

"As I said, I thought she'd be in Tallinn, or maybe California, by now. She phoned at six minutes past nine, whilst I was still enjoying my breakfast. The first meal of the day is so important, you know, in all sorts of ways. It's crucial not to rush it, to set the body's pace for the day, so you may imagine that I was somewhat irritated to receive a call just then. My irritation was soon superseded by surprise. She told me she was in Oban and wanted to meet as soon as possible, in connection with the books. Of course, I was wary about meeting her. Former KGB agents don't forget how to kill people. I suggested that she come round to my hotel, and I would take her to a suitably discreet establishment for a discussion and some lunch. I didn't tell her where, until she got into the car."

"She accepted the arrangement, then?"

"Yes. She clearly wanted to reassure me, by putting herself under my protection, as it were."

"So where did you go?"

"The Ardchattan Castle Spa Hotel. Do you know it?"

"I'm afraid not. I would guess it's the other side of Loch Etive, near the priory somewhere."

"Quite correct, sir. A very discreet five-star establishment, rather off the beaten track. I've stayed there myself when I've needed some peace and quiet. The cuisine is of the finest quality, I can assure you, and privacy is guaranteed."

"And what did she want to tell you?"

"She said someone had stolen the books and hidden them. She

actually suggested it might have been me! Of course, I put her straight on that one. Why should I hide the books? I want them returned, for a reasonable consideration, to the sort of institution from which they came."

"You mean a monastery or a synagogue?"

"Ha! You jest, sir. She suggested as the thief the Russian, Drekhkov, I believe, is his name, whom she alleged was in my employ. I made it clear he was nothing to do with me. She then claimed it might be Mr Carselaw. I found that very strange, as I didn't credit him with a great deal of imagination. We came back to the Russian. At this point I told her I believed she had killed the man and that I thought she knew exactly who he was and what he wanted. I'm afraid I cannot stand persons who think I am stupid enough to believe the simplest lies."

"You prefer complicated ones?"

"Honesty is always the best policy, sir, always!"

"I'm sorry. Do continue."

"Yes, she admitted, she had killed the man. Her story was that he was one of the couriers who had transferred the consignment, and they now wanted more money than had originally been agreed. He had removed the consignment from the safe and hidden it. Naturally, he refused to say where. She had no intention of paying more money, so she had to kill him. She reasoned that, as he had not been there long, and did not know Oban, he must have hidden the books in the shop or the flat above. She searched both but found nothing. But she recalled that when she first moved into the shop, she had a conversation with the lady who ran the other shop. This lady, whose name I don't recall, had told Mrs Carselaw there were cellars under both shops. She had checked her own shop but couldn't find any sign of a cellar. Now, remembering that, she thought I might know about the cellar. I couldn't recall anything about a cellar when I bought the shop. However, I despatched Ms Maarksen to Edinburgh to check out the details of the cellars. She phoned me this afternoon, not long before she phoned you. She told me just what she told you. Keeping both sides satisfied, eh?"

"Quite so. What happens now, then?"

"We've agreed to meet at the bookshop this evening at ten o'clock. I will let Mrs Carselaw into the other shop – as far as I know, I'm the only person with a key to those premises – and we'll search for the entrance to the cellar. So if you want to pounce, inspector, then is your opportunity."

"Do you believe Mrs Carselaw's story?"

"I have grave doubts, inspector. The lady is a practised liar. It has been her profession, you might say. It's possible this rendezvous is simply a means of enticing me to a spot where I can be killed, just like Mr Drekhkov. That's why Andreij will be there to protect me. He is very competent."

"What happens when you find the consignment?"

"Since neither of us now trusts the other, we agreed to a compromise. We will divide the books between us. I will take custody of the codex, since my investment is the greater. She will take the other two. She would arrange the sale, and give me my share of the price, at which point I would release the codex to her."

"Wouldn't she suspect you'd sell the codex yourself?"

"I believe she recognises that I am a man of my word. But there is also the fact that if I betrayed her, she could report me to the authorities. I am a public figure with a reputation to maintain. Unlike Mrs Carselaw, who, with her new identity, could disappear with all three books and never be heard of again. This is why I suspect some trickery this evening."

"Is this why Mrs Carselaw went to the trouble of finding a substitute to die for her and then taking up a new identity? To pull off this deal?"

"I asked her that myself. She said that she wished, once this business was over, to leave both Scotland and Estonia far behind, and carry on her life without anyone coming after her. A very clever plan, if I may say so."

"That suggests to me that she was planning to double-cross the people who sold her the books. And maybe you too. And maybe even Lind, if he's in this with her."

"A sound conclusion. And one that I myself also reached. We do think so very much alike, Mr Blue. You may understand then why I feel it appropriate to report these matters to the authorities."

"I appreciate your doing so, Mr Balfour. We will certainly be on hand. Our presence will be discreet. But we will need a signal when the moment is right."

"Yes, of course. Why don't I come to the door of the shop – I'll say I need a little fresh air. I'll wipe my forehead with a handkerchief, then go back inside. If you wait a minute or two, then move. I would appreciate it if you seized all three of us, so that Mrs Carselaw does not realise I have betrayed her. Then you can separate us at the police station, and let Andreij and myself go."

"Naturally we'd need to interview you first, but that would enhance the impression that someone else informed us."

"Very well. And I hope your superiors will note the fact that I am offering so much help to you in recovering these valuable works and apprehending a most notorious criminal."

"I will speak to my senior officer as soon as I return to the police station."

"Thank you, inspector. The more I know you, the more I appreciate your company. Come, let's raise a glass to our success this evening." Balfour opened the bottle and poured a measure of brown oily liquid into each glass. "I will demonstrate to you that it is not drugged," he said, and drank the contents of his glass in one long sip. "Ah. I'm never tired of this nectar." Then he refilled it and raised it. "Cheers!"

Blue overcame his natural reluctance to drink on duty. For the greater good, he told himself, raising the glass. The liqueur was good, heavy and not too sweet, slipping down easily without the throat-kicking violence of many drinks branded 'the famous drink peculiar to our village/district/country.' "I have to admit, this is very good," he said.

Ten minutes later he joined McCader in the bar, and they were bade farewell by a very merry Andreij. "See you later, my buddies!" he called to them as he made for the stairs, presumably to collect further orders from his boss.

McCader still looked perfectly sober.

29

They said nothing about their recent conversations during their way through the dark streets. Arriving back at the work room at the police station, they found Bhardwaj, tucking into a coronation chicken wrap.

"That was quick, Arvind," commented McCader. "It's only five to seven."

"Yes, sarge. They got a car and rushed me over to Dumbarton Central, having persuaded Scotrail to hold the Oban train there till I arrived. Neat!"

Blue summarised his conversation with Ishmael Balfour, and, before drawing any conclusions, asked McCader how he had got on with Andreij.

"He's been well trained. He put on a great show of being jolly, but only had a couple of bottles of lager, same as I did. And didn't give much away. Plenty of harmless yarns from his days with the Czech special forces and the joys of Bratislava. I was able to tell him all about my Albanian heritage and the things to see in Scotland. The only thing I did get from him is that he's been working for Balfour for seven years, and is full of praise for him. Balfour does a lot of travelling, and has business interests all over the place. It all seems above board, though clearly he wasn't going to tell me about anything dodgy. All in all Andreij seems a nice guy. I asked him about the imitation gun, and he found that very amusing. Mr Balfour is a great joker, he says. But I'd say he has a real gun too. I don't see Balfour being protected by an unarmed bodyguard."

"What about Lind?" said Blue. "He wasn't at the meeting with Aino, according to Balfour."

"Probably still on the way here," said McCader.

"To meet up with Mrs Carselaw, er, or Mrs Lind?" asked Bhardwaj.

"It looks very much like it," said Blue.

"Do you think Balfour's being straight with you?" asked McCader.

"Mostly. As we know, the more a criminal can tell the truth, the more he can get away with the bit that isn't true. I'm sure Balfour isn't as squeaky clean as he makes himself out to be. I suspect he's only telling us all about the book deal because he thinks we know about it. What if everything he told me is true, except for the time of the meeting this evening? What if it's set for seven or eight rather than ten? Then even if we turn up an hour early, we miss it. He gets his share of the loot, then hides it and tells us Aino never turned up."

"Or he tricks Aino and ends up with all three himself!"

"I don't get it," put in Bhardwaj. "We were thinking that Aino believes Paul Carselaw hid the consignment. Now she says to Balfour that it was Drekhkov."

"We don't really know what she's thinking. That's the problem," said Blue. "Maybe the whole basement thing is just a ruse to trick Balfour. Or us. So we better start watching the place now."

"Let me handle that, chief," said McCader. "I'll grab a sandwich and a coffee and get down there straight away. I'll alert you as soon as anything happens."

"Thanks, Enver." Blue knew that McCader's ability to merge unseen into any setting had been honed over several years whilst he worked for a government agency not mentioned in his personnel file. Nevertheless, this would be a challenge. "There's not a lot of cover there."

"It should be OK. The staircase at the end of the lane means that there will be occasional passers-by, and offers good cover too."

"Do you need to bring in some armed guys?" asked Bhardwaj.

"I don't think so. Nobody's been shot so far. And it would take a while to assemble the Armed Response Unit. By the time they get here the action will be over. On the other hand, we do need to be careful. We should be wearing some protective gear in case it does get nasty."

McCader was off, and Blue sent Bhardwaj down to the stores to pick up a couple of Kevlar body-protectors. Then they waited. After ten minutes they got a message from McCader telling them he was in the lane.

Ten minutes later Blue's mobile rang. "Hi, boss, Vunsells here. Someone's arrived at the caravan. They drove up in a car, parked, got out and went into the van. We couldn't see who it was in the dark, and they closed the blinds before switching on the light inside. What do we do?"

"Just stay where you are, and keep your eyes peeled. If anything happens, tell me right away."

"I could sneak round and check the car registration."

"No. She might see you. But keep an eye on the car in case you do get a glimpse of it."

"Will do, boss. Over and out!"

"So she's at the caravan now?" asked Bhardwaj.

"Looks like it. Though we don't know for sure that it's her."

"Who else could it be?"

"It might be Lind. He'll have got here by now. We need to be ready for anything."

They didn't realise what 'anything' might mean.

Quarter of an hour later – it was now 7.45pm – McCader called. "Hi, chief. Balfour's just arrived at the bookshop, on foot, accompanied by one other, whom I'd say was Andreij. Both were muffled up, but Balfour's shape is hard to disguise. Now there's a dim light in the shop. I think they've gone through to the rear, maybe the office. I'd say the meeting is going to start soon. I don't see them arriving two hours early for a ten o'clock event."

"Keep me posted," said Blue, and rang off.

His phone immediately rang again. "It's all happening here, boss," gasped Vunsells. "There's been an explosion in the caravan, and it's burning from one end to the other. Aelwyn has called the fire brigade and the cops. We tried to get as close as possible, in case we could get anyone out. But the blaze is just too intense. I hope to God no-one was in there. But we didn't see Aino leaving, and there were lights on. Maybe she was putting a bomb together. What do you want us to do?"

"Don't try to go in there. Keep any casual spectators away till the fire engine and the uniformed cops arrive, then the cops can take that job over. The fire people will have lights, and you can see if there's anything interesting around the van. Check the car registration number. Then see if you can find any witnesses. You won't get into the van till the fire's been put out and the whole thing has cooled down. That'll take several hours. We'll get the SOCOs in then too. But that'll be tomorrow morning, once it's light. No point in groping about in the dark." He ended the call.

"Wow! Do you think she *was* putting a bomb together?" said Bhardwaj.

"It's unlikely. She's not a terrorist. What would be the point?"
"Shouldn't we get out there, to the caravan site?"
"No. Right now we need to focus on what's happening at the bookshop. It's even possible the explosion at the van was intended as a distraction."
"You mean, so's we'd rush over there and not notice what was going on at the shop?"
"It's a possibility."
In five minutes the phone rang again. This time it was McCader. "Things are under way here. Two more arrivals. I'd guess it's Mrs Carselaw and Mr Lind. Though again, they're muffled up. They're all in the bookshop now."
"OK. We'll head over, but not come into the lane till you give the word."
Blue managed to round up three uniformed officers, two male, one female – the rest were at the fire at the caravan site – and he and Bhardwaj led them along Union Street until they reached the end of Stairfoot Lane, where they paused. Passers-by looked at them with some curiosity, so Blue led them across the road and onto the promenade, and told them to look out across the harbour, as if expecting the imminent arrival of a shipload of drug smugglers.

They heard the explosion from there, an ear-splitting crash. Then saw, in the pale glow of the street lights the cloud of dust and smoke billowing out of the end of the lane.
"Shit!" gasped Blue. "Come on, move!"
He led them in a run across the road towards the lane. The cloud had dissipated as it emerged into Union Street, moved along by the breeze, but the lane itself was still blanketed in thick smoke.
He told two of the uniforms to station themselves at the end of the lane, and not let anyone enter. They should also call the emergency services. He himself called the station to get any officers who could be found over, and pull some more out of bed. The third officer, PC Gregor McBain, a regular at the throwing events at the Highland Games, he signalled to follow Bhardwaj and himself into the thick smoke. He fished in his pocket and pulled out a mask which had sat there since the pandemic. It soon became apparent that the entire building had not collapsed. They

were not tripping over mountains of rubble filling the lane.

They were at the shop before they realised it, suddenly seeing, as a gust swirled the curtain of smoke aside for a few seconds, the gaping hole in the facade of the building where the shopfront had once been, dimly illuminated by the streetlight near the mouth of the lane. No-one could have survived that, thought Blue.

"Wait!" he told the other two. "Don't go in yet. We don't know what's in there or how safe it is. Let's find McCader first."

"Sergeant!" shouted Bhardwaj into the gloom. "Where are you?"

There was no response. Blue pulled a torch from his pocket and PC McBain followed suit.

"Let's feel our way along the wall opposite the shop. I doubt he'll have been standing right outside it." He muttered a prayer that McCader be still alive, as they made their way carefully to the wall and then moved along it. McBain cursed as he tripped over a chunk of stone, then cursed again when he realised it wasn't a piece of stone, but a human leg. It wasn't attached to anything. At least one dead, thought Blue. How many more?

Ahead of him in the smoke he could hear Bhardwaj coughing. And then a shout from McBain, "He's over here, boss!" And sirens in the distance, as if in another world.

At least McCader was in one piece. He lay near the staircase at the top of the lane, a pool of blood below his head. McBain was already checking for a pulse when Blue and Bhardwaj got there. "He's still alive, boss. Looks like something hit him on the head. Maybe other injuries too."

Sirens penetrated the smoky darkness. Blue sent Bhardwaj to find the ambulance, and five minutes later two paramedics arrived with a stretcher. "Thank goodness you didn't move him," said one. "He could have spinal injuries, or a fractured skull. We'll bandage his head to stop the bleeding and get him onto the stretcher." That was done quickly and carefully, plastic blocks put on either side of McCader's head to stop it moving, and he was carried off towards the ambulance. Blue thanked McBain and asked him to keep the lane sealed at the top end. Then he and Bhardwaj headed for the shop.

The fire engine could only reverse a few metres into the lane before it became too narrow, and lights were being carried over and set up at the scene. Where once had been a shop front there was now a gaping mouth with flames within. Blue recognised Matt Wetherby, the team leader, directing two men to play a hose at the flames. "Hi Matt. What do you think?"

"Hi Angus. Well, there was an explosion, plenty of people heard it. It's blown the front off the shop. But from what I can see, I'd say the rest of the building looks fairly intact. That doesn't mean you can just wander in there, by the way – nobody goes in there till I say it's OK. There could easily be internal damage to the structure that we can't see yet."

"What caused it?"

"Could be a gas leak, of course. There are two other possibilities. One is that some store or container of an explosive material has been ignited, through an electrical fault or some other unintentional action. And finally, it could be an explosive device, set off accidentally or deliberately."

"Any one of them you'd go for?"

"Too hard to tell right now. The fire investigator will check it out in the morning, when it's cooled down and safe to go in. Then we'll have a better idea."

"Where do you think the source of the blast was?"

"Again, that's something the investigator would tell us with more confidence. For me, I'd guess it was in the shop area, as opposed to further back in the building. I assume the shop area was only the front part of the building, and that there were other rooms behind. Something going off deeper inside wouldn't have blown out the shop front like it has, unless it were very powerful indeed, and then there'd be other signs of damage to the structure of the building. Floors collapsing inside, for instance. Again, we'd have to wait till it was safe, that would be in the morning."

"But there may be people in there, still alive."

"Not in the shop area, there won't be. The bits will be all over the place, some in there, some thrown out into the street."

"What about further back?"

"This type of building will have a communal rear entrance. I've sent a couple of guys round to see if they can get in and have a look round. They'll know where it's safe to go and where it's not. If there's anyone alive in the rear part of the building, they'll get them out. What do you know about the people who live in the flats?"

"As far as I know, none of them are occupied."

"That's a relief at any rate. What were you doing at the scene, anyway? If you don't mind me asking, that is?"

"Sergeant McCader was observing a meeting which we had reason to believe was attended by a person whom we suspect of one, possibly two, murders. I was waiting nearby, with a few officers, ready to pounce and apprehend our suspect. We didn't anticipate there'd be an explosion."

"Your suspect doesn't have a record of blowing things up?"

"Not as far as we know. But then, we don't know a great deal about this person."

"Were there other people in the building?"

"We think so. A meeting had been arranged. But we don't know exactly who attended it."

"That's helpful. We need to be careful in case there are further devices which haven't exploded so far. Thanks, Angus. Come back in half an hour and I'll tell you how things are going."

30

Blue told Bhardwaj to keep an eye on events at the shop, and went to the entrance to the lane, to make sure things there were under control. He needn't have worried. Chief Inspector Sandler from the uniformed branch had everything organised. Two police cars and a van were parked there and an ambulance stood ready in case of any further casualties. Uniformed officers were already knocking on doors to get witness statements. The flats over the shops at the entrance of the lane, and beyond the shop, had been evacuated in case the fire should spread or the buildings were compromised.

He phoned Elsa Maarksen: no reply. Had she been summoned to the meeting by Balfour? It was likely, since she was the one he'd sent to copy the ground plans in Edinburgh.

He called the station and asked for a SOC team as soon as possible. Even if they couldn't get into the shop, they'd have to check the lane outside for body parts and any other evidence right away, before rats and other carrion-eaters appeared.

He phoned Vunsells to let her and Sergeant Morgan know what was happening and see how things were at the caravan site. "The fire's almost out," she reported. "The fire guys pretty well drenched it, but there's not a lot left. Aelwyn and I have searched the ground around with torches and found nothing suspicious. The car's still here. It's empty. It's Mrs Carselaw's hire car."

"Tape off the caravan and the car when you can. I'll send a SOC team in the morning."

"Will do. Shall we stay here overnight?"

"It would be good if you did that. We don't know yet who was killed in the explosion, so it's possible that Aino is still alive, and she may come back for the car. Though I very much doubt it. I would guess she met up with Lind at the site, set the fuse for whatever device torched the van, and then left with Lind in his car. Nevertheless, if she is alive, she might just come back, so it's worth watching the place for tonight."

"Will do, chief. It sounds like you think Aino was responsible for the explosion. Assuming it was a bomb, that is."

"The caravan and the shop both going up on the same evening is too much of a coincidence. And I don't see Balfour wanting to blow his own building up."

"But why blow her cover, as it were, if there was still a chance the books might be there?"

"Maybe she'd checked the cellar already and knew they weren't. Balfour says he has the only key, but I don't see door locks being much of an issue for a trained KGB operative. Or the whole thing was simply a trick to dispose of Balfour."

"We're going to need a lot of SOCOs for the caravan and the shop."

"You're right. I can pull them in from Fort William if necessary." He saw the alert on his screen. "OK, Lena, I've got another call waiting, from Arvind. I'll talk to you later."

He rang off and took the call from Bhardwaj. "What's up, Arvind?"

"Boss, they've found someone in the building. Still alive."

"Don't keep me in suspense. Who is it?"

"I don't know. The fire guys went in the back, and just phoned Matt to say they'd found someone in one of the rooms. Unconscious but alive."

"Man or woman?"

"Man, yes, that's what Matt said, it was a man. They got him out of the building and called the paramedics. They're bringing him round via the back greens to the ambulance."

"OK, thanks Arvind. I'll look out for them."

A few minutes later he saw them. Two paramedics and two firefighters struggling with a heavy burden. That could only mean Ishmael Balfour. He approached them and showed his ID. "Who have you got there?"

"Don't know who it is," said one of the paramedics, "but he's bloody heavy."

"Can I see him? I think I can ID him for you."

"Be my guest."

Only the head was visible on the stretcher. "His name is Ishmael Balfour," said Blue. "How bad is he?"

"Unconscious, but breathing. Looks like smoke inhalation. Once we get him onto some oxygen in the van he should be OK."

"Any other injuries?"

"Doesn't look like it, but we'll have to check. Now we've got to go. Any more questions, ask the team leader."

Back in front of the shop, Blue found Matt Wetherby again, and asked how things were going.

"Progress, Angus. The fire's just about out. I think it was incidental to the explosion. Shelves, books and stuff that just got set alight by the heat of the blast. Luckily not intense enough to set fire to the ceiling timbers, so contained within the shop area itself."

"Anyone in that area would have been killed by the blast?"

"That's right."

"But you found someone further back?"

"Yes. I sent some guys round the back to see what was doing. Thankfully the back door hadn't blown out, so there was less of a draught to feed the fire. But the door at the back of the shop area was blown out, so plenty of smoke got through to the rear. It was relatively undamaged, though the walls had been shifted slightly, enough to jam the doors off the corridor. They forced them all, and only found one person, in the office, unconscious. They got him out and called the paramedics."

"What about bodies?"

"Too early to say yet. The room's still too hot to check. We've had a look around the lane here, and there are certainly some body parts lying around."

"I've got a SOC team on the way, to collect everything and check for any other evidence."

"Good. My guys really don't like walking around bits of people. We've been to explosions before, but you never get used to that."

Blue was there for another two hours, but little more came to light. He ordered a police officer to stand guard at the room in the hospital where Ishmael Balfour was being kept. He didn't want Balfour discharging himself and disappearing before he could be questioned. The SOC team soon arrived and set up floodlights to illuminate their inch-by-inch search of the lane. It had started to rain, and that didn't help, washing small slivers that were once human down to the gutter and thence to the drain. The dogged SOCOs recorded and marked each piece remaining, and anything else that lay on the ground. All this would have to go to the pathologist, to assemble the grisly jigsaw that might tell them something of what had passed.

Eventually he decided there was nothing more he could do. He would be wiser getting some sleep, to be ready for the morning.

He called Vunsells before he left, but she had nothing to report either. He went home and made himself a hot toddy in place of the meals he'd missed. He thought of phoning Alison Hendrickx, but was too tired. He lay in bed unsatisfied, and dreamed of things he'd hoped were long forgotten.

31

Friday 9 December

Up at seven, and in his office by eight, still dark and he knew there was no point in being there so early. Nothing would happen till it was light. Till the fire chief declared the shop and the caravan safe to explore, and the SOCOs came back to pick at the ashes, and the fire investigator rolled up at ten or eleven to work out what might have happened. Till the doctors would give him the okay to talk to McCader and Balfour. Till the pathologist told him how many were dead and who or what they might be.

Outside, in the dark, it rained. It had been raining most of the night.

First he phoned Vunsells. Nothing had happened overnight at the caravan site. Like him, she was waiting for the light.

Next he called Elsa Maarksen, but there was no reply.

Then he phoned Alison Hendrickx. He knew the explosion would be on the news. You could keep the news of a stabbing, or a poisoning, or even a shooting, from the press for a day or two if you had to, but not an explosion. She'd realised it was his case, that he'd be there and would have worked till late the previous evening. She didn't ask for details, but he was glad to give them, to tell the story to a sympathetic ear, to share the horror.

When he'd finished, she made no comments; he knew his job and would do it well. "I'll see you this evening. Maybe earlier if I can get things wrapped up sooner. Take care, Angus. I love you."

"Love you too, Alison. See you later."

At half past, a text message invited him to meet with Superintendent Campbell at nine. By then the Super had switched on and set up his coffee machine, and the just-ground beans had already given the room its characteristic odour of Mediterranean leisure. Rumour had it that the super now owned a flat, or maybe even a villa, somewhere in the north of Italy, to which he and his wife would retire. But it remained rumour, and the super took care to guard his private life.

Campbell listened carefully to Blue's account of events the previous day. "That's most useful Angus. Get back to me once you've talked with Balfour, and got the reports from the SOC teams and the fire investigator. Who do you think was killed in the explosion?"

"The SOCOs are reckoning at least two – don't ask me how they worked that out – but we've no definite idea as to who they are yet, or whether there are only two, or more. As far as we know, the only person injured outside the shop was Sergeant McCader. Thankfully he wasn't in front of the building at the time, or his injuries would have been a lot worse. As far as I know he was hit by some of the fragments. I'll see him this morning as well as Balfour."

"Who was there when it went off?"

"My guess is that along with Balfour at the meeting would have been his bodyguard Andreij, Aino Carselaw, maybe her husband Kalev Lind, and possibly even Elsa Maarksen. But any of them could have brought along others whom we don't know about."

"And Ishmael Balfour is the only survivor?"

"So it seems at the moment."

"Do you think he set something off? To eliminate Aino Carselaw and Lind? Sent them through to the front of the shop then dodged back into the office and set off a bomb?"

"That's possible. Though I'm not sure what he'd have to gain, as I don't think he knows where the books are. And there would be no point in blowing anyone up. Especially on his own property. I would be very surprised if he did it."

"Someone else could have placed a bomb, then it went off by accident at the wrong moment."

"That's also possible. We'll know more later today."

"One other thing. Explosions always attract interest. We'll have the press to deal with, of course. But we'll also get attention from Special Branch, the Anti-terrorist Unit and maybe the Security Service. They'll have to come to me first, and I can reassure them that it doesn't look like a terrorist attack. But the sooner we can prove that and tie the whole thing up, the easier it will be to get them off our backs."

"I understand, chief. I'll get things moving as fast as I can."

Back in his office, it occurred to him that Kalev Lind's hire car was still unaccounted for. He asked for a couple of uniformed officers to search the car parks and streets, working outwards from the bookshop. He guessed that to avoid leaving a trail Lind would have checked out of his hotel, which was still to be identified, so any belongings were likely to be in the car. Then he phoned the hospital and was told he could see McCader at ten. He asked Bhardwaj to come with him.

They were there by quarter to. He asked at reception how the sergeant was doing. A dctor was fetched who told him there were no major injuries. Fortunately, his lungs and ears had not been injured by the blast. He'd been hit by debris from the shop-front, including some glass and masonry. However, although something had glanced off his head, the scan showed that there was no fracture of the skull, the blow probably softened by his thick woolly hat. As to the glass, there were a few cuts to his hands, which he'd used to protect his face, but again, the thick clothes and Kevlar body protector he was wearing had minimised the damage. "All in all, he's a lucky man," concluded the doctor. "A few more steps along the lane, it would have been a different story."

"What about Mr Balfour?"

"Apart from smoke inhalation, no real damage."

"When can we talk to them?"

"Any time you want. Given who you are, we won't insist on you coming back at visiting time this afternoon. Upstairs, turn left. McCader's in Room 1, Balfour's in Room 3. But don't overdo it; they still need lots of rest."

Reaching the first floor corridor where the single rooms were, Blue noticed the woman police officer sitting on a chair by the door half way along. He recognised the slim figure with long blonde hair in a ponytail: PC Iris May. He asked Bhardwaj to wait outside, in case McCader was still weak.

The sergeant was sitting up in bed when Blue went into the room. Part of his head, towards the front, had been shaved and a few stitches were visible, and one hand was bandaged. Blue took the chair by the bed and didn't waste time. "Good to see you're OK, Enver."

"Hi, boss. Could have been a lot worse. They'll let me out this afternoon, they tell me."

"I'm glad to hear that. So what happened?"

"Not a lot really. I spotted some people arriving at the shop. First, at quarter to eight, Balfour and another, probably Andreij. Ten minutes later another two, both heavily wrapped. I'd guess they were Aino Carselaw and Kalev Lind, since no-one else turned up."

"That suggests Elsa Maarksen wasn't invited. Did any of them have bags or rucksacks?"

"Andreij and both Aino Carselaw and Lind looked like they had rucksacks. Tools, I thought."

"What next?"

"Must have been seven or eight minutes later, the front of the shop blew out. Luckily I was at the end of the lane by the stairs. I don't remember anything after that until I woke up here."

"You don't remember being hit by a piece of stone or brick?"

"No. The doctor says it's traumatic amnesia. The brain redacts the memories it doesn't like."

"And they'll let you go later today?"

"That's what the doc says. This afternoon, I guess."

"Spend the rest of the day at home with the family. Rest. Come in again tomorrow, but only if you feel up to it."

"I've had a lot worse than this, boss. Remember Islay. And before that, too. But OK, I'll see you tomorrow for sure."

He came out into the corridor to see Bhardwaj deep in conversation with WPC May. "Arvind, you can say hello to Sergeant McCader now," he said, and as Bhardwaj headed off, he turned to the WPC. "Good morning, constable. It's Iris, isn't it?"

"Yes, sir."

"Thanks for standing – or sitting – guard on Mr Balfour. Any activity here this morning?"

"No, sir. And no visitors."

"Good. I'm going to have a chat with him now. I may ask you to come in at some point and take a statement from him."

"No problem, sir."

Ishmael Balfour was lying in bed, apparently asleep, but as soon as Blue shut the door behind him, he opened one eye, then both. "Ah, the good Inspector Blue. At last a possibility of intelligent conversation. I don't suppose you carry a hip flask with you, with something you could slip into this cup of tea?" He pushed himself laboriously into a sitting position and indicated a half-empty mug of tea on the bedside table.

"I'm sorry, Mr Balfour. Police officers do not generally carry alcohol."

"Ah well. A pity nevertheless. What can I do for you, inspector?"
"I think you know the answer to that, Mr Balfour. What happened yesterday evening?"
"Ah yes. A most unfortunate set of circumstances. And I shall miss poor Andreij."
"Tell me the story, from the beginning."
"Of course. You'll remember the meeting was planned for ten. At twenty to eight Aino Carselaw phoned. She said simply that the meeting was rescheduled for eight, that each of us should come with only one companion, and that if there were any signs of anything suspicious, the deal was off. I was of course insulted that she should suspect me of anything underhand, and hastened to inform her that Andreij and I would be there. We took ourselves over there immediately."
"Can I ask why you didn't inform me of the change of plan?"
"Naturally, as a law-abiding citizen, that was my very first impulse. And yet I hesitated. What if she had paid those Russians at the hotel to monitor the phone, or had hacked into my cellphone? I simply couldn't risk it. I'm sure you understand that in such circumstances one must be most careful not to arouse any suspicion."
"Hmm. Please go on."
"Aino and Lind arrived about ten to eight, and we spent the next few minutes in the office. Aino proposed that we go through to the shop next door. She explained that she and Lind had brought tools to test for a cavity and prise up the floorboards if necessary. These were in their rucksacks, which they'd left in the shop area. In fact Andreij also had some tools with him. He had left his rucksack in the shop area too."
"So at this point all four of you were in the office?"
"Exactly. Then Aino said, 'Right, let's go through to the shop next door.' She led the way out of the office and Lind followed, then Andreij. But just as I was going through the door into the front shop, she said, 'Wait there a moment, I must pop into the toilet. Just wait here. I'll only be a minute.' And she slipped past me and went into the toilet."
"And shut the door?"
"Yes. It immediately aroused my suspicions. I wondered if she was going to sneak back into the office for some reason, and decided to go there and wait for her to leave the toilet."

"Did you shut the door to the front shop?"
"Yes. And the office door, as gently as I could. I waited until I heard the toilet door open and shut, but she didn't come into the office. I thought she must have gone back to the front shop. I went to leave the office, but as I reached the door I felt the explosion. Everything shook around me, there was a crash and then it all went dark. When I woke up the room was pitch dark and full of smoke. I could hardly breathe. I felt my way to the door, but couldn't open it; the blast must have twisted the frame. The smoke was coming in under the door and through a gap at the side of the frame. I banged on the door and shouted. I can tell you, inspector, I thought those moments were going to be my last on this earth. The next thing I knew is that I woke up again in an ambulance. They'd given me oxygen. I asked if I could go back to the hotel, but they insisted on bringing me here, and even put a police officer outside my door, as if I were some sort of common criminal. This morning the doctor examined me and told me I could be discharged as soon as the police okayed it. You may imagine that I protested, but he said it was out of his hands, I'd have to speak to the police. And now, my wishes are fulfilled, and here you are."
"Thank you, Mr Balfour. Tell me, after you heard the toilet door open and shut, did you hear Aino walking past the office door?"
"Hmm. No, I don't think so. I just assumed she did."
"During your talk in the office, did Aino offer any new information about the books?"
"She said it had been regrettably necessary to kill Drekhkov, but she was sure he had secreted the books nearby. I asked her how he would know about any cavity below the shop next door. She claimed her husband must have told him. I must say to you that I found that most improbable. I suspected that she had hidden the books there herself, and the discovery of them under the floor of the shop would be a staged event for my benefit. But I did not anticipate what happened."
"So why the bomb?"
"It was so simple, I should have seen it. She wanted rid of me. And Lind too, it seems. I believe now that she already had the books, and the whole point of the meeting was to get rid of those who might be in her way and would be able to identify her later."

"You don't believe she was killed in the explosion?"

"I doubt it very much. If the point was that I and Lind should die, it follows that she still lives."

"Did Andreij have a bomb in his rucksack?"

"Certainly not! He showed me the tools before we left the hotel. The only other thing he had there was an automatic pistol. Purely in case of emergency. As I've told you, I knew Aino was ruthless. That she has murdered Lind does not surprise me. I often wonder why there are such people in the world. If there is a deity, why does he inflict these people upon us?"

"Yet you were happy to work with her."

"Not happy. Yes, her focus and lack of emotion made her a good businesswoman. But I could never enjoy her company."

"Where do you think she is now?"

"If, as I suspect, she already has the books, she will by now be somewhere far away. But not necessarily beyond our reach. I have many ears on the ground in the book business, and, were she to offer these books for sale, even very discreetly, I would hear. But she is very clever. We must not underestimate her. I have done so, alas, to my cost."

"You do realise, Mr Balfour, that you may be charged for your part in this deal?"

"Ah yes. But what would you charge me with? Trafficking in cultural treasures? As yet, there is no such crime. Handling stolen property? We know the books were not stolen, but sold by the person responsible for them. Withholding evidence? But I've been completely open with you, inspector. The government of Belarus could issue a warrant for my arrest. But we have no extradition treaty with Belarus, and with good reason. Murder? But you'll find no evidence for that, for the simple reason that I didn't do it. You have only the fact that I'm still alive, which, I agree, from a circumstantial perspective could seem suspicious. And thankfully, in this country suspicion is not equated with guilt, or many innocent men and women would be languishing in jail."

Blue smiled. "You're right. We've nothing on you, apart from being involved in a dodgy book deal, and being close by when some people were killed. But you're an important witness, so we need you to remain here until we can solve these killings."

"My dear inspector, I wish to see justice done, and will happily remain in this area, for a few days at least. There is much around this delightful town that I have yet to see."

"Thank you, Mr Balfour, that's been very helpful."

"Not at all. I must say that I do relish our conversations, Mr Blue. And I really do hope that you find Aino Carselaw, wherever she is. She is a very dangerous woman. As soon as I am once again in Slovakia, I shall waste no time in seeking a replacement for poor Andreij. I am most sorry to lose him, and will do what I can for his family. He has a wife and children, you know. Such a pity."

"I'm going to ask Constable May to come in now and take a statement from you. She will record it using her digital recorder. PC Bhardwaj will accompany her."

"Are you worried that I'll accost her?"

"It's normal practice, sir. Please include everything you've said to me."

"Then may I leave?"

"Once Constable May has typed up your statement, and I'm happy that it tallies with what you told me."

"Don't you trust me, inspector? Surely we are both gentlemen."

"I'm sure we are, but there are procedures, and I'm obliged to adhere to them. When you're discharged, return to your hotel and remain there until I indicate that you can leave. As a material witness and possible suspect in what may be a terrorist-related case, you'll understand that I could have you detained in custody. It's been a pleasure, Mr Balfour."

32

He asked Bhardwaj to go in with May to witness Balfour's statement, and then to find out what was happening with the post-mortem examination of the body parts found the previous evening. Then he drove back to the police station, left the car, and walked to the bookshop. By now it was light, if the gloom permitted by the heavy cloud could be so described, and the rain still fell, no longer heavy, but persistent and penetrating. And cold.

The SOC team were at work in the shop now, having completed a second search of the lane. "Any further human remains had been cleared away by wildlife," said Steve Belford, "but we got one or two non-organic objects which could help identify the dead. A dental plate. A small metal badge. A room key. They've gone back to the station for analysis."

"OK. What's the situation here in the shop?"

"A lot of blast damage, and then fire damage. All those books just waiting for a chance to burn."

"Any evidence of a bomb?"

"Not yet, but that'll need a very detailed search, and we may need to get some experts in for that. The fire investigator will be here sometime this morning, and should be able to say whether it was an explosive device or a gas leak."

He was going to learn nothing more there for a while, so he returned to the station and drove out to the caravan site. A uniformed officer checked his ID at the gate to the site. The burnt-out shell of the caravan at the end of the row was obvious. He could see Vunsells and Morgan standing nearby, talking to two men and a woman. He greeted the police officers, who introduced him to the others, a SOC team sent down from Fort William that morning. The team leader, Jean McCarron, explained they'd only just begun to examine the site when the fire investigator arrived. "The rain'll not be making his job easier, mind," she commented. Blue could see dimly through the rain the figure moving about on what remained of the caravan, most of the walls, as well as the roof, having been destroyed in the fire.

Ten minutes later a heavily built man with a ruddy complexion wearing an overcoat and a trilby emerged from the wreck, and came over. Blue introduced himself as the CIO on the case to which the fire in the caravan was connected.

The man shook hands. "Duncan Blackstone. Pleased to meet you. Not much to say about this one. Nothing too sophisticated, looks like someone inside the caravan poured some accelerant over the furniture and floor in every room, then tossed a lighted match inside from the doorway. And no doubt vamoosed rapidly."

"Any bodies in there?" asked Blue.

"No. I'm sure of that."

"Could a timing device have been left?"

"No sign of any remains of one. I suppose it could have been something fairly primitive, like a candle burning down till it reaches some combustible material. I'll be done here soon – I need to get to Oban next. Somebody's tried to blow up a bookshop. Crazy."

"Yes," said Blue, "that's my case too. I'll probably see you over there."

Once he'd gone, Blue brought Morgan and Vunsells up to date on events at the bookshop.

"So what do we do next?" asked Vunsells.

"As soon as we know who was killed in the explosion, we'll know who wasn't. The big question is whether Aino and Lind were killed. If not, we'll have to find them."

"What about these valuable books?"

"We've still no idea who has them or, if they're still hidden, where they are. I hope to have some answers once the pathologist's finished his rather nasty jigsaw puzzle, but I suspect that won't be until this afternoon. There's not much you two can do here, so why not come back to the station after lunch?"

He headed back to the station. After a quick lunch in the canteen – he didn't fancy his favourite dining spot at the top of Pulpit Hill in the pouring rain – he got on with the task of updating his report, and there was plenty of updating to do.

At three the fire investigator phoned. "Just to let you know this shop business looks very much like an explosive device."

"A bomb?"

"We don't use the B word. I've found a few bits of the detonator; probably set off using a mobile phone. That's the way most of them work nowadays. Unless it was suicide by one of the victims."

"That's very unlikely."

"Or it went off when it wasn't supposed to. Anyway, you'll get my report on both the incidents in a couple of days. I'll give you a ring if anything different emerges."

Ten minutes later Bhardwaj phoned to say he was back from the post-mortem.

"Anyone else up there?" asked Blue.

"Lena and Sergeant Morgan are here too."

"Get yourselves some coffee. I'll be up in a minute. You can share your report with all of us."

He went to the canteen where he found Vunsells getting three coffees. He added a mocha for himself and paid for them. Up in the work room, he asked Bhardwaj to report.

"Bit of a tricky job for Dr Carmichael. He didn't show me all the bits, just called me down after he'd finished. He's pretty sure there are only two people there, and both male. There was apparently a thigh with a Czech Special Forces insignia tattoo on it, which suggests Balfour's henchman Andreij. The other is probably Lind."

"No clues in what's left of their clothing?"

"No. The doc says there'll need to be DNA tests to confirm their identities."

"OK. Thanks Arvind. We'll assume for the moment that Andreij and Lind are now dead. That means that Aino Carselaw is still at large, and a suspect, along with Balfour, for the bombing."

"Who's the most likely?" asked Vunsells.

"My money would be on Aino. If she wants to maximise her gains from the books, wiping out all the others makes sense."

"Even her ex-husband, or still-her-husband?"

"We're fairly sure she killed Paul Carselaw, and Boris Drekhkov, so killing a few more would be par for the course. Plus, if she was KGB-trained, she'd know how to put a bomb together. And her escape seems to tie in with Balfour's statement."

"What about Balfour?" asked Bhardwaj.

"As far as I can gather, all he wants is his share of the deal. And he seemed quite attached to Andreij. I don't see him as a mass murderer. But we could be mistaken."

"So the only person we're looking for now is Aino Carselaw," said Morgan. "My missing person is missing once again."

"That's about it," said Blue. "Everyone else seems to be accounted for, one way or another. So we need to find Aino and the books."

"I don't think she's got the books," said Morgan. "If she had, she'd have disappeared as soon as she'd got hold of them. She might have killed Lind, as he'd be more likely to come after her, but she could have done that discreetly, without all the fireworks. She wants those books, so she'll stay around here till she finds them. That gives us a chance to find her. She won't go back to the caravan site, so we'll have to start looking again for where she might be staying. I can get that moving."

"Thanks Aelwyn. Arvind, can you …?"

His phone rang. "Inspector, it's Elsa Maarksen here. Sounds like I've missed some action."

"You have indeed. Where are you? I tried to phone earlier."

"I went down to Glasgow to meet a potential client yesterday. I only came back this morning, and then went to the hairdresser. Prosaic, but necessary."

"Were you invited to a meeting yesterday evening between Aino and Mr Balfour?"

"No. I phoned Mr Balfour to tell him about the map, that the cellar was under the shop next door. He thanked me and said he didn't need to see the actual map, I could give it to him next time we met. And that was that. What happened? Everyone's talking about an explosion last night. It was the main topic of conversation at the hairdresser. I went round to the bookshop to have a look, but a policeman wouldn't let me into the lane. He wouldn't even tell me what was going on."

It can't have been PC Beattie, thought Blue. "Aino set fire to the caravan she was staying in. Then a bomb went off at a meeting at the bookshop. Looks like Mr Balfour's bodyguard and Kalev Lind were both killed. Mr Balfour was found in the office, still alive. Aino seems to have made off just before the explosion. Which does suggest that she did it. We're looking for her now."

"How bad is Mr Balfour?"

"Not too bad. He's in hospital, under guard."

"That's a relief. I'll contact him once he's out. Is there anything I can do to help?"

"Not at the moment. It's routine police stuff now, to track Aino down. Traffic cameras, and so on."

"No sign of the books, then?"

"Not yet. Aino told Mr Balfour she didn't have them, but that's not necessarily true."

"Could Mr Balfour have them?"

"I don't think so. He wants to stay on the right side of the law, so I think he'd tell us if he'd got hold of them. And he wouldn't have needed to go to the meeting. Aino's our target at the moment. Thanks for the offer of help. I'll talk to you later."

He called Steve Belford, who was co-ordinating both SOC teams, but there was little news there. The team at the caravan had found nothing of interest in the wreckage; it looked like Aino had cleared all her possessions out of the caravan before torching it. And the work at the shop was still ongoing. Steve would get back to him tomorrow.

He asked Bhardwaj to contact the airports and ferry terminals and tell them to hold Aino if she turned up there, either under her own name, or her new Finnish identity as Anneka Ländemann. Then back to his report.

He went back up to the workroom at half past four. Sergeant Morgan's hunt for Aino's accommodation had delivered nothing so far. Neither had the traffic division. And nothing from the airports and ferries. There was a sense in the room that nothing was going to turn up soon.

"Thanks for your efforts, everyone. Let's leave it there for today. We'll meet tomorrow at nine."

33

He was home by five, and happy to see Alison and Corrie. Over a glass of whisky, while Alison took a cup of green tea with mint, he brought her up to date on the case. "So we really end up back at my two questions," he summed up. "One, where are the books and two, where's Aino? They may be in the same place, of course, but my gut tells me she hasn't got them yet, and perhaps in fact nobody knows where they are."

"Let's go back a bit. You reckoned the last person who might have known where they were was Paul Carselaw?"

"I think there's a strong possibility."

"And Aino went to meet him because she thought he had them."

"That was one theory. Aino doesn't do anything for no reason. And it seems a rather roundabout approach if she simply wanted to kill him."

"But the killing looked a rather spur-of-the-moment thing?"

"Yes, we felt if Aino had planned to kill him it would have been a lot less messy. And risky. What makes sense is that Carselaw persuaded Aino he knew where the books were, and she arranged to meet him, either to collect the books or for him to tell her where they were. All for a price, of course."

"So why did she kill him?"

"Three possibilities. One, he'd given her the books on the boat, and she wanted to dispose of him to reduce the number of people who knew about them. Two, he didn't have the books with him, but he told her where they were, so again he could be disposed of. And three, he told her he didn't have the books and didn't even know where they were; once again, he could be got rid of."

"But you don't think the third is likely?"

"No. I think he gave Aino some proof that he had the books, maybe a picture. Otherwise why would she meet him? And there would be no point in killing him if there was a chance he could still lead her to the books. She must have been confident that he'd told her all he knew."

"OK, Angus, let's say Paul has the books. He agrees to meet Aino to hand them over at the marina on Bute, in return for a suitable sum. Why Bute?"

"A place he knows and she doesn't. And the marina's fairly public, so there's less chance of her trying anything. But maybe he has second thoughts about taking the books with him. He's afraid she'll double-cross him: take the books, but not hand over the cash. Maybe even kill him."

"Hm. Here's another idea: he decides to double-cross her. He'll take the money and tell her where the books are, except that he'll give her the wrong location. Then he'll have the money and the books. So he hides them and then goes to meet her."

"That's also possible. But we've searched all the likely spots and there's no sign of the books. The obvious place would be the safe under the train layout. But we know they weren't there when he was killed. We searched the place as soon as we heard about the murder."

"Right. Then what about this? He packs the books in his rucksack and heads off to the boat. But only then does it occur to him that she might double-cross him. Or he gets the idea of double-crossing her. It's too late to go back to the house, so he puts them somewhere else, that's on the way. Somewhere that's secure."

"Such as?"

"The marina at Gallanach Bay. If they have, say, a locker room, his locker would be perfect. Or he could leave them with the manager, what was her name?"

"Emma McIntyre."

"Then he gets on his boat and sails to Bute. He gives Aino a wrong location for the books. Maybe he adds the combination to open a padlock, or hands over a key he pretends is for a left-luggage office. But she doesn't realise he's lying. She doesn't think he has the imagination. And having got, as she thinks, access to the books, she decides on the spot to kill him."

"I guess that would fit what we know. It's a bit of a long shot. But worth looking at."

"OK Angus, let's go."

"Now?"

"Yes, right now!"

"Er, I've been drinking. Just one glass, but..."

"No problem, we'll take my car."

Twenty minutes later they drove down the single track road to the marina at Gallanach Bay and parked in the marina car park. It was still raining, now a thin but penetrating rain. The office was still open, and Emma McIntyre greeted them at the door. "Hi guys! How can I help you?" Then recognition. "Ah, Inspector Blue. And, er…"

"Dr Hendrickx," said Blue.

"Yes, of course. So, inspector, did you find Mr Carselaw?"

"We did. At a marina on Bute. He'd been murdered."

"Oh my God! How awful. Do you know who did it?"

"We have a fair idea, but I can't comment right now."

"No, well, of course. Er, so what can I do for you?"

"We may need a formal interview with you later, regarding Mr Carselaw's activities here at the marina. But for now, we'd like to know if he had a locker, or any other storage space, here."

"I'll have to check. We do have a locker room. It's in the building at the back of the car park. There are showers there too, toilets, and disposal facilities for portable toilets." She pointed to a long, single-storey building, white-painted breeze blocks and a flat roof. The windows were horizontal slits of frosted glass high up in the front wall. The door was in the centre.

"Come into the office out of the wet and I'll have a look." They followed her into the warm room, heated by a compact heater on the floor, attached to a gas bottle. She tapped a few keys on a laptop sitting on the desk below the window, and nodded. "Yes, he's got a locker, number seventeen."

"Do you know if he used it often?" asked Blue.

"No, I'm sorry, I've no idea. And we don't have CCTV in that building."

"Do you have any CCTV cameras that might show him going in there?"

"There's one in the car park that might do that. But it's been out of action for the last couple of weeks. We're still waiting for the guy to come and fix it."

"Hmm. May we look in his locker? There may be important evidence there."

"Do you need a warrant for that?"

"Only if you don't want to be co-operative, Ms McIntyre. This is a murder investigation, so it won't take me long to get one. But I'd rather look in there sooner than later, if you don't mind."

"I'm sure it'll be fine. I keep the duplicate keys in a locked box. I only ask because the day before yesterday, that would be Wednesday, about half past six in the evening a woman came and asked the same thing. She wanted to see Mr Carselaw's locker.

She said she was his wife, but when I asked for some photo ID, her picture looked completely different from her, so I said she'd have to ask him to lend her his key, or get him to come with her. She said he had gone off and she needed to get something from it. Well, I didn't want to get involved in whatever was going on between them, and I wasn't sure if she was Mrs Carselaw anyway, so I said there was nothing I could do. She wasn't for giving up, and I didn't like the look of her – not quite threatening, but maybe thinking about it – but luckily at that moment, one of the boat-owners, Mr Jenkins, came in looking for some change for the drinks machine. I told him to hang on so he'd be there when I asked the woman to leave. She was quite reluctant, she gave Mr Jenkins a scowl and then just flounced out."

"That's very helpful. Did you see her get into a car?"

"No, sorry, I was getting the change for Mr Jenkins. When he'd gone I locked the office door in case she came back. But she didn't."

Blue showed her the picture from the CCTV on the Bute ferry. "Does that look like her?"

"Well, it's a bit grainy, but it could well have been. The hair was certainly like that. I noted the incident in the log-book, just in case she came back, or anything came up, well just like this. There must be something in the locker that she wanted."

"That's what we want to check."

"Oh my God, did she kill him?"

"I can't comment on that, Ms McIntyre. Now, what about the key?"

"Oh yes, it's in here." She took a small key from her pocket and opened a steel box, about eight inches wide and three high, sitting on a shelf at about eye height, then took out of it a loop of wire with lots of keys attached. "Come on then, let's brave the rain."

She led them across the car park and into the building, flicking a light switch which showed a bare corridor to left and right, lit by dim light bulbs. In front of them in the small entrance hall was the drinks machine and a notice board. She turned to the left and stopped about ten yards along, by a plain wooden door. Opening it, she turned on another dim light, and pointed to the lockers against the walls, two rows, one above the other, each locker about eighteen inches wide and two foot six high. Number 17 was on the left hand wall, near the back, in the upper row. She flicked through the keys on the loop till she found the right one, and opened the locker door.

"Don't touch anything, please!" said Blue. "Can you stand back now? Dr Hendrickx is going to take a couple of photos."

Ms McIntyre stood back hurriedly, and Alison fished out her phone and took three shots of the interior of the locker. Then she stood back too.

Sitting in the locker was a rucksack of dark blue waterproof material. Blue gently lifted it out. It was heavy. There was nothing else in the locker. "Let's go back to the office, shall we?" he said. "So that we can have a better look at this. Can you lock the locker again, Ms McIntyre?"

Back in the office, with Alison and Ms McIntyre watching, he opened the rucksack. He took a small LED torch from his pocket and shone it in. He looked in and nodded. "Yes," he said, "this is a useful piece of evidence."

"Can you tell us what it is?" said Alison.

"Looks like an archive box. We'd better go straight to the station and get it logged in as evidence. It can be stored there securely until we open it."

He fastened the rucksack again. "Doctor Hendrickx, can you take a photo of Ms McIntyre and myself with the rucksack, so we'll have a date and time stamp on it."

Once that was done, he slung the rucksack on his back and thanked Ms McIntyre for her help. "Someone will be along tomorrow to take a statement about Wednesday's incident and get Mr Jenkins' details. And if the woman claiming to be Carselaw's wife comes back, lock yourself in the office and call the police. We believe she may be dangerous."

"I am indeed!" came a voice from the doorway, and a figure stepped into the office. A figure holding a gun.

34

Blue recognised her from the pictures taken on the ferry. The long red hair was now short and black, the eyebrows black too, and dark glasses masked the eyes. She was wearing a black waterproof jacket and jeans, walking boots, and a black woolly hat with a pompom. And in her black-gloved right hand sat a black automatic.

"Mrs Carselaw," said Blue. "I'd been hoping to meet you in the flesh."

"Well, now you have. Hands above your heads, please."

"What brought you here?" asked Blue, as he raised his hands.

"When she" – she waved the gun at Ms McIntyre – "refused to open the locker, I thought that sooner or later some official will come to look. I watched this place – the trees across the road give good cover. So you are Inspector Blue, who impresses Ishmael so much. And who is she?" She waved the gun briefly at Alison before turning it back towards Blue.

"This is Dr Hendrickx, our forensic archaeologist," said Blue. "She's here to examine the books in this rucksack."

"So let's do that. I don't want to waste my time if these are not what I'm looking for. Take the rucksack off and put it on the desk."

Blue did so.

"Now, you two" – she gestured with the gun at Blue and Ms McIntyre – "sit on the floor in that corner!" She nodded towards the far corner of the office where a grey filing cabinet sat. "One on each side of the cabinet. And keep your hands up!"

Blue and Ms McIntyre did so, not without difficulty.

"That's good. Now, any trouble from either of you two, and the archaeologist dies. And please believe me when I say she will die. I do know how to use this weapon."

"Mrs Carselaw," began Blue, "why not...?"

"Silence! Do you really think you can persuade me to give this up, when I have worked so hard to obtain it? Another word and your friend here dies. Do you understand?"

Blue nodded.

"Please, Dr Hendrickx, open the rucksack, and lay what is inside on the desk. If you try anything, I will shoot Inspector Blue."

Alison opened the rucksack, and carefully removed a brown

cardboard box, about a foot wide, a foot and a half long, and perhaps four or five inches deep. There was no writing or label on it.

"Good. Put the rucksack on the floor. That's it. Now open the box."

Alison lifted the lid carefully and laid it by the box. This action revealed what were clearly books wrapped in thick clear plastic. "May I comment, as an expert?" asked Alison.

"Go ahead."

"Thank you. This looks like an archival grade storage bag, folded over at the end. That's good. This plastic will not leach chemicals into the books. I'm not going to take the books out of the bag – it's safer to keep them in it, especially if you're hoping to sell them on. This will show they've been sensibly wrapped, presumably at their point of origin."

"Read the titles," ordered Aino. "They're on the spines."

"The books are all bound in the same dark leather, with titles tooled in gold," commented Alison. "Below each title is a coat of arms. It's the same one on each. That suggests that at one time they were all in the same library or collection."

"I know all that! The titles please."

Alison lifted the bundle out and turned it until she could see the titles clearly. "OK. The biggest is one called *Codex Gnesnensis*." She pronounced the title slowly, reading each syllable. "The next is *Libri Iudaeorum*. The third is *Annales Equitum Germanorum*. Are they the ones you were looking for?"

"They are!"

"What are they worth?" asked Blue from the corner.

"Ah, the policeman comes straight to the point. The codex is worth several million dollars. The others are not so valuable, maybe a million dollars altogether."

"Worth killing for?"

"Oh, yes. And please believe me, inspector, I know how to do it."

"KGB training?"

"So you know about that?"

"Is that why you married Paul Carselaw? KGB orders?"

"I did not object. Getting to the west was a big thing in those days. No-one realised that two or three years later it would be easy."

"But how did you put up with being married to a man you didn't love?" asked Alison.

"The good of the cause," said Aino sarcastically.

"Where would you have gone if you'd just been allowed to be yourself? To marry for love."

"Fantasyland, eh? *Kurat!* Why am saying all this?"

"You need to say it to somebody," said Alison quietly. "Who are you really, Aino?"

"Somebody who died a long time ago."

"And wants to find herself again, a long way from here. That's what the killings are all about, Aino, isn't that right? Getting rid of the people who made your life something that it shouldn't have been. Kalev Lind and Paul Carselaw. Who would you have been without them? Where's the real Aino Kuusk?"

"Long gone. But even zombies need to be happy somewhere."

"Happy? You won't ever forget what you became. Please, Aino, give it up. Be yourself again."

"Nice words, doctor, nice words. I've enjoyed talking to you, I really have. I should have killed you right away. But there's always a need to talk, isn't there? To find someone who understands. The trouble is, you can't get past what's happened. No-one is going to forget all those murders. And I'm not going to spend the rest of my life in jail. No way. Better to be a contented zombie in a faraway place. But now I have to go. And you know, you've made it harder for me to kill you. But I do need to kill all three of you, you must understand that."

"We don't count?" said Blue.

"No. What's left of me is still in control. It's been good talking to you, Doctor Hendrickx. I'll kill you last. The inspector first, I think. It's been men who've been responsible for all the bad things in this world."

As she swung the gun towards Blue, there was a tap on the window. She swung the gun away from Blue, towards the window, squinting as she tried to look outside into the darkness.

"That's the thing about windows," said Blue. "You can't tell who's looking in, watching everything. Maybe they've already called the police."

The tapping came again, heavier, as if the end of a walking stick was being wielded. Then a gloved hand appeared from below the window, clenched in a ball, and knocked loudly.

"*Kurat!*" shouted Aino. "Who the fuck are you?" and loosed three shots at where she'd seen the hand. The noise of the shots in the office was cataclysmic, mixed as it was with the shattering of glass as the windowpane collapsed.

Then the light went out. Blue had seen the door opening slightly as Aino fired her salvo, and the gloved hand flicked the switch up.

Aino swung her gun towards the door, but she was too late, the heavy door was flung inwards, and they could hear the thump as it hit her square in the face, the clatter as the gun fell to the floor, and the thud as Aino followed it.

The light was switched on again.

Elsa Maarksen closed the door behind her and trained her own gun on Aino, who was now lying on the floor, blood streaming from her smashed nose into a puddle beneath her head. She was clad in black rubber boots, dark blue trousers and jacket, and one of those hats that covers the back of the head and down round the ears, as well as a peak, also in dark blue. And dark blue gloves of some fine material. She still managed to look well-dressed. She smiled at them. "Just keep very still, everybody. No-one moves, please. I don't want to have to shoot anyone."

"We're not moving," said Blue. He pointed to Aino's gun, lying beside her. "May I?"

Elsa leaned down over the groaning figure on the floor and retrieved the gun. "I think it's better if I hang on to all the weaponry. I think you and Ms McIntyre should stay just where you are. Alison, you can sit in the chair behind the desk. Very slowly please."

Alison sat down. "Thanks for saving us. That was very close."

"My pleasure, Alison. You three don't deserve to die."

"What made you come here now?" asked Blue.

"A good question, Angus. But then, you're a good cop, so you ask good questions. Let's say I've been keeping an eye on this place ever since you and Alison were here earlier. I felt, as I'm sure you did, that if Paul Carselaw was involved, and the books weren't at their flat, either on the boat or somewhere here was the best bet. I saw Aino come here the day before yesterday, and get turned away without success. Frankly, if she had got the books then, it would have saved a couple of deaths and a lot of damage, as I'd simply have taken them off her at that point. Still, all's well that ends well, eh? Ah, and there are the books. Did you check them, Alison? I watched you take them out of the rucksack."

"Yes, there are three. A codex and two incunabula."

"Push them over here, please."

Alison pushed the plastic-wrapped bundle along the desk. Keeping the gun in her right hand, Elsa pulled the package up onto its end, so that she could see the spines. "Okay, this looks right. The titles are correct, and the sizes fit. There's the coat of arms of the University of Kraków too. But we'll need to take a look inside, just to be sure." She pushed the bundle back to Alison. "Can you open up the archive bag and take them out? One at a time."

"Surely we should be doing that in a proper environment, with gloves and masks?"

"Yes, you're right of course. But I'm afraid there isn't the opportunity for that right now."

"You intend to take them yourself?" asked Blue.

"Oh yes. Well, not actually for myself, though that's very tempting. But it wouldn't be good for my reputation if I cheated a client."

"Ishmael Balfour."

"Yes, he thinks he's employing me, but no. Ah, you've unfolded the archive bag, so they can be slid out. Bring out the codex first. Just use your fingertips to open it at the beginning. Angus, please remain still, I'm watching you. Don't spoil this by forcing me to some precipitate action which, believe me, you wouldn't enjoy. Let's all be happy with the number of kneecaps we have at the moment. Ah. Yes, isn't it beautiful?"

"It's wonderful," said Alison, as she turned over the thick vellum and gazed at the first page of St Matthew's gospel.

Liber generationis Iesu Christi filii David filii Abraham.

Those were the words. But what she was staring at was the illustration surrounding the first word, the image of the gospel-writer, a monk standing at a high wooden desk studying a book, his finger tracing the words on the page. The colours were strong: blue and red, deep black and gleaming gold. At the bottom of the page, in a smaller scale, a man, by his dress clearly a noble, clutching a crown in one hand at his side, looked up towards the writer.

"May I look over her shoulder?" asked Blue. "I won't try anything. I give you my word."

"Yes, please do. And you too, Ms McIntyre. It is worth looking at."

Aino Carselaw was now groaning, and pushing herself into a sitting position with her back against the wall. The blood still ran from her smashed nose down her chin and dripped onto her lap. She stared up at Elsa.

"Ah, Aino, you're recovering," said Elsa. "Angus, do you have something you can give her to staunch the flow?"

Blue pulled a handkerchief from his pocket. "Will this do?"

"Excellent! Just drop it near her. Aino, you can pick it up, and press it to the wound. And do keep still, please."

"The man is the symbol of the evangelist, isn't he?" asked Alison.

"Yes, but in this case he may represent King Bolesław II of Poland. He holds his crown at his side, however, to show that even kings are inferior to the saints, and must defer to Christ's teachings. Even if he didn't actually practise them. Kings are very good at making the right gestures, and mouthing the right words. And keeping the church onside was important; it was a powerful element in the structure of the state. Another means of ensuring the obedience of the less well off."

"How old is it?"

"We think the late eleventh century. It was written at the cathedral of Gniezno, hence the name. The text is the New Testament in Latin, hand-written on vellum and, as you see, richly illustrated. A preface suggests that it may have been produced for King Bolesław, who was crowned in Gniezno in December 1076. It passed through various royal hands until 1399, when it was gifted by King Władysław II and his wife Queen Jadwiga to the library of the University of Kraków."

"So how did it get to Belarus?"

"It was lucky to survive the next five hundred years, during which Poland disappeared from the map. I guess the university kept very quiet about it, to avoid the interest of the Russian tsars. Things became more open when Poland recovered its independence in 1918. Then in 1939 the Germans arrived. Given that Poles were regarded as *untermenschen*, not worthy of culture, the university library was seized and shipped off to Greater Germany. This book was then allocated to the University of

Königsberg, in East Prussia, and was briefly displayed during the celebrations of the University's four-hundredth anniversary in 1944. However, within a few months the entire city, including the university, was in ruins, thanks to British bombing and the Russian advance. It's probable that many of the library holdings were moved to a bunker or other safe place before the destruction, and thus fell into the hands of the Russians. It was apparently then sent to the University of Slonim south-west of Minsk. I didn't know where it had got to until I was informed of this sale."

"It's amazing that it's survived."

"You're right. Okay, can you put it back now, and bring out the others?"

Alison slid the codex carefully back into the plastic bag, and brought out the second volume. Again she opened it carefully and turned to the title page. *Libri Primi Iudaeorum*. "The first books of the Jews," she translated.

"Yes, the five books of Moses: Genesis, Exodus, Leviticus, Numbers and Deuteronomy. Published in Łódź in 1496 by Abraham Strahl. The text should be in Hebrew and Polish, with wood-block illustrations, coloured by hand in each copy. Turn the next couple of pages. Yes, there it is, Hebrew on the left sheet, Polish on the right. Good. That's fine. Now the third."

Alison slid the book back and brought out the last of the three. *Annales Equitum Germanorum*. "The Annals of the German Knights. The Teutonic Knights?"

"Yes. It's a version of Henry of Livonia's *Chronicon Livoniae*, written in 1227-29, an eye-witness account of the conquest of the area which is now Latvia and Estonia by the Teutonic Knights. Turn over again. There we are: published in Danzig, 1494. Turn over a few more. Ah, yes. See, in the margin. Someone has added his own notes. From the handwriting I'd say sixteenth or seventeenth century. It'll take a while to go through them. With luck it will turn out to be someone who had important evidence to add to the text. Okay, please put it back now, then put the bundle into the box and back into the rucksack. I think it's time I was off."

"Elsa, if you're not working for Balfour, who is your client?" asked Blue. "I thought you were on our side."

"Oh, I am, Angus. I want to see these books back where they belong, in the Library of the University of Kraków. My client, and this is strictly off the record, I never said it, is the government of Poland. There is a unit which seeks to recover books stolen by the Nazis or the Soviets during World War 2. They got wind of this deal, and commissioned me to see what I could do. I come well recommended, you know, and I'm not cheap. But you have to admit that it's worth it for them."

"But if we'd got them," put in Blue, "that's where they'd end up. Our government would hand them over. I doubt they'd send them back to Belarus."

"I'm sure you're right. They won't go back to Belarus. But that is not my client's concern. Britain, you see, has a sad reputation for having very sticky fingers. It's very reluctant to hand anything back that's been stolen or pillaged during the centuries when it was a real world power. Think Elgin Marbles. That's only the biggest example. The only stuff that's actually been repatriated is trivial material, things they have little interest in anyway. From Africa, for instance. But Greece, Rome, the Middle East, even Asia, that's a different matter. This bundle will go, I would imagine, to the British Library. If Poland specifically requests them, the authorities will say they are being retained temporarily, 'for assessment and conservation.' But this process will go on for a long time, years, decades, forever. And if Poland presses, they will quibble about the facilities at the University of Kraków, say the environment is unsafe, or there are no academics there who are up to the task of studying them. The list of excuses is endless. So it's much easier for me to simply take them with me and hand them over to Polish government officials. I won't say exactly how I'm going to do that, of course. But take it from me, these books will be in Poland, where they belong, in two or three days."

"I see your point," said Blue. "But the books are important evidence in our case against Aino here for four murders."

"Ah yes. Justice must be achieved." She swung the gun towards Aino and shot her between the eyes. A red-yellow explosion burst behind her head, and she slowly slipped down to her right until she lay on the floor, leaving a splash of yellow and red, brain and blood, on the wall, and a red trail marking her slump to the ground.

"Well, that didn't take too long, did it? Justice done! I really must go now. Angus, it's been a pleasure to know you. I do hope we meet again sometime. And when the books are displayed in Kraków, do go and see them. Oh, by the way, please give me your phones. I wouldn't want you summoning the authorities too quickly. I'll leave them out in the car park somewhere – I'm sure you'll find them in the morning. Ah, I see there's a land line here too. Well, I'll just remove the phone from it and put it with the others. Angus, could you find Mrs Carselaw's phone, please, and give it to Ms McIntyre?"

Blue searched in the dead woman's pockets, and produced an iPhone, which he handed to Emma McIntyre.

"Now, Ms McIntyre," continued Elsa, "put the phones into the rucksack, then fasten it and push it over here."

She slung the rucksack onto her back with her left hand.

"Goodbye all. Please don't try to follow me. I will do what it takes to cover my trail. And I really don't want to hurt any of you. We are on the same side, after all."

She smiled at Alison and Emma McIntyre, then opened the door and left.

35

As soon as the door shut, Blue knelt down by Aino's still form and checked for signs of life. He wasn't surprised to find none. After all, half of Aino's brain was smeared on the wall behind her.

"Let's see what's outside," said Alison, heading for the door. It wouldn't open. Something was jamming it from the other side. "It feels like she's shoved a wedge under the bottom," she reported.

Emma McIntyre resolved the situation by picking up the chair by the desk and throwing it through the window, taking out much more of the glass. Using a boathook which had been leant against the wall by the door, she removed the rest of the glass, then placed the cushion which had been on the chair onto the window ledge, and clambered out. A minute later she opened the door, and they were free.

But too late to have any idea where Elsa Maarksen had gone. And too dark to find a phone which might, or might not, be anywhere in or near the car park. Telling Emma and Alison to wait at the office, Blue jumped into Alison's car and headed for the police station.

Blue was not greatly surprised when, over the next few days, no trace could be found of Elsa Maarksen. The Austrian police could not find her in Austria. As he also expected, the Polish authorities denied all knowledge of her.

Four days after her disappearance, a postcard arrived at his home in Connel; it showed the cathedral of Kraków, and in the space for the message there was only a hand-drawn version of the smiley face emoticon.

Through the agency of Blue's Polish colleague, *Kapitan* Tadeusz Pilsudski, he learned that at the latest meeting of the Cultural Heritage Committee of the Polish Parliament, which took place a week after Elsa's disappearance, it was reported under 'Any Other Business' that three volumes deemed to be of significant cultural value, a codex and two incunabula, had been donated to the library of the University of Kraków by an anonymous donor. No details were given.

Kalev Lind's hire car was located in the car park of the Aldi store in Oban. In the boot were three cardboard boxes containing the books stolen from the bookshop.

Ishmael Balfour was not charged with anything, and soon returned to Slovakia to see to his business interests. He did, however, promise to return at a later date.

Eastwards Books was refurbished and reopened at the beginning of January, with Anna Zeresova as manager. The flats in the building were upgraded; Anna was given the one above the shop at a very favourable rent. The others were offered for long-term rent, with the proviso that tenants must be full-time residents of Oban.

Blue and Dr Hendrickx decided that in the spring they would go for a holiday to the island of Saaremaa, and visit the Kaali meteorite crater. Blue found on the internet a Swedish documentary 'Saaremaa, Hidden Jewel of the Baltic' (with English subtitles) which convinced them there were plenty of interesting things to see.

The End

Endnote

I hope you enjoyed *The Dead of Oban*. The first thing I want to say about it is that it's fiction. Of course, you already knew that. Stories have been around for a very very long time. I once read a piece by a well-known writer claiming that stories arose because stone-age hunters wanted to advise others on how best to kill mammoths, etc. This is patent nonsense! Stories are stories because they are not true. Their purpose is entertainment and enlightenment, in that order. Stone age man (and woman) did not spend every hour of every day hunting mammoths and scraping skins and making tools and looking after children. Like most mammals, stone age people had periods of down time, especially in the long winter evenings. Gathered around the log fire, did they spend their time arguing about the best way to catch a mammoth. Some of it, yes. But more time would have been spent listening to, and telling stories. Why? Because people like stories. They like them because they make them feel good, and sometimes they make them think too.

Storytelling has been practised since the dawn of man as we know him (and her), i.e. a hominid capable of conscious thought and using language to communicate, and some basic principles have been established fairly near the beginning. One is that there's a story arc, that is, the story has a beginning which sets a scene and some characters, a middle in which the characters are set a task or face a problem requiring to be solved, and an end, in which the task is completed, or the problem solved, and the characters obtain their just rewards, or otherwise. The ending provides the listeners with a resolution to the issues within the story and gives them a sense of satisfaction. This model has continued from ancient times and is still going strong in most novels and short stories written today.

However, we know that the sort of resolution found in stories doesn't always happen in real life. Real life doesn't progress towards resolution, and real people don't always meet the fate we feel they deserve. Real life is not fiction, and fiction is not real life. Most crime writers know that police procedures don't often work the way they do in novels; many investigations are long, tedious, involve dozens of officers carrying routine enquiries, and don't always deliver any results. Crime writers accelerate the whole process and slim down the manpower to make it a readable story, one that will retain the interest of the reader and satisfy them when they get to the end.

Fiction is made up, but it has be realistic, or rather, plausible. And the more so if it is set in a real time and place, such as Oban in the present day. In this book Oban and its hinterland is a real backdrop for the story, and if you've been to that area you'll recognize many of the places. However writers have to tweak reality to make the story work. Thus Oban police headquarters has been raised up from a rather modest building in an unassuming street to a large former hotel set on the promenade, staffed by a much bigger force that Oban can in reality deploy. And some locations have to be invented, to make the story work. Thus Stairfoot Lane with its bookshop exists only in the mind of the author, as do the marinas at Gallanach Bay and at the Kyles of Bute. The flats at Ganavan are real, but Aino and Paul Carselaw do not live in any of them, and the internal description of their flat is my own invention.

All of the characters in the story are fictitious, and the events are creations of the author.

The issues raised are however real. The theft or destruction of cultural objects, including books, is real, and has been going on for thousands of years. The Baghdad Museum was looted in 2006, and many artifacts stolen (though thankfully many of the most valuable had already been moved to safer locations to preserve them from war damage). Poland's libraries and museums were looted by the Nazis, and some of that loot swept up by the soviet forces in 1944-45. Codices and incunabula are very valuable items which attract thieves and very rich private collectors as well as the institutions which want to preserve them for posterity.

And in reality the good guys don't always win.

The information used in the story comes from many sources over many years. One book I would mention however is The Library: a Fragile History, by Andrew Pettegree and Arthur der Weduwen (Profile Books, 2021), a fascinating and very informative history of book collections from the beginning until now.

My thanks go to my wife Vivien, my muse, First Reader, and fearless (but constructive) critic; and also to Seonaid and Huw Francis at ThunderPoint Publishers, who enable the transformation of a story into a book.

And if you do ever happen to be on the island of Saaremaa in the Baltic Sea, make sure you visit the Kaali meteorite crater; it is just what it says on the tin.

About the Author
Allan Martin

Allan Martin worked as a teacher, teacher-trainer and university lecturer, and only turned to writing fiction after taking early retirement.

He lives in Perthshire and with his wife regularly visits the Hebrides and Estonia.

He has had several short stories published, notably in *iScot* magazine and *404Ink* magazine.

He has also translated from Estonian a closed-room mystery, *The Oracle*, originally published in 1937.

His first novel, *The Peat Dead*, was published in Estonia in 2021.

The Peat Dead - Book 1
Allan Martin

Shortlisted for the 2019 Bloody Scotland McIlvanney Debut Scottish Crime Prize.

ISBN: 978-1-910946-55-8 (Kindle)
ISBN: 978-1-910946-54-1 (Paperback)

On the Scottish Hebridean Island of Islay, five corpses are dug up by a peat-cutter. All of them have been shot in the back of the head, execution style.

Sent across from the mainland to investigate, Inspector Angus Blue and his team slowly piece together the little evidence they have, and discover the men were killed on a wartime base, over 70 years ago.

But there are still secrets worth protecting, and even killing for. Who can Inspector Blue trust?

"A mystery so redolent of its island setting that you practically smell the peat and whisky on the pages." – Douglas Skelton"

This atmospheric crime novel set on Islay gripped me from the start. A book that shows decades-old crimes cast long shadows." – Sarah Ward

The Dead of Jura - Book 2
Allan Martin
ISBN: 978-1-910946-68-8 (eBook)
ISBN: 978-1-910946-67-1 (Paperback)

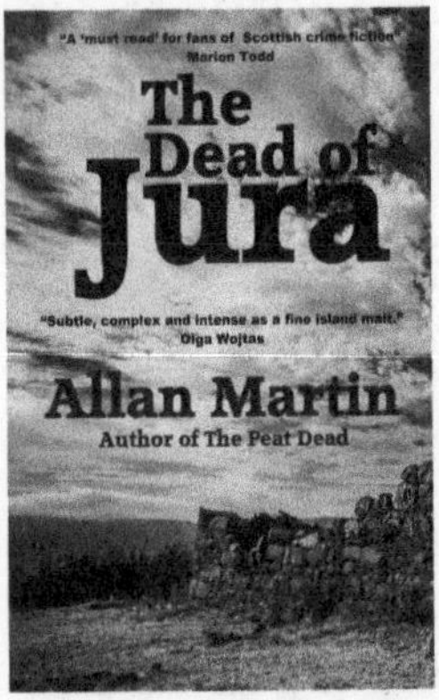

Jura: where the rich and the powerful come to play away from the prying eyes of the press.

But when there is an assassination attempt on a Cabinet Minister whiles he's on his island estate, questions must be asked, and Inspector Angus Blue and his team return to the Hebrides to investigate.

Deemed a matter of 'National Security' by London, local protocols are overruled, and Special Branch officers are sent to hunt down the assassin. By the time Inspector Blue and his team arrive the estate staff have been scared into silence, and the crime scene has been disturbed.

His investigation hampered at every turn, Inspector Blue must discover what Special Branch are hiding - and who they are protecting.

The Dead of Jura is the second novel in Inspector Angus Blue Series. elderly woman is found battered to death in the common stairwell of an Inverness block of flats.

"A 'must read' for fans of Scottish crime fiction" – Marion Todd
"Subtle, complex and intense as a fine island malt." – Olga Wojtas

The Dead of Appin - Book 3
Allan Martin

ISBN: 978-1-910946-83-1 (eBook)
ISBN: 978-1-910946-82-4 (Paperback)

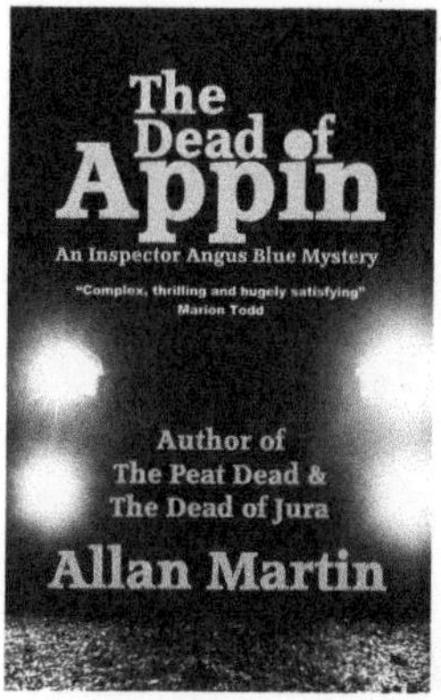

Just outside Oban, within sight of the Connel Bridge, there's a burnt out car containing the charred remains of a human body.

A woman is missing – but is the body hers?

In a high stakes game of business and politics, what secret does the bustling port of Oban hide that is worth killing for?

The Dead of Appin is the third book in the Inspector Blue series.

"Intricate and exciting. Scottish crime fiction at its best." – Marion Todd

"The Dead of Appin is another cracking instalment in the Angus Blue series. Embark on whisky flavoured adventures in the west Highlands as Blue is drawn into a dangerous world of intrigue and corruption. Addictive from page one!" – G. R. Halliday

"A complex mystery starring the unforgettable Angus Blue as he explores political corruption and grisly murders in the Scottish highlands. And he cooks too! Don't miss it." – Emma Christie"

In The Shadow Of The Hill
Helen Forbes

ISBN: 978-0-9929768-1-1 (eBook)
ISBN: 978-0-9929768-0-4 (Paperback)

An elderly woman is found battered to death in the common stairwell of an Inverness block of flats.

Detective Sergeant Joe Galbraith starts what seems like one more depressing investigation of the untimely death of a poor unfortunate who was in the wrong place, at the wrong time.

As the investigation spreads across Scotland it reaches into a past that Joe has tried to forget, and takes him back to the Hebridean island of Harris, where he spent his childhood.

Among the mountains and the stunning landscape of religiously conservative Harris, in the shadow of Ceapabhal, long buried events and a tragic story are slowly uncovered, and the investigation takes on an altogether more sinister aspect.

In The Shadow Of The Hill skilfully captures the intricacies and malevolence of the underbelly of Highland and Island life, bringing tragedy and vengeance to the magical beauty of the Outer Hebrides.

'...our first real home-grown sample of modern Highland noir' – Roger Hutchinson; West Highland Free Press

The Birds That Never Flew
Margot McCuaig

Longlisted for the Polari First Book Prize 2014

ISBN: 978-0-9575689-3-8 (Kindle)
ISBN: 978-0-9929768-4-2 (Paperback)

'Have you got a light hen? I'm totally gaspin.'

Battered and bruised, Elizabeth has taken her daughter and left her abusive husband Patrick. Again. In the bleak and impersonal Glasgow housing office Elizabeth meets the provocatively intriguing drug addict Sadie, who is desperate to get her own life back on track.

The two women forge a fierce and interdependent relationship as they try to rebuild their shattered lives, but despite their bold, and sometimes illegal attempts it seems impossible to escape from the abuse they have always known, and tragedy strikes.

More than a decade later Elizabeth has started to implement her perfect revenge - until a surreal Glaswegian Virgin Mary steps in with imperfect timing and a less than divine attitude to stick a spoke in the wheel of retribution.

Tragic, darkly funny and irreverent, The Birds That Never Flew is a new and vibrant voice in Scottish literature.

"Not Scandinavian but dark, beautiful and moving, I wholeheartedly recommend" – scanoir.co.uk